I0760305

SOUL BOUND

First published in Great Britain in 2023 by INKED ARROW BOOKS.

Published by INKED ARROW BOOKS

Contact: rhianedwardsauthor@gmail.com

www.rhianedwardsauthor.com

First Edition 2023

ISBN:
978-1-915719-08-9

Cover by 'Get covers'

RHIAN EDWARDS

SOUL BOUND

Complete Trilogy
Books 1-3

ALSO BY

SOUL BOUND SERIES
(YA urban fantasy)
Ascending in Chaos
Avenged by Fate
Alliance of Enemies

The Alliance (prequel short story)

KINGDOM OF DRUIDS
(NA fantasy romance)
Reign of Blood and Shadows

PREQUEL STORY

Don't miss the heart-breaking prequel short story, available when you sign up my newsletter: https://rhianedwardsauthor.com/newsletter/

This is how the story starts.
This is the alliance.

As tensions rise between wolves and magic, Kieran Alastair senses his Alpha control slipping.
The alliance is their last hope.
But not all agree.

A rouge mage signals the start of a powerful enemy against the alliance, one who shows too much interest in four-year-old Killian.

Heir to the shifter throne and an integral part of the alliance pact, Killian must now survive shifters and magic users against an alliance as they desperately try to destroy the one the thing that will put the two races at war forever: him.

RHIAN EDWARDS

SOUL BOUND SERIES

ASCENDING N CHAOS

1

ASCENDING IN CHAOS

For Chester: the cheekiest, softest, cuddliest Chocolate Labrador known to man. Considered himself human.
He just had to make an appearance here.
Loved, adored, and missed.
September 2005 – September 2018

PROLOGUE

BLAKE

North England

SWEAT COVERED HIS BODY like a second skin, gluing the cotton sheet to his bare torso as he tossed and turned in bed. His distress went unknown in the depths of night while the dream plagued him. Heart hammering at a hundred miles an hour, Blake clenched the bedsheets in his fists, breaths coming out in short, quiet pants.

His dark hair was plastered to his forehead and his head thrashed from side to side. His skin itched like it didn't belong, and he scratched at his narrow chest, almost drawing blood.

Blake's breathing accelerated, becoming strained gulps.

He sat upright with a painful gasp, panting desperately and trying to calm his racing heart as it attempted to leap out of his chest.

Blake slowly opened his sleep-filled eyes to find the room engulfed in light. He snapped them shut, wondering if he'd left his light on.

Placing a shaking arm over his face, he cautiously opened his eyes, ready for the onslaught of light. To his surprise, it was completely dark in his room – just as he'd left it. He could only just make out the silhouette of his small desk and wardrobe against the opposite wall.

He grabbed his phone to check the time. Midnight. A shiver raced through him. Something didn't feel quite right. His heart slowed from its sprint and his breathing calmed, but his mind was racing. Ticking. Scratching. He felt caged, and he fought the urge to run.

Blake flopped back on his bed and pulled the sheet up. Maybe he was coming down with the flu or something.

Unusually exhausted, it didn't take long for him to fall back asleep.

KAYLA

170 miles away, near the Welsh border

DARK HAIR FELL FROM her bun and spread around her head like a halo. While it was dark outside, her curtains remained open and cast bright moonlight across her light green walls and wooden flooring. Her dreams were pleasant and sweet as she slept with a smile on her face.

A gentle breeze lightly ruffled her hair and wrapped her sun-kissed skin in a comforting embrace. Even in her sleep, she registered the tingling sensation buzzing at her fingertips.

The wind picked up and sent sharp tingles of warning down her spine. The smile fell from her sleeping face, replaced by a frown. Her head turned from left to right, tangling her luscious locks.

She sat upright with a painful gasp, greedily gulping oxygen. What was that? A sensation lingered that she couldn't quite place as she lifted her trembling hands and studied them closely.

She ran a hand through her hair and looked at the window, surprised to find it shut. She was sure it had been open a moment before.

The clock on her bedside table displayed midnight and it dawned on her that it was her birthday. Great. She was seventeen, and she still had no magic. Could she be the only offspring of two magic users not to gain any powers? How fair was that?

Frustrated at her lack of abilities, Kayla slumped back against her pillows. Her mum had once told her the fantastical story of their origins; it was a tale Kayla had treasured for as long as she remembered, but with her magic being non-existent, she wondered if there was something seriously wrong with her.

Closing her eyes, she couldn't help but bring forth the fond memories of story time with her mum as she drifted off to sleep.

"Please, Mummy! Oh please!" Kayla begged her mum for the story she

had already heard a thousand times before.

Sitting next to Kayla in the small bed, her mother's lilting laugh chimed in the air.

A small chuckle escaped. "Okay, okay." Her arm curved around Kayla's body, pulling her daughter in close. Kayla snuggled against her mum's side, finding comfort in her flowery scent. "There was once a sorcerer our Creator made to look after the world and the inhabitants who lived there. The sorcerer had so much magic at his fingertips that it flowed from his body wherever he went. He could forge connections with objects and give words power, his mind could assist others in need, and he could talk with Mother Nature. He was happy. He was whole. But he soon became sad."

"Why did he become sad, Mummy?" Kayla asked, knowing the answer.

"He became sad because there was no one else like him, no one to share in his joy. But one night he met a beautiful woman. Her hair shone like sunlight and her eyes were as bright as the fresh green grass. They fell in love."

Kayla gasped with wonder at the prospect of a love story. "They fell in love!"

"Yes, my sweet girl. They did. It wasn't long before they came to realise they were going to have a baby. They were overjoyed. They couldn't wait to have a family. However, the Creator found out and said that the sorcerer wasn't meant to fall in love. Wasn't meant to have a family. He had been created – designed – to stay with the land, the animals, the people, and protect them. Forever. The Creator said the child wasn't meant to be. The sorcerer begged and pleaded with the Creator to keep the child."

"But Mummy, the Creator made us all!"

"Yes, but this was unforeseen. The Creator isn't cruel, and agreed that the child could be allowed to live – but for a small price. The compromise was that the baby wouldn't be just one baby, but three. The sorcerer and his love would have triplets, and his magic would pass to them as three different gifts."

Excitement emitted from Kayla's bright eyes. "Is this where the gifts are made into our magic?"

"Absolutely. One child had the power of a mage and could use magic of the mind. Another was a witch who could put power behind words. The last was an elemental with magic connected to nature. Mind, heart, and soul. The children would use these gifts to continue protecting the people of this

world – just as the sorcerer was originally intended to do. They would pass it on to their children and so on."

"Does anyone ever miss having all three magical gifts, Mummy?"

"Oh, honey. We were gifted with something so precious; we are matched with the magic that speaks to us most."

Kayla pursed her lips in thought, trying to determine if her mind, her heart, or her soul was magical. "Whose magic do I have?"

"We don't know yet. You're a special mix of me and your daddy so your magic will take after one of us. That's how the magic works when two magic users of different strains have a child."

"So I could be a witch like you or a mage like daddy?"

"That's right. Do you know which one you would prefer?"

Kayla thought carefully and answered, "I don't mind. It will be the right one."

"Why is my daughter so wise?" her mum whispered to herself, and Kayla smiled, proud of her clever nature.

"Whether you are a witch or a mage doesn't matter, because you will be precisely who the Creator envisioned."

"Envisioned?"

"Planned."

Kayla sucked on her bottom lip.

"What if the Creator gets it wrong again?"

"Do you want to know a secret?" her mum asked, and Kayla nodded her head with excitement. "I think the Creator knew exactly what they were doing all along."

Kayla's eyes went wide. "Why?" she breathed.

"Free will." When Kayla pulled her brows down in a frown, her mum continued. "I'll explain it to you one day, but free will is so important to humans."

"But Mummy, we're magical, not human!"

Her mum chuckled again. "You have so much to learn, sweet girl. But for now, it's bedtime."

She tucked Kayla tightly under the covers and headed towards the door, switching off the light.

"Mummy?"

Her mum stopped in the doorway. "Yes, baby?"

"I can't wait to meet my magic," she said, yawning.

"Your magic is already a part of you, Kayla. You'll see."

Her mum closed the door and young Kayla fell into dreams of magic, fire, and golden eyes.

CHAPTER ONE

KAYLA

"*HAPPY BIRTHDAY TO YOU, happy birthday to you, happy birthday dear sweet Kayla, happy birthday to you.*"

Her parents sang the birthday tune as they pushed open her bedroom door. Groaning, she sank lower into the blankets, pulling the white covers over her face. It wasn't that she was embarrassed – okay, she was a little – it was more that it was just too damn early in the morning. How were they always this cheery? She needed sugar. And lots of it. Some might have been dependent on their morning coffee, but not her. No. The newly turned seventeen-year-old could have done with a doughnut or another similar confectionary delight.

"I think our baby girl is embarrassed, Caroline!" Her dad's brown eyes sparkled with mirth.

"Not of us! We rock!" They high-fived each other as they whooped and jumped on her bed, snuggling in close. They pulled down the covers and kissed her cheeks at the same time. Slivers of her light green walls greeted her, reminding her of the matcha tea bun she'd devoured last night.

"Ugh, thanks, but it's not a special birthday, you know. I'm only seventeen."

"Only seventeen!" her mum cried, dramatically placing a hand on her chest.

"Every year is a special year with our daughter!" her dad added.

"*You are the dancing queen, young and sweet, only seventeen!*" her parents sang in unison, crooning one of ABBA's well-known numbers.

"Oh my word, you guys!" Kayla tried not to smile but the corners of her lips tipped up at their antics. They all burst out laughing when the small brown cocker spaniel they'd taken in last year sprang onto the now overcrowded bed. "Smithy! Great, now even the smelly dog is on my bed."

"Oh Smithy, you wonderful creature!" Her dad scratched the dog's head and her mum rolled her grass-green eyes. Smithy finished his rounds of greeting the family and padded across the hardwood floor, sniffing around the white desk for crumbs left from the previous night's snacking.

Her mum had been adamant for so many years that they would never welcome stray animals into the house. It wasn't that her mum was cold-hearted, but with the work they did, they had enough responsibility without worrying about another creature.

Her parents protected those within the magical community who found themselves in trouble. More so, her parents didn't distinguish between the two paranormal races of the world: magic users and shifters. It was something Kayla was immensely proud of, especially as their paranormal society was fraught with tension, secrets, and death after the dissolution of the shifter royal family twelve years prior. She was only a child when it happened, but whatever alliance the shifter royals had been working on was lost the night the royal shifter family were assassinated. She shivered. The only real thing she remembered was sadness. As a result, hordes of people were caught in the middle as both sides fought to become the superior race, and many of them came to her parents for help.

It angered her that extremists on both sides were more than happy to hunt their own kind. If someone supported an alliance between the races or worked with the opposing race, they were targeted. Kayla swore she would try to foster peace between the races where she could – if she could. She chewed on her bottom lip.

Smithy's sloppy kiss on her arm drew her out of her spiralling thoughts. She tutted. Her dad praised the dog, and she couldn't deny how much happiness the stupid mutt brought him. The dog went everywhere with him; even the shifters they worked with got along with Smithy.

She picked at a spot on her bedcovers as if it would help her build the courage to ask the question that haunted her every day. She would never be able to continue her parents' work if she didn't get her magic, and last night's dream only reminded her of that.

"Guys, I wanted to ask you something. My magic still hasn't materialised, and I wondered if it was possible that I just might not have any? I always thought I had it, and I believed I could feel it, but lately . . . I dunno, I just feel like maybe I'm a dud." It pained her to voice her fears. Magic users, much like shifters, accessed their true nature when puberty hit. She was long past those days – thank God – but no magic. Nothing. Nada. What good would she be to her parents and their line of work without magic?

"Nothing of the sort, sweetheart," her dad said with conviction, waving off the idea that she was a 'dud,' as she'd so delicately put it.

"I, too, believe you have magic somewhere inside of you, honey. You just have to be patient. All good things come to–"

"Those who wait. I know, Mum."

"Right! Pancakes?" her dad asked, bringing a small grin to her face. Sugar.

"Birthday pancakes?"

"With cream, sprinkles, and maple syrup? Of course! Only the best for you! Coming right up!"

Her parents jumped up with gusto and waltzed – she wasn't joking, they quite literally waltzed – out of the bedroom, humming some ballroom tune. Kayla shook her head and grinned at their goofiness.

"*You are the dancing queen, young and sweet, only seventeen, oooo yeah, mmmhhmmm, you can dance, you can jive, oh!*" Kayla sang under her breath as she walked down the street after school. The song had been circling her head all day since her delightful parents had put it there, but they'd made up for it with the sickly-sweet birthday pancakes.

She looked up from her feet and saw a distressed elderly man standing over his car engine.

"Are you okay, sir?" she asked when she got closer.

He wrung his weathered hands and turned to her, silver eyebrows knitted in angst. "My car. It won't start and my wife, she's in hospital, you see, not feeling so well, and the visiting hours will be over soon, and I promised I'd be there."

"I can help. My dad taught me a thing or two about engines." It was true. Mostly how to hotwire one to make an escape should she ever have a need for the skill, but he'd given her a basic rundown of the working components of an engine, too. "Why don't you sit in the driver's seat and try turning it on so I can listen?" The old man did as she asked and disappeared behind the car's blue bonnet.

She rested her hands on the edge of the hood and tried to identify the problem. The man twisted the key, but the engine wasn't turning over. She shouted to keep trying, but all she heard was a clicking sound. Her focus was solely on the engine and, having never used magic before, she failed to detect the slow and steady rising of her magic's excitement as it drew near the surface. She leaned towards the noise, and angry flames erupted before her, engulfing her hand. Despite the heat, a cold, icy feeling settled in the pit of her stomach. She gasped, stepping back and staring in wide-eyed horror at her smooth, unblemished skin.

The fire was magical.

"Do I smell smoke?" the old man questioned, but she was too stunned to answer. Had she just done that? Had she just set fire to the car? "Is everything all right?" the man asked again, getting out of his vehicle. He yelped when he saw the flames and looked to her for help. "What do we do?"

Kayla took a deep breath and stepped forward. Surely if she'd done this, she could un-do it. She tried resting her hand over a section of the car that wasn't covered in roaring flames and thought about what she wanted. Her mum always said magic had to have intention.

Before she could do anything, however, the water from the cooling tank exploded, dousing the flames and her arm. She sputtered in shock, expecting scalding water, but remained unharmed – again. The man stared at her.

Kayla fled, running as fast as she could towards home.

Her heart pounded like a racehorse. Whatever magic she'd just done – and there was no doubt that it was magic – it shouldn't have been possible. It wasn't mage or witch magic. She *should* have mage or witch magic. Her thoughts tumbled haphazardly through her disoriented mind until she remembered the story her mum told her – the one that once held her in awe but now chilled her to the bone.

Kayla blinked away the tears threatening to spill from her anxious brown eyes as she picked up her pace, needing her parents' help and counsel more than ever.

What had she done?

CHAPTER TWO

KAYLA

"MUM! DAD!" KAYLA SHOUTED, running into the house and slamming the front door behind her. Footsteps hurried towards her from within the heart of the home while she tried to take deep breaths. Her magic wasn't right. She didn't get her magic when she'd hit puberty, and now she had it, but it was all wrong. What if she was a mistake? What if she, too, was unnatural and unplanned and the Creator came for her?

"Kayla?" Her mum appeared from the kitchen, reading glasses on top of her head. Kayla ran into the familiar comfort of her arms and buried her face in her mum's hair to muffle the sounds of her shocked sobs. Her mum stroked her back, shushing her as she encouraged her to explain what had happened.

Her dad emerged from the kitchen, too, a frown curving his mouth. "Kayla? What's going on?"

Kayla forced the sobs back as she told the story of the old man and his car, her parents sharing worried glances while she spoke.

"That doesn't sound like witch or mage power," her mum said, her voice just above a whisper.

"What does that mean? Is that possible? Am I some sort of freak?"

Kayla asked in a high-pitched squeal.

"Oh no, honey. You could never be a freak. We'll figure this out, okay?" Her mum reassured her, absently rubbing her daughter's arm as she turned to her husband. "Perhaps we have an elemental in the family tree somewhere and it's skipped a few generations?"

Her dad didn't look convinced. Kayla felt the same; magic didn't work like that.

"I'll set up the news and social media alerts," he said after a few moments of thought. "Get ahead of any potential mentions of magic within the human community." His eyes held a world of worry when he turned away from her, hurrying to his desk in the corner of their small living room.

"What have I done, Mum? We're not supposed to use magic like that. We're not supposed to expose ourselves to humans." Kayla trembled like a small child during a storm.

"It's okay, it's okay," her mother cooed. "Your father and I will keep our ears to the ground for any whisperings about magic in the human society, and it'll be okay."

"But what am I? I shouldn't be an elemental. I should be like you or dad. Am I a mistake?"

"I don't know what to say. You should be like one of us, yes, but you are our daughter, and we will figure out your magic – whatever it is. Perhaps it has something to do with why it's so late. But listen to me, Kayla. Nothing about you is a mistake, you hear me? You are exactly who you are meant to be." Kayla looked away and nodded, trying to accept her mother's conviction even if she didn't feel it herself.

KAYLA FINISHED UP HER extra-curricular responsibilities – helping younger children with maths at the after-school club – and began her usually enjoyable walk home. Today, however, Kayla's thoughts were overrun with worry about her magic. Discovering her magic should have been an enjoyable experience – exciting even – but after what happened the previous day, her stomach was in knots. She meandered through the clean streets, admiring the perfect lawns of the nearly identical homes of her neighbourhood. Humans had such simple lives; they never had to worry about their magic.

She was unnatural.

She shouldn't exist.

Dread filled her stomach as she opened her front door and followed the sounds of hushed conversations.

Her dad pushed away from the computer to help her mum burn paperwork in the fireplace on the opposite side of the living room. His voice matched his frantic movements. "It's going. We have five minutes while the files transfer."

"Mum? Dad? What's going on?" Kayla asked, walking further into the house.

Both of her parents spun on their heels, startled at Kayla's sudden appearance, their faces lined deep with fear.

"Kayla, go pack. Essentials only. Now," her mum ordered as more paper was thrown onto the crackling fire.

"I don't understand . . ."

"Yesterday with the old man, there must have been a journalist nearby because you're in the paper." She grabbed the day's paper from the sofa and showed Kayla the front page. A blurry black and white image of Kayla with her hands in front of the flaming engine stared back at her. It looked like she was controlling them, which was far from the truth. The headline read: 'Are witches among us?'

"But you can't make me out? Right?"

"There are rumours that a group of hunters – shifters, we think – have been mobilised. If they find us, we don't have a chance," her dad said, coming up beside them. "Pack now, Kayla. We're not leaving anything to chance."

But they were too late.

The back door burst open and two shifters in their animal forms crashed into the hall, their snouts curled up in snarls to reveal gleaming sharp teeth. Three men followed, all equally tall, muscular, and lethal. The two wolves loped through the kitchen, their heads low to the ground. Their short brown fur stood on end in ridges down their backs, and low growls emitted from their throats.

"The mage first. No survivors," one of the men commanded in an authoritative tone. He stood to the side with the other men flanking him, all in dark clothing. The leader stared at Kayla, his bright yellow wolf eyes flashing at her in his human form. His blonde hair was cropped short, highlighting the squareness of his face. A shiver sprinted down her spine when he sneered at her, but her focus was torn away from him when the two wolves moved forward.

In the flash of an eye, her dad was in front of her, taking the full force of two attacking wolves. One wrapped its teeth around her dad's arm and shook viciously while the other bit into his shoulder. Her dad cried out and managed to get a hand on the wolf behind him. For the first time in her life, Kayla felt the crackle of energy surge through the air. The wolf closed its eyes and went slack, dropping to the floor.

Her mum opened her small, leather-bound spell journal she carried everywhere, quickly reading words from it and focusing on the wolf who pinned her father to the floor. As her dad writhed in agony, trying to buck the wolf off his arm, the halo of blood around him grew wider. Whatever her mum was trying to do, it wasn't working quickly enough.

A growl ripped through the kitchen and Kayla spun to see that one of the three men by the back door had shifted. The murky grey wolf ran at her, his eyes flashing with murderous intent. Her heart hammered in her chest as she raised her hands in defence.

She didn't know what she expected to happen, but it certainly wasn't a stream of fire shooting from her palms and wrapping the wolf in a blanket of death. The stench of burning fur made her want to retch, but she lowered her shaking hands and turned her head as another wolf opened its jaws, aiming for her mum's ankles. She yelled out a warning too late; her mum went down, landing awkwardly on the hard floor.

Kayla froze, not knowing what to do when yet another wolf flew into the room. There were too many wolves. They were surrounded.

The wolf at her mum's feet dove onto her body. The wolf's claws slashed at her mum's chest and a garbled scream filled the air. Kayla blinked back the brief, paralysing fear and threw her hands towards the wolf, willing the fire to burst forth. Nothing happened. She shook her hands in frustration.

"C'mon!" she shouted. Flames leapt from the roaring fireplace to grab a hold of the wolf on her mum's bloody chest.

"KAYLA!" her dad shouted. True fear spilled across his face as he threw his hand out. A wolf she hadn't even seen flew away from her, landing in an unmoving heap. She looked back to her dad, but relief was the last emotion she saw in his eyes. The wolf on her dad's arm lunged for his throat while he was distracted. The light disappeared from his eyes as blood pulsed from his neck.

Kayla screamed.

The flames devouring the wolf on the floor swelled with burning hunger, racing up walls and across the floors, searching out the beasts, following the trails of blood. She ducked, avoiding the scorching flames and thick smoke rapidly filling the room.

"Mum!" she yelled, competing with the wails of the remaining wolves as the fire consumed them. Dodging thick smoke, she crawled to where her mum lay on the floor. "Mum!" she shouted again when she reached her. Her mum winced, pulling off the necklace she was wearing. It was a small sunflower-shaped pendant with a delicate yellow stone in the centre. Closing her eyes, she muttered words Kayla couldn't hear. Kayla knew it was a spell. "Mum, we don't have time for this. We have to go!" she pleaded, hovering her hands uselessly over the wide, open wounds.

"Done. Take this," she croaked, pushing the pendant into Kayla's hands. "Go, go now, Kayla!"

"What? No, c'mon Mum. Hold onto me!"

"I can't. I'm not going to make it, and this fire is magical and unruly. It'll get you before you can get me out." Tears leaked from her eyes. "I'm not going to survive anyway, darling, but you can – you must. Take my spell book and find him, find the shifter. Find Killian. We hid him after his parents were killed. He is the key, your key, Kayla. He's the key to stopping all this madness between our races. You must find him." Her voice was hoarse and her skin paled, becoming ashy.

"What? I-no-I-what? Mum, you're not making sense!" she cried, and her mum grabbed her hands and held them between her own, bringing them to her lips.

"I'm sorry. I'm sorry we don't have more time to explain, but you have to go, Kayla, while you can still get out . . . the journal . . . tell you . . . Killian . . ."

She sobbed, "Who? What? Mum!"

"Killian . . . is . . ." Her mum's eyes fluttered shut. Kayla's mouth dropped open on a silent scream, tears blurring her vision.

"Mum?" she whispered.

Kayla glanced over at her dad's still body, flames starting to lick at the new source of energy. She turned back to her mum and leaned in close, placing a delicate kiss on her forehead.

"I love you," she whispered, gulping back a sob. She stood up and ran as fast as she could without looking back. The journal in her hands hummed with sorrow, but as she turned down street after street with no purposeful direction, the book slowly calmed down. The moment the journal fell silent, Kayla dropped to her knees and wept.

CHAPTER THREE

KAYLA

TO: anderson@sixth-form-academy
SUBJECT: code renew
MESSAGE:
Dear Miss Anderson,

I found your contact details within my mother's journal. Instructions suggest 'code renew' has been activated and I'm to join the academy. I trust you understand this and appreciate why I cannot explain any further details over e-mail. Is there a way for us to meet in person?

Kind Regards,
Kayla Mitchell

....

TO: k-mitchell
SUBJECT: re code renew
MESSAGE:
Dear Miss Mitchell,

I am so sorry to hear about code renew. Rest assured I will do all I can to help you in your endeavours. I have already begun proceedings to enrol you at the academy. When might you expect to arrive?

All my best,
Gaby Anderson

....

TO: anderson@sixth-form-academy
SUBJECT: re code renew
MESSAGE:
Hi Gaby,

I should be able to arrive by Wednesday if that is okay? It would be beneficial if I could start right away.

Thanks,
Kayla

....

TO: k-mitchell
SUBJECT: re code renew
MESSAGE:
Hello again Kayla,

Absolutely. I can have that arranged. Do you have a place to stay? You are more than welcome to stay with me.

All my best,
Gaby Anderson

....

TO: anderson@sixth-form-academy
SUBJECT: re code renew
MESSAGE:
Hi Gaby,

That is great, thank you. I am looking for another student who might be at the academy.

No, I do not have anywhere to stay. It would be great if I could stay with you. Thank you for your offer.

Kayla

....

TO: k-mitchell
SUBJECT: re code renew
MESSAGE:
Hello Kayla,

My pleasure. With regards to finding a specific pupil, I may not be able to help you too much, but I can explain more about that when I see you in person.

I look forward to meeting you on Wednesday. Please come into the school office where I can register you myself.

Take care,

Gaby Anderson

....

KAYLA SAT BACK FROM the computer screen and wiped her tired, weary eyes with the heels of her hands.

The library was getting quiet. She wasn't used to working in a public space, but she'd ditched her phone just in case it could be traced to her location. The shifter hunters may not have had the kind of resources for that, but she couldn't take the chance.

She folded up the letter her mum had written to her in the event of her death and tucked it back inside the journal. It still shocked her that the letter and its contents existed in the first place. How could she have known so little? Annoyingly, the letter didn't provide any information about who Killian was and why he was so important, only a set of instructions that included contacting Gaby Anderson. She understood the need to keep delicate information hidden, but Kayla knew nothing and she wondered how the heck she was going to find this 'Killian.'

It had only been a week since that night; her parents' murders were still being blasted all over news outlets and social media. They weren't being described as murders, though. Newspapers reported it as a 'tragic accident.' Tragic accident, her ass.

She had been able to pick up some essentials using one of her parents' work credit cards she'd found in the journal. They'd used it for risky purchases such as new identification documents, so she knew it was safe to use.

Packing away the journal in the backpack she had bought herself, she logged off the computer and exited the library to catch the next train north.

Keep moving.

Both her instincts and her father's lessons echoed the sentiment. On Wednesday she could join the academy, find this Killian, and hopefully figure out what her mum had meant about him being the key. Maybe this Anderson woman could also shed some light. And after that? Well, after that she intended to meet up with the person her parents had entrusted with their files. Those files held documents about their contacts and the people they helped, and she hoped she could find someone who knew about the original Alliance.

With a clear plan in her head, she boarded the train and prepared for the journey.

CHAPTER FOUR

BLAKE

BLAKE STOOD WITH HIS arms braced on the stone wall of the boys' changing room showers as water ran down his back. Blinking the mist out of his bright azure eyes, he tried to clear his thoughts. His heart pounded. He drew a deep breath into his lungs and the stale stench of pubescent boys filtered into his nostrils. He knew some washed religiously but others – not so much.

The results of a heavy workout hung in the atmosphere, so he was grateful for the thick steam now curling its way around his tall, somewhat lanky build. Now that Blake was halfway through his sixteenth year, he was trying to build muscle. His frame could withstand more weight, but he was struggling to keep hold of any mass he put on. It wasn't like he didn't try, he just had a ridiculous metabolism.

Or so his dad kept saying.

That was the thing about his dad. He tried hard to make Blake feel okay about his body, but when his dad managed a gym and had the physique he trained for, it was hard to not feel bitter about it. Blake respected his dad, but it didn't mean he wasn't envious. He shared very few similarities with his father. For instance, his dad was tall – taller than he was – and had a decent frame that was packed with muscle. Perhaps the past few years had seen a slight decline in his father's muscle mass, but still, for his age, his dad was built like a soldier. They trained together all the time. The whole family were into fitness, and holidays revolved around camping and long hikes, but his dad always made the time for a father-son training session. His parents even installed a home gym, which Blake used every night.

Once, in an effort to obtain the coveted, muscle-bound body of his dreams, he'd upped his protein, tracked his nutrient intake, and even tried shakes. They did not agree with him, and he chalked the whole week – complete with vomiting – up to an expensive mistake. Still, he struggled to keep muscle mass. It just seemed to fall off anytime he thought he'd achieved something. It didn't make him weak, though. In fact, he was one of the strongest players on the teams he played on – of which there were many.

The sound of laughter pulled him from his thoughts and he scooped back his thick brown hair, wiping water from his face.

"Collins!" a male shouted, banging on the shower cubicle door. "What are you doing in there? Your make-up?"

The tell-tale low timbre of male sniggering rumbled outside the cubicle door. Some of the guys mocked, whistled, or jeered in agreement. He rolled his eyes heavenward.

The steam affected his vocal cords as he shouted back gruffly, "Just trying to wash away the stench of your miserable loss." He could visualise how his best friend Josh would smirk at the other guys, shake his head, and walk away, embarrassed about being called out for his defeat in the game they had just played. Josh was the temporary captain of the opposing players – a team made up of the year below them – and they were an undeniable mess.

It was their sports coach who had asked them both to return and train the others. Now that he and Josh were in sixth-form, the hockey team they used to play for was down two of their best players, and they were called in during their lunch break as a favour. They couldn't pass up the opportunity to lord it over some of the younger lads who had been right pains up their butts for the past couple of years. Those same boys were now, unsurprisingly, struggling to win a game without them.

He turned the water off and snatched his towel from the hook, drying his chest before securing it around his waist. Having showered in a boys' changing room since he'd started in year seven, he had no issue striding out of the cubicle half-naked. Several of his teammates stood in various stages of undress as they either got changed into their sixth-form suits or their sports kit.

The school was famous for its variety of sports on offer, and he and Josh took full advantage of this by playing on most the teams. Hockey only went up to year eleven, but they were part of the sixth-form rugby and football teams, and they were in the middle of trialling a lacrosse team too.

"They do my nut in, Blake. All of them, the lot!" Josh huffed from beside him, his brown eyes full of irritation. Blake exited the cubicle and moved over to the locker, nodding his head in agreement.

"Yes, but coach asked us for a favour."

"Well, you can bloody well go on their team next time. Worst team I ever captained. They don't listen to a bloody word I say!"

"Have you tried not being so bossy?" Blake asked, slipping on some boxers under his towel. He pulled his navy trousers off the hanger as Josh slumped against the locker.

Josh shrugged. "Shut your mouth, Collins. It's not like I'm bossy, but if we're being honest, a captain has to be bossy. It's like, everyone knows that rule."

"Don't you think a captain should coach too? Offer encouragement? Have you tried that?" Josh turned and narrowed his eyes at Blake as he buttoned up his crisp, white shirt. "What?" he asked defensively when his friend continued to glare.

"As we're mates, I'm gonna pretend you didn't just tell me to be nice to that group of hooligans."

Blake frowned at his best friend. "Hooligans?"

"Yep. Hooligans."

"Moving on . . . I need to go drop some forms off at the office before class. Come with?"

"Holy Moses! You still scared of Mrs Rogers?" Josh smirked.

"I wouldn't call it scared so much as . . . yeah, fine. She scares me, all right!"

Josh laughed, doubling over at the waist. Blake packed his gym bag, slung it over one shoulder so it hung low over his hip, and put his backpack on over his jacket. Sixth-form required suits for the guys, and it was a massive pain for those who played sports and had to get changed throughout the day.

Josh was still laughing at him, but Mrs Rogers really gave him the creeps – she always looked like she was watching him too closely, and lately she'd been threatening to put him in after-school detention for no apparent reason.

Josh slapped his hand onto Blake's shoulder. "Mate, I'll come and defend you from the evil Mrs Rogers . . ." Josh tried really hard to keep it in, but the laughter bubbled up and out of him as he bent over again, holding his sides. Blake stood with his arms folded over his chest as he waited for Josh to gather himself. His best friend was still chuckling as Blake slung his own gym kit over his shoulder and they exited the changing rooms.

The boys made their way through the crowded hallways, and a group of young girls froze mid-gossip to stare at them when they walked past.

"Hey, Josh," one said, blinking quickly as she looked him up and down. Blake rolled his eyes at the wink Josh gave her.

"Man, you don't let up, do you?" Blake half-laughed as they continued down the hall.

"They're into you, too, if you just looked," Josh replied, fist bumping one of the other lads from their old football team. Blake sighed and tapped his elbow into Josh's side.

"How many times do I have to tell you? I'm just not interested in any of the girls here."

Josh left well enough alone for the short walk to the office door. Blake knocked and Ms Martinez opened it, beckoning them inside. She was in her thirties and was always warm and welcoming. Thank God it was her. Mrs Rogers really did give him the heebie-jeebies.

"What can I help you with, boys?"

"I've got the forms that Miss Anderson wanted from my dad, the updating details form?" Blake mumbled, rifling through his bag for the thick envelope.

"She's just with another student if you want to take a seat and hand it over to her?" She wasn't being rude, but she clearly had no intention of doing a job that she wasn't there to do.

"Cheers," the boys said in unison, watching her hips sway as she walked away.

Josh quickly smacked him on the arm and smirked. "You're in luck. I don't see Mrs Rogers." The boys stepped into the large, open room. The walls were lined with six desks, each occupied by someone typing or talking on the phone.

"Oh ha-ha. You'd be the same if–"

"That's not how it works here." Miss Anderson's sterner-than-usual voice caught their attention. The pair looked over at her desk. Miss Anderson, a job-orientated woman in her fifties, folded her arms and tapped her foot impatiently. She was the mirror image of the young girl who stood before her.

Blake took his time studying the young woman. He didn't recognise her from school, but she wore the crested blazer of their sixth-form academy. The girl was fairly small, but then again, Miss Anderson was a tall woman, so he couldn't compare the two. Nevertheless, Blake was pretty sure she would only come up to his shoulders.

A shiny curtain of chestnut-coloured hair hung poker straight down her back. The unknown girl swept a lock behind her ear, huffing exaggeratedly, revealing her face in profile. Straight nose, well-defined brows – he only noticed the latter because a lot of the girls in school were in the middle of a fashion fad of making their eyebrows super thin, and it was super unattractive. He only caught a glimpse, but he swore her eyes were brown too. Her complexion took on a frustrated, rosy glow.

"Fine. Just give me the class schedule and I'll figure it out myself." She thrust her hand out, impatiently waiting for Miss Anderson to give her the timetable. Miss Anderson smiled sweetly.

"I'll see you later, Kayla."

"Whatever," the girl mumbled, shoving the timetable into her bag and turning away. The boys had yet to sit down and stood awkwardly in the middle of what would have been her clear exit to the door. She stopped short of them and pushed her hands out and to the sides, not unlike a cabin crew member motioning to the exits on a plane. "Move it, dweebs."

"Feisty. I like it." Josh grinned. The girl zeroed in on Josh and marched forward. Blake sidestepped to give her room, but Josh – who clearly knew nothing about women – stood his ground, looking like he was enjoying the interaction. As she pushed past Josh, she flinched and gasped, frowning as she hurried away with concern in her eyes. Blake wanted to follow and ask if she was okay, but Miss Anderson called him over.

CHAPTER FIVE

KAYLA

KAYLA FOLLOWED MISS ANDERSON – Gaby, she insisted – into the small, two-bedroom terraced house after her first day at the academy. It had taken her some time to get used to the layout of the school, and she still hadn't adjusted to her new last name. Both she and Gaby had agreed it would be best to at least change her surname for now. It pained her, letting go of a connection to her parents, but it was just for a short while – at least she hoped.

Gaby put her bag, coat, and keys onto separate pegs in the narrow hallway, so Kayla followed suit, keeping her backpack with her.

"I'll show you to your room. It's not much, but it has the basics," Gaby said, moving up the stairs.

"Thank you again, Gaby; I appreciate this. It beats staying at a hotel. Speaking of which, let me give you some money towards rent."

"Oh, don't be silly. Your parents gave so much to our supernatural community; it's only right I give back just a little to their daughter." Gaby stopped by one of the three doors on the landing. She opened it to reveal a small bathroom, and the second door led to Kayla's temporary room.

Inside was a single bed, a chest of drawers, and a desk with a lamp. The bed had blankets and towels on it already – folded and artfully arranged.

Gaby had obviously gone out and fetched Kayla some school supplies, as a pot of pencils and pens, along with some notebooks, sat on top of the desk. Fresh flowers rested in a vase on the single window ledge.

Kayla's voice was thick with emotion when she spoke. "Thank you, Gaby."

Those small touches made her realise she was cared for. After being an orphan for only a handful of days, it helped cut through the grief a bit. She tried not to focus on her loss, but being here, being cared for, brought up those feelings.

"As I said, it's not much, but hopefully you'll be okay," Gaby said, wringing her hands nervously. Kayla smiled at her, easing the concern on the older woman's face. "Brilliant! Shall we do the rest of the tour now and get some dinner? I say tour, but it will be over in only a few minutes." She laughed.

"Sounds like a plan."

A simple kitchen-diner and a living space with a small sofa and a single armchair made up the downstairs of the house. The TV was relatively small by today's standards but big enough for the living room. The house was decorated to the tastes of a single woman in her fifties, but Kayla found it oddly comforting. Stacks of books sat haphazardly on the coffee table, blankets draped over the arms of the sofa, ready to wrap around and snuggle in while reading or watching TV, and candles littered the empty fireplace. That last fact relieved her just a bit. Since the night her unnatural magic had set fire to her house, she hadn't been able to call on it again, and she didn't want anything near her to encourage it either.

"I hope you're okay that I changed your last name from Mitchell to Smith. I know we didn't discuss what to change it to, but I thought Smith was more common – just in case others are still after you."

"That's sensible, thank you."

"I also wanted to apologise for getting off on the wrong foot," Gaby began as they moved into the kitchen and started preparing veggies for what looked like stir fry. Kayla tried to help, but Gaby shooed her away and made her sit at the table while she cooked. "I know you were upset that I didn't give you the information you wanted earlier, but I *can't* give you the names of the shifters as I don't have that information. As soon as I enrol shifters or magic users at the school, your dad wipes my memory of their true identities. We thought it would be a fail-safe measure to ensure no one is able to get to them."

"My dad? He wiped memories? Just that specific information? I thought he could only alter people's perceptions of memories?" Kayla rambled through the questions quickly and didn't miss the look Gaby gave her – the one that suggested her dad may not have always been truthful with her.

"So you see, I physically don't have that information for you, but I will help where I can."

Kayla blinked and focused on the task at hand, filing away the revelation about her father for later.

"Mum asked me to find Killian. Do you know who that might be? Have you heard of him? I know you said my dad wiped your memories but maybe if you concentrate?"

Gaby stopped stirring the pan and closed her eyes, but after a few moments, she shook her head and sighed.

"Sorry. He wouldn't have left a trace of him in my mind."

Kayla pulled the sunflower-shaped pendant out from under her top. "What do you know about spelled tracking pendants?"

Kayla pulled it over her head and handed it to Gaby.

"Spelled tracking pendant? I'm a mage, so this really isn't my area of expertise, but I'd say, especially if your mum did this, that it works only for you." She handed it back and Kayla put it on, feeling better as soon as the necklace was resting against her chest again.

"How does it work? Do you know?"

"From my limited knowledge, they help lead you toward whatever it was spelled to find. It will probably give a sign when you are close to the object or person, but other than that, I'm just guessing."

"When I pushed past that guy standing in the office earlier – the shorter, muscly one – the pendant flashed hot for a moment. I think it was telling me he might be Killian."

"Josh? He's one of the sporty ones, isn't he? Yeah, I could see him being a wolf. He shot up and bulked out fairly quickly this year, and that's quite common among the shifters."

"So it could be him?"

"Yes, but I can't know for sure, and you can't just go and ask him outright either. If he's human, that could have just as disastrous an effect."

Kayla flinched. She knew protecting their paranormal society was paramount. She'd have to try and find out if he was a shifter through other means. Perhaps she could get him to reveal some shifter qualities?

Gaby placed a bowl of stir-fry in front of her, her voice startling Kayla out of her plans. "It certainly sounds like a possibility though."

"I guess I'll have to do some more digging to find out if Josh is really Killian. I still don't know who he is and why my mum thought he was so important," she said under her breath.

"I wish I could tell you more, but I just don't know. Your dad made sure I'd never know who was in the school. Seemed like a good idea at the time."

The two ate in silence and then Kayla excused herself to her room. She took some time before bed to study her mum's spell journal. When the lights went out and she lay in her cold, foreign bed, she let herself cry for her parents as she had done every night since the incident. The only thing that eased her grief the tiniest amount was knowing the shifter hunters who'd attacked her family had all perished in the fire.

Tomorrow was a new day, but for the time being she was just a lonely girl weeping for her mum and dad.

CHAPTER SIX

BLAKE

ENTERING HIS HISTORY CLASS after break, Blake was surprised to find the girl from the office seated in the room. Her gaze stopped on Blake and Josh when they arrived, and she carefully tracked them as they found their seats. Josh, not in the least bit put off by what had happened in the office the day before, sauntered over to sit at her table.

She was tapping her pencil as she studied them both – mostly Josh – but he could sense she was eager to ask something. Despite the curiosity clearly present on her face, the girl stayed silent.

Josh tried to engage in conversation, but she seemed to think better of it and faced the front when the teacher walked in.

The teacher scanned the room and stopped at the girl. "Ah, we have a newbie. Great stuff. I see you're probably at the best table for catching up as Mr Collins is rather adept at historical work." He spoke fondly of Blake, who ducked his head at the attention. Reaching retirement age, Mr Adams was without a doubt one of Blake's favourite teachers. He was respected, commanding, and above all else, fair.

Mr Adams went down the register, only looking up to smile encouragingly at the new girl as he said her name. "Kayla?"

"Here," she replied softly. The name suited her.

"Ladies and gentlemen," Mr Adams said after he finished the register. "To help the lovely Kayla here and to re-fresh our own memories, I want you to work in groups to create a short presentation on the life of the last Russian tsar: Nicholas the Second. I want you to focus on his early life, his family, his effect as a ruler, and ultimately his death. What acts did Nicholas commit that led to the dissolution of the Romanov reign and the death of his family? You'll work with the other students at your table, so start with the basics today, and next week you can begin putting together your presentations."

Blake looked around the table. There were five of them: himself, Josh, Kayla, and two other girls who didn't look especially impressed at the idea of group work. No one spoke, so Blake took charge as he always did – a by-product of being a sports captain, he supposed – and directed the two girls to focus on the tsar's early life and family, suggesting he, Josh, and Kayla look at his reign and death. The two girls seemed pleased with the arrangement and logged onto their laptops.

"So, Kayla . . ." Josh began, and Blake inwardly cringed at Josh's attempt at a 'sultry' voice.

"Let me stop you right there. This is not going to happen," Kayla stated openly, addressing Josh's god-awful attempts at flirting. "I'm here for one thing and one thing only, and it is not whatever you have going on inside your head." Kayla's eyes widened a fraction, shocked by her own attitude. Her mouth fell open, but no words came out.

Blake tried to interject, attempting to save the project and his friend from further embarrassment. "Shall we catch up on the tsar?"

Kayla closed her eyes for a few seconds. When she opened them, her face had softened. "I'm sorry. That was harsh. I've not had the best of times recently; I didn't mean to snap when you were just being nice. Friends?" she said directly to Josh and held her hand out to shake. Josh frowned but clasped her hand in his and shook it.

"No problem. I'm Josh."

Josh reached into his bag to get his notebook and pens out, but confusion flashed across Kayla's face as she studied her palm.

"You all right?" Blake asked, and she lifted her eyes to look at him. She shook clear the cloud of confusion.

"Yeah, sure."

"I'm Blake, by the way."

"Kayla."

"I know."

She inhaled quickly. "What?"

Blake pointed to the teacher. "Register?"

"Right. Yes. Of course," she muttered, digging in her bag and pulling out a biro.

Josh looked at Kayla and then at Blake, having missed their introduction when his back was turned. Blake knew he was asking him what he'd done, so he mouthed 'nothing' and shrugged his shoulders.

"What do you already know then, Kayla?" Blake asked and Kayla flinched, dropping her pen on the table.

"Excuse me?"

"About the tsar?"

Her pinched features relaxed.

They spent the lesson mapping out their research points and splitting up the areas to study.

"Everyone cool with what they're doing?" Blake asked, and both Josh and Kayla nodded.

"Hey, Kayla, I was thinking we could meet up tonight in the library to work on the project if you want?" Josh asked her while they were packing away at the end of the lesson. If Blake wasn't mistaken, his friend seemed almost nervous – it was so unlike him. Kayla quickly glanced at Blake, possibly wondering if he was about to crash their little study session. "Blake can come too, right, Blake?" Josh quickly tagged on.

"Sorry man, can't. I'm tutoring tonight."

"What do you say, Kayla?" Josh asked again.

"Um, yeah, that'd be cool."

A smile lit up Josh's face. "Great! Meet you there after school?"

"Sure," she replied, tucking some hair behind her ear as the bell rang. "See you later."

IT WAS FIVE THIRTY when Blake finished his tutoring, which was later than normal, but he didn't mind. He walked home at his usual unhurried pace, enjoying the mild evening. A soft, welcome breeze reminded Blake of the camping holidays he took with his family. He'd always connected better with nature than the city, and he felt lucky to live towards the edge of the town where houses were further apart and green areas were respected. Kayla crossed the street ahead of him, pulling him from his thoughts. Wasn't she meant to have been with Josh?

"Kayla!" he called out without thinking. She spun quickly, face serious and body tense, but she sagged a little when she saw who it was. Her eyes darted about before settling back on him as he took a few long strides to catch up. She looked wary and clutched her bag's straps while he approached. "Thought you were at the library? With Josh."

"We finished. He had to suddenly . . . leave."

"Huh," he grunted. He would have expected Josh to walk her home at least, especially as it was dark. Not that she wasn't capable; it just wasn't the sort of behaviour that had been drilled into him by his dad. "Where are you going?"

"Not far."

"What a coincidence, I'm going 'not far' too!"

A smile ghosted her lips before they settled back into a tight line.

"I don't need anyone to walk me home, Blake," she said, fixing him with a stare.

"I'm sure you don't *need* anyone, but it's what friends do," he replied, watching as she rolled her shoulders back, about to argue. "I normally walk past the park. If you're heading that way, some company would be nice."

A calculated look entered her eye, but he couldn't figure out why. She mulled something over in her mind until she gave a single, sharp nod.

"I'm going that way. Company will be . . . nice."

He didn't understand the look of worry shadowing her face, but he didn't question it and matched his stride to hers as they began to walk down the street.

"How was tutoring?"

"Study session go okay?"

They both asked simultaneously.

"Sorry, you go," she said with a slight chuckle. He smiled.

"Just wondered if your study session went okay. Josh showed you the library and all that?"

"He sure did."

"I'm surprised he let you walk back by yourself. If you're already here, your house is a fair distance away from school."

She responded curtly, "You're going this way."

"I like the fresh air."

"Me too."

Silence filled the air like static energy.

"Learn much?" he asked after a few moments.

"Enlightening," she responded, worrying her bottom lip between her teeth.

He had a feeling she wasn't talking about their history project. Josh had better not have laid it on too thick or pushed her too far. He was Blake's best mate, which meant Blake knew exactly what Josh was like, and there was no denying his best friend liked Kayla. He clenched his fist when unwelcome thoughts entered his head.

"What do you tutor?" she asked.

"Maths. We have a volunteer programme at school. I'm currently helping out this year nine kid who is struggling with algebra."

"Oh," she mumbled, surprise lacing her tone. "I like algebra," she tagged on, and his lips quirked up.

"You're one of the only people I know who does. I find it some of the easiest maths to do. It's pattern building and logical thinking."

"I like how the numbers and letters work together."

"That's precisely why so many hate it. Josh is constantly hammering for my help, saying, 'Letters shouldn't mix with numbers. What are we doing? English?!'" Blake grumbled in a deep tone, mimicking Josh. Kayla let out a quick laugh, the musical notes lingering in the air.

"But that's the beauty of it: two opposites finding balance." She frowned again. She did that often. "Are we really having a conversation about algebra?" she asked after a brief silence, her tone a bit lighter.

"Yeah, you're a right nerd," he said. Her head whipped up, a shocked, humorous look on her face.

"Says you!"

He barked out a laugh just as she came to an abrupt halt. He'd taken one step ahead but stopped and glanced back. The seriousness on her face sobered him.

"Kayla?"

"I'm sorry, Blake, I . . ." He wasn't certain why, but regret marred her features.

"What's up?"

She squared her shoulders again and forced a smile.

"This is my street," she said, pointing the opposite way he needed to go. He carefully studied her face for a moment but nodded.

"Cool. See you at school."

She tried forcing another smile, but it came out as more of a grimace. She turned on her heel and marched down the road.

Why was he so fixated on her apparent lack of openness with him? He'd only just met the girl. She certainly didn't owe him anything. He watched until she disappeared from sight, running an agitated hand through his dark hair.

CHAPTER SEVEN

KAYLA

KAYLA STEPPED INTO GABY'S house, leaning her back against the door after she'd locked it. She blew out an unsteady breath. He'd watched her leave for the longest time; she wasn't used to having eyes on her like that. He made her feel . . . nervous, she realised. Nerves like she'd never felt before. She placed a hand over her fluttering abdomen, hoping to quiet the butterflies.

She pushed Blake out of her mind and moved into the living room where Gaby sat with a cup of tea and a crossword puzzle. Gaby looked up as she entered.

"You're back! How was school? The library?" she asked with an interested smile. Kayla had seen Gaby at lunch and told her she'd be late getting back. She knew the woman was waiting to be filled in.

"School was fine. Josh though . . . when I shook his hand in class, I didn't get the same heat from the pendant. Why could that be?" Kayla asked, absently fiddling with the pendant as she sat down.

"I honestly don't know. Do you still think it's Josh? Could it be anybody else?"

Kayla sat back in the plush armchair and shrugged.

"I've only spent time with Josh and Blake. I thought it had to be Josh."

"Blake?"

"Josh's friend."

"Blake Collins! Of course! Not sure why I forgot who he was." She shook her head, smiling.

"What do you mean?" Kayla asked as her heart sped up. What was with her at the moment?

"Oh, nothing. Just that he and Josh have been co-captains for various sports teams. Both exceptional sportsmen from what I hear."

"Shifters are usually sporty, so Josh's muscular frame makes sense. Blake's frame doesn't. He's too . . . slender. By his age, he would have shifted so his body would be piling on body mass – they need it to sustain and repair from shifts. Right?"

"From what I know of shifters, yes."

"Do you think I should continue down the Josh line of thinking?"

"I'm about to say something you'll probably roll your eyes at, but I say go with your gut instinct."

Kayla did roll her eyes. "Gee. Thanks."

"Do you have another class with Josh tomorrow?" Kayla nodded. "Well, tread carefully but talk with him some more, and if you're still really unsure after . . . I can try and contact a witch, see if they can help you narrow down the search."

"Really? That would be so helpful. Thank you."

"I'm pretty useless otherwise."

"Don't say that!"

"What are you going to do once you've found who you're after?" she asked. Kayla didn't miss that she was trying to change the subject.

"Figure out who Killian is so I can understand why my mum wanted me to find him so much and then get to the person my parents sent all their work to. I need to know if they have any information on the original alliance. Mum said Killian was the key to bridging the gap between the two races. That makes sense, doesn't it?"

Gaby frowned. "That might be difficult. The surviving supporters of the alliance have gone deep into hiding. Nobody knows the exact parameters of the alliance that the shifter royals were trying to create."

"And there's no one from the original magic user council left either," Kayla huffed, folding her arms and sinking even lower in the chair.

Gaby leaned over and patted her on the knee, a warm smile on her face.

"They'd be proud to see you taking an interest in their work. It's a very noble thing to want to continue what they did."

Kayla felt guilty; it had nothing to do with being noble and everything to do with staying connected to them in some way, fulfilling her mum's dying wish.

"I can get you a counsellor? Someone to speak to?" Gaby gently queried, interrupting her thoughts.

"I'm fine," Kayla replied, taking slow, even breaths to cover up the fact that her heart was squeezing tight.

"It's barely been two weeks, sweetheart."

Kayla flinched. She tried so hard to cope with her parents' deaths during the day, but now that it was getting closer to her bedtime, she was struggling to hold it all in. If she cried now, Gaby might force her to talk to a shrink, and that was the last thing she wanted.

"I know, but this is keeping me busy, honestly. I'm just . . . I'm just not ready to talk about it yet."

"Okay," Gaby responded, but her tone made it obvious she would revisit the subject later.

"I know it's early, but I might head up to bed," Kayla said, rising from her seat.

"I'll see if any witches might be able to help you with the tracking pendant. Good night." Gaby smiled, her voice gentle.

Kayla nodded and left the room, not quite trusting her voice.

As she lay in bed, eyes stinging with tears, her thoughts turned to memories of helping her parents with their work. They'd trained her to follow in their footsteps.

"I miss you guys. I wasn't ready to do this on my own," she whispered as she drifted off to sleep.

Kayla walked in from school, throwing her bag in the corner by the shoes. She checked her watch and was about to run upstairs to change when her dad walked in from the kitchen.

"Hey, baby girl!"

"Hey, dad," she replied as she swung around the sofa.

"Good day at school?"

"Yeah. I'm just going to change and then I'll be ready."

"Any magic rumbles today?"

She groaned, hastily running up the first few steps. "Gah! I'm not talk-

ing about puberty with you!"

"It's not puberty. It's magic," he replied, a smile on his face.

"Same thing for magic users, Dad. Same thing," she shouted, stomping up the rest of the stairs. As she ripped off her school uniform in frustration, she speculated about when her magic was going to show up.

It was her fifteenth birthday, and she was officially a complete loser. Apparently, she was the only offspring of magic users to not get any magic. Both her parents were quite powerful, so why had she still not received an inkling of her own? She'd shot up in height, grew leg hair for Pete's sake, and even had boobs now – thank the lord for some miracles – but magic? Nothing to show for it. She knew it was there. Deep down, she could feel the magic moving inside of her, rushing through her veins like blood. It just had to surface. That was all.

Her parents were so kind and forgiving, but she could tell they were worried about her future. How could she hope to take over her parents' work – hiding magic users and shifters from assassination and prosecution – if she didn't have any magic to help?

She slung on an old pair of jeans and a jumper for the meeting her dad had set up. The only thing she knew was that a young boy and his father were coming to their house for help because the boy's mum had been killed for being an Alliance activist. They were looking for somewhere safe to live.

Three knocks at the door alerted her to their arrival. She quickly jogged down the stairs as her dad rose from the couch. He nodded to her, silently asking if she was ready, and she smiled back.

Nerves fluttered furiously around her stomach; this was important to her. Her parents were trusting her, and she didn't want to let them down. Magic or no magic, she had to prove she was capable of this.

As he opened the door, she anxiously tucked her hair behind both ears. This was the first time her dad was letting her speak to one of their clients alone. Kayla's job was to take the young boy out for some burgers and get him to open up. That way, her dad could use his magic to help him overcome his fears. The more knowledge her dad had, the more effective he was.

Normally, she did this with one of her parents, but with her mum away working with another client and her dad needing space to speak to the father, she was left to handle the task alone. The door opened and she shuffled her feet, fidgeting in place. Her parents trusted her; she could do this. She wanted to help people just like her parents did. She had this. Her pep talk came to an end when she saw the clients.

"Mr Richards, come in, please. It's so good to see you again." The men shook hands while the young boy stood awkwardly. His dark brown skin stood in rich contrast to her dad's fair colouring. His dark eyes held a world of pain, and looking into them nearly took her breath away. Her heart ached for him. She knew she had to help.

The eleven-year-old boy appeared to be on the cusp of puberty. His trousers skimmed the tops of his trainers and the first signs of pubescent acne dotted his chin.

"Hi Oliver, I'm Kayla. I thought we could go get some food while these two chat about boring adult stuff?" The boy stared, his deep brown eyes flicking between her and his father.

"Go on, son. That sounds like a great idea," he said to Kayla as he laid his hand on top of his son's close-cropped hair and kissed him gently on the head. "Have a good time, okay?"

The boy shrugged and followed Kayla out. She was closing the door when her dad mouthed 'only the route we discussed' as a quick reminder. She nodded and tried not to roll her eyes. She'd had the route drilled into her head for months. It was the route with the most CCTV, the most populated streets, and led to the busiest fast-food chain the town had to offer.

Kayla stuffed her hands into her pockets as she tried to make conversation.

"So, my dad says that you've stopped going to school?"

Silence.

"Got any hobbies?"

Silence.

"What are your mates like? Have you seen them since . . . you know?"

Silence.

God, she was rubbish at this.

They entered the busy chain and ordered their meals, taking a booth by the window when they finished.

"Sucks huh? Your mum. She sounded really brave."

"Stupid more like," he grumbled, pushing two fries into his mouth. It wasn't what she was expecting, but at least he had said something.

"I don't think fighting for what you believe in is stupid."

"Perhaps you're stupid too."

"Hey, I'm just trying to help. No need to be rude about it!" she scolded

and immediately regretted it. The boy had just lost his mother. "I'm sorry. I didn't mean to snap."

"That's okay. It's kind of different from how everyone else has been treating me."

"You were there, weren't you? The night she was . . ."

Oliver sneered into his food. "Killed? Yeah."

"How do you feel about that night, about losing your mum?"

"I told you, she was stupid and I'm angry. I'm not upset. I'm mad that she did what she did and got killed because of it, and now I've got no mum and my dad has lost his bond mate," Oliver answered sourly.

"Bond mate? Aren't they quite rare?" she questioned, thinking back to how her mum had said bonded pairs within shifters were few and far between. Oliver nodded.

"My dad? He's dying. If it wasn't for me . . ."

"Dying?"

"His heart. It's breaking. I hear him cry at night when he thinks I'm asleep. I hear him cry in the shower when he thinks I can't hear. He doesn't eat, and he barely sleeps. He needs to know I'm safe and . . . well, I'm probably going to be an orphan soon."

"Hey! Don't talk like that! He just needs to start somewhere fresh, somewhere safe with you . . ." she trailed off, sensing she wasn't going to get any more from him. They ate their burgers in silence while thoughts of failure circled her head like vultures.

When Oliver spoke again, he did so quietly. "They ripped her apart like she meant nothing, those shifters. Shifters shouldn't be able to do that to other shifters without consequence. It's like they had no emotion, no connection. I just don't understand."

Her voice softened, her heart breaking for the boy. "I think it's because shifters don't have a royal family anymore. The rifts within and between our races are so wide."

"Mum wanted peace between us, shifters and magic users back in harmony. She died because she was trying to find a distant bloodline to the royal family to establish an alliance between the two races again. It got her killed. She wanted peace and she was murdered by her own kind." He sniffed and rubbed his eyes.

They were quiet on the way home, and it wasn't until she was speaking to her dad later that evening that she asked about bond mates.

"Oliver said his parents were bonded mates, and that if it wasn't for him, his dad would have died already. Is it true that bonded mates need each other to survive? Can you help him?"

"That's a difficult question, Kayla. I can't help him, no. It's not like being soul entwined. Bonded pairs can be broken, but the longer they are together, the more bonded they become, and they simply die of broken hearts when one passes. There's nothing anyone can do."

"What's soul entwined?"

"It's a legend among the shifters who believe bonded mate pairings come from the soul entwined from centuries ago. The soul entwined were shifters whose souls were literally bound together. But nothing of the sort has been proven. Being soul entwined was just a way for the shifters to assert their superiority over magic users. Some shifters anyway. Bonded pairs are a thing, however, and though they are not as common as they once were many, many years ago, those who experience it are truly lucky."

"Do magic users have anything like that?"

"Not in that way, no, but I don't need a bond to prove how much I love your mother. My magic hums when she's nearby. That's all I need to know," he said, smiling to himself. "I better go and work my magic. Thank you for finding the source of his pain." He squeezed her shoulder comfortingly as he left to find Oliver.

Kayla woke suddenly and tried to push away the image of her dad tampering with Oliver's memories. Had he done more to Oliver than she'd realised? What exactly was her dad capable of?

Leaning over, she switched the lamp off.

"Why, Dad?" she whispered into the dark. "Why didn't you tell me what you could do?"

CHAPTER EIGHT

BLAKE

BLAKE PUSHED OPEN THE sage coloured front door and shrugged his bags off, dumping them by the coat stand. He hung his jacket on a spare hook and wandered into the living room as he rolled up his shirt sleeves. His younger brother sprawled on the couch with an X-box controller in one hand and one leg resting on top of his knee, eyes glued to the screen. The twelve-year-old was unlike Blake in many ways. For one thing, he was blonde.

Unfortunately for his brother, puberty was already starting to rear its ugly head. Thankfully, Blake was coming out on the other side and was losing the teenage acne. However, his own embarrassing experiences didn't stop Blake from taking the piss out of Charlie when his voice broke for the first time.

His brother twisted the controller to the right and repeatedly hit one of the buttons.

"Die already!" he screamed as two zombies attacked his player. The screen changed and blood-red liquid covered the scene with the words GAME OVER stamped across the TV.

"Lose again?"

"What the hell, Blake? Sneak much?" Charlie responded sourly, sitting up to make room for him. Without a word, he handed over another controller.

"How was school?"

His younger brother gave him a sideways glance. "Why do you want to know?"

"No reason. Just trying to take an interest in your education."

"Uh-huh . . . you just want to know what I know," he said smugly as he started a new game. Charlie was best friends with Mrs Rogers' son, the one who knew everything in the school office, and the two boys always spied on new students. Blake wanted to ask about Kayla, but before he could figure out how to bring her up, the game began. Distracted, the boys forgot what they were talking about as zombies raged around them. It was a high level, one that held the duo prisoner.

"Go around dude! Around! I'm getting cornered!"

"I'm low on ammo!"

"Shit beans, I lost an arm!"

"I'm out!"

Both boys tossed the controllers on the low coffee table and slumped back in defeat.

"Same time tomorrow?" Blake asked, holding his fist out to the side.

"You bet," his brother responded and bumped the fist with his own.

Noise coming from the hallway suggested their mother was home. "Charlie? Charlie, can you *please* go get changed for practice?" she called out, walking into the living room. His brother was due at football practice in forty minutes, so he ran out of the room and stomped up the stairs. The boy was *not* light on his feet.

Blake followed him out. His mum took off her coat and scarf, hanging them up neatly before she attempted to pick up the shopping bags at her feet.

"Here, let me help you with that, Mum," Blake said. His mum beamed at him and let him carry the majority of the bags into the kitchen.

"Thank you, honey. Good day?" she asked breezily while putting the groceries away. Blake reached over to snatch a box of biscuits from one of the open bags, but she slapped his hand away. She pointed to the kitchen island stool and told him to get out of her way while she worked. She stored items carefully by colour, size, and product type, and anyone who messed with her system got a right rollicking. Seriously, no one cooked in the house for fear of his mother's wrath. He only ever assisted in the kitchen with his mum taking the lead, and his brother Charlie? Not so much. His mum had settled for just teaching one of her sons how to make a decent meal.

"Not so bad," he mumbled in answer to her question.

"And by that, you of course mean . . ." she prompted.

"You know, for once you could pretend that what I say is what I actually mean."

"I can't stop being your mother, can I?" she said smartly, passing him a glass of freshly poured orange juice. Blake rolled his eyes and took a gulp.

"I met a new girl the other day. Or rather, she just appeared out of nowhere at school."

"A new girl you say?" his mum repeated, hiding a grin.

"Why are you saying it like that? Anyway, Josh likes her so . . ."

"Is there some sort of 'bro-code' I'm not aware of?"

"Not so much. We both saw her at the same time, so it's not like he can make a claim to her or anything."

"He couldn't anyway, sweetheart, because she's a person. You can't claim people," his mum replied pertly.

"Yeah, I know. What I mean is she showed some interest in him."

"And you like this girl?"

Blake knew his cheeks were going red. He talked to his mum about everything, but some subjects were getting harder to discuss – girls being one of them. He ran a hand through his hair, making it stand on end.

"No, yes, sort of . . . I don't know. I only met her two seconds ago. I've not had a chance to get to know her."

His mum chuckled as she moved to the sink to wash some vegetables.

"You should trust your gut instinct, Blake."

"You *always* say that."

"And I'm *always* right."

Blake playfully stuck his tongue out behind her back.

"Put your tongue away!"

"How did you know?"

His mum spun around, pointing at her eyes and then at the back of her head. He groaned and she tutted at him.

"Are you going to speak to Josh about this girl?" she asked while she lined the food up to chop.

"Maybe. I'll just get to know her first. I think she's been through a lot recently."

"How so?"

Blake shrugged. "Just a look in her eyes."

Charlie walked in carrying his football boots. "Is that the new chick?"

"Women are not chicks, Charlie," their mother scolded.

Blake scowled at his brother. "Why are you being so nosey?"

"What was her name again?" Charlie asked as he scrunched up his nose in thought. "Kayla, wasn't it?"

"Yeah."

A loud clattering rang through the kitchen. Blake jumped off the stool and looked towards his mum. The knife she had been chopping with lay discarded on the floor.

"Mum?"

"Sorry!" She rushed to pick the knife up. "Finish prepping tea, Blake?" she asked, darting out of the room. Apparently, Charlie needed driving to football practice at that precise moment. Even Charlie looked confused.

His mum and Charlie left, leaving Blake alone. After finishing tea, he went outside and tossed the netball into the hoop, waiting for his dad to pull up. Blake grabbed the ball as it rolled back towards him, and he perked up at the sound of a car door slamming. He knew his dad would join him in the backyard momentarily.

"Hey kiddo," his dad called, shutting the side gate behind him. He still wore his gym gear despite being the manager at the gym – especially on days when he held personal training sessions.

"Who are you calling kiddo, old man?" Blake smirked as he threw the ball in his dad's direction.

"Old man? I think you'll find I can still whoop your ass," his dad said, effortlessly tossing the ball up and into the net. Blake shook his head in mock annoyance.

"You're on!"

The two played a game of hoops, the first to reach ten winning the game. It was something they did regularly, and Blake was even starting to believe that some of his wins were genuine.

The two sweaty men walked into the kitchen via the back door. One went to grab a couple of apples from the fruit bowl while the other poured two glasses of water from the fridge. When they were sitting on a pair of bar stools, his dad questioned him about Kayla.

"Did Mum ring you or something?" Blake asked wearily as his father pressed him for answers. "She's just a new girl."

His dad avoided his eyes when he spoke, and it made Blake's stomach sink in trepidation. "I need you to trust me, please. I know this is going to sound crazy, but can you stay away from her? Just for now?"

"Why?" the question was out of his mouth before he could think. The request was so far out of left field that it made him wonder if he was missing something vital.

"Please, Blake," his father pleaded.

Maybe it was the desperation in his tone, or perhaps it was the fact that he was clenching a fist, but Blake found himself nodding.

"I'll not actively seek her out if that's what you're saying," he replied after a pause.

"I'd appreciate it," his dad said. He strode out of the kitchen, leaving a confounded Blake behind.

BLAKE JOGGED DOWN THE stairs early the next morning, already dressed and ready for school. He grabbed his gym bag and put his earphones in, planning to get to school early to use the running field while it was empty. He needed some exercise. There was too much energy roiling inside of him, and he needed a release.

He silently moved down the hallway towards the kitchen where his parents talked in hushed voices. As he got closer, he slowed his footsteps. He wasn't eavesdropping, really. At least, that was what he told himself.

"She may not be Lewis's kid," his dad said.

"Derrek, we don't hear from Lewis for weeks, and then someone called Kayla just happens to turn up? Lewis has never been late before. We're nearly a week over and I can sense–"

"Blake!" his dad announced loudly, overly cheery, effectively ending Blake's eavesdropping. Blake walked into the room and towards the fridge. Opening it, he grabbed the butter.

"You guys all right?" he questioned slowly. His mum was jumpy – nervous, even. It was totally out of character for her. "Mum?"

"Yes, yes, all good. Don't worry about us." Her smile was tight, forced, as she shared a silent look with his dad.

He buttered the toast when it popped up, and his dad poured himself a coffee.

"Who's Lewis?" Blake asked, figuring he may as well just air it out. Surely his dad knew Blake heard a part of the conversation.

His dad froze momentarily before replying quickly, too quickly. "Just an old friend. Nothing for you to worry about."

"Okaaay."

"Have a good day at school!" his mum said, her voice pitched too high. She kissed his cheek and left before he could reply.

"Were you guys talking about Kayla?"

His dad walked over and clasped a hand on his shoulder.

"Remember what we said last night," he said, avoiding Blake's question.

It was the second time Blake was more than a little confused at his parents' behaviour. What did they have against the new girl at school – someone they'd never met?

CHAPTER NINE

BLAKE

BLAKE WASN'T PAYING MUCH attention to his surroundings, and he was only vaguely aware that he was somewhere near the dining hall as his head filled with his parents' conversation. He was convinced they were talking about Kayla. Was she the kid that they mentioned?

It was the weirdest his parents had ever behaved. His mum was jumpy and on edge, and his dad warned him to stay away from Kayla. He didn't understand why. Maybe he would ask her instead?

He'd already admitted to his mum that he liked Kayla, but his interest wasn't purely romantic. He suspected Kayla was hurting, and something inside of him wanted to help her. He didn't understand where the feelings came from or why he felt so inclined to be there for someone who was essentially a stranger. Plus, there was the fact that he knew his best friend liked her, too. He wasn't ignorant.

His head spun, so much so that he was oblivious to the conversations going on around him until her name broke through his thoughts.

"Kayla, isn't it?" a girl said.

He was passing a group of four girls huddled together, not so subtly pointing at a bench. Looking over, he spotted Kayla hunched over her lunch, nibbling on her sandwich. Her hair hung in a curtain around her face, covering most of her features.

"She's the one that was sniffing around Josh, wasn't she?" one girl sneered.

"Surely, she *does* know that she can't just come in and take over? There's a system," another girl responded, tutting as she swung her hair over her shoulder.

Blake was taken aback. He didn't realise the girls here were like that. Shouldn't they be trying to welcome a new student?

"I heard she's living with someone from the office staff; taken in like a stray." A hushed laugh followed.

Blake heard enough. Warning or no warning, his stomach churned with the need to do something, so he changed direction and marched towards Kayla, his long strides eating up the ground. He stopped in front of the bench, and she froze, sandwich halfway to her mouth. She slowly lifted her head to look up at him as he loomed over her.

Seeing the wary look in her eyes had him softening his glare – it wasn't aimed at her, after all.

"Can I help you?" she asked bluntly.

"Want to eat lunch with me?"

Her brows furrowed and she glanced at the group of girls he'd stalked past. She seemed to breathe out and slump a little before looking back at him.

"It's okay. You don't have to take pity."

"It's not pity; I'm trying to be a friend."

"Huh," she huffed, putting down her sandwich. "Look, Blake, I appreciate the walk home last night and I appreciate what you're doing now, but I'm fine. Honestly."

"Are you?" He didn't mean to ask that so snappily, and heat flared in her eyes, but it was somehow better than the wariness she always displayed.

"Yes."

He tried a different tactic. "Those girls were talking about you."

"I'm fully aware, but I'm not here to make girlfriends," she said, glancing their way again. Blake looked behind him and the girls balked, squeaking as they turned tail. "You must be popular to have that effect on them."

"It's mostly Josh's influence. They just know me because I captain a lot of the sports teams."

She raised her eyebrow at him. "Why 'mostly Josh'?"

"You've seen him, right? Now look at me." He smiled at her, trying to get rid of some of the tension coiled tight in his body.

Kayla took her time responding. "If you don't go get some lunch soon, there'll be nothing left."

"Trying to get me to leave?" he teased.

"Maybe."

"If you don't come with me, I won't bother with lunch."

"Trying to get me to come with you?" she teased back.

"Maybe."

Her smile swiftly fell. "Why?"

"I couldn't stand them talking about you behind your back . . ." He stared at his shoe, grinding it into the grass. If he didn't know better, he'd say he was nervous. For what?

Kayla stood up, swinging her bag over her shoulder.

"Lead the way," she sighed.

They walked side by side into the lunch hall and stood in line for food. He looked down at her as she crossed her arms and scanned the room.

"What eventually made you come with me? You ever even been in here before?"

"I heard your stomach rumble," she replied distractedly. "This is my first time in here. I don't like . . . crowds."

Blake raised his eyebrows at her, but she didn't see. He grabbed a tray when he got to the counter and ordered the beef stew with dumplings and mash and extra vegetables. She looked down at his tray.

"Hungry?"

"Got a big appetite. I'm a growing boy!"

She rolled her eyes but smiled.

"You need anything?" he asked when her gaze spread over the food.

"I'm good, got my sandwich."

"Just a sandwich?"

She nodded.

"That doesn't sound like much."

"Well, I'm not a growing boy." She was so deadpan as she spoke that his bark of laughter surprised even himself. She jumped at the noise.

"Sorry," he said sheepishly, but she grinned with him. He leaned over to grab the apple pie and custard dessert option; her head followed the bowl. "Want some?" he asked, automatically reaching over to get another.

"No." She rushed to get the words out.

He paid, and they moved to find a seat together, settling at the end of a table sitting opposite one another. Without waiting, he dug into the stew while she brought out her small sandwich wrapped in foil. He frowned.

"Is that really all you're eating?"

She glanced quickly at his food before looking at him again.

"Yeah." It was the wistfulness in her voice that troubled him.

"You're not worried about . . . money?" he lowered his voice at the end.

She shook her head, tucking some hair behind her ear. "It's not that. It's just I-I need to . . . just plan ahead, that's all. And I like food to go – just in case."

She didn't look at him, and he wondered what she meant. In case of what?

"What's your favourite food?" he asked to break the tension as he tucked into his pie.

She finished her sandwich and sighed longingly. "Anything with sugar."

"You like sweet stuff? What's your favourite dessert?"

Her eyes flicked to his pie.

"Pie?"

"Pie," she agreed, smiling. At least she wasn't mad at him, he supposed.

"What's your favourite TV show?" he asked, and she grinned wider. He ate in silence as she talked about some cartoon and then some comedy show about an office – he wasn't sure he'd seen either, but she was so animated. She looked relaxed, he realised.

"What's your favourite sport? You play here, don't you?" she questioned.

"Rugby is my favourite. It used to be hockey, but that sport only goes to year eleven so I've had to refocus, and rugby . . . this may sound weird, but it's great for releasing pent up energy."

"Doesn't sound weird at all."

"We've got a game coming up, actually. I'm quite nervous. I'm captaining it."

"You'll be great."

"How do you know?"

She shrugged nonchalantly.

The bell rang through the hall, followed by the sounds of chairs scraping and feet shuffling. Neither of them moved until he cleared his throat.

"I have to get going. Thanks for this," she added as she hurried off to class.

CHAPTER TEN

KAYLA

KAYLA HAD TO MAKE sure she sat next to Josh during her second to last lesson of the day: geography. Great. She really sucked at geography, but she was thankful for the opportunity to speak with Josh again. She'd chastised herself all last lesson for being preoccupied at lunch with Blake. Her plan had been to eat, then locate Josh and strike up a conversation with him. Instead, she'd spent the hour chatting with Blake. He was nice and funny and distracted her from all the negatives in her life, but she had to focus on finding out if Josh was Killian or not. She'd made a deathbed promise, after all.

What was her life coming to?

Josh sauntered into class and spotted Kayla when she waved him over. He beamed at her as he sat down.

"Hey!" He grinned, opening his bag to get his books out. "Cool with us being partners today?"

"Sure." Oh jeez. She didn't have the gigantic textbook he was pulling out from his bag. She was about to ask Josh if he didn't mind sharing – and something told her he wouldn't – when a shadow fell over the table.

"Kayla?" A guy she recognised from another class handed her a white polystyrene food container, looking slightly embarrassed. "It's not from me. Hey Josh!"

The guy struck up a conversation with Josh about some sports game last night as she opened the lid.

A cold slice of apple pie sat inside, and a scribbled note was written on the underside of the lid.

For your sugar addiction

Just accept it

Blake

She smiled to herself, shutting the container before anyone saw the writing. The guy who delivered it left with a nod as she thanked him.

"What's that?" Josh asked, trying to peer over shoulder.

She rushed to put it in her bag. "Oh, nothing."

"How are you finding everything?" Josh asked, leaning his chin on his fist to watch her. His eyes glinted with intrigue as he studied her, and she him. He definitely had the stature of a shifter; she just didn't know how to find out without asking point-blank.

"Yeah, not bad. Thanks for the library tour yesterday."

"Not a problem."

"I hope you weren't in trouble for being late or anything?"

"Nah, my mum's cool. Sorry I had to take off though," he replied, tearing his eyes away from hers.

"What's your mum like? Got any siblings?" she asked, trying not to raise her pitch. They were normal questions for Pete's sake. *Be cool,* she told herself.

"Mum's awesome, but it's just me, her, and my nan. My dad died a few years ago, and then Nan came to live with us."

"I'm so sorry," she said and put her hand over his, searching for any contact she could get. Again, there was no flash from the pendant and she frowned. Josh must have misinterpreted her meaning as he sandwiched her hand between his.

"There's no need to apologise. Happened a while ago."

"How?" she breathed and closed her eyes. "God, that's insensitive of me." She tried tugging her hand back, but Josh held on.

"That's okay. He was ill." He smiled at her and let go with one final squeeze. "What about you?"

"Me?" she squeaked. Their lesson began before she could answer, and she sighed with relief. It was the perfect excuse to avoid his question.

It was hard to focus on what the teacher was saying, and she doubted she would have understood anyway. Shifters didn't get sick unless they were poisoned with silver. Two shifters weren't needed to produce offspring, however. Only one was necessary, so the shifter could be his mum.

She needed more answers. She hoped their next lesson – compulsory physical education – would help. She'd already checked to make sure she was in Josh's class.

KAYLA WALKED OUT OF the girls' changing room and into the sports hall, awkwardly trying to pull her shorts down to cover more skin. Her old school had allowed students to wear joggers and that was much preferred. Josh had accompanied her to the class but had to use the boys' changing rooms for obvious reasons.

Blake chatted with a few of his friends, and she gave him a small wave when he noticed her – against her better judgement. She was here to discover if Josh was Killian, and she needed to focus. She was about to make her way over when Josh walked through the boys' door and jogged up to her. She shook her head, glad to be side-tracked from the weird compulsion to join Blake.

"How good are you with obstacle courses?" Josh asked with a flash of his teeth.

She narrowed her eyes at him. "Why?"

"Because the teacher loves them and makes us compete against each other in teams."

"Oh goodie."

His roaring laughter made her flinch.

"Sorry," he said, putting a hand on her shoulder. No flash of heat. "Stick with me and I'll help you."

"Thanks," she said. Her heart beat faster. Why were there no more signs? Had she just imagined the whole thing?

If things weren't confusing enough, Blake chose that moment to walk over, a frown etched between his brows.

"Josh," Blake said, and they nodded their heads in greeting. "You okay,

Kayla?"

"Yes," she answered far too quickly. Heat coloured her cheeks as she looked between Josh and Blake. Both squared their shoulders, and Josh flexed his biceps as he crossed his arms over his chest. A muscle ticked in Blake's jaw. She wasn't exactly sure what kind of silent communication was going on, but she was relieved when the teacher arrived and blew the whistle.

Then, a different kind of torture began.

The teacher announced they were doing a bleep fitness test. A freaking bleep test. Running back and forth between two points before a bleep sounded, and if it went off before you got to the other side, you were out.

Now, she considered herself fairly fit, but she loathed and detested running. If she wanted to clear her mind, she'd do yoga, and she'd even gone for a run with music on once or twice . . . but pointlessly running from one side to another? She was in for it. It also seriously reduced her chances of talking to Josh if he was ahead of her. She just had to hope that watching him run would give her some clue. Shifters were known for their stamina – that could be an indication. If he dropped out early to keep under the radar, she could look for signs he wasn't actually fatigued.

They lined up. Josh lightly bumped her shoulder with his.

"Don't worry. I'll help keep you going."

"By carrying me? Because there's no way I'm going to last long with the number of people here who play sports on the regular."

"Don't tempt me." He winked as Blake walked past. Blake didn't look at either of them as he settled between a couple of guys further down the line. She frowned, confused by the sudden cold shoulder.

Bleep.

Oh shit.

She started to run and made it to the other side quickly. She even had time to turn around and prepare to go again when Josh casually jogged up to her, trying to hide his grin.

"You might want to pace yourself. The first few bleeps are pretty slow."

She nodded. Damn, she must have looked a right fool.

Bleep.

This time, she kept pace with Josh's slow, lazy jog and peeked towards

Blake who looked like he was taking a leisurely stroll. To be fair, he did have long legs, so she was certain he had an advantage.

She focused on Josh, and casual conversation flowed between them while they navigated the first handful of bleeps. She picked up her pace and Josh matched her stride, but he seemed unaffected. He talked some more, and all she could do was listen. Blood started to rush in her ears and her breathing hastened when the first few people dropped out. Thankful she wasn't one of the first ones, she pushed through a few more bleeps.

When she approached one side, Blake turned and waited for the bleep. She misjudged her step as she locked eyes with him, his gaze a swirling mass of unidentified emotion, and she tripped over her own goddamn feet. She fell into Josh who stumbled against Blake, and then she landed on her butt.

A flash of heat surged through her chest. The pendant. She looked up as Josh loomed over her with Blake just behind.

"I'm sorry," she breathed. Excitement and the exercise itself squeezed her lungs tight.

Bleep.

"Quick, go!" She pushed the two boys and they sped off, easily catching up to the other side. Those that were left were mostly from sports teams, Josh had pointed out to her. She was happy several girls were left in the test, too, but numbly made her way over to the bench and chugged half a bottle of lukewarm water.

The girl next to her let out a soft sigh, resting her head upon her hands and leaning over her knees. Her perfect blonde hair was done up in a long, spiralling ponytail and her makeup was flawless as if she hadn't even done any running. Kayla looked down at herself, noticing the sweat soaking through her shirt and the tendrils of hair sticking to her skin.

"You're doing it wrong," the girl chimed in conspiratorially. She leaned closer. "Drop out early next time and then you get to watch." She winked and went back to observing the runners.

"Huh?" She hadn't meant to say that out loud, but the girl turned her head and looked Kayla up and down. It was an appraisal, but she didn't feel as judged as she had by the group of girls at lunch.

The girl spoke, snapping Kayla out of her post-exercise daze. "You're new, aren't you?" At least she sounded friendly. Kayla nodded. "You can't escape the fact that this school prides itself on sport; that means we have a lot of sportsmen – and women, if that floats your boat."

Kayla couldn't help herself as her eyes flashed towards Blake and Josh running side by side, neither looking out of breath. Another runner dropped out.

"Boys, I take it. Which one?" the girl enquired with a smile in her eyes. She steamed ahead without waiting for an answer. "I'd bet on Josh. I saw you two chatting earlier, and he seems smitten. I'm Charlotte, by the way."

"I'm sorry. I don't mean to step on any toes," Kayla replied when her breathing returned to normal.

"Oh, you're not. He's single right now. He's just yummy to look at," the girl finished as she went back to staring at him unashamedly. "He came back . . . when was it? Oh yes, year ten he came back looking like . . . well, that. One hell of a summer – am I right?" she asked, seeking solidarity. Kayla mumbled something vague in response.

By Charlotte's calculations, Josh had probably shifted around fourteen, putting him on the later side of development but still within a normal range – unlike her own stubborn magic which appeared far later than usual. She quickly pushed down a huff of annoyance that threatened to spill out and focused on thoughts of the pendant flashing when she fell into Josh. She had to be on the right track. New hope filled her.

"Are you going to the rugby team's party this weekend? Hopefully it's a celebratory one!"

"Err, not sure," Kayla replied. She hadn't even heard about a party, but she quickly tried to work out if it would be an ideal opportunity to speak to Josh. It was outside of school but still in a public setting.

The last two participating in the test were Blake and Josh. There were only a handful of seconds between each bleep, and Blake barely made it across the line when the bell rang. The teacher blew the whistle.

"All right Blake and Josh, enough of that. Class dismissed!" the teacher shouted, tucking the clipboard with their scores underneath her arm.

Several people went up to the boys, so Kayla followed. Charlotte got there first and put her hand on Josh's muscular chest before she sauntered to the girls' changing room, hips swaying exaggeratedly. Josh's eyes tracked the movement and Kayla coughed pointedly.

"Well done," Kayla announced, pulling Josh's attention away from Charlotte. Josh shot her a sheepish grin. "That was impressive. Was that like a record or something?"

"Nah, Blake and I are always the last left."

"Have you ever tried seeing how many more bleeps you can make?"

Josh crossed his arms over his chest, his biceps tightening as a slow, teasing smile played on his lips.

"Why? Wanna see me work out?" Before she could answer, Blake turned sharply from where he stood a metre away and stormed off.

"Is he okay?" she asked Josh. Blake disappeared through the boys' changing room door.

Josh shrugged, but concern entered his eyes. "No idea."

CHAPTER ELEVEN

BLAKE

BLAKE STORMED THROUGH THE changing room doors. He knew he was being irrational – he knew it – but he couldn't explain the feeling bubbling up from his very core. Anger. He had to get away before he snapped. He was almost scared of the power coursing through his body. The fury made him feel invincible.

His heart raced and his stomach twisted into knots. He didn't understand why. Blake rushed into a shower cubicle, hoping to rinse off his bad mood beneath the cold water.

"Blake? You okay, mate?" Josh's concern was obvious through the cubicle door.

"Yeah, just needed a shower," he answered. His words were thick with the last dregs of rage. It didn't help that the illogical anger surged again at Josh's voice.

Josh huffed, knowing Blake too well to believe him, but he didn't push it. Josh retreated and Blake sagged against the icy tiles. His eyes snapped open when his friend's footsteps changed direction.

"Oh hey, I invited Kayla to come watch the rugby game tonight."

Blake growled inwardly; he did not need the distraction. It was a big game. They were up against a boarding school they played frequently, and the last match had been a disaster. They were desperate for a win, and Kayla being there was the last thing he needed.

HE PULLED A DEEP breath into his lungs, welcoming the cheers as they echoed through the stands. He could almost feel his heart pumping blood around his body. Adrenaline raced through his muscles, providing the stamina he needed and heating his body against the cool chill of the evening. The smell of freshly cut grass mingled with fumes of coffee and popcorn. The sun may have set beyond the floodlit field, but Blake was wide awake. He grinned. The sweet release of tension was one heck of a feeling. He was captain of the winning team. There were only minutes left in the game, but they had it in the bag. Blake, however, wanted to make damn sure it was a landslide victory, so he refused to ease up on his team.

He had perfect control over his players: where they were placed and what actions they needed to take. Many of them had been playing under Blake for several years in various sports, and they worked together seamlessly. They didn't need words when their eyes communicated and their body language spoke for them.

He didn't want to admit it, but he had glanced into the crowd surrounding the playing field a few times, looking for the one girl he was supposed to avoid. Kayla stood with some students he recognised from their history class, watching the game intently. She tracked Blake and Josh, he assumed because she knew them, but they weren't the only ones. He was observant, and he noticed some of the key players on the other team held her interest, too. Namely, the opposing captain.

James was the biggest jerk known to man. He'd always goaded Blake and Josh. They tried to ignore him, but it was getting harder to look past his blatant disrespect. He'd really pissed off Blake during the game, and Josh's anger was visibly rising. James illegally tackled two of Blake's players but got away scot-free because the referee was biased. It was a good thing the referee couldn't take away the brilliant game they were playing. Sure, the ref had disallowed a few tries, but even with the unfair ruling, his team were winning. It plastered a great big smile on his face.

The ball was making its way down the pitch in favour of Blake's team;

he was certain of its path and he knew Josh would intercept and score, so Blake took the opportunity to cast another quick glance at Kayla. Her eyes were already on him, and as their gazes collided, she quickly looked towards James. Blake swallowed a growl as the hulking, blonde-haired thug gave him a menacing grin. James smirked at Blake, winked, and ploughed into Josh from behind, taking him down to the ground.

A gasp whispered through his mind, and though it should have been impossible to hear one person over the roar of the crowd, he knew it was Kayla. He stared in her direction as he rushed over to where Josh lay in a heap.

"Josh! You okay buddy?!" Blake shouted. The whistle blew, signalling the end of the game. Of course the referee 'missed' the tackle.

"You bloody idiot!" Josh roared towards James, spittle flying from his mouth. The two were tangled together on the field, one trying to get the better of the other. The air around them filling thick with tension and testosterone.

"You think you're the only one here, Josh?" James teased, his blue eyes flashing icily. Blake roughly shoved the sweaty brute off his friend and helped Josh to his feet. A small crowd had formed, made up of a few players from each team and some students, including Kayla.

One of the coaches shouted to them as he followed the rest of the team inside. "Pack it in, boys. Leave it for the next game." They clearly weren't picking up on how riled both James and Josh were.

"Okay, that's enough now. Nothing to see here," Blake ordered to the last few stragglers while he and Josh stayed put. Two of James's teammates stood on either side of their captain. After Blake's command, most of the players left to get showered and the crowd dispersed – all except Kayla. Blake glanced her way and his brows drew together. He jerked his head in what he hoped was a 'please, get out of this' kind of motion.

"There's plenty of us around," James repeated, and even though Blake didn't quite understand what he meant, the threat in his tone was clear.

"I think you ought to back off, James," Blake said.

The tall, burly player turned his venomous sneer on Blake. James was huge, bigger than he or Josh, and so he didn't really want to get into a fight. Especially since Kayla didn't seem to be a good judge of danger.

"Or what? You're hardly a risk to the likes of me."

"Don't threaten him!" Josh growled, shoving at James. Blake appreciated Josh's attempt at restraint, but he recognised his best friend was about to erupt.

James glanced down at his chest where Josh had pushed him and took an unnecessary step back. When he looked up to Josh, Blake swore he growled. Before Blake could think to do anything, Kayla stepped between Josh and James.

"Wait! Stop this. We don't need to be throwing around idle threats, do we? Let's just move on," Kayla said with confidence.

"Idle? Hardly, love. Now, I'd move if I were you."

"Oh, and why is that?" Kayla asked, leaning into one hip and folding her arms across her chest. Blake recognised the attitude from the first time he'd seen her and worried how James would react to it.

"Little lady, do not get in my way. You will *not* survive," James hissed. Heat rose from the pit of Blake's stomach. He clenched his fists, hoping the unwelcome bout of rage towards James disappeared quickly. He couldn't afford to lose his cool.

"I can take care of myself," Kayla argued back, but her voice lost volume. James snarled and lunged forward quicker than Blake thought possible. Kayla's sharp intake of breath ripped through his senses. Her arms flung up in a protective stance but James grabbed each of her wrists and brought her close to his face, taking a long inhale as he did.

"I don't think you can, *witch*!" he seethed, and Kayla struggled to get out of his grasp. Kayla's terror was clear. The boys moved forward in unison, grabbing onto James's arms and yanking them off Kayla. She wrenched away from him at the same time and pulled her hands close to her body, cradling them protectively. She blinked back tears, but it was the angry, inflamed handprints staining her wrists that made Blake see red. He spun towards James.

"How dare you think you have the right to hurt a defenceless girl!" he screamed as he drilled his finger into James's chest.

"She's hardly defenceless–"

"You put your hands on her without her consent and harmed her. You deserve to rot in hell, James!" He slammed his fists into James without thinking, but his fury must have come on the heels of an adrenaline boost because James flew backwards as Blake landed his last blow.

James struggled to rise without the help of his friends as they stared open-mouthed at Blake. Even Josh was giving him a strange, calculating look and Kayla frowned. Blake froze, thankful that James's friends encouraged him to leave, snarling at Blake as they did. With a bruised ego, James eventually limped off the field, but he sneered venomously at Blake as he went.

Blake spun around to where Josh and Kayla stood to find Josh with his hand on her shoulder, talking softly as if she were a frightened doe.

"Kayla I . . ." Blake began, and she jumped as the sound of his voice brought her out of whatever place she had gone to. She looked up at both of them and stepped back when she realised Josh's hand was on her shoulder.

"I'm sorry," she whispered, before turning and quickly walking away.

"DAD? YOU GOT A SEC?" Blake asked when he entered the Collins' home gym. His dad was bench pressing weights with a notepad beside him. He was probably making a plan for one of his personal training clients. His dad placed the bar in the holder and sat up on the bench, bending to grab his towel so he could wipe his face.

"'Course, son. What's up?"

Blake motioned his father off the bench so he could replace him.

Without speaking, his dad replaced the weights at the end of each bar – lighter, of course – and became Blake's spotter. His dad took a few minutes to coach him through the reps, aware that Blake needed to talk but willing to give his son the space he needed. He loved his dad for that; he was an extremely patient guy who had nothing but time for his sons.

Blake pushed himself through the last two sets before finally letting his dad take the bar. Blake sat up and wiped his face with a spare towel.

"It's Kayla," Blake said slowly. His dad froze momentarily but continued to clean and put away equipment. "She was at the game. I didn't start anything with her like you asked but . . . there was sort of an incident."

"What kind of incident?"

"Just . . . the other team's captain – James – was trying to rile up me and Josh. He even tackled Josh illegally at the end of the game, but Kayla got between us, and James grabbed her."

"What happened?" His dad turned to face Blake. He was paying close attention and he stood statue-still.

"Josh and I rushed James and I-I . . . I punched him."

"Are you in trouble?"

"No, I don't think so. Well, not with Coach or anyone like that. Maybe James, though. Dad, he *flew* backwards. I didn't know I was that strong!" The panic rose again, but it receded when his dad squeezed his shoulder comfortingly.

"It's okay, son. He sounded like he was asking for it, and you were just being protective. That's a good thing; it's who you are. You're probably just a late bloomer and that muscle is starting to make an appearance," his dad finished. Deep worry lines carved into his forehead.

"It just didn't feel right. I got so angry at him marking her with his hands that I lost it. He even called her a witch!" His dad's face paled. "Dad? You okay?"

"Yeah, yeah, it just sounds like this James is a thug but please, please Blake, stay away from him and don't engage if you see him again. The likes of James . . ."

"The likes of James?"

"I mean people who think they deserve everything. I have some stuff to do right now. You going to be okay?"

"Yeah, sure."

"Make sure everything is wiped down when you leave," his dad called over his shoulder as he left the room.

CHAPTER TWELVE

KAYLA

KAYLA STUDIED THE BLUE and purple marks staining the skin on her wrists. They were fading, but for a while, it looked like she'd been in some kind of car accident. She shivered at the memory of James putting his hands on her; she didn't want to come across him again, that was for sure.

It had been five days since the rugby game, which had been an utter disaster. To top it all off, she had completely freaked. Way to go, Kayla. Thankfully, she did glean some new information.

First, she was pretty sure Blake was also a shifter. He clearly had an alpha presence on the field; the way he exerted himself and led his team with clarity, conviction, and control more than made up for his difference in body type. Then there was the fact that he'd lost his temper – definitely a shifter trait – and pushed James. It had only taken one punch to throw the guy across the field, and James wasn't exactly a small guy to begin with. It made her suspect they hadn't seen the last of James who – and she really couldn't believe her own damn bad luck – was also a shifter. He'd scented that she was a magic user, so he clearly had a good nose – even for a wolf. He also didn't seem like the type to just let a 'witch' go. And wasn't it interesting that he called her a witch? *She* didn't even know what she was.

She had to find out more from Josh. If James was going to come around again, she needed a plan. She had an inkling that Blake was also a shifter, but Josh was still her primary guess at Killian. The pendant had flashed twice when she'd been in contact with Josh, and she couldn't ignore that. Perhaps today she would get to speak with Blake about Josh as the two seemed like close friends. If nothing else, it would be good to see Blake. She shook her head. It wasn't smart to think like that. Once she established that Josh was Killian, she probably wouldn't see Blake again.

Guilt hollowed her stomach. The pie he'd given her was still on her mind; she'd scribbled a note to say thank you and posted it in his locker, but she hadn't spoken to him in person. He'd mentioned being friends, but she hadn't really come to the academy for friendship. She'd never been one to get close with people anyway, and she was looking for answers – for Killian. Putting off her search was something she could no longer afford to do, even though she would miss living with Gaby. The woman was kind and graceful and made her feel looked after. Would she have that feeling again, now that her parents were gone? Leaving also meant saying goodbye to Blake, who protected her and made her laugh – two things she'd sorely missed since the loss of her parents.

AFTER LUNCH, KAYLA WALKED into her English class – the one she'd avoided for a few days after the rugby game – and saw Blake sitting by himself. He was doodling in his notebook, ignoring everything around him. He idly ran a hand through his thick brown hair. It was fairly long and flopped more to one side than perhaps the style should have allowed. He was what Kayla would have called 'cute' had her life not been turned upside down.

Taking a breath to calm her nerves, she walked over to him.

"Mind if I sit next to you?" she asked. Before he could answer, and before he could say no, she sat. Not wanting to waste any time she turned to face him in her seat. "I just wanted to say thank you for the other day." And she was. James was a right douche.

"Um, that's okay?"

"No, I mean it. You didn't have to stand up to him like that."

"Who, James? He's a dumb thug who wants everything to go his way."

"Well, I fear there could be retribution for what happened, but regardless, I totally agree with you."

The teacher walked in – a substitute – and gave the instructions for the lesson. They were to work in pairs to analyse and annotate Shakespeare's 'Shall I compare thee to a summer's day?' sonnet.

"You good with us working together?" Kayla asked, feeling more at ease than she had in weeks . He blinked at her, and she worried he was about to push her away; she didn't know why that bothered her so much.

"Yeah, sure."

She exhaled in relief and started the task with him, surprised at how well they seemed to work together. She'd studied the text before, but Blake was full of surprising facts and insights.

"Hey, so I wanted to ask you about Josh if that's okay?" she said, focusing on the sonnet between them. She didn't want to be blunt, but she was getting so involved with talking to Blake that she was losing sight of what she really needed to discuss.

He audibly sighed, sounding slightly annoyed. "Why not?"

"How long have you been mates?"

"Since I can remember. We went to primary school together, too."

"So you must be close?"

"As brothers."

She raised her eyebrows. It was an interesting choice of words, especially as shifters considered their pack family.

"As close as brothers . . . soooo, you would know if he began acting differently?"

"What do you mean 'acting differently'? He's into you if that's what you mean." He sounded bitter, she realised, and she stilled at the unexpected tone. She knew Josh had taken a liking to her, despite her best efforts to keep things platonic.

"I don't mean to lead him on. I meant what I said that first day. I'm here for one thing and one thing only."

"And what's that?"

She needed to change the topic. "Josh seems to have an awful amount of muscle for a what? Sixteen-year-old boy?"

"You are so weird."

She smiled in response. "I've been told. But seriously, compared to you, Josh is stacked."

"Oh hey, way to make a guy feel inadequate!"

"Ah, I'm sorry. I didn't mean it that way. Looking at you, I can see you're built pretty averagely compared to him. Oh gosh, I mean, there's nothing wrong with being normal, right?" She wished she could crawl into the deepest, darkest hole she could find. There was absolutely nothing wrong with Blake. He was quite attractive even, but Josh had the muscular definition of a shifter. She wanted to know what Blake thought about that and she needed his insight. But most of all, she liked spending time with Blake even if it couldn't last.

Blake tried to hide the smile stretching across his face. "Oh, do continue. You're very adept at digging your own grave."

She buried her face in her hands and mumbled through them. "I'm doing this all wrong. I really don't mean to insult you. I just . . ." She tried to calm the blush creeping its way across her cheeks.

"You're interested in him, I get it . . . If you must know, I work out a lot. I just have a wicked metabolism."

Oh god, even Blake thought she was interested in Josh. The conversation was not going the way she'd planned – at all. For some reason she couldn't explain, she really didn't want Blake to think she liked Josh in that way.

"Shall we start again? I just wondered what Josh is into to make him so big. Drugs?" she asked, hoping the humour might diffuse the furious embarrassment she felt.

"Nope."

"Just works out a lot? Same as you?"

"Yep."

"But you look very different."

"What can I say?"

"Fast metabolism?"

"That's what my dad claims."

"He's really fast."

"Some would say."

"Does he ever miss days of school?"

"Hardly ever sick, so no – except when he pulls a fast one and takes a day off to play his X-box. Seriously, why are you so interested if you're not trying to date him? Are you writing an article on him for the school newspaper or something?"

"I'm just thorough."

"How about I ask you some questions now?"

She had to say something to distract him, and fast. Lying didn't come naturally to her.

"Do you think I can come to the party Saturday? I heard some others talking about it earlier."

"The rugby team party? The one Taylor is hosting?"

"That's it, unless I'm mistaken." Charlotte had been the one to tell her about it, and she thought socialising might help her connect with Josh and get him to open up about who he really was. She just had to do it in a way that didn't lead him on.

"Nope, you're right. Why not? Josh would love to see you there."

She smiled as she packed her things away. "Great! I'll see you later?"

"Sure."

Kayla left in a hurry when the bell rang, not wanting to see Blake's disappointment. He probably thought she'd only asked him to get closer to Josh.

Before her next lesson, she rushed to the class Josh was leaving. In her haste, she didn't see him until she was bumping into his chest. His hands shot out and grabbed her shoulders to steady her. There was no flash, but she was breathless from running. Maybe that was why.

"Kayla! Hey!" He smiled brightly.

"Are you going to the party on Saturday?" she asked quickly, falling into step with him as they moved towards his locker.

"Sure thing, you?"

"Yeah, if that's okay?"

He opened his locker and nodded. "It would be really great to see you there." He'd emphasised the 'really,' making her fidget uncomfortably. "Do you need a ride there?"

"Ah, no, that's okay. I need to go into town during the day and catch up on some work before I come over anyway." And by work, she meant she had to read a book on tracking spells that Gaby had found for her. Neither of them could work out why the flashes were so sporadic.

"I can take you to town if you want?"

In truth, she needed a dress for the party. Her essentials hadn't included clothing suitable for the event. She pulled her bottom lip in between her teeth while she thought it over, not wanting him to think it was a date or something. His gaze lowered to her mouth, and she promptly released her lip.

"As friends?" she clarified.

Josh's hooded eyes cleared enough for him to reluctantly nod his head. She got the feeling it wouldn't stop his crush, but at least she was being consistent.

"Sure, that would be good. Thanks," she finally responded just as Blake walked by without even stopping to say hello. She turned her body slightly when he passed to . . . well, she didn't know what she was going to do, but he stopped with his back to her.

"Great. I'll pick you up around eleven?" Josh asked, and Blake carried on down the hallway. Kayla sighed and plastered a smile on her face.

"That's fine. I can meet you at the park." She didn't want anyone knowing where and who she lived with.

Josh's smile blossomed with her agreement, and it annoyed her that he was clearly still into her in a way she didn't want him to be. What more did she have to do?

CHAPTER THIRTEEN

BLAKE

"WHY CAN'T WE JUST order something online!" Charlie moaned as they exited yet another shop on the busy high street. They were shopping for their mum's birthday, and Blake wanted a new shirt for the party that night. Charlie was also desperate for new trainers, and as they'd just purchased a pair, his little brother was ready to leave. The boy dragged his feet with exaggerated frustration.

"Because then we wouldn't have this beautiful bonding experience," Blake responded back, equally sour.

"Ew, man, we don't need any of that shit."

Blake clipped his brother on the back of the head with a smirk.

"Mum would have hit you harder had she heard you swear."

Charlie shoved him with his elbow and they both spewed laughter as a young couple walked by, heavy judgement upon their faces. His younger brother maturely stuck his tongue out when they passed.

"Rude," Charlie tutted.

"Says you! You just stuck your tongue out at them!" Blake chided, grabbing his brother around the neck and ruffling his hair.

"Stop! Stop! My hair!" Charlie cried in the high-pitched wail of a boy on the brink of puberty.

"My hair! My hair!" Blake mimicked. "What are you? A girl?"

A startled gasp made him release his brother straight away to avoid colliding with someone who sped out of a clothes shop. He looked up to see dark hair and a pair of brown eyes.

"Kayla?"

"Blake," she said breathlessly. The shopping bag she was holding swung on her arm.

"Um, this is Charlie, my brother," he said, gesturing to Charlie while his brother smoothed his hair. Blake glared at his brother when a look of recognition, along with a mischievous glint, entered his eyes.

"Ahh, *this* Kayla," Charlie said. "Nice to meet you." Kayla's eyebrows shot up.

"This Kayla?" she asked, narrowing her eyes on Blake. He ran a hand through his hair and reminded himself to give his brother hell later.

"I thought you were out with Josh?" He immediately wanted to bang his head against a brick wall; why did that have to be the first thing to come out of his mouth?

"I was. He had a call – some emergency, I think," she mumbled, tucking and untucking the same bit of hair behind her ear.

"What? And just left you out here alone?"

"It's the middle of the day in a busy part of town. I'm just fine," she said slowly.

"Chill, man. This ain't the 1800s," his brother whispered from the side of his mouth as he smacked his arm into Blake's stomach, smiling sweetly at Kayla.

"Right. Well, I'll leave you to it." She began to turn away.

"Wait!" Blake rushed over to her. Wait? What was he asking?

"Wanna hang with us?" Charlie effortlessly tagged in. Kayla looked from Charlie to Blake.

"Okay," she finally agreed, and Blake sagged with relief. At what, he wasn't so sure.

They spent the next hour or so looking for a gift for his mum's birthday and settled on a cashmere scarf which Kayla helped choose. Kayla and Charlie got on well, easily even, laughing with each other as she tried on different scarfs for them before helping to narrow down some options. His brother caught him looking at her a few times, watching her talk as she used her hands to tell a story – a habit, he supposed – and

Charlie would smirk. Little shit.

They decided to grab a milkshake from a café, finding seats at one of the small round tables.

"I need a piss," Charlie announced out of nowhere, climbing to his feet.

"Oi, language!" Blake barked absentmindedly. Charlie rolled his eyes and sauntered out. "Sorry, our mum would have my ass if I didn't pick him up on it," he said when Kayla frowned quizzically, her head tipped to one side.

"He's a good kid."

"Most the time, yeah, when he's not being a thorn in my side."

She stirred her milkshake with the flimsy paper straw. "It must be nice though, to have a sibling."

"You an only child?"

She nodded. "Yes, but I loved my childhood. I never missed out, always had company, and I was loved. So very loved."

Her eyes swam with tears, becoming brighter. He sensed her trying to rein in her control; it was clear she didn't want to cry in front of him, so he changed the subject.

"I'm sorry Josh left you." Internally, he winced. Not the subject he should have switched to.

"It's okay. You're not his keeper."

"No, but he's my best friend, and I'd expect better of him. I dunno. Recently..."

She frowned at him. "Recently what?"

"Nah, it's nothing. Good milkshake?"

She studied him closely for a moment, that calculating look entering her eye as it so often had before, making him want to squirm in his seat under her scrutiny. What was she thinking about? The glazed look disappeared with a small shake of her head and she shot him a smile. She slurped up more milkshake, closing her eyes and moaning.

"God, these are so good," she whispered.

"Sugar?"

She looked up with a laugh. "Sugar," she agreed.

Charlie chose that moment to come bouncing back.

"What you two talking 'bout?" he asked with a conspiratorial smirk aimed at Blake.

"None of your business!" Blake retaliated. Kayla giggled.

"Shall we get going before you boys start brawling?"

"We don't brawl!" Blake tried to explain but the more he did, the more she laughed. The beautiful melody lingered in the air as they walked home together.

CHARLIE CALLED BLAKE'S NAME as he stepped out of the family bathroom. Wrapping a towel around his waist, Blake finger combed his hair and walked into his bedroom.

"What?" he answered, pulling out his new black polo shirt and a pair of jeans.

"Have you seen this?" Charlie asked. He waltzed into Blake's room, holding out a note in their mum's handwriting.

"The note? Yes."

"Then why do you look like you're getting ready to go out?"

"Because I am, idiot."

"But the note says–"

"I'm going to a party. It's been on the calendar for ages; we can have dinner together tomorrow night. I'll even cook."

"Boy, are you going to be in trouble if you're not here when Mum and Dad get back."

"Where are they anyway?" he asked, spraying on liberal amounts of his 'good' deodorant and slipping on his best jeans.

"Gone to get food supplies, I think. Mum just texted saying they'll be an hour or so. Why do you think she wrote a note about family dinner?"

Blake shrugged while he put on his shirt. "Who knows with Mum and Dad? But I'm going to the party."

"You don't even like those parties!" Charlie declared, and Blake just stared at his little brother. He knew the moment the lightbulb had gone off inside Charlie's head. "You want to go because of Kayla!"

"You don't know what you're talking about."

"Yes I do, and don't deny it. You know Mrs Rogers' son is my best mate, right?" Charlie winked at his brother and folded his arms casually. Blake caved.

"Fine. What *do* you know?"

"What's it worth?"

"Your washing-up chore for a week." Silence. "And two loads of laundry."

"Deal. She comes from out of town. Her file is kept by Miss Anderson, so we don't know much, other than the fact that she doesn't live with her parents."

"Who does she live with?"

Charlie shrugged. "When Mrs Rogers asked Kayla about her parents, she flipped and told her to contact her present guardian."

"Could explain why she didn't want me to walk her back the other day and why she was happy being left at the park earlier. Maybe she doesn't want anyone to know who she lives with?"

"Dude, I don't know. Just ask her."

BLAKE CONSIDERED WHY KAYLA was so secretive on his walk over to the party. What happened to her parents for her to be living with somebody else anyway?

His phone buzzed in his pocket. The message was from his brother.

CHARLIE: U are so gonna be dead bro!

BLAKE: whatever dude.

Knowing that he was, in fact, going to be dead meat when his parents realised he wasn't home, he switched off his mobile, pocketing it in his jeans as he entered the front door of the house party.

Music boomed, and various bottles of alcohol littered the surfaces of the living room. A large crowd of kids he knew from school swayed and danced to the beat. It was not a party that the host's parents knew about let alone were home for it.

"Oh heeeeeey, Blake!" A drunken slur greeted him. One of his ex-hockey teammates appeared in front of him. "Glad you could make it."

"Sure."

"Grab a drink, dude. This party is rockin'!" the guy said, punching his fist into the air and sticking his tongue out. Blake laughed at his drunk friend and wandered off to find a drink, preferably a soft one. While he was breaking rules to be here, he wasn't stupid enough to drink alcohol underage. Not only would his parents kill him, but they'd bring him back to life just to kill him again.

Before he got to the kitchen, however, a hand stroked up his back and slipped down to his butt. He knew it was Charlotte. She was the most uninhibited of the year group, and she tried to get with Blake at every party. She wanted to add him to some list she always bragged about.

"Charlotte," he said warily. "Had a drink?"

"You bet, handsome!" she purred, moving to his front as she continued to stroke his side. He could smell the fumes on her breath but he smiled politely. Blonde curls spilled over her shoulders, stopping just above her ample chest. Trying not to stare, he focused on her heavily made-up face – something he didn't find especially attractive.

"Look, Charlotte, we do this every time. I'm not that kind of guy."

She pouted. "But c'mon, Blake, you're the only hockey player left," she moaned, referencing her record. He didn't know why she thought she had a chance.

"I get that, Charlotte, but still . . . would you mind?" he asked as she plastered her body to his, pursing her lips. He assumed she thought the expression was sexy. He didn't want to get involved but he was a guy, and her chest was pressed against him. He gulped, moving both hands out in surrender.

Glancing over her head and wondering how the heck he was going to get her off him, he spotted Kayla walking in the front door. She scanned her surroundings carefully. She wore a dark, knee-length dress with a black jacket and flat ankle boots. Instead of the straight style he was used to seeing at school, her hair hung in soft waves, held back by a thin, metallic band. He knew she wasn't wearing much make-up because he couldn't see it from his spot near the kitchen. He thought she stood out against most of the other girls – in a good way. When she spotted him, he smiled instinctively.

She frowned ever so slightly at the girl wrapped around his waist, so he shrugged and tried to look as helpless as possible. Kayla rolled her eyes and came over in what he hoped was a rescue attempt.

"Charlotte, right?" she asked as the drunk girl attached to his chest opened her eyes and focused on Kayla. "I heard that umm . . . Harry was looking for you."

"Harry?" Charlotte exclaimed, springing away from Blake and tottering towards the dining room.

"Oh, thank God. I did *not* know what to do – she tries it every time."

"I kinda felt sorry for you," Kayla admitted, looking away.

"Well, I appreciate it. I'm guessing you didn't know that Harry was actually at the party?"

"No, though I vaguely remembered overhearing some girls gossip about a Harry and I took a stab in the dark. It worked though, didn't it? You're a free man again!"

"Drink?" he said with a laugh, and she nodded. They both moved to the kitchen to find something without alcohol.

"You not drinking?" she asked when he bypassed the alcoholic beverages.

"I try not to. I'm in enough trouble as it is with my parents," he said as he found a bottle of Coke in the fridge and started to pour drinks for the two of them.

"My parents would kill me if I drank."

"Your parents strict?" he asked casually; he knew from Charlie that she didn't live with them. He was beginning to recognise when she wasn't going to say anything. Her eyes were downcast as she reached for the cup and brought it to her lips.

"So, is Josh here tonight?" she asked, and his stomach sank. That was it. The only reason she ever spoke to him was because of Josh. The same guy who abandoned her earlier that day.

Sighing loudly, he replied, "Yeah, somewhere. You're welcome to go and look for him. Tell him I said hi."

"No need," Josh said, approaching the two of them and looking Kayla up and down with an appreciative smoulder. "You look great! Sorry I had to leave earlier. Something unexpected came up. Family stuff, you know the drill." Josh ran a hand through his hair, never quite meeting Kayla's eye. What was up with him?

Kayla put her drink down and moved closer to Josh, looking nervous as she did so.

"Josh, do you think we could go speak somewhere . . . private?" Her eyes flicked towards Blake so quickly that he almost missed it.

"Yeah, I'm sure there's a room upstairs we can find." Kayla winced as Josh took her hand and led her away. Blake was pretty sure Josh didn't even notice her discomfort.

"Cool. Yeah, I'm just going to . . ." Blake trailed off as they disappeared out of sight. "Way to play it, Blake," he mumbled to himself, grabbing his drink and sauntering into the front room again.

Even though the music was loud and the house was packed with people, one voice rose above the crowd and made him go cold. Blake stopped just inside the dining room and swallowed his rage as James strolled through the party with his mates from the rugby match. They paused at the pool table in the conservatory. He knew they were there to cause trouble – call it a gut instinct.

"You know where that Kayla chick is?" James asked one of the guys around the pool table. He got a shrug in response. James nudged his two teammates and pointed to the kitchen.

Blake spun on his heel and darted up the stairs, taking them two at a time. He turned left on the landing, letting his instincts guide him. He didn't have the luxury of time. Pausing by one of the doors, he pressed his ear close – there was no way he was going to waltz in during some make out session. He heard her voice.

"Josh, please. I said no."

Blake pushed open the door and found Kayla and Josh standing face to face. Josh held Kayla's hands between his own and he looked like he was pleading with her, but Kayla was trying to pull herself away from him.

"What the hell is going on, man?"

Chapter Fourteen

Kayla

THE LAST PERSON SHE wanted to see her in her current situation pushed into the room. Blake hurried inside, shutting the door behind him. The double bed was pressed up beside her and Blake was now blocking her exit to the door.

"I'm being serious, Kayla. I've never felt like this before," Josh carried on as if Blake hadn't come into the room.

"Josh! Seriously? You've known her like, ten seconds!" Blake looked between them both and she hoped he realised that it was Josh being the unreasonable one, not her.

"Back off Collins, I mean it!" Josh ground out between clenched teeth. Blake recoiled at the sharp edge to his tone.

"I think you've had one too many drinks, pal, and we have bigger things to worry about. James and two of his buddies are downstairs looking for you, Kayla."

Kayla froze. Her gut instinct kicked into overdrive, and she knew she had to get out of there quickly. She was almost positive that James was a shifter, and she wouldn't be surprised if his friends were, too. While she knew she didn't have anything to fear from Josh or Blake, James and his pals would kill her given the chance.

"I can protect you, Kayla. You've got nothing to worry about," Josh said as he studied her face.

"Josh, we don't have much time. Is your real name Killian?" Josh furrowed his brow in confusion. She yanked her arms away from Josh and pulled her necklace off. The pendant, tied to a thick black cord, had been well hidden by the neckline of her dress. She placed the necklace over Josh's head and they both stared at it.

"It's not you," she said, her hopes deflating. She had expected a reaction – something, anything – but nothing happened. What had that flare been the day she'd first met Josh and brushed past him?

"I'm not quite sure what's going on here, but we should all probably leave before–" Blake started.

"Before what?" James's cheerful voice announced. He stood in the doorway, flanked by two of his friends. Kayla yanked the necklace off Josh as both he and Blake scrambled to her side. James was terrifying, especially as he clearly wanted to hurt her. James seemed like one of those elitist shifters who thought they were better than everyone else; his actions towards her thus far indicated that if he confirmed she was a magic user, he'd stop at nothing to destroy her.

"James, you're not welcome here," Blake said, his voice calm and level.

"Hey, pretty lady. I need to know what you are. If you could clarify which strand your abilities fall under, that would be most welcome," James said, looking directly at her. She couldn't move. She couldn't speak. James knew. He was going to kill her, rip her apart like her parents. Her breathing sped up a notch and the room began to spin.

Blake growled, "James, seriously. Back off."

"Leave it, Blake." Kayla could feel James's irritation rise, and needing to steady herself, she instinctively placed a hand on Blake's arm. As she made contact, the pendant in her other hand flashed hot, the hottest it had ever been.

It was him.

It was Blake.

Killian was Blake.

It flashed those other times because it had been close to Blake. She'd always assumed it was Josh's presence that set it off.

She tried not to give anything away, fearing for Blake if James were to find out. James didn't exactly strike her as someone who valued equality among the races. She clutched the pendant close to her stomach and kept her hand on Blake's lower arm. Blake's confusion and anger were steadily mixing, and she didn't want him to attack. She had no idea if his shifter strength and abilities could help him take on someone like James.

James smirked.

"I think we may have gotten off on the wrong foot. Why don't Josh, Blake, and I leave, and we won't bother you," Kayla said, trying to think on her feet. The urge to protect Blake gave her a purpose and chased away some of the fear.

Josh growled.

Kayla gulped.

Josh was close to shifting if the growl at the back of his throat was anything to go on. At least she knew she was right about him being a shifter. But would he retain enough of himself to not attack her when he shifted?

"I don't think we'll go for that option. Mmm, you smell like a witch, and all you have there is Josh! Judging by the looks of him, he's a pup with only a handful of changes under his belt. Me? I've mastered my shift. Oh, and there's something else you should know. My family have a speciality," he said, tapping his nose. "We are extremely good trackers. When I got home after the game, my pa immediately scented an old bloodline, one thought to have been erased some years ago. He used to work for *them* you see, and he was pretty familiar with *their* scent. But he was more than happy to help facilitate the breakdown of that family in order for us to become who we are today. He also recognised another scent: yours. We are not equals, witch. I am better than you, and I am more than willing to prove it. Right. Now." James growled and lowered his head. The first flash of yellow took over the irises of his eyes, and Kayla stepped forward, angling herself slightly ahead of Blake.

"James, I am not a witch, but I will stop you if I must." It didn't matter that she actually *was* afraid of him, and she didn't exactly know *what* she was either. she just had to sound confident enough to get them out of there.

Blake grabbed her arm, but she pulled away, keeping her focus on James. "Kayla? What are you doing?" he hissed.

Josh yelped and fell to his knees. Blake went to help him, but Kayla barked at him to stay put. She didn't know why he listened to her, she was just thankful that he did.

"Well, well, well! Look what we have here. I thought it was just Josh I was looking for, but your adrenaline levels are skyrocketing, Blake. And that scent..." James closed his eyes and inhaled. "Oh yes, there are changes within you. I'd bet anything you're the Alastair heir. I'll admit, I'm rather surprised."

"Alastair? What do you mean?" Blake asked as James crept forward. Kayla mirrored him and slid to the side, manoeuvring herself in front of Blake. The fact that James knew about Blake chilled her to the bone.

"Seriously, Kayla, what are you doing?!" Blake whispered angrily.

"This just gets better and better! Kayla, darlin', move. My pa's team is already on their way to Blake's house. He gets to deal with his family, and I get to deal with him. So, while I'm ninety percent certain the heir is the dweeb standing behind you, I'm going to have to grab both of them, just in case. Then I get to show you why we're the superior race. I don't have to take *you* alive, after all."

"There's just one thing you're forgetting," Kayla said. "I'm not a witch."

Before she could even hope that her magic would appear, a growl erupted from Josh and his skin rapidly turned, peeling away and morphing into something else. She'd never seen a full-on transformation before, and even though she knew it would be painful – especially so for the first few shifts – she wasn't prepared to witness it. Josh's fingers curled and strained as he moaned, his nails sharpening into claws. His jaw cracked and elongated.

And then he was a wolf.

His fur was a light brown and his lip pulled into a snarl as a fearsome growl rolled up his throat. Blake stepped back, horror lining his face, and Kayla's suspicions were confirmed. Blake didn't even know the shifter world existed.

She had no time to see if he was okay, no time to assess the situation, no time to react. Josh's wolf leapt at James, aiming straight for his jugular.

CHAPTER FIFTEEN

BLAKE

EVERYTHING CHANGED IN THE blink of an eye and Blake was frozen at the centre of it all. Josh, his best friend, had transformed into a wolf. Blake blinked, struggling to process what he was seeing. For a moment, he was afraid the wolf was going to rip James apart, but in a matter of seconds, James and the two boys beside him had shifted into wolves, too. Wolves! And they were much larger than Josh – or at least the animal Josh had turned into.

What the hell was happening?

Blake opened his mouth, but no words came out. One of the wolves darted across the room, its gleaming teeth pointed at him.

Kayla screamed, and the wolf slammed into an unseen wall mere inches from Blake's face. It wobbled its head dizzily.

"Blake!" Kayla shouted, shaking him from his stupor. He saw his own terrified expression reflected in her eyes.

His voice shook as he asked, "What's going on, Kayla?" The two of them watched as the wolves fought in the small confines of the bedroom doorway. "Is that Josh? Is he okay? Should I be worried? He's a wolf. My best friend is a wolf?" His own questions flew around his head – he wasn't sure if Kayla even answered them. He turned back to her, peeling his eyes away from the violence, but it was impossible to tune out the growls and snarls and yelps.

"Not really. I don't know if I can stop them."

But one of them was his best friend. A wolf. Josh was a wolf.

"Try! You did something to that other wolf, didn't you?" He was guessing, but a part of him insisted that Kayla stopped the wolf from ploughing into him earlier.

"Yes, but I wasn't sure it was going to work, I–" She let go of him and pulled a small journal out of her pocket. She flicked through the worn pages and muttered some words from the passage she'd stopped on. She looked up. He followed her line of sight, but nothing had changed. There were still wolves in the bedroom. How were there wolves in the bedroom? He was struggling to weave together what he saw with his own eyes and what he knew – thought – was reality. "Goddamn it! Why are you always so temperamental?" she yelled, making him jump.

One of the bigger animals rammed into the side of the brown wolf – Josh's wolf – and he tumbled out of the room and onto the landing. "Josh!" Blake shouted as instinctual fear for his best friend crept in. Kayla said the same words again, angrily this time, and the non-Josh wolves were pulled into the furthest corner of the bedroom by an invisible hand. Kayla and Blake legged it out of the room and she pulled the door shut just as the wolves lurched to their feet. She placed her hand over the door handle and read from another page in the book. Was it Latin? Was James right? Was she a witch? The lock lit up with a faint white glow and rattled when the wolves hit it from the other side.

"It's secure for now," Kayla breathed, resting her head against the door.

Blake looked over as Josh's wolf twitched and its fur started to recede. The paws were replaced by human hands and his snout re-shaped into the familiar face of his best friend. The human version. Josh sat up, fully clothed, wincing at the claw marks on his arm and across his face.

"The bastard got me!"

CHAPTER SIXTEEN

KAYLA

"JOSH!" KAYLA EXCLAIMED, RUSHING to crouch near him. "Are you all right?"

"Yeah. Hey, so, about the fact that you're a magic user . . ." he looked at her pointedly.

"It's not like you told me you were a shifter! That would have made everything so much easier!"

"Someone needs to tell me what's going on," Blake said quietly. It made her worry more than if he had shouted, demanding answers.

"Blake, I–"

"You're a witch?" This wasn't strictly true, but she didn't think Blake could handle specifics right now, so she nodded. "And you're a – a werewolf?" he asked Josh.

"Shifter. Yes."

"And neither of you told me?" Blake's eyes held more than confusion. He was hurting, convinced of their betrayal.

Kayla looked to Josh for help. She didn't know what to say to help Blake understand. Judging by his reaction in the bedroom, he had no clue he was also a shifter.

Josh answered for her. "It's the first rule we're ever taught, Blake. I wanted to tell you, man, I really did, but if it got out, I could have had magic-user hunters on my ass; they hate us."

"Not all magic users hate shifters!" Kayla said, trying to justify herself.

Blake continued with his questions, clenching his fists. "What's James then? Why does he want us dead if he's . . . if he's one of you?"

Josh shrugged. "There is a lot you don't know," he replied.

"Then tell me!" Blake commanded.

Kayla tried not to flinch. "I don't know what James is. Possibly a shifter hunter, and it sounds like his dad might be, too," Kayla said. She toppled into Josh when the door rattled and growls reverberated from inside. "We need to leave!" Kayla cried as she sprung up, Josh giving her a helping hand.

"No, seriously guys. I need an explanation! What's going on? Who are the hunters? What are they hunting? I don't get any of this!" Blake tugged at his hair. Kayla opened her mouth to answer, but she was interrupted by the sound of wood splintering. Josh slammed his back against the door.

"Kayla, get Blake out of here. If he's an Alastair like James believes, he needs protecting. I'll hold these guys back!"

"Josh no, you might get hurt!" she cried.

Blake darted towards Josh, and Kayla feared he didn't truly understand the severity of the situation. How was she going to get him to calm down? "That's just what James said! I'm not that. I'm not anything!" Blake shouted at Josh.

"No. You're better." Josh looked Blake in the eye and nodded even as sweat trickled down the side of his face. The barricaded door shook again and Josh groaned. "I'm serious, Kayla! I'm strong enough to hold them back but not indefinitely. Get Blake out of here! Protect him!"

"C'mon, Blake," she whispered, grabbing his hand. He didn't budge, staring at his best friend whose arms were rippling with exertion.

"I got this, man, go!" Josh shouted. Blake refused to leave, and Kayla's tiny frame was far too weak to move him on her own. Josh locked eyes with her, obviously thinking the same thing. He turned back to Blake. "I can hold my own against these guys for a bit, and they'll probably rough me up, but they'll tear her apart for being different." His firm words flipped a switch within Blake, and he finally let her tug him away.

They flew down the stairs and out the front door, and she was grateful the loud music and crowded party provided cover for their getaway. She sped down the dark, empty street with Blake right beside her.

He stopped. "Wait!"

Kayla spun to face him and threw her arms wide.

"Wait? No, we need to get out of here! They're coming for you, for us!"

"But my family. James said his dad was going for my family!" He sped off in the opposite direction.

Damn his shifter speed! Thankfully Blake slowed down enough to let her see where he was going next. At least he had *some* thought-making processes working.

She knew she should be running the opposite way or taking a more hidden route, but instead, she chased after a shifter in the open street – a shifter who didn't even know he was a shifter. What had Mum gotten her into?

She followed Blake down a curving road and saw him standing on the pavement in front of a house with a green door. She slowed to a stop, struggling to catch her breath.

"My parents . . . Charlie, they were home. They were home," he whispered to himself, and Kayla saw it, too. The front door had been kicked in.

"Blake, I'm so sorry, but we have to go. Shifters have been here. They *will* kill you." Of that, she was sure.

"My parents . . . Charlie," he repeated. He shuffled forward in some sort of daze. Kayla sighed heavily at Blake's lack of self-preservation. She stalked after him when he pushed inside, and they inched down the hallway shoulder to shoulder. Pictures of smiling family members lined the walls of the cosy living room, but the happy memories were overshadowed by signs of struggle.

The coffee table was smashed to pieces and the TV had been ripped from the wall. One of the sofas had tipped over, and a torn jumper lay across it. Books, magazines, and mugs were scattered across the room.

Blake dropped to his knees, one hand covering his mouth. Kayla knew he was shattered, broken like she had been when her family was attacked. She squeezed his shoulder and told him to stay put while she checked the rest of the house. A similar scene of destruction littered the dining room, where it looked like his family had been having a meal, but the kitchen was largely intact. Upstairs was clear, apart from one room that had been tipped upside down. She guessed it was Blake's. The shifters would have tried searching for any clue of his whereabouts.

She moved back downstairs as Blake flipped the sofa around and picked up the TV, propping it gently against the wall. He was deathly pale.

"I'm sorry, Blake, but it looks like there's no sign of your family. I think they were taken by James's father – he probably wants to try and lure you in. I'll explain what I can about the hunters later, but we need to leave this town as soon as possible. Why don't you go and pack a bag of essentials?" Blake looked at her, his face blank, emotionless. It was very unlike the Blake she had come to know.

"I need to find them."

"I can make some enquiries, but we have to leave. Blake, do you realise the danger we're in?"

"Do you realise my family have been taken? Because of me? Why? Why, Kayla? You seem to know so much!" His voice rose in anger.

"I'm not sure I understand any of this myself."

"But you knew what Josh was. You did something to lock those werewolves–"

"Blake, I think you're going into shock, and I just need you to try and hold it together while we get out of here."

"Why am I in danger? Why do you keep saying that those *things* want to kill me?"

"This is really not the time–"

"Make the time, Kayla, because I'm not going anywhere until I understand what's happened to my family!" he shouted, jabbing his finger at her.

She blew out a breath, trying to keep calm. She had to remember that she'd been in his shoes not long ago, except her family had died. Would she be acting the same if there was a chance they were still alive?

"Shifters and magic users have been fighting against each other for some time. Each side thinks they're the superior race. I think you're the key to solving that."

"And why do you think that?"

"Because my mum told me that as she . . . just before she died. She told me to find you and I did, but that is literally all I know. I don't know who you are. I don't know how you're different." She left out the part about thinking he was a shifter, too; she didn't think he could take much more in his state. "Now please, Blake, please go and pack some clothes."

"Only if you agree to help me find my family first," he replied. Kayla opened her mouth to speak but he cut her off. "My family first, and then I'll help you figure out whatever this feud is between the shifters and the magic users."

It wasn't what she had in mind, but without him, the whole plan to bring the races together fell apart at the seams. She nodded, and he went upstairs to pack.

CHAPTER SEVENTEEN

BLAKE

WHEN BLAKE RETURNED, KAYLA was examining a family photograph on the wall. She had straightened up the room even though he'd only been gone a few minutes.

"Hey," he said softly, but she still jumped.

"Sorry, nervous. You got what you need?"

"Not sure, but it'll do," he said. He took the frame off the wall and turned it over, retrieving the picture from inside. "This photo was taken when we went on holiday a couple of years ago."

"You don't really look like your parents," Kayla said, leaning over his arm to peer closer.

"Yeah, we get that a lot, but you should see us on game night. Competitive nutters, the lot of us," he said, smiling. She watched him closely and the silence grew tense. "I'm sorry I was sharp with you. I'm just struggling to . . ."

"Yeah, I know."

"Where are we going?" he asked, hoping that was enough of an apology.

"Back to where I'm staying to get my things. I need to leave a note for Gaby."

"Miss Anderson?" he asked, furrowing his brow. They left the house and set a quick pace down the darkened streets. Kayla monitored the area as they walked.

"Yes, I'm living with her. I didn't exactly have anyone else to stay with." She avoided eye contact, but whether it was because she was staying vigilant or because she was uncomfortable, he couldn't tell.

The two marched to the house in companionable silence. It wasn't until she unexpectedly halted and threw her arm out that he looked up. They came to a standstill, and Blake glanced down at Kayla.

"Umm, is this--?"

"Shh," she hissed. "You good to run if we need to?" He shifted his backpack and nodded.

She cautiously pushed open the door. The creak that ensued sounded like a gunshot in the silence.

"Don't you have any of that 'magicky' stuff you could use?" he asked. Tension rolled off her in waves.

"Not how it works," she muttered, shaking her head. "It's dark. She said she would be leaving the light on for me, and the door was unlocked."

"Crap."

"Yeah."

They crept in, careful not to make a sound, and slipped down the short hallway into the living area. The light was off, but Blake could make out enough. Broken furniture and shattered decor lay everywhere, just like his home, and there was a wooden chair in the middle of the room. He found it odd until Kayla switched on the light. Gaby was facing away from them. She hadn't moved, and a coppery scent hung thick in the air.

Kayla moved forward but he grabbed her forearm and gently pulled her into his chest. He knew she wanted to argue with him, but he pointed to the dark stain pooling beneath the chair.

"Blood, Kayla." He didn't know what else to say. Kayla's face drained of colour and she nodded, pulling her arm out of his grasp. She shuffled around to the front of the chair and her reaction turned his veins to ice. He trailed behind her and stood at her side, forcing himself to look at Miss Anderson's dead body. "I don't understand," he whispered. Kayla inhaled sharply, her body shuddering next to his as she clutched his hand.

"We . . . we need to get, um, I need to get my things . . ." she said faintly, but she didn't move. He guessed she, much like himself, couldn't take her eyes off Miss Anderson.

She had been tortured, that much was clear. Blood was splattered across her face, her fingers were bent at odd angles, the nails on her right hand were missing, and she was covered in shallow cuts. What had she been tortured for? Why?

"Blake? Can you come with me?" Kayla asked, and he nodded. He wasn't sure he wanted to be on his own, anyway.

They silently made their way up the stairs and into a small, single bedroom. Blake didn't know what to do, so he sat on the edge of the bed as she grabbed her backpack and gathered her things. She slid into a pair of jeans, and even though she did so under her dress, he turned his head away.

The annotated Shakespeare sonnet they worked on together in class had been left on top of her bedside table. He smiled to himself, thinking she was nerdier than she'd let on, but the brief flash of happiness dried up in an instant. A few hours ago, his life was normal, and now werewolves and magic existed, and his best friend could turn into an animal and Miss Anderson . . . a chill slid down his spine and his stomach rolled as he remembered the scene below him.

"There won't be any trains this time of night, but we can't stay here. We're going to have to sleep at the station so we can get the first train in the morning," Kayla said, pulling him out of his thoughts.

He turned to face her. She had replaced the dress with a fresh, long-sleeved t-shirt and was in the process of zipping up a sweater. She placed the journal in her bag, and he wondered where she'd hidden it during the party.

"How are you so calm?" he asked.

Kneeling by her open backpack, she paused. "This isn't the first time something bad has happened to me." Her lips pressed together, and Blake knew she wasn't going to continue. She cast a glance around the room. With a loud exhale, she stood up, grabbing her backpack as she did. "Let's go, Collins."

"Have you got everything you need?"

"This is everything," she said in a small voice.

He followed her down the stairs, but she didn't leave like he expected her to. She went into the kitchen and started opening cupboards, pulling out boxes and rifling through the fridge.

"Hungry?" He frowned, putting his hands in his pockets. He couldn't stop thinking about the body just metres away from him.

"No, but we will be. This will save us some money."

"Money? Oh god, Kayla, I don't have any. I didn't think!"

"Don't panic. I have some for us. Hopefully it'll be enough, but we shouldn't waste an opportunity when we see one. Got room in your pack?"

He nodded, and she pushed over some cereal bars, fruit, and chocolate.

"Better than nothing, right?"

Once they'd put what they could into their bags, they moved down the hallway. Kayla stiffened as they passed the living room, staring at the front door.

"You okay?" he asked gently. She sniffled, and her voice sounded thick when she murmured a response, but he pretended he didn't hear it.

KAYLA FOUND THEM A spot behind the train station that was well hidden and not too windy. It was past two in the morning, and he was starting to feel the effects of the night take their toll. He was tired.

With their backs against the wall, they sat shoulder to shoulder – or head to shoulder, rather, as he was much taller than Kayla.

The silence ate away at his thoughts until he blurted out the question that had been on his mind for hours. "Do you think Josh is all right?"

"I'm sure he is. He seemed like he knew what he was doing. If he stayed in the house with the others and didn't leave alone, then he'll be fine – I hope. Protecting our secret comes first, so James and the other two wouldn't have gone downstairs as wolves. That would give Josh a chance to escape. Try not to worry," she added, looking up at him.

Blake nodded, satisfied for the time being. He wanted to ask about the wolves and why James was after them, but she shivered when she leaned against him.

"Why was Miss Anderson killed?" he asked instead. Perhaps understanding more might help him make sense of what was going on.

"I don't know, to get to me? To you?" She shook her head and sighed, tucking a loose strand of hair behind her ear.

"Do you think it was the same people who took my family?"

"I don't know, probably. James said he knew who I was. He mentioned that his dad was a tracker, so he probably followed my scent to her." Her voice was quiet, but he didn't know how to alleviate her guilt.

"I'm sorry."

"For what?"

"You looked like you were close." He could feel the grief coming off her, and it hurt him to see that much pain in her eyes. No one should know that kind of pain at her age. No one.

"We didn't know each other for long, but she was the first adult . . . she was the first place I felt safe, like I was being taken care of again after . . . oh God, this is so stupid," she cried, tears spilling onto her cheeks. She rested her head on her knees and let them fall.

She wasn't stupid. Someone she cared about had been murdered. He placed an awkward hand on her back and gently rubbed small circles between her shoulders. It was something his mum did when he was stressed as a child. It used to calm him down, and he hoped it was doing the same for Kayla.

They sat like that for a while until she straightened up, wiping at her face. Her eyes were red around the edges, but he didn't say anything.

"I don't get what you're trying to tell me about shifters and magic. These things shouldn't exist," he said after a while.

"We do exist, and it's never been smooth sailing between us, but things are worse than ever right now."

"Let's just say that I'm getting on board with the fact that we humans aren't alone in the world. Explain what's going on between you and the shifters. Help me to understand what I'm . . . in the middle of."

Kayla sighed. "Shifters and magic-users have always quarrelled because each side thinks they're the better race. You wouldn't believe how entitled some of them are. Things were steadily getting worse between the races, so twelve years ago, the shifter royal family and the magic-user council at the time decided to create an alliance."

"What alliance?"

"That's the thing. Nobody knows because the shifter royal family were all assassinated at the celebration of the signing. Nearly everyone who witnessed it was killed or has gone so deep into hiding that they've never been found."

Blake's mind was reeling with information. He ran a hand through his hair and blew out a long breath. "Okay then. And that made things worse, I'm guessing?"

"Oh, yes. Before the failed alliance, people worried about the races fighting each other, but the assassination of the shifter royal family somehow helped to cement the idea of race superiority into many people's heads. Any sort of camaraderie between the races was punishable by death. That's why we have to be careful – both races could come for us if we're seen helping those not of our kind."

"Jesus."

"Yeah. I'm hoping my parents' files can help us, but to get to them, we've got to go to Oxford. They sent them to a trusted friend for safekeeping."

"Why would your parents have files that could help?"

"They rescued people, shifters and magic users, and hid them from one another. They saved people and gave them new identities. Because of that, they had contacts and associates all over the place, so one of them will surely have heard about a family being taken by shifters. Hopefully, they'll know something about the original alliance."

Blake noted her use of the past tense when she spoke about her parents, and he held back on asking what happened. He couldn't ask her to speak about her family when he was hoping his own was still alive – not when hers clearly wasn't.

"Why my family, Kayla? Why me?"

She chewed on her lip.

"What do you know, Kayla?"

"I think you're a shifter, too. I think you're somehow related to the Alastairs."

"What? That's crazy. I think I'd know if I was one of them!"

"Yes, you would. And you should have already had your first change, several even, under your belt."

"You're wrong, and James is wrong. I'm not a shifter. I'm not an Alastair!"

Kayla shrugged. "Not directly, no, but maybe distantly. I know someone who was looking for an Alastair relative to help establish an alliance after the first one was thwarted. Maybe you're distantly related?"

Blake snorted.

He didn't answer. She was wrong. He wasn't a beast – he wasn't one of them.

"Get some sleep if you can, Blake. We can talk more tomorrow."

She grabbed her pack to use as a pillow and pulled her hands inside her jacket. Closing her eyes, she dozed off quickly, but hours passed before the pull of sleep knocked at his mind where hideous monsters roamed freely inside his nightmares.

CHAPTER EIGHTEEN

KAYLA

KAYLA AWOKE WITH THE sunrise and nipped to the station toilets. When she came back, Blake was still asleep, hair plastered down across his forehead and an arm flopped over his head. She smiled at the typical teenage boy behaviour. Grabbing her pack, she went to purchase their train tickets.

She needed a walk, so she decided against the vending machine in favour of the convenience store a mile or so away. She picked up a water and a Ribena, hoping Blake liked the drink. Stocking up on more food crossed her mind, but they had enough in their packs, so she carried the bottles back to the station.

The woman at the counter smiled far too much for Kayla's liking and handed her two single tickets direct to Oxford leaving at 10:40am. That gave her, after checking the clock in the station, just over an hour and a half to wait. She really hated waiting.

Thinking Blake would probably still be asleep after their night, she walked to a popular fast-food chain that wasn't far away and ordered two pancake boxes as a treat. God knew they both needed it, and it could help Blake feel a bit better considering he had to process far more than she did.

Carrying four bottles and two lots of pancake boxes wasn't easy, and it took some careful managing to cross the road and walk the short distance to their spot behind the station. Thankfully it was still well hidden, even in the daylight.

Rounding the corner, Kayla found Blake on his feet, his jumper creased and his hands buried in his hair. When he saw her, his posture sagged, and his arms fell limply by his sides.

"You okay?" she asked, concerned.

"Yeah, um, I woke up and . . ." He didn't have to finish. He'd woken up, and she was gone with her pack. He thought she'd left him, and if she was being honest, she would have thought the same.

"Sorry, Blake."

"No, that's okay. I just thought for a moment that last night might have been . . . are those pancakes?" he asked quickly, changing the subject.

She smiled and held them up as best she could.

"You bet!"

He stepped forward to help her with the bottles, and they sat cross-legged on the ground, facing each other. Kayla took off her jacket and lay it over the pavement; she'd rather feel the cold on her arms than her bum.

Blake drizzled the syrup pot over the contents of his box and took his first bite, closing his eyes.

"These are the best goddamn pancakes!"

"Food can do that after sleeping rough."

"You sound as if you speak from experience," he said around a mouthful of pancake.

"Yeah, it's an experience I don't really want to keep repeating."

"Last night, what you did . . . well, what is it exactly that you did?"

Telling him about magic wouldn't *really* break the rules – he already knew about shifters and witches, after all.

"I used magic. I'm a magic user," she said, watching closely for his reaction. She was surprised when she only found curiosity.

"Like a witch?"

"Not exactly. There are three types of magic users: witches, mages, and elementals."

"Woah, so are they all different?"

"Yes. A witch uses spells and special objects like herbs to do magic.

Words are power to a witch, and their magic comes from the heart. A mage can conjure and do magic without spells, as their power comes from the mind. They think of something and it's done, but the degree of power can vary with the strength of the mage. And then there are elementals who control the elements: fire, water, earth and air. They can only control what already exists. They can't conjure up any fire, they can only control a fire that's already lit. Their magic comes from the soul. They feel it in their very being."

"That sounds powerful!"

"Elementals? Most aren't that powerful. Earth is the weakest element. They can mostly support plants in their growth – it's not as if they can cause an earthquake or anything like that. Air is probably the next one on the scale, but again, you can't go around creating hurricanes. You could possibly control the wind in a storm, but that's all. The most powerful elements are water and fire. Elementals tend to have a stronger link to either fire or water, but they can control all the elements. Mages are considered the most powerful in our community."

"So, you must be a witch because you used that spell book?" She looked down at her empty pancake box. Could she really tell him about her messed up magic?

"I'm not sure," she admitted eventually.

"What do you mean by that? You must know, right?"

She tucked some hair behind her ear and put the empty box down. "Yes, I should. Like shifters, we come into our magic around puberty, so it can vary from person to person. You inherit magic from your parents. My parents were slightly different in that my mum was a witch and my dad was a mage, but marrying within the magic user community isn't too uncommon."

"So you'd be one or the other. But I'm sensing that's not the case."

"Not quite. The first time I used magic was about two weeks ago. The day I turned seventeen." She stopped to let it sink in.

"You were late coming into your magic?"

"Yes, and . . . I set a car engine on fire and doused it magically with the water from the radiator to extinguish it." She rushed through the explanation.

"Elemental magic?" He guessed, and she nodded in response. "But you should be a witch or a mage?" Another nod. "But last night you used a spell and it worked?"

"I panicked. I've been training with my mother my whole life and I had her spell journal, so I just tried it and . . . it worked. I'm not sure what I am."

"Well, we can figure it out. We'll just add it to our list," he said, quite casually given the situation.

"Our list?"

"Yup!" he said, holding out his hand to tick things off on his fingers. "Find my family, find out why people are after me, find out about your magic, and figure out this alliance."

"Okay, our list. Doesn't sound too bad."

"Piece of cake! When's our train?"

She looked down at her watch: it was about twenty minutes away.

"Not too long. Let's go inside, find a bathroom to freshen up in, and wait on the platform."

"Sounds like a plan to me," he announced, getting up to put both of their boxes in a nearby bin. When he came back, he grabbed his pack and started to follow her to the station entrance. "Wait!" he said, stopping suddenly.

She spun in alarm. Panic flared in his eyes and the colour drained from his face. "What's wrong?"

Blake closed his mouth and gulped. "Miss . . . Miss Anderson. What about her?" he whispered.

Kayla's stomach summersaulted again at the thought of leaving Gaby like that, but they had no choice.

"She'll be found eventually. The police will put it down to a robbery gone wrong, or someone in the magic community will come and cover up the – the – scene. Either way, we don't have a choice."

"That sucks. It's not right."

"I know."

Blake's face softened at her tone, and he reached for her hand.

IT WASN'T LONG BEFORE they were settled on the train and heading south towards Oxford. She was really hoping that when she got there, they would be able to find the person who her parents entrusted with their legacy.

They sat side by side, Blake leaning against the window while she took the aisle seat. He was fidgety, and the further they got, the more restless he became.

"Are you all right?" she finally asked when he shuffled next to her yet again.

"Yeah, just not comfortable. I can't believe you made me ditch my phone," he snapped.

"I'm sorry. It's just safer. In case they can track it."

"I want to ask you something," he announced, abruptly changing the subject. "Why do you think I'm one of . . . them?" he said, lowering his voice at the end so other people wouldn't hear. It wasn't like the train was packed, but she didn't think she would be able to explain a conversation about werewolves. She brought her head closer to his.

"Because of this," she answered, pulling her necklace out of her shirt. "My mum sent me after a shifter, spelling the necklace so that I could track and find you. It alerted me when I touched your arm for the first time."

"At the party?"

"Yes."

"Could it be wrong? I don't think I'm one of these shifters," he said, looking at her hopefully.

She didn't want to be the one who took away the light in his eyes, but at the same time, he needed to be prepared – especially if he was going to change soon. That was another problem. An untrained shifter who hadn't had their first shift? Big issue. She needed to focus on finding his family first, and hopefully they would be able to reveal some answers.

"Perhaps."

Blake nodded and said he was feeling sleepy, so he tucked his arms to his sides and rested his head against the window. Kayla flicked through a magazine someone had left behind, but she soon grew bored. She decided to take a walk down the train, this time leaving her bag on the seat so if Blake woke up he wouldn't think she had left him again.

She made her way to the cafe section and bought a muffin, eating it at the bar so Blake didn't find out. She even had a nice conversation with the elderly attendee, talking about everything from the weather to his grandkids. After she finished, she meandered back down the train, taking her time before she got back to her seat.

As she sat down, she automatically flicked a quick glance over at Blake and frowned; he looked pale and there was a slight sheen to his skin. Leaning over, she brushed some of his hair away and placed her hand on his forehead. He was hot – a feverish kind of hot. He opened his eyes and squinted against the light.

She sucked in a breath. "Are you feeling okay?"

"No," he breathed out on a shudder.

Shit. This could not have happened at a worse time. The adrenaline from the night before must have accelerated the process. He was going to shift. She had so very little knowledge of shifters changing, especially for the first time, but what she did know was that doing it without an experienced shifter was beyond her capabilities.

"Okay, Blake. I need you to stay calm, but I think your body is trying to transition."

"Transition?"

"Yes . . . change."

"No, I-I just have the flu or something," he mumbled. He didn't believe her. Again. "I'll be fine."

"Blake, I'm being serious. You won't be fine, and I can't allow you to shift on the train. We have to get off."

"But we're nowhere near Oxford," he groaned, trying to settle back into his seat. Kayla pulled on his sleeve to keep him alert.

"Blake, stay awake! If you sleep, it quickens the transition."

"What? Why?"

"Because it's your first one. Your body is trying to do it for you. You won't be in control."

"I'm gonna be sick," he said sitting upright. Kayla jumped out of her seat and watched Blake stumble down the train toward the toilets. Grabbing both their heavy packs, she followed him and stood outside the door, waiting.

People started to stand up and pack their bags as the next stop approached. The toilet door slid open, and Blake stood in the doorway with his arms braced on either side of the small frame, his head hung low.

"Blake?" she asked tentatively, reaching a hand forward. When his head snapped up, his eyes for the briefest of moments, flashed golden yellow.

"Help me," he whispered feebly, terrified.

She couldn't let herself panic. She had to stay calm to help Blake; he was going through something much worse than she was right now.

"Okay, okay, lean on me," she instructed, putting her backpack on and helping Blake into his. She put his arm around her shoulders and hoped they looked like a normal couple, not like she was supporting his weight.

"I'm sorry," he whispered.

"Don't be." The train was slowing down as it pulled into the station. Her blood ran cold when four guys strode onto the platform, one of them directing two to the left while he and his partner took the right. The training her dad had insisted upon alerted her to their actions. They were hunters. And she was confident they were shifters. "Crap! Right, Blake, we might have some company on the platform, so I need you to keep your head low and just stay on me, all right? We need to move fast and we can't make a scene. My dad taught me a few basic self-defence moves if I was ever caught with my back against a wall, but we're going to follow his first piece of advice instead."

"What's . . . that?" he whispered.

"See a shifter? Run."

He nodded in response and the doors slid open. A few passengers disembarked first, but as soon as they stepped off, she set a fast pace. The turnstiles were tricky with Blake leaning on her, but she got them through before he could fall. She could see the exit. They were nearly free when one of the shifters from the platform blocked the exit, searching the crowd. She quickly pushed Blake into the station coffee shop and manoeuvred her way through to the back exit, hoping they hadn't been seen.

The fresh air seemed to be helping Blake, who leaned on her less and less, and there were no more flashes of gold in his eyes.

They jogged down the street, taking turn after turn, trying to move away from the crowds of people. She didn't think Blake was in danger of shifting anymore, but she had to be sure. It wasn't until they made it to a deserted, industrial area that she slowed down.

Now she had to figure out where they were and how they were going to get to Oxford.

"Kayla, I'm so sorry," Blake panted, trying to support his own weight.

He was still pale, but at least the feverish look in his eyes had disappeared. "I don't know what happened."

"The change was starting, that's what." She kept her words short and to the point, considering he didn't quite believe her.

"I–" he started, but he was cut short by a man ploughing into him, tackling him to the ground.

"Blake!" she yelped. She kept back as the two fought, knowing she'd be nothing but a distraction. Besides, the man standing at her side left no doubt that she should probably stay where she was. "What do you want?" she snapped as she faced the other shifter.

"We have orders to grab the boy, but we don't have any orders regarding you. You're fair game."

"I can be helpful," she replied, trying to think of ways to keep herself alive.

He sneered. "Not interested, girl." He was a big guy with muscles as thick as her thigh.

When he stepped closer, she slammed her heel down on his foot. He bent forward and she thrust her elbow into his nose. He fell back, grasping at his face, clearly shocked that a girl – a non-shifter at that – had gotten the best of him. She sent a silent thanks to her dad for the basic defence training.

"You bitch!" He shrieked at her, spitting out blood. She scrambled into the road but turned around when she sensed the broken-nosed shifter come after her. She didn't hesitate. The water pipe running down the side of the building sang to her. Focussing, she channelled her power, and for once it listened to her commands. Water shot out of the pipe at a rapid speed, slamming the shifter into a wall and pinning him against it. Turning to Blake, she whipped another torrent of water at the shifter on top of him. Blake jumped up, sputtering.

"Is this you?" he asked, his mouth gaping open. She nodded, afraid that the magic would stop working at any moment and the shifters would be released. "Let's get out of here," he said. She didn't argue.

They half-ran, half-walked out of the industrial area so they didn't look too conspicuous, and steadily moved towards the more populated city centre. If Blake wasn't going to change, they were probably better protected in a crowded area.

Kayla stopped abruptly, turning down an alley and sinking between two massive dumpsters.

"Kayla? You okay?" Blake asked, sitting down beside her. She didn't mean to, she honestly didn't, but she was so overwhelmed that she leaned into him and cried. Again. She had to stop doing that around him. He didn't seem too weirded out as he placed his arm around her. Feeling protected and cared for, she wept, if only for a few minutes. She wasn't used to bearing this much responsibility.

"I'm sorry, I shouldn't have done that." She sniffled, sitting up and away from Blake's warmth, wiping her face on her sleeve.

"That's okay. I think we're very much in uncharted territory here. You ever run away from people trying to kill you before?" He was joking, but he didn't realise the truth of his words until she stilled. "Oh shit. I'm such an insensitive jerk."

"You weren't to know."

"Your parents?" he asked when she leaned forward, resting her head on her knees and wrapping her arms around her legs.

"Yeah. I'd like not to have my life in danger for a little bit."

"God, I get it. That sucks. I'm sorry. If it makes you feel any better, I think you're doing marvellously." He smiled at her, but as she opened her eyes to look at him, she winced and sat up straighter. "Umm, what? That dude smash my face in more than I thought?"

"You could say that. You can*not* walk around in public like that. You have blood all over your nose and your mouth, and the skin around your eye is really purple. I'm surprised it's not swollen, too. I imagine that's your shifter benefits starting to kick in."

"Shifter benefits?"

She leaned towards him and pressed her fingertips gently around the bruising, bringing her face close to his. "Tenderness isn't as pronounced. And yes, benefits. Faster healing, heightened senses, strength – you know."

"How fast is that healing you're talking about, 'cos my face hurts like a skunk's arse stinks!"

She snorted and it quickly turned into laughter, real laughter. Of all the situations to find herself in, she had never expected this one. Blake smiled in response and his face lit up. It was just as she remembered from the party, before everything had turned to chaos. It was a smile that transformed his face. The smile warmed her heart and eased her grief, just a bit.

Chapter Nineteen

Blake

BEFORE THEY EXITED THE alley to join the busy street, Kayla stopped him and pulled up his hood. It wasn't an easy feat considering his height, but he didn't help, enjoying Kayla's struggle as she balanced on her tiptoes, her tongue sticking out in concentration.

"Stop looking at me like that! You're the giraffe, not me!"

"Sorry. You stick your tongue out when you focus on something. It's funny." Cute. He actually wanted to say cute, but he stopped himself. That would have been embarrassing.

"Well, keep your head down until we can find a bathroom or something to clean you up in."

"Where are we going? Back on the train?" he asked, their arms brushing together as they walked.

"No, I think that avenue has closed, at least for a few days. We need to make sure we don't have any. . . episodes . . . before we publicly travel again."

Right. And by 'episodes' she was referring to the shift that nearly overwhelmed him. Okay, so he *had* felt beyond helpless on the train. He had been unbearably hot, his stomach was in double, triple, quadruple knots, and the world had spun around him. If it wasn't for Kayla, he was positive he would have collapsed. But changing? Into a wolf? He really didn't – couldn't – believe it. Not yet.

"What's our plan?"

"Find a fast-food chain. People tend to take less notice there, and we can get you cleaned up and order some warm food. We've not actually eaten anything for hours."

It was then that he noticed the sky was dimming. Where had the time gone?

Kayla found them a restaurant like she said she would, and after reminding him to keep his head down, she marched them to the back where the toilets were. Thankfully, they were individual rooms, so they squeezed into one and locked the door. Kayla immediately took her pack off, rolling her shoulders when they were unburdened. She grabbed a pile of paper towels and wet them under the sink.

"Could you sit on the seat? I can't reach very well," she mumbled, and he grinned at her flushed cheeks. It was definitely cute.

He sat on the closed seat and she became the taller one as she attempted to wipe the dried blood off his face. He caught his reflection in the mirror beside them and winced.

"Is that what he did to me?"

"This is better than what it was a half-hour ago."

"Let me guess. Shifter benefits?"

"Yep." He sighed. "Blake, c'mon, you must believe me by now?" she asked, scrubbing near his hairline with a fresh towel.

"It's not that I don't trust you. I do, despite not knowing you very long. It's just . . . turning into some monster . . . that's not me."

Her face softened, and he wasn't sure he was fond of the pity he saw there.

"You won't be a monster. That's not how it works."

"Enlighten me then, because the only shifters we know turn into murderous freaking wolves."

"What about Josh? He's your friend," she said, and he sucked in a sharp breath. Not only had he been a crappy best friend and forgotten all about him, but Kayla was bringing him up – yet again.

"Oh, yes. Your boyfriend, Josh, the one who didn't tell me he could change into a wolf and the one who leapt at James's throat, probably with the intention of killing him. He seemed nice."

"Don't be like that. He didn't tell you because we're not supposed to reveal our true identities to humans; it's like rule number one."

"Pfff."

"Don't huff at me! In fact, he tried to help us at the party. He helped us get away."

Blake looked down so she didn't see his embarrassment. He understood what she was saying, but for some reason, thinking about Josh hurt him.

"Did you ever actually like Josh in the way he liked you?" he asked in a muted voice. He wasn't sure why it mattered, but it did.

"I told you both a hundred times that I wasn't there for that."

"So, you did."

"No, I didn't like him back that way. Happy now? Why does it matter to you so much, anyway?"

He shrugged as she turned to wet more paper towels. "Clearly today is just getting to me."

"Clearly."

"I didn't mean to be rude about Josh."

"Uh-huh."

"It's just, I get why he wouldn't tell everyone else. But I was his best mate."

"Okay."

"Are you just going to give me one-word answers?"

"Maybe."

"Kayla! I said I was sorry!"

"No, you didn't. Not for this, and it's not fair. All I've done is try to save your ass and then I get moaned at." She threw some of the bloodied paper towels in the bin and folded her arms; she was very close to him given the small size of the room.

"Well then, I apologise. Guess I'm just a class 'A' jerk."

"No, no you're not. But you do need to stop feeling sorry for yourself and playing the victim."

"But isn't that exactly what we are?"

"Yes, but that attitude doesn't help us. We have to find your family, figure out what's going on with your change, get to the bottom of my freakish magic, and somehow get two warring races to agree to peace. Remember our list?" she asked, and his spirits started to climb again. She was giving him an out, brushing past whatever spat they'd just had. And he knew he had to find his family above all else.

"Our list," he agreed, his face now scrubbed clean of blood. "Good job," he complimented, brushing his damp hair back with his hands. The skin around his eye was less bruised, too. No one would notice unless they were looking for it.

"Food?" Kayla asked, and his stomach rumbled embarrassingly in response. Kayla smiled. "Shifters are always hungry."

"So are guys my size," he replied as they somehow managed to get their backpacks on in the small space.

"You're not big. Tall, yes, but not big."

"Oh, not this again!" he joked.

"What? You don't have muscle yet. Shifters pack it on once they change, so you'll be a 'big guy' in no time," she said with a laugh. Swinging the door outward, she stopped short, causing him to bump into her. An old man stood outside scowling at them. Blake didn't have to guess what he thought they might have been up to.

"Stupid kids," the old man muttered as he moved inside the cubicle and Kayla and Blake made their way out. Once the door closed, they both muffled their laughter as Kayla directed them to a booth near the back of the seating area. An exit wasn't too far away, and it was busy with customers coming and going; no one would notice if they stayed a while.

Kayla instructed him to save the table while she went and ordered the food. He thought she might be a while, given the queue, but she was back in a matter of minutes with burgers, chips, and those cheesy bite things. He went to reach for one, but she slapped his hand away.

"Did you ask me to get these?"

"No," he replied sheepishly.

"Then stop giving me those puppy dog eyes. They're mine."

"Didn't know you were so possessive."

"About food? Always."

"So, captain, what next?" he asked. She frowned while ripping open a sachet of ketchup and drizzling it over her chips. She put a few in her mouth, chewing with a pensive look on her face. He didn't interrupt. He knew a lot of the planning fell to her, but he didn't have the knowledge she did.

"Amy," she said finally.

"Amy?"

"Yes, she's a shifter here in the city. My parents helped her a few years ago. She was one of the first cases I remember. She may be able to help you – us," she corrected quickly.

"You mean a shifter who can help a shifter?" he clarified.

She shrugged in response. "Well, it's just someone who can help us regardless. We need it. I feel like there are hunters everywhere."

"What I don't understand is why there are shifters trying to kidnap us. And what about these magic people? You said there was essentially a war going on."

"Users. We're called magic users as a collective."

"Okay, magic users. Shouldn't they be the ones to want me dead? Why are shifters attacking us if I'm supposed to be one of them?"

"I'm guessing magic users also want your head. That's why I've got to be careful about who I trust here. And I'm betting it has something to do with you acting as a bridge between both races, or at least that's what I got from my mum before she . . . well, just before. I reckon I'm just collateral damage."

"Let's say, for argument's sake, that I am one of these shifters. How do I bridge the gap between the races?" he asked, shovelling fries in his mouth. Kayla frowned at him disapprovingly.

"That is very good question."

"Your mum didn't elaborate?"

"Wasn't the time," she said, and he immediately felt guilty when pain flashed across her features.

"So, this Amy girl. We need to find her. How?"

"I'm hoping I can use one of my mother's tracking spells."

"Witch magic?"

"That's the one."

"What do you need?"

"A map of the city, please?" she asked, clearing away some space on the table.

He went on the hunt, and luckily for him, he found a wall of maps at the entrance of the building along with a variety of leaflets about things to do in the area. He grabbed the most detailed one and brought it back to their booth. Kayla sat with her feet tucked underneath her, concentrating as she bent over her journal. Blake stopped in his tracks.

He wondered how she was managing to cope and look so . . . put together when he was struggling to hold back the raw, jumbled mess of his emotions. She'd shed a couple of tears, but boy was she strong – stronger than he was – for getting them both through the chaos. He hated that she'd seen so much violence and grief, and he had the strangest urge to protect her from the world. He just didn't know how. One thing was certain: he would do better, be better.

"Okie dokes. Now what?" he asked, sitting down and sliding the map over to her. He tried to sound confident. "What spell are you going to do? Is it, you know, safe to do here?"

"Yeah, we're safe. It's not a very big spell, and no one is paying us any attention. It's a tracking spell that I can use because I know Amy's name. It should work, as long as there's no cloaking spell, that is."

"Cloaking spell?"

"My parents often advised against them as they can become a beacon of sorts. Instead of hiding in plain sight, there's just this magical void around the object or person being cloaked. Although, you must have had one on you, given how well you were hidden. Even you weren't aware, but I couldn't find evidence of a cloaking spell on you. I'm not sure how they did it. Anyway, I need a drop of your blood please," she said, looking up at him expectantly.

"Blood?" he squawked. He didn't think he was particularly squeamish, but the idea of using his blood for a spell made him queasy.

"Yes, I need shifter blood to find a shifter."

"But what if I'm not a shifter?"

Kayla sighed. "Then the spell won't work."

He reluctantly agreed, if only to prove to her that she was wrong about him being a shifter. Using a pocketknife she'd taken from her backpack, he watched her prick his index finger and pinch the skin so that a small droplet of blood welled up. She directed his finger over the map and let the droplet fall. While she murmured her mother's spell, he sucked on his finger to staunch the bleeding – it hadn't been that bad in all honesty.

She finished her spell and watched the map intently, as did he. They both leaned over the table, their heads almost touching. Just when he was about to lean back, thinking it hadn't worked, the droplet moved. The shiny ball of crimson liquid actually slid across the map, coming to a stop.

"I'm really one of them?" he breathed shakily. She nodded, looking like she wanted to apologise.

Leaning back, he ran his hands through his hair. It wasn't like he hadn't believed Kayla. He even knew deep down something had been up with him. And hadn't he always felt caged somehow?

Shit.

He was a werewolf.

A shifter.

"Are you okay?" she asked, bringing him out of his spinning thoughts.

He shrugged. "Yeah, just . . . I dunno."

"We'll figure it out, remember?" she said, placing a comforting hand over his.

"Who am I? You said I was Killian? Who's Killian? Who's me? That doesn't even make any sense."

"Hey, hey, look at me," Kayla said, squeezing his fingers. "You're Blake. This doesn't change that." Sincerity and absolute conviction shone from her eyes.

"Where is this Amy?" he asked. His voice was scratchy even to his own ears.

Kayla frowned and studied the map. "Not far, but I think we should wait until it's darker before we go."

"I agree."

They sat in silence, finishing off the extra burgers that Kayla bought, hungry from the day's events.

"You know, that spell was rather anti-climactic in a way," he said, scrunching up his burger wrapper.

"What do you mean?"

"There was no 'double, double, toil and trouble'." He screwed his face up and wiggled his fingers as if he were an old hag stirring a potion. She rolled her eyes. "Okay, all right, so it's not movie magic, but that was witch magic, right?"

"Yeah."

"So you've got to have part witch in you somewhere?"

"That would make sense as my mum was a witch, but I used elemental magic earlier when the two shifters came after us. Whatever my magic is, it's extremely unreliable, probably because I haven't been trained in it."

"Would it help if we found another elemental magic user?"

She paused for a moment. "Possibly, but I think that's fairly low on our list at the moment."

"Maybe, but we'll get you help. I promise."

"I don't think you can make that promise, Blake."

He couldn't figure out why her words cut him so deeply.

He watched her glance around the room for the hundredth time, cleverly avoiding his gaze. He was about to tell her that she could trust him when she froze, a frown carved into her face. He immediately sensed that something had changed.

"We need to move," she whispered and grabbed her pack.

Without questioning why, he followed suit and trailed behind her, glancing back inside to see what could have spooked her. Just as he turned his head, he made eye contact with a tall, dark-skinned man somewhere in his thirties. He stood rigidly and his cold eyes were trained on Blake and Kayla. The man wore a thick coat, but if he had to guess, the guy was heavy with muscle. He'd only been in the supernatural world for a day, but he was guessing the man was a shifter, too.

Kayla tugged on his arm. A pale, red-headed woman appeared from behind the man. She sneered at Blake, making a move to surge forward, but the man lifted his hand in a clear indication to stop, never tearing his gaze away from them. Blake shivered. He would not survive a fight with him. Of that, he had no doubt.

"Please," Kayla whispered, tugging again on his sleeve. The desperation in her voice forced his feet forward. The man and woman wouldn't spare her if they were caught.

CHAPTER TWENTY

KAYLA

KAYLA DRAGGED BLAKE AWAY from the restaurant; she'd known the moment she saw the redhead speaking to the older man that they weren't there for food. It was instinctual. She was thankful Blake had followed her without question, as any commotion could have alerted the hunters of their presence. What she hadn't counted on was Blake looking back, searching for something in the sea of people. When the hunters caught sight of them, her heart had jumped into her throat. The man was gigantic even in his human form, and there was no way the woman was anything less than lethal. Of that, she was sure.

"Are they coming after us?" Blake asked as they hurried down a street littered with people coming home from work or going out for dinner. She wished she and Blake were doing the same, but no. They were running for their lives, yet again.

"Yes. They didn't come after us straight away because there were too many humans around. Keeping our society a secret is more important than catching us, but they won't be far away."

"I don't see them."

"That doesn't mean they're not there. Honestly, it was a stroke of luck I spotted them. My dad . . . never mind. They are highly skilled hunters.

If they're coming after us – after you – they'll be experienced. I don't know what to do, Blake," she moaned, her heart thumping faster against her ribcage. The wolves were going to find them. They were going to kill her. They were going to take Blake and use him. Kill him. Kill the only possible chance for an alliance between the races. Her parents had died for nothing. Her hands clutched at her shirt, pulling the fabric away from her neck.

Just as her throat began to close, Blake shoved her between the sides of two buildings and pressed her against the wall, clutching the tops of her arms and leaning his face close to hers.

"Kayla, you're about to panic," he said, his voice slow and calm.

"I'm sorry. I just don't know what to do. This is too much, I–"

"Kayla," he said, giving her a little shake, "you can get us out of this. I know it. You've mentioned your dad a few times, did he train you for this or something? What did he teach you?"

"Evading capture."

"Okay, so what would he say? What would he do in this situation? Just pretend it's another training session with your dad."

Kayla closed her eyes. Blake's firm grip on her arms grounded her. She took a few deep breaths to try and calm her racing heart, and as she did, Blake's scent wrapped itself around her. Her breathing slowed and her brain began to work again.

"I can't use a tracking spell with them because I don't know their names . . . but what about water? I used elemental power, or whatever it is, with those pipes earlier, so perhaps I can do the same again. There was a bridge on the map, so if we head there, I might be able to use that power again. I hope. I also think it was a bit removed from the main town centre so there should be fewer witnesses."

"Hope is better than nothing. You did it before. You can do it again. Do you know which way to go?"

She nodded and dug the map out of her back pocket, showing it to Blake who still hadn't let go of her.

"Thanks. I'm okay now. We should go, because if we stay here too long, they could scent us out. Especially if one of them is a proficient tracker. Our best bet is to avoid them for as long as possible and get to Amy."

Blake nodded and released her. When he did, she felt the panic rise again, but he glanced down at her with piercing blue eyes full of concern, and she knew he was counting on her to get them out of this. She couldn't let him down.

THE STREETLIGHTS WERE PAINFULLY bright as they jogged through the city. Night had fully descended, and they wound their way through busy shopping streets, then residential areas, and finally an open park. Evenly spaced lampposts revealed a path snaking through the darkness. The cool night air settled on her skin like an unwelcome blanket. Each breeze sent painful shivers down her spine and her eyes darted from side to side, studying their surroundings. An empty park should have been a welcome reprieve, but instead, she felt exposed.

It had been an hour since they'd seen the two shifters; Kayla was praying they could keep clear of trouble for a bit longer before making their way to Amy. She hoped they wouldn't be followed.

She noticed Blake shake his head out of the corner of her eye and she quickly glanced his way. His close presence had been a comfort, but she was starting to worry. He was pale again and sweat beaded on his forehead. She was tired but she was holding steady; Blake was an athlete and a shifter. The past hour shouldn't have been too strenuous for him.

"How are you doing?" she asked, slowing her pace. He only nodded. "Blake!"

"My head's hurting again, and I feel sick, but that's it. I'm fine. I'll be fine."

"Hey, stop. Look at me," she ordered. She took his arm and pulled them out of the streetlight's halo so they weren't so exposed. Dragging him closer, she studied him for signs of a shift. His eyes were bloodshot, and his pupils were dilating and contracting rapidly. His chest rose and fell much faster than it should've, and he looked clammy. She placed a hand on his forehead and winced at how hot his skin was. "You're burning up."

"You don't think . . ."

"Yeah, I do. I think–"

"Wait, did you hear that?" he asked, turning his head, frown lines etched deep between his brows.

"Hear what?"

"That," he said, thrusting his hand towards a grove of trees in the distance. Nothing touched her ears, only the rustling of bushes, the occasional squawk from a bird flying overhead, and the odd rumble of an engine not too far away. "That!" he said again, looking back at her with wide eyes. His expression sent a spike of fear coursing through her body. "It sounded like a . . ." he paused. A blur of teeth and fur shot in front of her, taking Blake with it. It was the second time he'd been tackled that day. She didn't even have time to call out. Blake's shout of surprise ended in a grunt as he landed on the concrete, rolling with his assailant.

The night-black wolf got to all four paws and looked at Kayla with menacing yellow eyes. She knew it was the man from earlier. The wolf was one of the biggest she'd ever seen. Thick, bunched muscles strained around its neck and down its front legs. He growled and his lips peeled back to display a set of gleaming fangs, waiting to tear into her flesh. Kayla shivered as the wolf continued to stare at her, and when it took a step towards her, her heart stopped.

Blake roared, his voice still human but trembling with anger. He rushed the black beast and the two went down in a heap. The change must have been giving Blake some advantage because he was able to keep the wolf's snapping jaws away from his neck. As she moved closer to help, the red-headed woman sprang from behind her and leapt onto Kayla's back. They both tumbled to the ground.

She briefly wondered why the woman hadn't changed, but soft fur brushed against her fingers before the thought could fully form. The woman was shifting. Growls vibrated against her body and Kayla fumbled for the knife she'd stuffed into her back pocket. Reaching for the weapon, she shrugged her pack off and shuffled backwards, kicking the wolf in the head when the shift was complete.

Yellow eyes locked with her own, and the red wolf snarled low in its throat. Kayla gulped, fear gripping her as the wolf pounced. She brought her hands up, crossing her arms over her head with the open pocketknife facing out. She buckled beneath the heavy weight of the wolf as it landed on top of her, but a whine immediately followed. Lying on her back, panting heavily, she withstood the full force of the wolf's body before it dragged itself away, leaving a dark trail of blood in its wake.

Sounds of struggle reached her ears, and she knew she had to get to Blake. She flipped onto her front, forcing air into her lungs. Terror ripped through her as she watched Blake attempt to get up from where he lay. The black wolf placed a paw on his back and pushed him down, sending Blake crashing into the concrete.

Worried he was losing strength, she pulled herself into a sitting position and prayed her magic would aid her. She begged and pleaded with it, and nearly wept with relief when she felt the familiar tingle of its awakening. Knowing she had to give the magic purpose, she asked it to push the wolf off Blake. She visualised it and raised her hand to direct the magic towards the beast. She kept her breathing steady and commanded it to do her bidding.

A surge of magic exploded out of her, and the black wolf flew through the air, landing several feet away. She wasn't sure if the magic was elemental, mage, or something else, but the wolf didn't get back up. Kayla ran over to Blake, grabbing their fallen packs on her way.

"Blake? Blake!" she whispered as loudly as she dared. Blake groaned as she forced him onto his back. She quickly ran her hands over his jumper, pressing hard, but she couldn't feel any obvious breaks. His face was bloody, but he seemed otherwise intact. She grabbed his face between her hands and shook him lightly again, tapping both his cheeks. "C'mon Blake, we have to move!"

Blake opened his eyes, but Kayla's relief was short-lived. They were golden. It was only for a moment, but she knew the adrenaline wouldn't help him fight the change. If anything, it would encourage it.

"The wolf?" Blake mumbled. Kayla tugged him into a sitting position.

"Over there and out for now. I don't know if or when he'll wake up, so for the love of God, help me!" she said through gritted teeth. He climbed to his feet, but his injuries were extensive, and he leaned heavily on Kayla while she dragged their packs in her other hand.

"Where?" he mumbled.

"Just away from here," she replied, moving as fast as she could out of the park. Blake winced and whined as he tried not to put too much of his weight on her.

"I can't . . ."

"Shh, nearly there." The bridge from their original plan came into view, and the lapping sound of water was music to her ears. Before she could decide what to do next, an angry howl sent shivers down her spine.

He was awake, and he was coming for them.

Kayla didn't stop. She hauled Blake towards the riverbank. If they could get under the bridge, the water would hide their scents – especially Blake's if he was close to a shift.

The grass was soft and slippery, and she nearly lost her footing a few times on the steep decline.

A howl pierced the night again. She jumped, falling backwards and sliding down the rest of the way on her butt. Her feet hit the water. Thankfully it was shallow, but Blake landed face-first.

Together, they stumbled under the bridge and up the short embankment, pressing their backs against the stone supports. Blake slumped to the ground next to her. He moaned and screwed his face up.

"Kayla . . ."

"Shh. Concentrate on forcing the change back. That's all you have to do."

"Kayla . . ." His eyes flashed golden and he snapped them shut. "My sight. It keeps changing."

"That'll be the lupine sight. It's distorting, but all you have to do is close your eyes and will it back."

"Make it sound easy," he mumbled. She stroked the hair back from his pale face. What if he changed? Would he survive it without an experienced wolf to guide him? "Hot," he breathed, clumsily grabbing at the hem of his jumper. She yanked at the collar, and between the two of them they managed to get the heavy material off.

His wet t-shirt was plastered to his skin. The muscle spasms looked agonising. His face creased in pain and his forearms twitched, contracting and releasing. His body couldn't quite manage the change, though it desperately wanted to. She was no expert, but something was wrong. Fear took her breath away like a punch to the gut. She felt his gaze, sensed his question before he even asked it.

"What are you hiding?" he whispered, fatigued.

"Nothing."

"Liar." As he said it, a crack echoed through the air and his rib cage fell in on itself. He bent forward with a cry of pain, pressing his face against the muddy grass.

"Shh, shh!" She tried to coax, pulling his head up into her lap so she could offer some form of comfort – anything. She would have to cover his mouth if need be. They had to stay quiet and hidden until she was confident the wolf had left the area.

"I can't, Kayla. Go, leave me," he whimpered, trying to push her away.

She couldn't leave him. She wouldn't. "No. You're too important."

"How can we unite our races if we're both dead? Go, you can do it on your own!"

"No! I won't leave you!" She swallowed her panic. What was she going to do if he changed? She couldn't just abandon him. Her family saved people, they didn't leave them to die – and at the mercy of hunters no less.

She was about to argue with him again when sharp claws traipsed across the stone above them, tapping with each step. The sound stopped, and a series of nauseating cracks and pops followed. She looked down at Blake, worried it was him, but he remained still.

"Are you sure you scented them this way?" the male attacker asked, his voice rippling with cruelty. Another set of cracks and pops sounded and a different voice replied.

"Yes! God, that hurt like a bitch!"

The red-headed woman's voice was shrill and Kayla winced, realising she hadn't killed her. She wasn't sure if she was feeling relief that the woman survived or regret that she hadn't checked.

"Quit whining. You know injuries shift when you change from form to form."

"She stabbed me, Antonio. Stabbed me!" There was a brief pause, footsteps, and then a loud slap.

"And you were supposed to stop her. Where did you scent them?" The man's voice remained calm and composed despite the brief flash of violence.

"Here! I swear!"

"I don't detect anything. You're off your game. You'd better improve it or I won't have need of your services."

Blake's body stiffened with a soft snap. She quickly covered his mouth with her hands, and his eyes lit up with pain. He grabbed at her arm and leg, the nearest things he could reach for, and his body shook. Bending over at her waist and resting her forehead against his, she comforted him as loudly as she dared and prayed the wolves above hadn't heard. She felt

Blake's pulse slow to a more normal pace and she hoped his pain was fading.

The footsteps retreated and she blew out the breath she had been holding, slowly moving her hand away from Blake's mouth. She kept her head pressed against his, neither of them making a move to part, as the adrenaline left her body in a rush.

CHAPTER TWENTY-ONE

BLAKE

BLAKE MANAGED TO HEAVE himself into a sitting position, resting his arms on his legs as Kayla retrieved the packs she'd let go of when they fell. Luckily, the bags had slid out of sight and the two wolves never spotted them, but unluckily, they'd landed in the stream. Kayla negotiated her way back up the slippery bank with the water-logged packs. Her face said it all.

"How are you feeling now?" she asked, plopping down next to him and passing over his bag.

Even when they couldn't detect signs of life above them, they'd stayed still and silent for a good twenty minutes or so, refusing to move until they were certain the two wolves had gone. In that time, the spasms had tapered off and his eyesight returned to normal. He wasn't sure how he felt. It was one thing to know that he was a shifter who turned into a wolf, and it was another thing to experience it. Or not experience it, in his case.

Something was holding him back, despite his body pushing for the change. The spasms were like nothing he'd ever experienced as a sportsman; he'd never seen his muscles cramp or seize like that before, and the way his eyesight changed was dizzying. Between one moment and the next, the colour would bleed out of the world until everything was painted in shades of grey, with some hues brighter and more vibrant than others. He could also see clearly in the dark when his sight changed, which was odd.

He looked to Kayla whose eyes were dark; she was exhausted. Guilt ate away at him like poison.

"Yeah, I feel normal . . . mostly."

"Are your ribs all right?" she asked. He'd one hundred percent thought he was going to burst open at the time, but he touched his chest and his ribs were fine. He was tender, but nothing felt broken anymore.

"Must be."

"Oh no . . ." she breathed, opening her pack and pulling out her mother's spell journal. Blake leaned over to see the pages running with ink, half the words drowned. She stroked the page softly; he didn't need to be told that she was mourning one of her last links to her parents.

"Can you trace the words? Is the pen indent enough?"

"Umm, maybe?" she replied, sounding a bit lighter at the suggestion. She rubbed her nose dry with her wrist and put the journal back in her pack. "Well, we're wet anyway, so it doesn't matter if our packs are too."

Blake agreed and grimaced as he put on his wet jumper. It clung to him like glue and stank of dirty river water.

"Would love a shower right about now," he moaned. A brief wave of dizziness washed over him when he stood up, but it quickly passed. He would be damned if he let Kayla carry him again.

"You'll have to beat me to it if we find one."

They helped each other climb the steep bank to the road, and Blake offered his hand to haul her up the last section. His strength was returning and he knew Kayla noticed when she did a double take. She grinned at him – at least she wasn't mad at him for nearly getting them killed.

"Amy's place now, yes?" he asked, pinching the map from her back pocket and frowning when it ripped apart in his hands.

"Yeah, so that map has had it."

"Don't suppose you remember where she was, do you?"

"Course," she replied instantly. He frowned at her and she tapped her head. "Trust me, I have good orienteering skills."

"Cool, after you."

THE PAIR LOOKED UP at the block of flats before them. It hadn't taken them as long as Blake had anticipated to get there, so he hadn't had the time to sort his head out. He was about to meet an actual shifter, one who might not actually try to kill him.

Kayla made to move forward, but Blake reached out and grabbed her hand, pulling her back.

"What is it?"

"I'm . . . I'm not ready."

Glancing up and down the dark, empty street, she asked, "What do you mean?"

"I'm about to meet another shifter and it means that I can't . . . I can't ignore what I am anymore." He looked down at his feet, embarrassed.

"There's nothing wrong with being a shifter, Blake."

"Your kind hate me. My kind hate me."

"I don't hate you. My parents helped everyone – magic users *and* shifters, remember? That's what we'll be doing after we find your family, right?"

"I hadn't even thought about my family being connected to all this. Do they know? Do they know I'm a shifter? Is it hereditary?"

"Ummm . . ."

"What?"

"It is hereditary, yes."

"So they're shifters, too?"

"Maybe . . ."

"What do you mean 'maybe'?"

"Well, umm, my mum said they hid you after your parents died." She spoke slowly, as if she was afraid of Blake's reaction. He didn't understand at first, then it dawned on him.

"My parents *are* alive."

"Not your birth parents," she whispered.

He didn't know what to say. Words escaped him. Hadn't everyone always said how different he was from his parents? And what about the fact he had no memories of his youth? He always assumed he'd just been *too* young, but nearly everyone he knew remembered something from their childhood, just not him. How could he have not known?

"My family still matters. My parents are still my parents," he said with conviction. He needed Kayla to know that nothing would change how he felt towards his family.

"Of course."

"My parents raised me. My parents love me. Just because I'm not their blood doesn't mean anything."

"I get it, Blake. We're still going to find your parents and your brother, but we have to get you help first." He was about to speak, but she interrupted him. "You're no good to your family if you change mid-rescue." That made him stop and think.

"Who am I?"

She frowned. "Blake, of course."

"No, you said I was Killian. Who's Killian?"

Her face went soft, and her hand tightened within his.

"I don't know, but I do know that *you're* Blake. The guy who walked me home at night and bought me pie to feed my sugar addiction. The guy who's close with his brother and who let a random girl tag along on their shopping trip. The guy who makes people laugh and sees the light in even the darkest of situations. That's Blake. That's you. Killian may be important, and we'll figure it out, but this doesn't change who you are inside."

Neither spoke. He didn't think he could without his voice wobbling, and he couldn't let her hear that.

"So you'll call me Blake?" he asked when he was sure his voice was steadier.

"I could call you nincompoop – wouldn't change who you are," she said with a wink.

He closed his eyes for a second, gathering himself, and when he opened them, he found the resolve he needed in Kayla's smile.

He nodded. "Okay, I'm ready."

They crossed the road and pushed open the lobby door, finding themselves inside an average entrance hall. A broken light in the foyer cast shadows across the space. An artificial spray of flowers sat on top of a small wooden table in the middle of the sitting area, and a lamp near the mailboxes highlighted the names on the lockers.

Kayla let go of his hand and silently studied the mailboxes, searching until she found Amy's information. She relayed the number to him and they decided to take the stairs to the fifth floor, bypassing the elevator altogether. They were still jumpy after the night's events and they wanted to be prepared for whatever surprises were in store.

Climbing the stairs was much easier now that his body had recovered. His fitness regime gave him an edge over Kayla, and now that he wasn't attempting a change, he had to wait for her to catch up. He even offered to carry her pack at one point, but she just glared at him, spouting breathlessly about being an 'independent woman.'

After ten lots of stairs, they arrived at the fifth floor. Blake gave Kayla a moment to recuperate and slowly opened the corridor door, edging his head out to look in both directions. The green-carpeted hallway was clear of residents, and he dipped back into the stairwell to tell Kayla they were good to go.

"Which number?"

"Eighteen," she replied, rubbing her legs.

"What's up?"

"My thighs are on fire!" she whispered as they walked down the well-lit corridor. He chuckled and she threw her hand out, smacking him lightly on the arm. "I think you'll find I was supporting your broken ass earlier!" His snickers died down. "Yeah, you *better* stop laughing at me."

Blake spotted a dark brown door with the number eighteen fastened to the front. Kayla moved to stand by his side.

"Ready?" she asked, and he nodded before he could give himself the chance to bail.

Kayla knocked, squeezing his hand as the deadbolt clicked.

The door swung open to reveal a young woman in her late twenties, if Blake had to guess. She wore black trousers and a white shirt with a small coffee logo embroidered on the left side, and her blonde hair was scraped into a high ponytail. One bright pink streak was woven into the strands, accentuating the rosy hue of her pale skin. The woman crossed her arms over her chest and frowned at them both.

"Do you need something?" she asked, cautious but not hostile.

"Yes, hi. I'm not sure if you remember me, but I'm Kayla and my parents, Lewis and Caroline Mitchell, helped you a few years ago?" Kayla finished, and Amy's eyes went wide with recognition.

"W-What are you doing here? Am I in trouble? Am I unsafe?" she asked hurriedly, directing her questions at Kayla. In his peripheral, Kayla wrung her hands.

"No, you're fine, but we're not."

Amy looked between them both before quickly glancing down the hallway. For a moment, Blake thought she was going to tell them to get lost, but she stepped aside and beckoned them in with a concerned frown on her face.

He followed Kayla into the apartment. The front door led them straight into the living room. There was a small kitchen area to the right and a short corridor that he imagined led to a bedroom. It was cosy with all three of them standing in the main room. A worn couch sat against the back wall and faint music drifted from the old TV set in the corner. When he looked back at Amy, she shuffled from foot to foot, visibly uncomfortable.

"Thanks for inviting us in," he said, compelled to say something. Amy examined him, her eyes sliding up and down his body before settling on his face. Her scrutiny made the hair on the back of his neck stand up, and he snuck a quick glance at Kayla. She was frowning at Amy.

"This is Blake," Kayla announced slowly, and for some reason, his unease grew tenfold. "We're being hunted." That seemed to bring Amy's attention back to the matter at hand.

"Hunted? Shifters or magic users?"

"Both, I think. Shifters for sure, but magic users probably aren't too far behind."

"Both? What have you guys gotten yourself into? What did your parents say?"

"Um, my parents," Kayla said, voice wobbling as she tucked her hair behind her ears, "are no longer with us . . . shifters found them," she said by way of explanation.

"Oh my God, I'm so sorry."

"And now shifters are after us both, Blake especially. He's a shifter working with a magic user – so they're probably after me, too."

"Why are they after him specifically?"

"I wanted to speak to you about that. See, the reason I came to you is because you were the only shifter that I knew in the city. Blake is a shifter, but he hasn't had his first shift yet. His body keeps trying to force the change, but something is stopping him. I was hoping you could coach him through it?"

Amy tilted back on her heels, blowing out air as she did. "That's . . . that's a big ask, Kayla. Judging from his age, he should have already gone through a change. I've never coached someone through a first shift, let alone someone who's had magic thrown at them."

"Magic?" Blake and Kayla said in unison, sharing a confused glance.

"It's got to be the reason he hasn't changed yet. In theory, magic could block a shift, which is why he might be struggling to complete it."

"I've never heard of magic stopping a change."

"Well, I've certainly never seen it, but shifters always change around puberty. He's definitely past due, so the only thing that could be stopping it is magic."

"Will he be able to complete the change?"

"Maybe in time?"

"I reckon the last episode went further than the one before, so we can hope."

"We can hope?" Blake exclaimed. "This is my body we're talking about! Do you know how bloody painful it is?"

Amy crossed her arms over her chest again, but her face softened as she spoke. "I can imagine; most shifts come with pain of some sort, the first few being the worst, so I can only imagine what a prolonged shift would feel like."

"Will you help me?" he begged, and a small part of him was ashamed to be doing so. He just couldn't keep going through what he had already experienced, and it put him and Kayla at a massive disadvantage when they were being hunted.

Amy didn't answer.

"Amy, please. He needs help and I can't give it to him," Kayla pleaded.

"I'll see what I can do, but I can't promise anything. Do you need a place to stay? As long as no one followed you, the two of you should be safe here. Your parents made sure I got this specific apartment as there was a witch before me who spelled it to be soundproof. The spell remained in place after her death, so it's great for a shifter who might make noise during a change. I don't have to stress about finding somewhere else to shift and I can stay in my own home without worrying about anyone hearing me. When we're wolves, we can get a bit . . . wolfy, so to speak." Amy spoke directly to Blake, but he wasn't quite sure he understood what she meant.

"Thank you. We really appreciate that. We're only in the city because we had to get off our train, so we don't have anywhere to stay tonight."

"Well, unfortunately it's a one-bedroom apartment, but if you two are okay bunking in the living room, then you're welcome to crash here."

"Anything is better than last night," Blake muttered.

"Sounds like you guys have had a rough ride. I don't know what I can do to help, but I'll try my best. I owe your parents for the life I have now." Amy looked down at her feet. "Right, I'll go get you guys some blankets. It's late, so I imagine you're tired, but there's a bathroom if you want to freshen up." Amy moved down the hallway, leaving them alone. Kayla and Blake exchanged glances.

Blake held up his fist. "Best out of three?" he said with a smirk.

"Rock, paper, scissors? Seriously?"

BLAKE EMERGED FROM A much needed shower, still grumbling about losing the game. Amy had left some blankets and an extra pillow on the couch, which Kayla was using to set up their makeshift beds. Blake offered Kayla the sofa and he took the floor. His father would have had his ass if he made Kayla sleep on the ground. Thinking of him made Blake miss his family, and he imagined all of the horrible things that could be happening to them. He needed to figure out what was wrong with his shift so he could focus on helping them. Admittedly, a part of him wanted some answers from them, too, but it was selfish, so he pushed the desire to the back of his mind.

"Sorry," Kayla whispered, yanking him out of his spiralling thoughts.

"For what?" he whispered back.

"For not being able to do much. I feel . . . useless."

"You are *not* useless, not by any stretch of the imagination."

"Any stretch of the imagination?"

"It's a phrase my mum used all the time."

"I can hear it you know, the wistfulness in your voice. I can't help you with the change, but I can try to investigate where your family might be. Tomorrow I'll see if Amy has access to a computer and send some emails.

Someone my parents knew must be able to help. Speaking of," she said, getting off the sofa and rummaging through her backpack. She wore a thin strappy top and shorts, and he was a guy – he tried not to ogle but she made it hard to look away. He blushed when she came back over and was thankful the darkness covered his face.

Kayla found a pen on the coffee table and switched on the lamp by the sofa, going over some of the ruined writing in her mum's spell book. Luckily, she didn't see his stained cheeks.

"What are you trying to repair?" he asked, hoping his voice didn't betray his embarrassment.

"Contacts. Mum kept everything in this book. There are some email addresses here that I can try tomorrow."

"Are you thinking one of them will know something?"

"Because of the type of people my parents knew, someone is bound to have heard about a shifter family being held against their will. They make it their business to know these things."

Blake was quiet for a moment. "Do you think they're okay?"

"I think they were taken to lure you in. If the shifters kill them, they lose their bait. I guarantee they want you to charge in on a half-baked rescue attempt, and by keeping them alive, they give you a reason to come to them. They're hunting you, Blake, trying to find you. But that won't happen."

"Why are you so convinced they won't find me?"

"Because I won't let them."

"I couldn't do this without you. You know that, right?" he said, sincerely. She opened her mouth to speak but couldn't. He realised they hadn't yet looked away from each other.

"Unlucky you," she said, shrugging. She glanced to the side, breaking their eye contact. "Get some sleep, who knows what will happen tomorrow."

She switched the lamp off and turned to face away from him. He wanted to ease her burden, but he didn't know how. She carried it all on her shoulders.

"Goodnight, Blake," she said sleepily, and he smiled into the darkness.

"Goodnight, Kayla." He lay back down and tried to ignore the visions of monstrous wolves tearing his family apart.

HE DIDN'T KNOW WHAT woke him, but his brain registered the dizziness even when lying down. His limbs shook and sweat coated his body like a fine mist. Tangled sheets clung to him; he desperately tried to claw them away, but his limbs weren't co-operating.

His stomach spasmed and he curled inward, wrapping his arms around his middle. He wanted to call out. He knew Kayla was close, but for the briefest of moments his throat closed and left him without air.

"Kayla," he managed to croak, and he stretched a hand across the floor. He was nearly touching the sofa when another violent convulsion shuddered through his body. He could barely make a sound, and the more he tried, the more confused he became.

Noise – white noise – filled his mind, making it hard to think about anything. He grabbed his head and pulled his hair, caving in on himself as his heart sped too fast, trying to race out of his body. He clutched his chest and his vision went dim.

CHAPTER TWENTY-TWO

KAYLA

HIS VOICE ECHOED INSIDE her dream.

He needed her.

She spun, looking for him, but she couldn't see him. With rising panic, she knew she had to get to him quickly, but she couldn't find him.

"Kayla," he moaned, and her eyes flew wide open.

Blake was sprawled across the floor, reaching for her. She slipped off the sofa and turned him over, brushing the hair back from his eyes.

"Blake?" she whispered. He grabbed his head, rocking it from side to side.

"It hurts," he groaned.

Heat came off him like a radiator, and with one touch she confirmed her suspicions. His temperature was too high. That was his temperature. Too damn high. A sheen of sweat covered his skin and his white t-shirt stuck to the lines of his body. He clawed at the damp fabric.

"Hot," he whimpered. His eyes were closed and he had yet to look at her.

"AMY!" she shouted, not wanting to leave his side as she tried to soothe him.

"What?" Amy asked with a yawn as she came into the room wearing a hoodie, shorts, and bed socks. "Holy crap!" she yelped at the sight of Blake writhing on the floor.

"Help him!"

Amy slapped on the living room lights and watched Blake closely before coming to kneel on his other side.

"Blake? Can you hear me, Blake?" She enunciated her words clearly, but Blake pushed her hands away in favour of clawing at his top again.

"Hot," he repeated and sat up on a growl, tearing his t-shirt down the middle. He looked at the shredded top in shock.

"Better?" Amy asked.

"No," he moaned, grabbing his head. "Help me."

Kayla placed a comforting hand on his back and grimaced at the sweat and heat – he'd been there for her in times of weakness, so she could do the same for him. She could.

Amy got up and disappeared, only to return a few moments later with hand towels that she had soaked with water. She passed one to Kayla, who folded it and placed it on Blake's head. Amy went to drape one over his back, but as she stepped behind him, she gasped.

"What?" Kayla asked, worried. "What, Amy?"

Amy pointed and Kayla peered around to look. There was nothing out of the ordinary apart from a tattoo – admittedly, Blake was a little young to have one – but just when she was about to ask what was so bad about it, the ink moved. As it stretched, Blake moaned. His muscles bunched under the design on his right shoulder blade. The black ink swelled from the size of a coin to the size of a plate. A diamond shape connected to the outline of a rounded triangle below it, flanked by a mirror image of a curved 'C.'

"What's . . . wrong?" Blake gasped as he turned to look at Kayla.

"Your tattoo. It's growing."

He frowned.

"I don't have one . . ." He winced, and she watched the muscles in his shoulders contract and release. She massaged his back and Amy fell to her knees.

"Holy shit, Kayla, do you know who this is?"

"What are you on about?"

"That tattoo is a symbol of royalty. Alastair royalty."

"Royalty. He's a direct descendant? I thought he might just be distantly related!"

"You would have been quite young when the shifter hierarchy fell to pieces. I was only a teenager myself, but as a shifter that day . . . God, it was painful for us. I can't believe this. This is why people are after you!"

"But the entire Alastair family were murdered! Are you sure you're not mistaken?" Kayla rambled. She ran her fingers over the tense muscles of Blake's back.

Blake cried out and fell to the side. Cracking sounds echoed through the room as his ribcage broke and collapsed in on itself.

"This is bad!" she shouted to Amy.

"I can, I have, just, let me . . ." Amy stuttered as she searched the drawers in the kitchen. She was muttering expletives as she whirled around, but Kayla's attention was forced back to Blake when he grabbed her arm, his eyes wide with terror.

"It's okay, Blake. We're trying to help you," she said to comfort him, but his breathing was all wrong, too fast and too shallow.

He cried out again. She reached for his face, framing it in her hands to get him to focus on her. "C'mon Blake, stay with me. Just keep breathing."

As she spoke, his body quieted and the tension leeched from his face. Amy came skidding back in, mixing herbs in a small bowl.

"Okay, okay, okay, this should help. It's a mix of . . ."

"What?" Kayla asked when Amy stopped talking.

"He's calmer," Amy replied. Blake closed his eyes and took his first even breaths since he'd woken. "How . . .? Oh."

"Oh what?"

"You must take after your father. A mage, I presume?"

"I'm not following."

"You must be doing something to quiet his mind. Your power? Is it like Lewis's?"

"My dad was a mage, yes, but he just altered memories. . ." Even as she spoke, she processed Amy's words. Her dad was exceptional at mind magic, and she herself had just helped Blake. A low tingle pulsed through her body – a sign of her magic use. She had mage magic, too?

"Mmmhmm. You could have used that a while ago, the poor lad . . ."

"I didn't know I could do this. I still don't know what I've done. Have

I pushed back the change? Is he going to be all right?"

"I'm not sure I know the answers to those questions. You've done something to ease his mind, but his body is still trying to change. I can . . . err, scent it, and I can see the muscle contractions, although they are less intense than they were. Honestly? This is convincing me further that someone used magic on him to stop the change. When he was holding his head, it was like he was trying to claw at something. Normally our minds are much more in sync with our bodies."

"Who could do something like that? Prevent a change?" It wasn't until the words left her mouth that the thought occurred to her, and it altered her grip on what she believed she knew. "My dad. He could, couldn't he?"

"I can't answer that. He was powerful enough, yes, but whether he did or not . . . I've still never heard or seen this before, so if he did anything, it was extremely experimental."

Kayla leaned against the sofa, watching Blake sleep on his back, his bare chest rising and falling. Was her dad really responsible for what was happening to Blake now?

"Is he going to change tonight?"

"I'd say his body wants to; we just have to get his mind to agree."

"And what if they don't? Agree, that is."

Amy shook her head and mimed an explosion with her hands. Kayla winced.

The pair of them curled under the blankets next to him, waiting for a sign. Kayla hadn't asked about the tattoo and what it meant because her mind was a tangled mess. She wondered what her father may have done to Blake. She'd assumed her parents were the ones to hide him; her mum had sent her after him and spelled the necklace herself. Why would they want to stop his wolf side from appearing? And at what cost? To what end?

SHE BOLTED AWAKE, SENSING that something had changed. Blake wasn't lying on the floor next to her. Springing to her feet, she glanced into the kitchen and moved down the hallway when it was obvious he wasn't there. Pushing open the bathroom door, her relief was instant. He stood in front of the sink, gripping either side of the bowl. His arms were poker straight and his head hung low. She stepped into the room and their gazes collided in the mirror.

"How are you feeling?" she whispered, stepping closer. Dark circles shadowed his golden eyes and his pale skin gleamed with sweat. Heat emanated from his quivering muscles and he looked like he wanted to speak, but only a small grunt made it to her ears. He coughed and shook his head, trying again.

"Do it again, what you did," he finally croaked out, his voice rough.

"I'm not sure what I did, Blake."

"Pushed back."

"I pushed something back?" Blake nodded. "I think it's something magical in your head. It must be getting weaker as you have more of these episodes." Blake nodded.

"You can get rid of it."

"I don't think I can. It's very powerful mage magic and I'm not a mage," she said, trembling.

"You do all," he managed. She blinked. He was right. She had been able to do all three strains of magic. Could she help him?

"I can try Blake, but . . ."

"Please," he begged, turning to face her. The muscles in his jaw spasmed and he winced, gripping the porcelain sink tighter.

"Okay, I'll try," she whispered. Placing one hand on his shoulder, she reached for his forehead with the other. He leaned into her palm and she closed her eyes, trying to concentrate on her magic. She pictured a dark, murky cloud in his head, and she asked her magic to come forth. The slow hum sparked to life; she drew it up her arm and into her hand. As her magic crept into his head, so did her own consciousness.

Screens of varying sizes greeted her, all showing a different reel of images. Memories? They were mostly his family, but her father blinked in and out of focus on several of the screens all at once. Her father was doing something to Blake, pushing away the wolf. She couldn't see the wolf, but she sensed it cowering. Chained.

Knowing she had to fix whatever her father had done, Kayla pulled as much magic as she could from within – more than she'd ever felt before – and the slow hum became a rumbling purr. She pushed her magic out, driving back the swarm of dark clouds, and as she did, the screens all began to flicker. One by one, they started to show a sliver of the same memory until the image filled the space before her. It was her dad performing magic on Blake. The scene merged with images of her when they were on the train and their chase through the park. Her own face looked down at him through the screens, cradling his head as his body tried to shift under the bridge. They paused on one final image: Kayla holding his face and chasing away some of the darkness.

Loose chains clattered as a joyous howl of pure elation chorused around her. She looked for the creature who made the sound, but the screens flashed red, black, white, grey on and endless loop. She flinched out of his head and back into her own body.

Blake opened his eyes, and instead of flashing between colours, they stayed golden. His head jerked backwards, and he ripped his hands off the sink. She jumped back to give him room as loud pops and cracks made him lurch, dancing in time to cruel drums. Silky, ice-white fur started sprouting from his arms and chest as his jaw dropped, dislocating. Blake didn't even scream, but the pain was written all over his face. She was terrified she hadn't succeeded, that he was frozen in this horrifying state.

"Blake!" she shouted. His back snapped and he bent at an unnatural angle. The force of it flung his arms through the air, and one hand hit her, throwing her across the small space. She hit her head on the doorframe.

"Careful! Get out!" Amy shouted, running down the hall. She lifted Kayla with her shifter strength to get her out of the way. "He's changing!"

"I know. I used magic. I tried to dispel what my father did . . ." She stopped talking when Blake howled, and Kayla watched in horrified fascination as his dislocated jaw lengthened into a snout. White fur covered his face and he fell to all fours. "Is this normal?" she panicked.

"Very much so. It's very fast," Amy responded and instructed Blake to follow what his body wanted to do. She was coaching him through the last of the change.

Kayla gasped when his hands were replaced with paws and his back legs transformed into the hind legs of a wolf. His sunken spine pulled up and lengthened into a lupine body, reaching the height of the sink, and he was coated with a thick blanket of striking white fur. His ears elongated into peaks on top of his wolf-like head, a head that would come up to her stomach should she stand close enough to measure. His lips pulled back and he snarled as his human teeth sharpened into canine points.

The sleek, snowy wolf lifted his head and howled for several seconds. When he finished, his head lowered until his golden eyes locked onto Kayla's.

"Holy crap," she breathed, clutching onto Amy's arm as she studied the majestic animal before her.

Blake's wolf.

CHAPTER TWENTY-THREE

KAYLA

THE HUGE WHITE WOLF looked at her with wide eyes, his expression so much like Blake's that her heart slowed from its thundering pace. His silky fur shone under the lighting in the bathroom, his ice-white colouring reflecting off the light porcelain.

Blake moved one paw forward, but his back paws moved, too, and he collapsed to the floor. Amy laughed, and Kayla couldn't help smiling. If wolves could show frustration, the sound that came from Blake's snout was definitely it.

Amy coached him on the basics of paw co-ordination while Kayla observed in wonder at the sheer size and beauty of his animal. Admittedly, it was weird at first because it was still Blake.

Blake shook his head again, pinching his eyes shut.

"Is he all right?" she asked Amy.

"He's just transitioning to wolf sight, which is mega disorientating at first – don't worry so much."

Blake collapsed halfway out of the bathroom and whined.

Amy crouched beside him. "Don't be such a baby. These two," she tapped his front left and his back right, "tend to move at the same time, and then your front right and back left move together. Try it, you'll only be thinking consciously of it for a short while."

Blake did as she instructed at a painfully slow rate, but he moved out of the bathroom and down the hallway. Kayla let out a shriek of excitement and Blake jumped, spinning quickly, his new limbs tangled and sent him to the floor with a dull thud.

"Sorry!"

Blake continued to practise, gaining confidence the more he moved around. Kayla asked Amy why it wasn't something innately ingrained in them, knowing how to move on four legs, but she just muttered about Kayla knowing nothing. Kayla rolled her eyes behind Amy's back; Blake sniggered – as much as one could snigger as a wolf.

It was an hour before Blake flopped to the ground, eyes closing in protest. Amy decided she needed some sleep and said Blake would be fine in his wolf form for the rest of the evening. Kayla asked about him changing back but only got a vague response that he should be back in his human skin by morning.

Kayla watched Blake curl into a ball and grabbed a pillow to rest her head beside him – just in case he needed any help during the night. It wasn't long before his soft snores gently pulled her to sleep.

KAYLA WOKE UP WITH smooth fur tickling her face. She opened her eyes and found herself curled up next to Blake's sleeping wolf. He was warm even in his animal form, and Kayla took delight in the comforting feeling of being snuggled.

Judging by the sunlight creeping round the edges of the curtains, Kayla guessed it was morning and Blake was still a four-legged animal.

Kayla stretched, feeling content. She'd slept soundly cuddled next to the furry beast; it was probably the best night's sleep she'd had since her parents passed. There was something to be said for furry friends and cuddle therapy.

Noise came from the kitchen. She sat up, careful not to disturb Blake as he softly snored, and joined Amy at the counter. When Kayla wandered over, Amy poured some cereal and wordlessly got down another bowl, smiling when Kayla's tummy growled. The two sat at the table, digging into their mounds of Cheerios.

"Still wolfy?" Amy asked softly.

"Apparently so."

"Huh."

"What do you mean by that?" Kayla asked, mildly concerned.

"It's just that most first-time shifts aren't sustainable for very long. The body is usually fatigued and changes back. There seems to be more of an element of choice on the next shift, but then again, nothing about him is normal."

"About that. Do you think these hunters know who he is? Shifters have been after us, but I wouldn't say they were very friendly – they were happy to kill me, at least. Why would they want Blake if he could help with an alliance? I thought they'd want him dead, too."

"That's a loaded question for first thing in the morning. What do you know of the royals?"

"Not a lot, just that they were all killed and we descended into madness with no one to rule the shifters."

"Spoken like a magic user raised by magic users," Amy tutted, spooning more cereal into her mouth. "So basically, the royal family were trying to form an alliance of some sort between us and you guys."

Kayla nodded. "I know about the original alliance, but nobody knows what happened."

"Well, I was only a teenager who paid more attention to boys than politics, but when they were assassinated, my life changed. My parents were quite vocal about wanting unity, and that got them noticed. Eventually . . . I ended up needing your parents' help. Magic users wanted to kill any shifter they saw, and the most dangerous of shifters would kill any of their own kind that went against their ideal of being the 'one and only superior supernatural race.' It was a tough time; you couldn't trust anyone. It wasn't until I met your parents that I realised not all magic users were bad."

"That sounds like a horrible way to live."

"It was. It's still not great now, but at least I have an idea of who I can trust."

"So, with this alliance, what do you think the royal family were trying to achieve? What were they doing to bring the shifters and magic users together?" she asked, thinking about how her mum claimed Blake was the one who would bring peace to both sides. If he was a royal and had the ability to lead the shifters, that could very much turn the tide. *He* could be the bridge between races.

"I think the Alastairs were trying to find a way to unify us as supernaturals. Maybe magically? Maybe exert more control over the wolves? They weren't fans of using their abilities to control us though. Free will and all that jazz."

"If the royals could control the wolves, I'm wondering if Blake can do it, too."

"He might, but he'd have to take the oath to do it."

Kayla frowned. "What oath?"

"I thought you would know this, considering your family helped people like me. Did your dad use his magic on you or something?" she half joked, but Amy's face turned serious when Kayla didn't respond. Kayla's stomach dropped. It made sense. Her missing memories, her lack of knowledge, all of it. "Oh shit. Sorry, Kayla. I didn't mean . . ."

"No, it's um . . . it's okay. I think I'm beginning to see that my parents did a lot more than they let on," she said with a bitter edge to her tone. Her anger at being misled and having magic used on her warred with her grief. "If my memories are . . . different from what they should have been, then tell me about the Alastairs; I need to know what happened to Blake's family."

Amy shrugged. "They were all betrayed, and I thought they all died at the original alliance – some party or other. I can't remember what the little boy was called, but it stands to reason that they would have changed his name if he survived."

"Killian?" Kayla supplied unenthusiastically. Her dad must have wiped her knowledge of Killian Alastair.

Amy looked at her studiously. "Yes, it was Killian! Blake could be Killian, the only surviving heir to the shifter throne. This is big, Kayla. Huge." To emphasise, Amy spread her arms apart.

"In theory, could Blake help unite our sides?"

Amy shrugged. "As I said, I didn't follow politics. I wasn't very observant. I'm sure there was something that the Alastair family were trying to do to achieve this unity, this peace. Backfired just a tad though," she said, pinching her finger and thumb together. "If Blake can finish what the royal family started, without being betrayed like his parents were, then who knows?"

"We need to find some shifters, ones who might know what his parents tried to do."

"Good luck finding trustworthy ones. A lot of shifters have enjoyed the past twelve years. A surviving royal who could potentially control other shifters with his Alpha influence will not be welcomed by a majority of the shifter community. And you have to remember that most magic users don't like shifters. They will try to kill him before you even get a chance to explain."

"You paint a positive picture."

"Just being real. You have my support though, and he," she said, looking over at his sleeping form, "has my loyalty. I'm sure you just have to infiltrate an army of people who feel the same."

"Oh, is that all? Well, we still need to figure out what he can do to finish his parents' legacy. My mum said he was the key, and if he can take up the position of . . ."

"King Alpha," Amy supplied.

". . . King Alpha, then he might be able to do it. No wonder people are after him."

"Well, you guys can stay here as long as you want. I have work to get to," she said and cleared away their empty bowls.

"Actually, I have to find a computer to send some enquiries about his family. Someone my parents knew must have heard about a family being taken by shifters."

"His family were taken? Adoptive family, I presume?"

"Yes, and I promised I would help him find them."

"That's probably not a great idea, taking him to the shifters – they've probably done this to trick him, get him to work for them."

"That's what I said, and don't worry. I'll be going instead."

Amy raised a brow at her.

"I highly doubt he will let you go alone."

"He won't have a choice, and what do you mean by that?"

"Pff, never mind, hun. I'm running late and I'm out of mobile data on my phone, otherwise I'd leave it here, but you can take my library card. They have some computers there, so that's your best bet. I'd leave the pup here, as . . . well, you know. Large wolves aren't that common in city centres."

Kayla changed when Amy left. With the library card and some money in her pocket, she stowed the rest of her things in the apartment. Before she slipped out the door, she placed a note beside Blake letting him know what she was doing and that she would be back soon. Not able to help herself, she gently ran a hand down his silken back. Blake stretched contentedly beneath her hand as she marvelled at the feel of his fur between her fingers.

CHAPTER TWENTY-FOUR

BLAKE

BLAKE DREAMED OF RUNNING through the forest. Moss carpeted the ground beneath his paws as he thundered past legions of trees and leapt over their fallen comrades. Wind swept past, ruffling his silken fur. His eyes adjusted to the darkness, tracking an array of marks etched into the forest floor. He knew which direction the rabbit had gone, where the doe had turned off the trail, and where others like him had been.

He came to a clearing and stopped, his tongue lolling out of his mouth as he panted. In the middle of the grassy area stood a man and a woman, both with dark brown hair. They were tall, like Blake was in his human form, and they wore smart, tailored clothing, as if they were important. They walked over to him and stroked his fur.

"You are such a handsome fellow!" the woman exclaimed, her gentle face smiling down at him.

"The best our kind has yet to see. He will make a fine leader!" The man proudly boasted. Blake cocked his head to one side, wondering who they were talking about, when a blade thrust through the man's chest. The man looked down, eyes wide with shock. The woman screamed.

Blake couldn't tear his gaze away from the man as he reached behind him and pulled the blade out, yelling as he did. The woman turned her back to Blake and stood protectively in front of him, but she, too, was attacked by an invisible perpetrator. He shook his head from side to side, looking for the attacker, but there was nothing.

The kind couple's screams quieted to low moans. They fell together.

"Run!" the man whispered hoarsely, and Blake's feet moved of their own accord. He ran back through the trees, re-tracing his earlier tracks. Blake tried to stop, to turn around, to help, but his paws betrayed him, taking him deeper into the forest.

It wasn't until he smelled fresh blood that he was able to change direction.

Feeling more confident now that he had full control of his own body, he pushed through the strain of exertion, wanting to save whoever was in trouble from what had attacked the couple. He burst through the last line of trees, stumbling to a halt. The sharp drop a few paces away would have landed him in a river with fast-moving rapids and rocks that could grind his body to dust.

Past the sound of rushing water, he heard crying voices, shouts of shock, and pleas to leave. On the other side of the river, his parents and brother were trapped in a cage barely large enough for them to stand in. He pawed the ground and whined in frustration; he couldn't get across. He couldn't save them.

As he wore the grass thin, he nearly missed a man emerging from the forest – the man who had chased him through the park not so long ago. The tall, dark-skinned man stood near the edge, only a few metres away from Blake. Blake lowered his head and snarled, ready to pounce, but *her* gasp stopped him.

The red-headed woman pushed Kayla into the clearing, her hands bound with rope. When Kayla reached the man, he yanked her towards him, roughly covering her mouth with his hand when she cried out. Blake prepared to attack, but the man jerked Kayla's head backwards at an unnatural angle.

"Ah-ah. I'd stay there if I were you, because you have a decision to make. I can free your family, or I can free this one. I can't do both." Blake shook his head, confused. An ultimatum? He couldn't make that choice.

"One . . . two . . . three . . ." A dangerous glint appeared in the man's eyes.

He threw Kayla over the edge.

Time slowed down. Without thinking, Blake roared and leapt over the edge, plummeting after her as she fell towards the watery coffin below. Her eyes met his, sheer terror illuminating their depths.

"NO!" HE SCREAMED, JUMPING up from the floor. He was in Amy's front room. Had it been a nightmare? He brought his hands up and saw fingers and flesh – human, not wolf, then. He sighed in relief as the last few dregs of the turbulent dream washed away. He was safe, at least for the time being.

His head snapped up when keys rattled in the door, and Amy burst into the room holding containers of take-out. She froze mid-step. He was naked. He quickly covered his manhood with his hands, his face the colour of a tomato.

"Umm . . ." he began, not sure what to say. She shut the door behind her and dumped the boxes on the small kitchen table, keeping her back to him as he scrambled for the underwear and jeans in his pack.

"I see you're no longer a four-legged creature." Amusement riddled her voice.

"Umm, yeah. So it would seem. Sorry, I didn't know I would be naked. I wasn't when I . . . well, you know." He grabbed a t-shirt and threw it on over his head.

"Oh, I *do* know, and you should have on what you were wearing when you changed forms – part of the deal, thankfully. I guess whatever magic interfered with your change affected that part, too."

"Well, that was embarrassing. Sorry," he said, still blushing when he stepped into the kitchen. He watched Amy open tubs of Chinese food.

"Nothing I haven't seen before," she said dismissively, gesturing for him to sit down as she got plates out. "Tuck in. I bought loads because shifts can take it out of you, especially the first few. I figured you'd be hungry."

"Starving, actually," he admitted, spooning egg fried rice, sweet and sour chicken, and vegetable curry onto his plate. Amy smiled and sat down, scooping a portion of noodles for herself.

"Shifters," she stated, explaining the mound of food.

"Where's Kayla?" Blake asked, trying to forget her terrified face as she fell in his nightmare.

"Library, I think. Something about sending emails." That made sense, and he'd seen her pack in the living room next to his, so he wasn't too worried. Yet. "That was some experience, right?"

"You could say that. Is it always . . .?"

"That intense? Sorta. It will get easier though."

"I was only able to change because Kayla did something to me." He remembered her pushing away the darkness, releasing the chains from his wolf.

"A mage, just like her daddy. I think she was able to counter what her father had done to you. I'm not sure what that was though," she said, frowning into her dinner.

"If you had to guess, what do you think he did?"

"Something I've never seen before; he pushed the wolf so deep into your mind that your brain couldn't mirror what your body was naturally trying to do. My guess is that his magic was slowly wearing off. Perhaps that was how Kayla was able to use her own mage magic to help."

Blake stayed quiet, not wanting to reveal Kayla's secret about her abilities. That was for her to share.

"Last night, you said something about royalty. I couldn't follow all of it, but what did you mean by that? It sounded like you said I was a royal? That can't be right."

"That tattoo of yours is a symbol of the royal family, the Alastair family. Thought you were all dead, to be honest."

"I don't have a tattoo."

"Well, you do now."

His dream about the kind couple came back to him, and he frowned.

"Can you . . . can you explain more about the shifters . . . I don't know anything," he finished quietly, playing with his plate of food. His parents had hidden so much of the world from him. They even concealed his true identity. His stomach churned, a vortex of complicated emotions borne from the lies he'd been told his whole life.

"Sure," Amy replied gently. "We used to have a family – the royal family – who ruled the shifters. To a certain degree, they were able to control other shifters."

"What happened to them?"

Her face softened. "They were killed by others who didn't want an alliance between the shifters and magic users. I thought no one in the Alastair family survived, so with you here, there's a chance you might be able to stop this madness and unite us."

"What can I do?"

"Kayla was asking the same question earlier, and I told her that I don't know what your parents were trying to do, but whatever it was, it made many shifters unhappy. Now we have shifters hunting magic users, but also shifters hunting other shifters who have any sort of desire for an alliance. Magic users hunt and kill our kind, too. That's why people like Kayla's parents were so important."

"Helping both sides, regardless of who they were?"

"Yes. I'm sick of hiding just because my parents wanted peace between us and them. Shifters *and* magic users want my head – I can only imagine how much they want yours."

"Mine?"

"Because if you can do what your parents couldn't, we might not have to be so scared all the time. Many shifters and magic users don't want that – they think they're the better race and the other deserves to die."

"But again, what can I do? I wasn't brought up as this so-called royalty, let alone a shifter."

"The royal family – the Alastair bloodline, that is – has the ability to control other shifters. As our leader, our Alpha, your command would be law above all else once you took up the position."

"So why didn't my parents just command the shifters to agree with this alliance or whatever?"

"Because, according to my parents, your family believed in free will, the ability to choose right from wrong. Although . . ."

"Although what?"

"I'm not sure why your father – he was the Alastair – didn't stop the attack. Something doesn't make sense there, but I've never really had the chance to question it."

Blake stayed quiet, taking everything in. While he knew she was discussing his biological parents, he couldn't associate them with the family he'd grown up with. The family who needed him and were being held against their will – he had to find them. He pushed the royal shifters out of his mind for a moment.

"Hey, how are you doing?"

Blake huffed. "I don't know. I feel useless. I can't do anything right now. I'm no help to Kayla, and I'm no help to my parents."

"Well look, there's nothing you can do tonight until Kayla gets back and you can discuss things with her, but till then, do you want to just hang and watch movies? You look like you need a distraction," Amy suggested.

Blake nodded and followed her to the lounge, sinking into the old sofa next to her, hoping the comedy she put on would peel his mind away from some of the darkness that had begun to consume it.

CHAPTER TWENTY-FIVE

KAYLA

KAYLA HAD BEEN AT the library all day. Sat at the computer all day. Bored all day. The most exciting thing to happen was when she logged off and popped to the corner shop to buy a sandwich. Some lads around her age were caught trying to nick bottles of alcohol. The police were called and the boys tried to fight them off. She wasn't ashamed to admit that she sat on the bench nearby, ate her sandwich, and watched the whole thing like it was a TV show.

It wasn't until the library was close to shutting for the night that she had any response from the enquiries she sent. She'd nearly called it a day when the 'you have mail' ping stopped her from packing up. At first, she was worried, concerned the message might have been a trap, but she decided she had to take the chance – especially knowing exactly who Blake was and how important he could be to ending the deadly feud between their races.

The email came from a man named Michael. He gave an address within the city, and even Kayla admitted that was a stroke of luck. She internally debated whether to go alone or not while she logged off and put away her rubbish. With nothing else to do, she decided to go alone. Michael's email had been in her mother's spell book, and while her parents may not have told her the truth about everything, she trusted their work and their contacts.

The bus took her to a residential area, further out from the city than she'd expected. Walking along the darkening streets, she kept an eye out for Michael's address. The houses were spread out, and long driveways led to fairly large residences – the area was definitely more affluent than Amy's neighbourhood.

She spotted the number and slowly moved down the driveway, making note of how many windows had lights on inside. Thinking like that reminded her of her dad, which was the last thing she wanted. She still felt guilty for being angry at him.

She knocked and the porch light flipped on as a man answered the door. He looked to be in his thirties, with long dark hair that he wore tied back. He had a close-shaven beard and he clearly worked out, given the tightness of his clothes, but his overall stature didn't make her think 'shifter.'

"Kayla, is it? The Mitchells' kid?" he asked, a slight frown on his face. His voice was gruff. She had yet to determine if it was how he normally spoke or if he was just being wary.

"Yes. You're Michael?" she asked, trying to be polite, open, and kind, her mother's well-worn phrase to her growing up.

Michael stepped back, allowing her in. With only a brief moment's hesitation, she strode inside, feigning confidence.

The entry was spacious and a large dining room sat to her right. A long corridor led into a kitchen at the back and a living room branched off to the side of the house. She followed Michael into the last room where a lit fireplace crackled cheerfully. She prayed she wouldn't need to use any magic as she'd probably latch onto the fire. Three light blue couches were placed evenly around the TV that hung above the mantel. The place felt homey, not cramped, but loved and lived in.

There was no evidence he shared his home with anyone else except for the chocolate Labrador who hobbled over in the tell-tale sign of old age, tail wagging furiously. He lowered his head and rested it against her leg when he neared; she gently stroked him as he looked up with the biggest brown eyes she'd ever seen.

"Aren't you adorable," she cooed.

"Ah, don't mind old Chester. He's hoping you'll give him some fuss and food, and now that you've petted him and spoken to him? You're his new best friend."

"Well, I don't mind," she said in the voice she reserved for babies and dogs.

"He's also a good judge of character." She didn't miss the subtle tone of acceptance. "What can I help you with, Kayla? Your email was rather vague, but your parents were one of a kind. Felt like I owed hearing their daughter out at least. Hope you don't mind meeting me. I prefer to do business face to face." He gestured to the couches, and she sat on one as he took another. Chester tried to gracefully lie down beside her but ended up falling to a heap on her feet. Whatever worked for the old boy, she supposed.

"I'm hoping you might know of a shifter family being held hostage by other shifters."

"That's quite rare. Shifters would only do that if they had need for something else. Otherwise, they'd just kill the family."

"So, have you?" she asked again and watched one eyebrow raise.

"Yes, as it turns out I have heard. I make it my work to keep track of as much shifter business as possible. I have several other magic users who rely on my knowledge for safe keeping."

"You help others like my parents did?"

"Sort of. I keep them and myself abreast of shifter news. It can help others like me move to secure locations and so on. The shifters get one whiff of a magic user and they'll kill us, no questions asked. I used to share the relevant information with your parents, too, before I heard what happened." Kayla focused on the dog, happily snoring below her. "Do you mind if I ask you something?"

"What's that?" she whispered, not looking up at him.

"I know what happened to your home. Shifters attacked, but I don't know why. Do we need to be worried? Is there something I can help you with?"

She studied him, and no obvious signs of deceit lay there. In fact, she felt safe. Trusting her instincts, she spoke. "I accidentally used magic near a human; it made our newspaper, and the shifter hunters found us there. I managed to escape – just."

"I'm sorry to hear that."

Kayla stayed quiet for a moment. She didn't want to think about her parents given the information that came to light the night before. She was there to find Blake's family. "The family being held by shifters?" she pushed.

"Why do you want to know about this family of shifters? Are you continuing your parents' work?" He sat back on the sofa, lazily crossing one leg over the other.

"Not right now; everything was sent to someone they trusted to take over the whole business. I wanted to head there to make sure it was all safe, but I came across a shifter whose family was taken." She deliberately left out who Blake was for the time being.

"Personally, I wouldn't go near shifters holding others of their kind captive. Not only is that highly immoral, but they probably want this other shifter to come after their family. Who is this person? They must have done something to catch the eye of hunters." Kayla squirmed in her seat, not wanting to let on who she was trying to shield. "Okay, okay, I can see you're trying to protect someone," Michael finally said, letting her off the hook. "But in all seriousness, Kayla, shifters like that mean business. They'll most likely kill your friend and the family after."

"He won't give up on his family, though. Would you?"

"No, you make a good point, but he needs to be careful. Whatever he's done, he needs to prepare for the worst."

She sighed. "He's not even done anything yet."

"As someone who those murderous shifters are concerned about and want to silence, I would do precisely what they don't want me to," he said with a mischievous grin.

"Easier said than done. I think he just wants his family back and to pretend there isn't such chaos between us and them. The murders, the lies? They can't go on for much longer, can they? They're all I've ever known, but surely at some point they have to stop?"

"I believe it will only stop when one side has completely annihilated the other. The shifters want superiority, and as much as it pains me because I'm not one of them, a lot of magic users believe they are better than shifters."

"But isn't that the problem, Michael? I know too many people on both sides who don't want this hostility and fear. Not every shifter hates magic users, and not every magic user hates shifters."

"Unfortunately, Kayla, we live in a world where extremists run society.

That's true in both the human world and ours."

Kayla sighed, tucking some hair behind an ear. "This world sucks."

"That it does."

"So help me make it a little less sucky for my friend. I've just lost my family. Let's help ensure he doesn't lose his."

"You are a lot like your parents," Michael said, and Kayla hoped he didn't notice her flinch. She didn't want to lie, deceive, and perform secret magic on the ones she loved. "I'm waiting to hear back from an associate who was trying to pinpoint where the hostages are – we magic users don't want to be anywhere near that. He checks in with me every night, so I'll let you know what he found. That's the best I can do at this point. After that? I would still urge you not to go there."

"That would be great, thank you. Will you email it to me?"

Michael paused. "Now that I know you, yes," he finally responded after some thought. Kayla sagged in relief.

A quick rap at the door had her on alert, and she bolted upright as a shot of fear flooded her body. Without meaning to, she must have commanded the fire to flare as it sparked up high into the chimney.

"Oh God!" she said, mortified her magic betrayed her like that. The fire quickly calmed.

"Elemental?" Michael asked quizzically. He moved out of the room to answer the door. He was talking to whoever was at the door, so she sank back down onto the sofa. He was going to label her a freak and not help her anymore. "Ah Wyatt. Good to see you, although I wasn't expecting you?"

"Marcus sent me," a voice answered. Male, definitely younger than Michael.

"Better come in then."

The two men walked into the living room. The new guy, Wyatt, blinked in surprise when he saw Kayla. He was much younger than she'd first thought, closer to her own age in fact. He was tall and lanky, with dirty blonde hair parted to the side and styled neatly. He wore a loose-fitting green jacket and jeans, and the baggy clothing indicated he was probably a magic user. As young as he looked, he would have bulked out had he been a shifter.

She briefly wondered if Blake would start keeping the muscle mass he always spoke about not being able to retain now that he'd had his first shift.

"Woah, Michael. Not like you to have company as pretty as this . . . and as young," he said in an accusatory tone, glancing over at Michael, his eyes narrowing.

"Wyatt, meet Kayla. She's another elemental and she's here because she needed my help. I knew her parents before they passed. Wyatt is an associate of mine," he finished, looking back to Kayla.

"I'm sorry to hear that," Wyatt spoke to her softly.

Kayla gave a small smile in response.

"Elemental?" he asked, unaware of her unusual case.

"Yeah, sure."

"You don't sound it?" he said jokingly.

"Um, well, you see . . ." She struggled to get out the right words at just how weird she was. Being hunted by shifters who hated her was enough. She didn't want people who were on her side hating her as well.

"Kayla's parents were a witch and a mage," Michael interjected.

"Oh . . . that *is* highly unusual," Wyatt commented, rubbing his chin with his hand and pulling a 'so what' face.

"Unusual?" Michael started. "That's impossible. Are you sure your parents are your biological parents?" Kayla smiled inwardly at the question. That was the same query Blake had been faced with.

"Yes, they're my blood parents." Of this, she was sure. Their motives for hiding things from her, however, were a different matter.

"So, you control the elements? What's your speciality? Fire? Judging by how you reacted when the door knocked."

While she didn't feel threatened by Michael's questioning, she didn't really want the newcomer to know she'd jumped at his arrival. That was just embarrassing.

"I'm not quite sure. Possibly. It was setting a car on fire that got me noticed." She directed her words to Michael and knew he got her meaning. "I've only had this magic a short while. I was late coming into it." And that was all she was sharing. She was making certain she didn't admit that she could also do witch and mage magic because she'd already shared enough.

"Interesting," Wyatt mused.

"Very," Michael answered.

They both stared at her.

"What?!"

"Do you want to do an experiment?" Wyatt asked excitedly.

"If she's new to her magic, especially since she wouldn't have been brought up knowing much about the elemental path, maybe one of your experiments isn't the best idea," Michael cautioned.

Kayla's heart sped up a beat. "Experiment? What kind of experiment?"

"The one where we test which element you're strongest in!" Wyatt answered, his eyes lighting up in excitement.

"I'd say fire is a good place to start. Especially for you, Wyatt, if you're determined to do this and Kayla agrees."

"I'm strongest in water," Wyatt explained. "Shall we?"

"What? Now?" she squeaked, and Wyatt chuckled.

"Why not?" he said, flashing her a big smile, dimples and all.

"I don't want to alarm you, but my magic isn't that well controlled when it comes to fire. I set my own house on fire!"

"Sometimes flames can get a little out of control, but I'm on hand to help. I'm rather good."

"He's arrogant but he is good, I'll give him that," Michael added.

"Just try. Why don't you see if you can make the flames dance a little?" Wyatt's face was so honest, so open, and so kind that she felt as if her mum were telling her to try. To trust him. She didn't get any hint of bad intent from either of them and her dad had trained her to trust her gut instinct.

She opened herself up to the magic and tried to tell it to dance with the flames, just a little, like turning on a tap bit by bit. She closed her eyes to focus.

She remembered how her magic sang when she burst the water pipes, helping her and Blake to get away from the shifters who had tracked them from the train. The memory drew the magic from her centre.

She opened her eyes with a shout of surprise and watched as the flames began to multiply and crawl out from the fireplace.

"What the . . .?" Michael began. Wyatt acted quickly and thrust his hand out, pushing the flames back into the grate. With his other hand, he siphoned the water out of Chester's water bowl and doused the flames. They immediately shrank down to soft glowing embers.

"Okay, so that's impressive," Wyatt said.

"I'd say more than impressive. You added to the fire, Kayla."

"I know, I know. This is bad. I shouldn't be able to do that as an elemental!"

"No Kayla! This is awesome! Do you know how powerful you could be if you honed this? Wait till we try the other elements!" Wyatt whooped with a boyish kind of joy.

"Actually, I think I should be getting back to my friends. I've been gone a while. Michael? Please let me know anything you discover about what we discussed," she said, standing and zipping up her jumper. Chester even pushed himself up when Kayla made to leave. She gave him a quick cuddle to say goodbye.

"Well, it was nice to meet you, Kayla. If you ever want to discuss elemental magic, ask Michael to hook us up!" He winked and Michael smacked him on the back of the head like a big brother – affectionately, but with the full force of disappointment. "Ow! Not like that. I didn't mean . . . oh never mind."

"Be careful out there, Kayla. There's been more unrest lately," Michael cautioned.

Kayla nodded, leaving the house as they began to discuss something in more serious voices. She hoped they would become firm allies as she and Blake tackled the divide between the races.

IT WAS LATE WHEN she got back to Amy's apartment. She'd caught the last bus back to the centre, but it didn't go all the way to the flats where Amy lived, so she had to walk a fair bit in the dark. The clock in the lobby suggested it was nearly eleven at night when she pushed open Amy's door.

She was greeted with loud music. She hadn't heard it from outside thanks to the flat being spelled. Blake stood on the sofa, holding Amy up by her ankles as she stood upside down on her head. Amy smiled and waved one handed at Kayla.

"Oh hey! Was wondering where you were at! Go Blake!" she instructed, and Blake lifted her up, his arm muscles straining. She used her body to swing up and around, landing on Blake's shoulders and ducking so as not to hit her head on the ceiling. They both cheered when she achieved it, but Blake wobbled and they tumbled to the floor in a heap, laughing hysterically.

A pang of annoyance raced through Kayla; there *she* was, worried, doing research and meeting contacts to find out what happened to Blake's family, and here *he* was getting cosy and having a laugh with Amy?

"What are you guys doing?" she bit out.

Blake grinned. "We've been practising this move we saw on a gymnastics show!"

"It's way more difficult than you might think, but I figured with us both being shifters, we might have the strength to pull it off, and we sorta did," Amy added, eagerly high fiving Blake.

"You're an experienced shifter. Blake's turned once. Once. And you think he's capable of pulling stunts like that? What if you'd gotten hurt?" she said, directing the last question to Blake. Amy's face fell.

"Look, I didn't mean to offend anyone. Yeah, I'm just gonna go to bed. Night!" she finished and quickly exited to her room. Kayla put her hands on her hips. Yes, she looked like her mother, but she was really, really pissed. And hurt, but she didn't know why.

"I feel like you're upset," Blake began.

"No, not upset. Just wondering why I'm bothering to help you if all you're going to do is play silly games with Amy. Why don't you ask her to help you?" She was being unnecessarily harsh. She knew it, but she couldn't stop the stream of unwanted hurt from entering her voice.

"Look, I'm sorry if I upset you. It's the last thing I want. We were just having a laugh. I really needed a few moments away from all this."

She didn't think he meant to spread his arms between him and her. She knew he meant everything that had happened and not that he needed distance from her, but it still stung.

"I don't care, Blake. I'm tired, it's been a long day, and I want some sleep. Someone I contacted knew about a family being held hostage, but he didn't know where. Hopefully, he'll find out tonight, and when he emails me with that information, you can do what you like with it."

She grabbed her pack and changed into some bed clothes in the bathroom. When she came out, she tried her best to ignore Blake, who sat on the floor in cotton trousers and a fresh top. He obviously wanted to talk to her, but she leaned over and switched the lamp off, plunging the room into darkness.

"Kayla . . .?" Blake said softly. She ignored his attempt at engaging her in a conversation, knowing if she caved, she would say sorry for snapping when he should be the one saying sorry.

She was obligated to see their plan through, but afterwards she would go to Oxford to find the person who had her parents' lifelong work. She'd assist them and do what she could to support others in need.

After a few minutes, Blake sighed and nestled into his makeshift bed on the floor.

It was irrational to feel hurt, but she wouldn't let herself cry. She wouldn't.

CHAPTER TWENTY-SIX

BLAKE

BLAKE WOKE UP TO find Kayla packing her bag and checking its contents. His guilt from the night before had bled over into the morning. Hurt was written all over her face, and she was right to feel that way; she'd been working non-stop to help him locate his family while he wanted to have a relaxing evening. The problem was that he didn't know how to apologise, and she wasn't really speaking to him anyway.

"Kayla?" he asked, hoping she might talk to him now.

"Amy's already gone to work. I'm packed, so I'm ready when I get that information you need. I've checked the train times in the newspaper, and as long as Michael has emailed me, I'll be getting on a train this afternoon."

It was a lot of information to process, so much that he just sat, dumbfounded. She was serious about leaving him? The thought was sobering. He didn't think he was ready to face his new world without Kayla there. Did that make him a selfish person? "I'm going to the library again to check my emails, and I'll pass on what I find."

"Can I come? To message Josh, see how he's doing?" It sounded lame, but it was the best he could come up with. He wanted to ensure he went with her, and besides, he should really see how Josh was doing. Kayla frowned at him but agreed.

She got breakfast for them both in silence. She waited for him to sort his stuff out in silence. And they walked to the library in silence. She signed him in as a guest using Amy's card, and they found two computers opposite each other. There were ten in total, five on each side.

He looked around his monitor while Kayla logged on to her computer. He couldn't see her screen, but she was staring at it intently as she typed. There weren't many people in the small library. Behind him, several rows of books sat on dark wooden cases, bolted to the floor.

"You were here all day yesterday, huh?" he asked. She glanced at him, making a shushing sign with her finger. He looked around, but nobody had even glanced their way.

"Yes," she whispered back and got back to typing.

"What did you do after? The library closes well before you got back."

"Went to meet one of the contacts I messaged."

"You went alone?" he asked incredulously.

"Yes."

"Why the frigg would you do that?" he exclaimed, his voice rising slightly. She rolled her eyes.

"Calm down, will you? I was meeting a magic user. I was perfectly safe as I wasn't with a shifter."

"So you're saying that I'm the reason you've been in danger?"

"Well, no, but sort of . . ." She shook her head and focused on her screen.

"Weren't you already running from hunters when you found me?" he asked, knowing his anger was coming from a place of frustration.

"Michael said you probably shouldn't go after your family as you'll be killed, and to be frank, I agree. You've only changed once. You're in no state to go up against experienced shifters."

"You're suggesting that I just let my family die?" She didn't answer him or even look at him, and he got angry. He typed out a quick message and sent it to Josh's school email address, careful to leave out key information in case someone else read it. "Right, I'm done. I'll see you back at Amy's."

"Whatever," she said dismissively. She paused, hands hovering over the keyboard, so much so that he thought she was going to say something. But she didn't. She went back to typing out her email, and he left.

As he walked back to the apartment, he nearly turned around to apologise but remembered that she'd pretty much said he should let his family rot. Once he had information on where his family were, he would track them down, Kayla be damned.

In his foul mood, he didn't see the car following him, its dark, tinted windows concealing the inhabitants.

HE SPENT A FEW hours getting food and walking around town, and he ended the morning with a run through the park to burn off some of his relentless buzzing energy.

It was middle of the afternoon when he actually got back to Amy's flat. He pushed open the door, praying Kayla was back from the library. His run helped him think, and he knew he'd acted badly. She only said what she did because she was upset with him and had every right to be. He needed to make sure she knew he was sorry and that he was grateful for what she'd done. He wanted to stick with her. After all, he'd made a promise to help her after they found his family.

Opening the door, he called out, "Kayla?"

Blankets and cushions were strewn across the living room, and books were tossed around as if they held no worth. The kitchen cupboards were raided and empty. He immediately became worried and alert. Hearing noise from the back bedroom, he soundlessly crept forward. He braced himself and opened the door, but he threw his hands up as a baseball bat zoomed towards his face. He caught it at the last moment and his assailant pulled back on the force, cursing as she did.

"Blake? You scared me half to death!" Amy chastised, throwing the bat on the bed and continuing to shove clothes into a big duffel bag.

"What's going on?"

"I've been made – or you have. Either way I'm out of here."

"Wait, hold up. What?"

"This guy came into the café, specifically requested I serve him, and let me know in no uncertain terms that he knew who I was and who I was helping." She moved over to a chest of drawers and pulled out underwear. "He mentioned the Alastair name, Blake. They know a member of the royal family survived the assassinations."

"This is bad, isn't it?" He ran his hands through his hair as he followed Amy into the bathroom so she could gather basic supplies.

"Bad? Yes. If they know you exist, and they've connected me to you, then you've been found, too. I'd go grab your girl and scram."

He followed her back into the bedroom.

"She's not my . . ." He stopped himself. "They may not have linked you to us, and maybe they were just being friendly?"

She stopped what she was doing to stare at him. "You don't survive as long I have without picking up on threats. Besides, when he said he would have me drowning in a pool of my own blood, it was a dead giveaway. Shit. Probably shouldn't say 'dead' right now as that's precisely what he wants." She frowned and zipped up her duffel bag.

"What do you mean? What happened next?"

"I got another waitress to cover me and snuck out. Now I'm here and panicking."

"Jesus."

"I wouldn't be leaving the place I've called home for years without good reason, Blake. I don't travel with others. It's too risky for me, but you and Kayla need to leave. If they tracked me to my place of work, they can track me here."

Blake rubbed a hand over his face and rushed to make sure both his and Kayla's packs were sorted. As he finished, Amy came staggering down the hallway carrying too many bags.

"Here, let me help," he offered, but she shook her head.

"No, I have to be okay by myself. I have a taxi waiting downstairs to get me out of here. Will you be okay? Promise me you and Kayla will get gone, like now. And promise me you'll stay safe?"

"I'm not sure I can promise all that, but I'll go and get Kayla now."

Amy smiled and hugged him. "Good luck, King Alpha. When you need help in this fight, let me know. I'll come out of hiding. Until then, we all need to stay safe."

Amy squeezed him once more and left. It was only after the door slammed shut that he realised she'd called him King Alpha.

CHAPTER TWENTY-SEVEN

KAYLA

KAYLA SAT BACK AT the computer, tapping her fingers against the desk. She'd messaged everyone she could, but waiting was the hardest part.

Ping.

An email from Michael had her rushing to open it.

....

TO: k-mitchell

SUBJECT: information

MESSAGE:

>Open attachment

Kayla,

I hope this finds you well. My associate got back to me with the address; I shall add below. Please consider my strongest concerns about you and your friend going here. I appreciate that it is his family, but these shifters are quite skilled. My associate recognised a few – they are ruthless assassins for hire. I don't know why they would want your friend, but whatever the reason, they do plan to kill him. You, too, if you go. I would hate to see another comrade fall.

All the best,

Michael.

....

She scribbled the address on a scrap of paper she found in the bin and googled its location. It was about an hour north, in the opposite direction of Oxford.

Sighing, she figured their next hurdle would be finding a car. Blake probably didn't know how to drive and she'd never had an official lesson. Just the odd one from her father.

As she started closing down the computer, another 'ping' alerted her to an incoming email.

....

TO: k-mitchell

SUBJECT: Get out

MESSAGE:

I've just heard about a young girl and a boy being targets of the same group of shifter assassins who have your friend's family. This must be you. Get out now. I got the impression the shifters were already on the move.

....

"Oh no," she breathed out, hurriedly shutting down the computer. She set a quick pace back to the flat. If they had been discovered, the shifters would head straight there, and Blake had gone back on his own.

She began to run, worried she'd be too late. The last thing she'd said to him was to leave his family and that she didn't care about him. It was totally untrue. She'd been a right bitch, and if those were the last words he heard from her . . . she didn't – couldn't – let herself think about it.

Wasting no time on the lift, she took the stairs two at a time and unlocked the door as quickly as she could, slamming it shut as soon as she was inside. Blake held their packs, a panicked look on his face.

"We have to go now!"

"Amy thinks she's been made. We need to leave." They both spoke at the same time, frowning at each other when they finished.

"What?" she asked him.

"A shifter hinted to Amy that he knew she was involved with an Alastair and that they know I'm alive. She's already left and so should we. I was just about to come and get you."

"You were?" she asked incredulously. She couldn't believe he would have given how she'd been acting earlier.

"Why did you say we need to go? What to do you know?" he asked.

She moved closer to slide her mother's spell book inside her pack.

"Michael emailed and said a young girl and boy were targets of the same group of shifters who have your family. It doesn't take a genius to know that's us."

"Wait, you found out who has my family?"

"Yes, but we need to find somewhere safe first and decide what to do with that information–" She was cut short when soft scratching whispered at the door.

She froze, looking to Blake and silently wondering if it was Amy. He shook his head. He frowned and looked at the door, but as she turned around, he yelled and pulled her close to his body.

A group of shifters rushed into the flat, jumping on them with speed and force. Blake took the brunt of the attack, slamming her back to his front and cocooning her within his arms, but the strength of the shifters was overwhelming.

She grabbed onto him, and her heart burst from her chest when he was ripped away from her. His angry roar echoed, followed by thumps and cracks. Another shifter grabbed her hands and yanked them behind her, making her arms twist at unnatural angles.

"Blake!" she screeched. He lay curled on the floor, the skin split by his eye. He looked up at her and they locked eyes, their fear mutual. A fist slammed down into his face again, and his eyes rolled back. A garbled 'no' rushed out of her, but her words were swallowed when a bag covered her head, enclosing her in darkness.

CHAPTER TWENTY-EIGHT

BLAKE

BLAKE CAME TO AND panicked at his lack of sight. He was briefly relieved when he realised his head had been covered by a hessian sack. His hands strained against the plastic zip tie forcing his arms behind him. He ascertained that he was in the back of a van or some form of moving vehicle, and was slumped on a cold, metal floor. Vibrations rumbled through him as he tried to sit up, groaning as he did. He bumped into another body, and everything in him told him it was Kayla.

"I can't believe how easy that was!" a deep, gravelly voice said from near the front of the vehicle. Blake guessed it was one of the shifters who had taken them.

"How did James fail so spectacularly when it was that simple to grab him?" The guy chuckled at his own joke.

"The dude was given far too much responsibility, if you ask me. A kid at a party, and he couldn't even take him down?"

The other man huffed. "He shouldn't have been given the job. Just because he has connections doesn't make him better than us. How many magic users have we killed? How many shifters, come to think of it? We could have grabbed him no problem."

Beside him, Kayla stiffened at the mention of killing magic users.

"I can still see the look on his face when he got his ass handed to him after turning up empty-handed at the rendezvous point!"

Empty handed? That meant Josh had gotten away! The rush of relief was instant.

"That was priceless! Oz was so pissed James had screwed up. I didn't think he could get more pissed till we went back to the kid's house and discovered the boy was already on the run again."

Deep laughter boomed from the front.

"Kayla?" Blake whispered, hoping the laughter would cover him.

"Blake? Are you okay?" Her small, strangely timid voice greeted him; he was about to answer when loud banging echoed around them.

"Shut your mouths, or I'll happily knock you out again. Got it?" one of the men spat.

Blake straightened so he was shoulder to shoulder with Kayla and gently rested his leg against hers, knowing that was all he could do.

He assessed his injuries and was surprised to find them less severe than he had anticipated; his back was scratched and the skin was broken in places, but he felt lucky – or maybe it was the shifter benefits Kayla had spoken about. He figured he'd been unconscious for a while, as his body had healed the worst of it.

The vehicle came to a jarring halt only moments later, and the front doors opened and closed. Someone climbed in from the right, jostling them from side to side. Kayla's body was dragged up and over him. She yelped and squirmed, falling into his lap.

"Hey! Leave her alone!" he shouted angrily. He heard a grunt and he smiled to himself, assuming Kayla was trying to fight back as much as she could while bound.

"The little wench!" A gruff voice exclaimed.

"If she does it again, stab the boy in a fleshy part. See if she keeps it up," a bored voice commented.

The sounds of struggle ceased, but footsteps crunched over gravel. Before he could ask what was happening, his feet were yanked and he was dragged out, landing with a sharp thud against the stone. He winced, trying to twist on to his side to stop the pressure on his back, but a hard blow to the head knocked him out cold.

CHAPTER TWENTY-NINE

KAYLA

KAYLA'S EYES FLEW OPEN and her breath came out in short, sharp bursts. Sat on a chair, her arms were haphazardly bound to the armrests with duct tape, but at least the bag was off her head.

A door behind her creaked open, but she couldn't turn to see who entered. The small room only had a single bulb dangling from the ceiling, casting an eerie, artificial light on the plain cream walls. A large shadow loomed ahead of her; whoever stood behind her was big, male, and most likely a shifter.

A gravelly voice said, "You have been a God damn pain, you know that? I'm Oz."

Her pulse roared in her ears. That voice. She knew it.

"Show yourself," she whispered. The man chuckled and stepped into her line of sight. Her mouth went slack. It was the blonde shifter, the leader of the group who attacked her parents and killed them. "You!" she spat.

The man sneered, enjoying her pain as she relived the horrifying moments. She thought he'd perished in the fire.

"That's right. Me." He leaned into the full light and she snapped her head back in shock. The right half of his face was distorted, the flesh raw and mottled. If he had been human, he would have been in intensive care, not walking about with half-healed burn wounds. "Correct, little girl. You caused this."

She gulped down some of the revulsion, making way for a slow smile to spread across her face. The man frowned, the scarred skin stretching tightly.

"At least I left a mark."

Anger flared in his eyes and he slapped her across the check. Her teeth rattled in her jaw, tears welling at the sting.

"Bitch! You have no idea what I could do to you!"

"Try me," she coolly responded, sounding braver than she felt inside. Where was Blake?

She was about to ask when the door opened again, and someone came to join the man. There was no mistaking they were father and son as they stood side by side.

"James?" she asked in disbelief. His smirk told her he was enjoying her confusion. The men who took her and Blake spoke about James in the van, but she hadn't expected him to be there. Or to be related to the guy who'd killed her parents. New hatred for James sparked to life.

"Hello again, Kayla. I see you've met my dad."

"I've had the displeasure," she retorted. James curled his hands into fists, but instead of hitting her like she expected, he huffed and looked to his dad.

"I still get to do what I want with her after, right?"

"Course, son."

"What do you guys want? Where's Blake?"

"Worried about your boyfriend?" James teased.

Oz stepped up to her. "I should thank you, actually. When my son mentioned a magic user, I couldn't pass up on the opportunity. I'm an exceptional tracker and found where you were staying, and what an unexpected surprise. A fun one, though. She was a tough woman, wouldn't rat you out, but I could scent you all over the place."

Kayla gasped. "You . . . you killed Gaby?"

"With pleasure."

"I'm going to kill you!" she screamed, jerking against her restraints. They deserved justice: her parents, Gaby – all of them. The first signs of her magic appeared, and she grasped for it desperately; she didn't know whether it was elemental, witch, or mage magic she was hoping for. She just wanted to hurt him. It followed her command as she drew it up her arm. She stretched her hand as far as she could while bound but a sharp sting in her upper arm sent a cold, icy sensation seeping into her veins. The magic drained back into her body, out of her reach. "What the hell!" she cried out in frustration. James stepped back from her, smiling menacingly. He held an empty syringe in his hand.

A thick, fuzzy cloud descended on her mind and the room drifted in and out of focus.

"What is Blake?" James's dad demanded. "They were all killed, so why is he important? Who is he?"

She heard his words and processed them slowly, the drug affecting her thoughts. What she did know was that she couldn't divulge anything. She had to keep her mouth shut. If they both thought Blake was a distant Alastair, he might stand a chance. At the very least, it would give him more time. They couldn't know he was a direct heir.

"Why are you holding us?" she managed to grind out. Even in her groggy state, she didn't miss the shared look between them.

Before she could ask another question, a phone rang. James's dad reached into his pocket and answered it, stepping closer to the door. James leaned into her personal space.

"You are seriously going to pay for what you did to my dad, girl," James spat through gritted teeth.

"For what I did? Me? He killed my parents!"

James shot his hand out and grabbed a fistful of her hair, yanking her head back and exposing her throat. He bent his head until his nose touched her neck and inhaled, growling low in the back of his throat.

"James!" his dad shouted. James reluctantly let go of her and straightened. James's dad opened the door and instructed two shifters to take her to 'the cell'.

"Want us to keep her bound, Oz?" one of the shifters asked as he came to stand over her. She wasn't even sure she could pick out any discernible features given how hazy her head felt.

"No, she's incapacitated for now," James's dad, Oz, responded.

When one of the shifters made to rip the tape off her arms, James shoved him aside.

"Let me," he almost sang, giddily ripping the tape from her skin. A short cry of pain fell from her mouth, but she bit her lip to hold a second sob from escaping. She wouldn't give him the satisfaction.

CHAPTER THIRTY

BLAKE

WHEN BLAKE REGAINED CONSCIOUSNESS, the sack was off his head and his hands were untied. However, he knew he wasn't in a state to do anything; his head throbbed to the beat of his heart, and when he gingerly touched the back of his skull, his fingers came away sticky and wet. How long could shifters suffer from a concussion?

He took in his surroundings from where he lay on the cold, tiled floor. It was a small room, no bigger than a metre and a half by two metres at his best guess, but it was devoid of all furniture, and there was only a small window nestled up high in the wall. Dark paint peeled away from the ceiling and dusty cobwebs littered the corners. There was one metal door that had no handle, meaning it was designed to keep people inside. He briefly rolled to his back, but it protested, so he turned back to his side again, wincing as his head throbbed.

Lying on the floor made him ache. He worried for his parents, his brother, and for Kayla, who he hadn't seen since she was taken out of the van. The last memory he had of her was the sound of her kicking one of their captors, and it made him smile. She was such a badass. The image soured quickly when he remembered their argument.

Guilt swamped him. He hadn't thought about how much she'd done for him; he'd acted like a child when she'd spoken to him in the library. He was ashamed and knew his dad would be scolding him for being so spoiled and selfish.

What he wouldn't give to see her again and let her know he was sorry.

Strangely, the idea of her leaving him in the new world he'd only just discovered made him miserable. Despite the situations they had found themselves in, she had given him sparks of joy: her smile, her words, her kindness and compassion. Most people would have given up on him long ago and saved their own skin. But not Kayla.

Regretting how he treated her and only just realising her true worth, he worried that he wouldn't get to see her again.

The sun disappeared, plunging the room into a murky darkness. Luckily, the moonlight was shining at just the right angle, illuminating the room with an oddly comforting silvery glow.

A key clicked in the lock, and Blake stood to attention. Dizziness washed over him for a moment before everything righted. He waited in trepidation; should he be ready to fight, to argue? Could he fight? Would he need to kill? Nothing prepared him for the sight that befell him as the door swung outward.

Kayla stood, or rather slumped, half supported by two shifters. Her head hung limp and her feet dragged across the floor, but they threw her inside like she was nothing. Blake awkwardly caught her so she remained upright. She moaned and brought her shaking hands up to rest on his chest. He didn't have time to say anything to the guards before the metal door slammed shut again.

"Kayla?" he said gently, and she stirred in his arms. He circled her waist, taking most of her weight. She tried to pull her head back to look at him and he helped her, cupping her cheek gently and brushing back her hair. He gasped. Her beautiful face was marred with fresh bruising, staining her cheekbone to match her bloody split lip. "What did they do to you?" he asked, anger simmering low in his belly.

"Drugged," she just about managed to get out. "Looks worse."

"Let's sit you down and check you over," he said, leaning her against a wall and sitting down beside her. Her head fell to his shoulder and he let her stay there, trying to scan her for any other obvious signs of injury.

"Tired," she whispered.

"Just sleep," he replied, and her head drooped against him.

THE SUN WAS RISING when Kayla lurched forward with a strangled cry. She'd slept on his shoulder for the entire night, barely moving. In fact, several times he'd worried she'd stopped breathing, and for the few seconds he struggled to find her pulse, his own heart had stopped.

She slept like the dead.

"Kayla?"

She sank back against the wall, resting against his side.

"Sorry."

"For scaring me?"

"Yeah."

"More concerned than scared," he said, not letting on about checking her pulse so many times. "How are you this morning?" he asked. She stared straight ahead.

"I've been better, certainly." He noted her voice was weaker than normal, but she was holding it together, all things considered.

"What did they do to you?"

She was quiet to begin with, but he gave her time.

"Not as much or as bad as you're thinking. They slapped me twice because I wouldn't cooperate, and they threatened a bunch of stuff."

"Like what?"

"I don't think it's best if I get into it now," she replied and shuddered slightly. Whatever it was, it wasn't pleasant for her. She pulled her lip in between her teeth and closed her eyes. "It was his dad – James's dad – who killed my parents and tracked me to Gaby. I led them straight to you," she cried, burying her head in her hands.

Anger for Kayla boiled his blood, but he took a calming breath. His anger wouldn't help Kayla right now.

"Hey, look at me," he said softly, gently pulling her hands away from her face. She kept her eyes downcast. "I promise you that we'll make it right. They won't get away with what they've done."

"I need them dead," she whispered.

"I'm on board with that." She let out a shuddery breath when he agreed with her wish.

His instincts urged him to look into her eyes, and he reached out to turn her face to his. He held her chin in his gentle grasp; her lip was less swollen, and her cheek wasn't quite as angry as it had been last night, but a light purple tinge coloured the area.

She watched him closely, giving him full access to her soft eyes, and before he could register what he was doing, he leaned in. Their breaths mingled as he watched her eyes close; a whisper of contact between their lips was all they had before the loud, disrupting clank of keys in a lock shocked them apart.

They sprung up and took a step away from each other as the metal door swung outward. Two people stood on the other side, escorted by shifters with iron grips on their upper arms. The shifters roughly pushed the couple inside and slammed the door shut again. The room had just gotten inexplicably smaller.

"Mum? Dad?"

CHAPTER THIRTY-ONE

KAYLA

SHE DIDN'T HAVE TIME to dwell on the almost-kiss in light of the new revelation. Mum and Dad? Recognition hit her: the couple in Blake's family photo. The woman stepped forward and embraced her son, and Blake hugged her tightly. His mum pulled back, holding his face between her hands and studying him closely.

"Are you okay? Have they hurt you?" she asked, tears in her eyes.

"No, I'm okay, Mum. Are you guys all right?" His father wrapped an arm around him, clapping a hand on his shoulder.

"We're okay, son. Nothing we can't handle."

"What about Charlie?"

A quick sob escaped his mum.

"We haven't seen him. We know he's here, but we haven't been allowed to see him."

"They show us pictures. It's a part of their torture!" his mum angrily explained.

"He appears to be doing all right though, from what we can tell."

Blake ran his hands through his hair – a tell-tale sign of stress.

"Why did they put you in here with us? It doesn't make sense," Blake said, and a lightbulb went off in Kayla's head.

"To tease you." Kayla stepped closer, resting her hand on his bicep. It was stupid to need the contact for comfort. "They want to know who you are. I don't think they've figured out you're a direct heir to the throne – but by giving you time with your parents, they're probably thinking it'll be motivation to do what they ask." Blake looked down at her and nodded in agreement when she finished. Okay. At least they were on the same page.

Blake's mum studied Kayla with a small frown between her brows.

"Speaking of, why didn't you guys tell me I was a shifter?" Blake snapped. Both his parents froze, looking to each other with their mouths hanging open.

"How did you find out?" his mum breathed, and Kayla wished she could be anywhere else.

"My first change was a pretty big clue, Mum!" Blake argued, his voice rising, and Kayla worried what it would do to the wolf inside him. She could only imagine how the adrenaline would affect him.

"Blake, you've got to calm down," his dad said.

"No, you lied to me. I don't care that you're not my birth parents," he said, and his mum's face paled. "What I care about is you hiding the fact that I'm a shifter. I had no idea what was happening to me. My body was trying to shift, but my mind wouldn't let it because of what you did."

His mum cried out, her hands coming together in front of her as if she were praying. "It was for your own good, Blake. You have to believe us!"

"My own good? Please *do* explain how it was for my own good!"

"Son, when you shift your scent changes, and there are shifters who would have recognised your family's scent. We couldn't take that risk," his dad said, trying to justify their actions.

"So you erased my memories? You got Kayla's dad to do some magic on me so I'd conveniently forget?"

Both of his parents gawked at her.

"You're Lewis's kid?" Blake's father asked.

"Yes."

A look of recognition came over their faces at the same time, and Kayla wondered if she'd met them before. Her memory had been wiped by her dad, so there was no way for her to know. It was yet another realisation that her parents hid more from her than she ever could have imagined. She pushed the feeling of betrayal deep inside.

"And if it wasn't for Kayla, I wouldn't have been able to shift. I would have been stuck in the god-awful in-between stage for who knows how long!" Blake continued, oblivious.

"Blake." Kayla tugged on his arm to get his attention. "If you get too worked up, you'll trigger the change." Her words – her voice – seemed to take effect as understanding dawned in his bright eyes. He took a few deep breaths and turned back to his parents who watched him with worried expressions.

"Honey, we're sorry. We did what we thought was best. We had to hide who you were so people didn't discover you."

"And who am I? I need to hear it from you."

"You're our son–"

"But who was I before I was your son?"

His mum looked away, holding back tears. His dad placed a hand on her shoulder.

"You're the heir to the shifter throne, Blake, and we were honoured to protect you and love you as our own. We are truly sorry for how things have turned out but please, please know that we love you and your brother so much."

"And what about Charlie? Is he really my brother? Is he your blood son?"

"No, he's another shifter orphan who we agreed to help. He doesn't know any of this either. As far as Charlie is concerned, we are his parents and you are his brother."

Blake paced in the crowded room and sank down against the wall, pulling his knees up and resting his head in his hands. Kayla didn't know what to say, and she shuffled from one foot to the other in an awkward dance.

"Are you okay?"

Kayla jumped when Blake's mum spoke to her in a gentle tone.

"Err, yes, relatively speaking."

"Thank you for helping our son. You must be a mage, too, like your father?"

Kayla smiled but gave no other answer, not wanting to let them know about her unique magic.

They didn't get the chance to ask her anything else because the metal door unlocked and opened. There stood not one or two, but five shifters looking as mean and horrible as they undoubtedly were. James was positioned in front of them all, a smug smile plastered on his face as he caught Kayla's eye.

Blake's dad took hold of his wife's hand and Blake came to stand at Kayla's side; his presence took the edge off her frayed nerves. His arm brushed hers when he spoke.

"James," he snarled. James ignored him and pointed at Kayla.

"The girl."

Chaos erupted.

Blake pushed her behind him and started to fend off a shifter who made to grab her. At the same time, his parents rushed forward and put their own shifter strength into the mix. The small space left her with nowhere to go, and with shifters fighting in close quarters, she wasn't safe. She tried drawing on her magic, but it was as unreliable as ever.

"Enough!" James boomed, holding up a gun and aiming straight at her head. She gulped, and the three shifters on her side froze. Their captors backed out of the room with sly gins pasted on their faces. "The girl walks to me, and the rest of you don't try to stop her. Got it?" No one moved, so James pointed it at Blake instead. "If you don't move, Kayla, perhaps I'll shoot him in the leg? Your compliance worked like that before, or am I wrong?"

She didn't want to risk Blake. She forced her shaking legs to move forward. As she passed Blake, who stared at James with barely contained hatred, she grabbed his hand and gently squeezed, hoping to reassure him. She didn't expect a quiet growl to come from deep within his throat as he kept his eyes trained on James.

She stepped over the threshold and looked back at Blake, whose eyes were full of worry and anger. It was the last thing she saw before the door slammed shut.

What happened next occurred so quickly she had no time to process anything. The door closed just before she was backhanded across the face, the force of it throwing her against the wall. A scream escaped her before she could think about the consequences.

As shouting and banging sounded from within the small room, the men outside laughed. Kayla sat dazed on the floor but was hauled up by one of the shifters nearby.

"Thanks for helping, love," James spat at her. "Take her to the interrogation room," he ordered.

Kayla was marched down the dim hall of the building and shoved into the so-called interrogation room, her heart thundering in her ears. She tried to make sense of what was going on. It was the same room she'd been in the previous night, and she was pushed into the same chair she'd been strapped to earlier. Oz, James's dad, waited inside.

"Right, so here's how it's gonna work," he said as all but James left. "I need those same questions I asked you last night answered, and I'm quite frankly running out of patience." He twirled a chair round to straddle it in front of her as he spoke. "So, we'll try this again. Who is the boy?"

"And why should I tell you?" she bit out, earning herself another slap. With how strong shifters were, it could've been a lot worse, but if they kept slapping the same cheek she was going to end up with a fracture. "Why don't you just drug me again and be done with it?"

"No need. The drug's still in your system so you can't do none of that magic of yours."

The realisation hit her like another slap in the face: it was the drug – not her magic – that prevented her from attacking the guards in the cell. She felt a strange surge of relief. With the knowledge, however, came the question of how long it would be before she could do magic again. If she could do any, what would it be? Her magic was unstable at the best of times, let alone after having been drugged. "Oh, you hadn't figured that out yet? Maybe not as smart as you thought, hey?" Oz mocked.

"What does it matter anyway? You're just going to kill us all."

"Mmm, potentially. I have to know who that boy is first."

"Why?" she asked again as her brain started to work overtime. Why would her captors not know who he was? She remembered Michael saying they were ruthless shifters for hire, perhaps they didn't quite know what all the fuss was about? "Hasn't your boss shared that information with you?" she asked, hoping to bait him.

James got into her face again. "None of your concern."

"It is if you need me to answer." Oz stared at her, working his jaw in obvious frustration. "The person who hired you hasn't told you anything and they asked you to keep them all alive, but now you want to know why." She was smug at her guess, but probably shouldn't have been.

"Think you're so clever? Have you spared a thought about yourself?

We have no instructions about keeping *you* alive." He paused, letting the information sink in, and she knew she was at their mercy. She believed him when he said they didn't have orders to keep her alive. She wasn't important. Blake was.

"You know how angry he was when you ordered me out of that room at gunpoint?" she began, hoping to stall for time. What for, she didn't know. "Think about how angry he'd be if you killed me. You don't know who he is, but trust me, he's not to be messed with. Why do you think the person who hired you hasn't given you the green light on killing the family, huh?"

It was a risky idea, talking to him like that, but she hoped stretching the truth a bit would spare her life. She knew she couldn't just hand over information about who he was to these shifters.

The person who contracted them knew who Blake was, but she couldn't figure out why Blake was being kept alive: why not just order his death on the spot? Surely any Alastair, no matter how distant, would be a threat?

Oz stood up and moved his chair away, cracking his knuckles as he stood in front of her.

"Oh love. You really shouldn't have pointed that out. You see, I may still have some use for you alive . . . I can use you to get him to tell me what I need to know without even laying a finger on him."

Kayla gulped.

Lunging quickly, he grabbed the back of her head by her hair, lifting her out of the seat and smashing her face against the wall. A crack vibrated in her nose, and the blood gushed like a waterfall down her face and clothes. The coppery liquid flooded her mouth.

As she coughed, he threw her to the floor and straddled her body; she tried fighting him off, but he was a shifter and she was without her magic. She was powerless.

He wrapped his big, meaty hands around her throat and squeezed so tight she couldn't breathe. She kicked her legs in protest, her lungs screaming, and just as the edges of her vision tinged black, he let go and sat back.

"That should do it," he announced, and he tossed her limp, wheezing body over his shoulder. She watched the rooms pass by, upside down, hung over his shoulder. Somehow, she knew James followed. "All right, love. Let's see if I get what I want now," he said with a confident drawl, tapping her ass. The creaking metal of the door to their cell echoed through the hall, and then a startled gasp caught her ear. From what she could tell, it was Blake's mum who had reacted, but she couldn't see Blake.

The shifter slung her off his shoulder and into the room where strong arms caught her and laid her down gently. Looking up at Blake's face, she knew what the shifter's game plan was. She couldn't let this get to Blake.

"Fine," she managed to croak out. She wanted to say more but couldn't.

"Shush now, honey," his mum whispered.

Blake's dad rushed forward. "What do you think you're playing at? She's just a kid!"

Blake brushed her hair out of her face and tried wiping the worst of the blood away from her nose with his sleeve. The skin around his eyes tightened with pain.

"I want to know who he is. If you don't tell me . . . well, we'll have to do more to the girl." The threat hung heavy in the air, and Blake's face hardened. She knew that look. She reached up, wanting to communicate that she was okay, but his eyes flashed golden. Oh boy.

"Blake, no. Control it," his mum said, but Oz noticed he was on the cusp. A syringe plunged deep into his neck as his ribs began to snap like the night under the bridge.

"Oh no you don't. This should effectively put a stop to any shifting. I'll be back later for some answers. Perhaps some time will help you think about what your priorities should be." The door slammed behind James and his dad, leaving them alone again.

Blake cried out and jerked backwards, bones still cracking.

"Blake?" his mum shouted and clambered over Kayla to help her son. He cried out as he had done when he first shifted. "That drug should be stopping his change like it does ours. Why is it not working, Derrek?!"

"His mind . . ." Kayla croaked, trying to sit up and feeling dizzy as she did. "The effects of my father's magic are still there."

"And he's the heir to the Alastair bloodline, Lucy, there was only so long we were going to be able to suppress the wolf. He's too powerful. His wolf will be fighting the effects of the drug."

"What do we do?" Lucy asked, panic rising in her voice.

"Soothe him as best we can," he replied, kneeling next to his son. He tried to reassure him, but Blake arched up on a loud shout.

Blake groaned. "Kayla . . ."

Both his parents looked to her.

"I think he wants you closer," Lucy said with a sad smile on her face.

"No, he wants my help," Kayla answered, her voice raspy but functioning. She crawled over, ignoring the bout of nausea rising in her stomach. "Blake, I'm not sure I can do this again. The drug they gave me yesterday is blocking my magic."

A sheen of perspiration covered Blake's face as the fever set in, but his eyes found hers, absolute faith gleaming in their depths.

"Please," he begged, and she knew she had to try. She managed to bring herself to a kneeling position beside him and pushed back the hair plastered to his face. Putting one hand on his brow, she closed her eyes and tried to visualise her magic flowing into him as she did before.

It wasn't long before she faced a wall of resistance, like she was trying to burst free from her own chained prison. She knew she was pushing against the constraints of the drug she had been given. She pushed harder, hoping enough of it had worn off, and concentrated on unleashing her magic.

A relieving rush of freedom flew through her as the last dregs of the drug disappeared. She quickly directed her magic towards Blake, but it bounced against another invisible barrier.

Agony and frustration flowed from the other side, his wolf restless and agitated.

She commanded it to break its chains. Nothing happened.

"I release you," she whispered, but the only response she got was Blake's pained moan. "I release you!" she ordered again, and the wolf burst from its shackles.

Lucy's reflexes were quick, snatching Kayla backward when Blake transformed. His limbs thickened as he flipped onto his front and pushed up onto all fours. His back arched impossibly high before lengthening, a tail stretching out behind him. His legs shortened and paws replaced feet as his gorgeous mane of striking ice-white fur sprouted and covered his body. Blake turned his head, and his golden eyes found her own.

CHAPTER THIRTY-TWO

BLAKE

BLAKE KNEW HE WAS changing. From the moment he caught Kayla, her body shaking in his arms as she wheezed, he felt the wolf wake up – rise up – at her distress. The wolf was not happy Kayla was hurt; the wolf felt Kayla was family and should be protected. The wolf pushed through Blake's mind quicker than before, but a cold sensation spread through his neck. His wolf whined in protest, once again chained.

His mum's voice sounded through the fog and his dad explained he was an Alastair. He recognised the word, and his wolf did too, but he couldn't remember where from.

He pictured Kayla and how she could help him. His wolf strained at the bindings as he sensed her presence nearby, trying to get to her.

As if she could hear him, she was there, her words floating through the murky abyss, calling to his wolf. His wolf whined and strained, pulled and howled, trying to get free so he could run to her. But the chains were so heavy. So tight.

Her voice became clearer and louder and commanded him to be free. His wolf listened intently but struggled to escape from his chains. Her magic sought him out, coating him with her strength. When his wolf broke free, Blake withdrew, allowing his wolf's form to take over.

The pain was less intense the second time around. In one way it was freeing – energising. When the wolf stood before his parents and Kayla, he sighed in contentment. Blake and his wolf were one, as they always had been without knowing, finally able to work together.

He scanned the people in front of him and settled his eyes on Kayla. His wolf leapt for joy and wanted to run up to her, but Blake was more careful, so they stayed still, watching her closely. He and his wolf were satisfied that her injuries were not as grave as he'd previously thought, but thinking about that man's hands on her filled him with rage. He and his wolf agreed he would not go unpunished.

"I'm okay," she said calmly, and he realised he'd growled. He whined and trotted forward to nudge her hand with his head. She rested it there, absently stroking, while she spoke to his parents. He would have listened, but he closed his eyes to focus on the sounds outside the room with his heightened shifter hearing.

CHAPTER THIRTY-THREE

KAYLA

"HE'S AS MAGNIFICENT AS we'd thought he'd be," Blake's mum said in awe. Her face split wide open with a smile as she watched her son trot forward. Kayla placed her hand on his head, understanding his need to know she was okay.

"Isn't he? I've not seen many wolves," Kayla replied.

"He seems taken by you."

Kayla's head snapped up.

"It's only because we've spent some time together and he knows I can help his change," she said. She could not have felt any more awkward. "We should think about a plan," she added, trying to distract them from that line of thought.

"Hopefully now that Blake is in wolf form, we might have a chance of surprising them when they next open the door," Derrek said.

"Can't you change, too? Jump the shifters before they know what's happening?"

"No, we've been drugged with the same drug they used on Blake, but we're not Alastairs. Our wolves aren't strong enough to fight against it."

"They're sleeping," Lucy clarified.

"I could maybe help?" Even as Kayla said it, she doubted it. She was beginning to think she was only able to help Blake because she knew him.

"It's a kind offer, but we are very different from Blake. It wouldn't work. I'd rather have you conserve your magic to aid us getting out of here."

"Blake," his father demanded in an authoritative tone and Blake's eyes blinked open, looking up at his dad expectantly. "You good for helping me take down whoever opens that door next?" Blake clumsily moved his head up and down. She guessed he needed to work on that skill. "I know you're new to this, but we may need your senses to locate Charlie. I know that's a lot to ask and I know how important you are, but he's my son, too, and I would appreciate your help." His dad's voice softened, emotion lacing his words.

Blake snorted, and Kayla easily translated. "I'm taking that as his agreement." It got quiet, uncomfortably so. She moved her weight from foot to foot, swaying into Blake. "Um, so, we probably have some time . . ." And she really didn't know what to do with that time. Playing the waiting game sucked. She never did like waiting.

"Can I just say that everything we did, we did for the safety of our boys," Lucy blurted. Kayla blinked in surprise, wondering what she was getting at. "I'm talking about getting Lewis to use magic on him. We all believed pushing back his change and protecting him from this world was the best decision. It meant he could have a normal childhood."

"When were you going to tell him? Would you ever have let him change?" she asked, knowing she might as well ask the questions she knew Blake was wondering about.

"On his seventeenth birthday. It would give him a year to prepare himself for this world and the challenges he would face. Lewis would help him change for the first time when he turned eighteen and be able to take the King's oath. It's just . . . it was getting increasingly difficult to alter his memories and keep his wolf at bay. Lewis was having to come by more often. I think he would have been close to naturally changing anyway."

"You do realise that even though my father hadn't done any magic on him recently, Blake still massively struggled to shift. I dread to think what might have happened to his body if he hadn't been able to complete the change." Lucy inhaled sharply. "Look, I'm sorry. I didn't mean to upset you. I just don't get why you and my parents kept all of this from us and altered our memories. The world is so very dangerous. We should be ready for that, not disadvantaged."

"We were selfish and wanted as normal a childhood as possible for him. But you're right, you're right," Derrek admitted.

"I don't doubt you guys are great parents and just wanted the best for Blake and Charlie, but perhaps you need to tell him, explain to him what you did so he can understand. I don't have that option . . ." she said, trailing off.

"Has something happened to your parents? To Lewis and Caroline? Before we were taken, we couldn't get in contact with Lewis – we were getting worried." Lucy asked, and Kayla stared at the floor. Blake bumped her leg with his nose and she patted him on the head again.

"Shifters killed them," she said quickly. The next thing she knew, Lucy wrapped her in a giant 'mum' hug.

"Oh honey!" she gushed. Missing maternal comfort in her life, Kayla took the opportunity to sink into the hug. Tears gathered but she kept them back. She had to stay strong to make it out of there. Lucy leaned away but still held onto her, gently tucking some hair behind Kayla's ear. "I'm so sorry that happened, but I'm so thankful you're okay. When we get out of here, if you need anything, you come to us all right?"

Kayla smiled gratefully. "You're very optimistic."

Lucy laughed. "I've raised two boisterous boys! It's the only way you can be!"

Blake snorted – apparently he understood that.

Keys jangled in the lock, and their heads snapped in unison towards the door. As it swung open, the guy on the other side froze in shock.

"What the? You shouldn't have–" he began but Blake pounced on the man and knocked him backwards. The guard hit his head against the hard stone floor and groaned; Blake stood on his chest and growled, baring his teeth.

"Blake, wait!" His dad rushed to stand beside them. "You'll have plenty of burdens soon enough. Let me take this one from you now . . . please," he begged. Blake slowly retreated. His dad hauled up the body and dragged him inside the room where his wife and Kayla stood. He looked to his wife, and Lucy took Kayla by the arm.

"Come on, Kayla," she said, guiding her out. She was confused, and the loud snap that followed made her jump. She tried turning around, but Lucy held her with strong arms.

"You, you killed him," Kayla whispered with a weird mix of relief and horror. It was similar to how she'd felt the night she thought she'd killed the red-headed woman who was after her and Blake.

"I had to. Given a chance, any of these shifters here will kill us. It's kill or be killed," Derrek said solemnly when he shut the door.

Lucy led them down the hallway. "I remember being taken for questioning once, and I swear I heard Charlie down here," she said. Blake whined.

"Everyone stop," Kayla whispered. "What, Blake?" He used his nose and pushed her back; she retreated and encouraged his parents to do the same. He padded forward slowly and turned the corner.

"Why have you shifted?" A male voice asked when Blake disappeared from view. Derrek moved to follow, but she grabbed the back of his shirt and shook her head. They had to have faith in Blake. "Seriously man, cut it out." A sharp growl was followed by a gurgled scream. The scream didn't travel very far, but all three of them shot around the corner to find an unconscious man in a heap beneath Blake's paws.

"Blake?" Kayla asked, concerned for him. Blake's dad pushed open the door and stepped over the body.

"Dad?" A younger, male voice sounded from inside. Blake's dad and Charlie walked into the hall. The boy ran to his mum, ignoring the unconscious man.

"Are you okay, honey?" Lucy asked, grabbing her young son's face between her hands.

"Yeah, I'm okay. They mostly let me play games. Are you and dad all right? Where's Blake?" he asked, looking around. He jumped back when he saw the wolf.

"Charlie, it's okay. It's okay," Lucy soothed. "We have a lot to explain, but for now we just need you to listen to us. Blake will not hurt you."

"What do you mean Blake won't hurt me? Where is he?" he asked, looking warily from his mum to the wolf.

Blake slowly walked over to stand beside Kayla; she put her hand on his head again.

"Hi Charlie, I'm Kayla. Do you remember me?" He nodded, keeping a wary eye on the animal. "This is Blake," she said carefully. Charlie frowned and looked to his parents.

"She's not lying," the boys' dad said.

"We should go. We can deal with this later," his mum stated, taking Charlie's hand and moving him away.

As Kayla and Blake followed, another snap sounded behind them. Derrek jogged up in his wolf form, over-taking them so he could lead.

They walked fervently down the corridor, passing what appeared to be abandoned office set-ups. Dust coated the rooms littered with files, and desks with old, box-style computers sat within snaking tangles of wires.

Blake shook his head a few times.

"Are you all right?" she asked quietly. He flashed her a quick look and snorted; she assumed that meant yes, but she was beginning to know different when it came to Blake.

After another turn, a large door looking very much like an exit came into view. No signs indicated otherwise. They made their way towards it, but their clear path didn't last much longer. Two shifters walked in through the door, the outside world just beyond them.

The two shifters halted when they saw the group. Blake rushed one of them before he had a chance to shift; his parents went for the other. In such close quarters, Kayla worried her magic wouldn't behave. She stepped back with Charlie to allow the others room.

Blake yelped and stumbled, giving the man an opportunity to wrap his arms around his furry neck.

Kayla ran forward and grabbed the man. She didn't mean for it to happen. She didn't mean for fire to race out of her hands and cover the man in a deadly outfit of flame. It was just like when her family had been attacked, and the fire took off on its own path. She scrambled back, mortified as the man wailed and screamed, finally succumbing to the blaze. He fell to his knees, a statue of agony, before toppling over. The flames withered and died out, leaving a blackened corpse behind. She looked beyond the corpse into Blake's golden eyes. He blinked and groaned as he shifted, shedding his beautiful white fur. His snout shortened, and his human face took shape. It only took a second to realise his human form was naked, crouched low on the ground.

"Oh my God! You're a werewolf!" Charlie shouted, pointing at Blake's naked form.

"Here," his dad said, tugging the plaid shirt from the man at his feet.

He tossed it to Blake who hurriedly put it on while his dad tugged the jeans off the dead guy, too. Blake pulled a face but yanked on the trousers.

"Are you okay, Charlie?" his mum asked while Blake dressed.

"Am I okay? My brother turned into a freaking werewolf! I thought he was like her pet or something," he said, and a smile lit up his face. "That was so cool, man! And you! Are you a witch or something?" he asked Kayla, eyes awash with excitement. She didn't know what to say, still horrified that she had killed someone in such a cruel way. Blake came over and touched her lightly on the arm.

"You all right?" he asked softly, looking into her eyes. She was relieved there was no judgment, only concern. She could deal with it if he didn't judge her. She shuddered.

"Am I gonna turn into a werewolf? Am I?" Charlie asked his mum with far too much excitement.

"Not now, Charlie," she chastised. "Blake? Kayla? Are you both all right? You're not hurt?"

"No, I'm not hurt," Kayla responded flatly as Blake shook his head.

"We should go, and quickly," Blake's dad instructed. He opened the door that led to the outside world. Lucy and Charlie followed him with Kayla and Blake taking up the rear.

Kayla stepped outside and revelled in the sunlight. It was glorious after being held captive, and with Blake and his family beside her, she wasn't quite as weighed down by the people who had died at her hands.

A van sat on the gravelled driveway; Derrek went to check if it was open. Kayla was just about to say that she might be able to hotwire it when somebody clapped behind them. She whirled, and Blake immediately took a small step in front of her.

CHAPTER THIRTY-FOUR

KAYLA

JAMES AND HIS FATHER stood side by side with another shifter, one who'd been happy to see her abused by Oz earlier.

"Thought you could get away, did you?" Oz spoke.

"Why don't you let the others go and you can keep me?" Blake's dad offered but James's dad shook his head.

"You're not worth as much as he is," he said pointing at Blake. "The rest of you, we no longer care about."

"But I get to keep the girl, right?" James asked, rubbing his hands together like a greedy kid.

"As long as she's dead by the time the others get here. Nobody escapes me," his dad responded.

Kayla gasped and grabbed hold of Blake's hand. At the time, she wasn't sure whether it was to ground him from lunging at them, or to comfort herself. Blake squeezed her hand, not taking his eyes off the other shifters. His form was rigid and poised for action. His palm pressed against hers and it brought her comfort, but she was plagued with worries about his ability to shift. She sent a bit of magic into him, hoping it was enough to release his wolf. She knew it worked when his hand tightened and a small growl rumbled from deep within his chest.

She knew she would have to do something to give Blake time to change, and she focussed on her magic rather than the words being exchanged. Praying her magic would obey, she concentrated on the fire element like she had with the fireplace at Michael's house. Could she do it? Could she consciously create fire? Sweat formed in nervous beads at the base of her neck, slowly travelling down her spine. The sensation gave her an idea, and she started drawing on her power like a tap, drip by drip. Her magic normally had a mind of its own, but she had to control it. She couldn't accidentally hurt Blake or his family.

Blake's father grunted with the familiar snap of bone. In her peripheral vision, he tensed and she sensed the drug he and Lucy had been given to stop their shifts was wearing off. He was fighting the last of it. Lucy was smaller, so she doubted Lucy's body had processed enough of it yet.

James and his dad cracked their knuckles in unison, malicious smiles erupting on their faces.

"Let's get 'em. Just keep the boy alive," Oz instructed. They started forward and Kayla took a small step in front of Blake, raising her free hand.

"No," she whispered, directing the force she had been building towards them. A stream of fire jetted from her hand and landed in a ball a few yards from their advance. The shifters started changing with more agility than she'd seen with Blake.

Worrying about Blake and his father having enough time to shift, she willed the fire to spread, just like the fireplace at Michael's. She imagined a wall of amber and crimson, a wall of flame and destruction, and she watched the blaze expand and grow several metres in each direction. James's wolf tried to run through the fiery curtain, but he yelped and fell back.

Letting go of Blake's hand, she ordered him to change with her magic; he dropped to the ground in a crouch, just as his father did.

Their shifts were sluggish, but they completed them just as the wall of flame died down to a simmering ember. The three wolves who paced on the other side leapt over.

Blake and his father ran full speed at the oncoming trio, but a dull grey wolf side-stepped the Collins and headed straight for her. Her breath caught in her throat. She quickly backpedalled, but the wolf was on her in seconds. Charlie cried out for his mum, but she could hear nothing else apart from her wildly thumping heartbeat.

The wolf surged through the air. She held her hands out defensively, willing the fire to come back, but she couldn't concentrate in time. The wolf descended on her, his jaw wide and teeth prominent. Pain lashed through her arm when he clamped down; she fell backwards and he stood heavy on her chest, pushing the air from her lungs. He growled and shook his head.

She cried out as her flesh tore and the wolf gurgled on the bursts of blood that shot into his mouth. Trying to get a grip on his fur, she attempted to shoot some magic at him – anything – and was momentarily relieved when he unlatched and jumped like he'd been shocked. The wolf looked down on her with a bloody grin, but before he could go at her again, Blake's wolf jumped on his back and locked his jaws around the wolf's neck.

Blake growled wildly and held on with an iron grip. The wolf beneath him thrashed from side to side, alternating between vicious growls of fury and whines of pain. Blake was beginning to lose his grip, but with one sharp shake of his head, the wolf went limp and Blake let him fall to the ground. His head rolled at an unnatural angle and he reverted to his human form, revealing James's lifeless body.

Blake stepped over him and approached Kayla, splatters of blood stained across his mane of white fur. A soft whine came from the back of his throat as he softly bumped his nose to her arm. She brought it close to her body while Blake shifted back; it was the fastest he'd managed so far, and pain hardly marred his features. He wore the jeans he had on before the shift but no shirt. He looked down at himself.

"Almost," he said jokingly. Some of the gruffness from his wolf had yet to disappear from his voice. His gaze dropped to her arm. "Kayla," he breathed.

"I'm sorry you had to do that. I just . . . I just froze."

"You did great. You helped me and my dad shift. Without that, they would have had us." He paused, figuring she didn't believe him. "Teamwork. It was teamwork."

She looked at his face and a shadow passed over it. She swore it was guilt. She could accept teamwork if it helped him.

"Teamwork," she agreed.

"Your arm?"

"Painful."

"Here," he said offering his hands, pulling her to her feet with little effort.

Kayla glanced over at the two dead bodies as Derrek's wolf trotted towards Lucy and Charlie. "What happened?" she asked Blake as they walked over to where his family stood. He kept his arm around her lower back; she could walk, but she appreciated the comfort of his touch.

"Dad took out the first wolf pretty quick and came to help me with Oz. He was a good fighter and far outmatched me. Luckily, the two of us wore him down, and when you screamed, Dad was able to take over so I could get to you." Blake stopped, his arm tightening around her just a fraction.

Kayla didn't know what to say, how to respond.

"Blake! Kayla!" Charlie shouted, and the family turned to face them.

"Mum, Dad, Kayla's arm . . ." Blake gestured to her torn and bloody arm, small strips of flesh hanging loose.

"That is so gross," Charlie said but stared anyway. When Blake slapped the back of his head, he apologised.

"Derrek, we need to slow down that bleeding," Lucy said. She turned to her husband who used his elbow to smash the van window and open the door. He rummaged around and brought out a simple first aid kit.

"We can use something from in here to wrap it up, but you'll need to be seen by a specialist. We can get to the shifter doctor we know within a few hours if we drive straight there."

He wrapped her arm in a bandage as gently as he could, but she still winced.

"I can't. I need to head to Oxford and check that all my parents' work is safe. I have to continue what they asked me to do." She didn't look at Blake as she spoke, couldn't, because she was too afraid that he'd want to stay with his family now he'd found them. She wouldn't even blame him if he did; she wasn't sure what her own decision would be if their roles were reversed. "You guys need to get somewhere safe; Blake is a coveted shifter and not in a good way. People will use you again to get to him. Besides, you have . . ." she coughed, nodding her head towards Charlie, "to help, you know."

"But–" Lucy began.

"Lucy, she's right. We'll just be a burden on her, and we can't ask her to do that. She's done so much for us already. Seriously Kayla, you've saved my family." Derrek told her sincerely, finishing up with her arm.

It was bandaged but she still held it close to her body. Whether it was to keep everything close to her chest as she imagined herself being on her own again, or because of the pain, she couldn't truly distinguish.

"Guys, umm, I won't be coming with you," Blake announced. Kayla opened her mouth as Lucy and Derrek frowned at him.

"What do you mean? You need to stay safe!" His mum said in a shrill voice.

"I know, but if I'm as important as everyone believes me to be, then I need to do what I can to help. We can't go on like this for much longer. There'll be no one left. I also promised Kayla that if she helped me find you, I'd help her. I'm a man of my word, just as you taught me to be," he said, looking to his dad. He and his dad shared some sort of silent communication before they embraced.

"I'm so proud of you, son. I knew you'd do great things, but," he leaned back and gripped the back of Blake's head, "you stay safe as you can, don't do anything stupid, and protect each other. You're about to go up against some powerful people. I wish I could help more."

"You will, by making sure you, Mum, and Charlie stay safe. Charlie will need support, and I'll sleep better knowing you guys are out of harm's way."

"Do you know what the original alliance was about?" Kayla interrupted, thinking they may be able to provide some information. Lucy and Derrek shared a quick look and Derrek answered.

"I wish we did, but there wasn't much time for discussion when Blake came to us, and to be honest, we didn't want to know. We thought the less we knew the better. We just focussed on hiding and protecting the shifter prince." Kayla's shoulders dropped. She'd been hoping for a head start for once.

Blake's mum grabbed Blake into a hug, Derrek followed, and Charlie wrapped his arms around them all. Lucy leaned back and beckoned Kayla over.

"You too, honey." Kayla was hesitant, but Blake opened his arm and she joined them, tucking herself under Blake. "Will you let us know how you are? Both of you?" Lucy asked when they stepped apart.

"Yeah, um, is there anything I can write on? I'll give you an email address."

The van produced a scrap piece of paper, an old receipt by the looks of it, and a pencil, so she scribbled down Michael's email and passed it over to Lucy. Derrek and Blake had the sombre task of moving the dead bodies inside so they weren't left out in the open.

"Your magic is so wicked," Charlie commented while she watched Blake haul James's corpse over his shoulder. A brief look of remorse clouded his eyes before they filled with steely determination.

"Umm, thanks."

"About that," Lucy said, "you've used mage magic and elemental magic. I'm not sure I've seen that before, or if it's possible. If I hadn't seen it myself, I wouldn't have believed it."

"It's a bit of an anomaly, and I'd appreciate it very much if you didn't say anything to anyone while we try to figure it out." She tried not to dwell on how she'd referred to her and Blake as 'we.'

"I wouldn't dream of it. It could put you both in more danger." She paused and leaned in close to whisper so Charlie couldn't hear them. "You will look out for him? He's still my son and . . ."

"You don't need to explain. I will. If he can help unify the shifters, building a bridge of peace between us, then he's the most important person I can think of right now."

Lucy smiled and squeezed her hand. Blake and Derrek came out of the building; Blake had one backpack slung over a shoulder and he held the other by the straps.

"My pack!" she gasped in delight, and Blake smiled at her, handing it over.

"We found them when we did a final sweep of the building. Thought you'd lost your mum's spell book, didn't you?" She dug out the journal and hugged it close with her uninjured arm. She tried to swallow her tears of relief.

"Thank you."

"Right, where can we take you? And do you need any money? What can we do? Let us help you one last time," Derrek asked.

Blake turned to her expectantly, and wasn't that like the Blake she knew?

Kayla rolled her eyes, smiling. "To the city please."

Charlie and Blake climbed into the back with Kayla while Lucy and

Derrek sat up front. Charlie loved the freedom of the back of the van, but Kayla and Blake shared an uncomfortable look as they remembered the last time they were there.

BLAKE AND KAYLA WATCHED his parents drive off. They'd let them out near a busy shopping street, and the goodbye had been brief but sweet so as not to linger in traffic. Anxiety was etched across Blake's face.

"They'll be okay. I've given them Michael's details, as I'm sure he'll help. I'll email him myself and make sure he understands what is at stake."

Blake nodded. "We'll need more allies in this too; is Michael prepared to help us?"

Kayla nodded, convinced. "He will."

"We need to find someone who knows about this original alliance, don't we?" Blake asked, and Kayla nodded as she quickly scanned the streets again.

"Yes, but we also need to figure out who hired Oz and James to take you and your family. Don't you think it's strange that they were given instructions *not* to kill you?"

Blake tilted his head to one side, pondering what she'd said.

"You're right, as usual. So where to, Captain?" Kayla rolled her eyes at him. "What? You make the plans; that's how we work."

"I'm going to have to teach you then, aren't I?" she said as they started forward. Cash. They needed to get cash for what she wanted to do.

"Looking forward to it," Blake said quietly. Hiding the blush that crept across her cheek with her hair, she smiled.

END OF BOOK 1

RHIAN EDWARDS

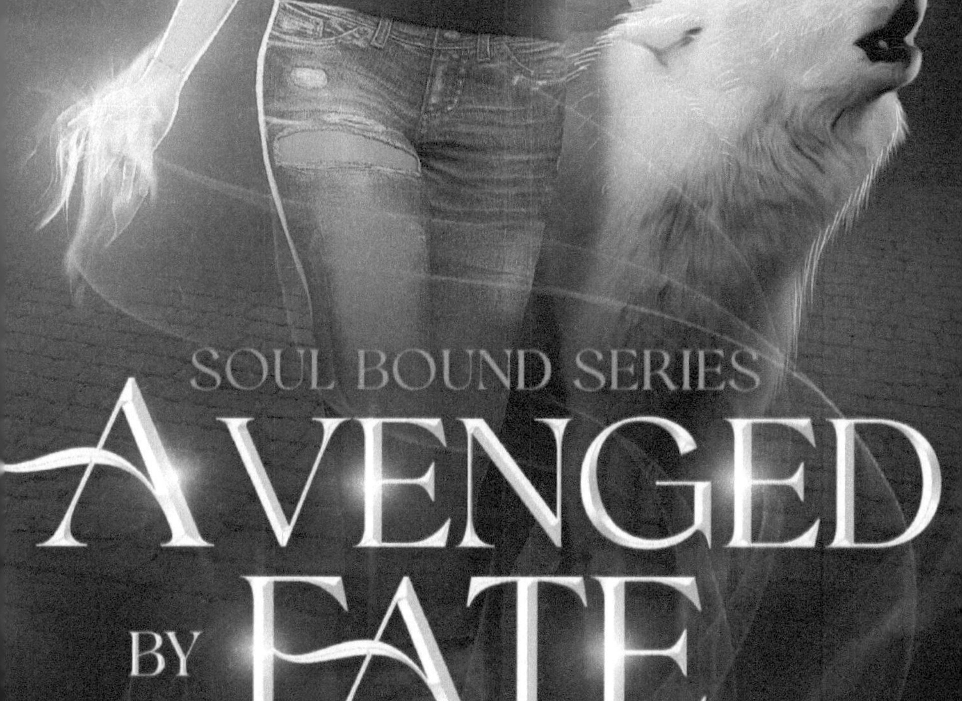

AVENGED BY FATE

For my Alpha readers, my longest friends, thank you for reading my trashy first drafts and being gentle with my soul, but never sparing me from the truth. Blake wouldn't be as loveable without you.

CHAPTER ONE

KAYLA

IT WAS THE PARTICULAR INCIDENT she was currently running from which irked her. She was meant to be meeting with someone who supposedly knew about the original alliance. It had taken weeks to find another lead, using underground paranormal resources that weren't all that safe, but it had turned out to be magic hunters luring them into a trap. If she wasn't so exhausted, she'd moan in frustration.

Her heart thundered like a drum in her chest. Only the sound of her own laboured breathing reached her ears. Her muscles screamed for a break, but that would end in her death. She had to keep going.

Somehow, she'd ended up separated from Blake as they raced through a thicket of dense trees just on the outskirts of the town they had been in to meet their contact – the one she'd discovered was fake. Why running into the wooded area was a good decision, she didn't know. *They* had forced her in that direction.

The group of magic hunters had been on her and Blake's tails for months, constantly getting in their way ever since she'd accidentally exposed her magic. They wanted her power for themselves, and she was worried about how they would take it from her. More than that, they had no desire for Blake; they wanted to kill the Alastair heir and any hope of an alliance with him. From what the two had discovered, the group had no desire for an alliance and instead wanted to eliminate all shifters. The heir to the Alastair shifter royal throne was one person they were especially eager to stop.

A familiar tingle started in her fingertips and worked its way up her arms as her magic hummed, searching for a way out.

Not now, she thought. She couldn't let her magic alert anyone who was close enough to her position. She didn't turn to look behind her, but she sensed the magic hunters were spread out and searching for her. She had to make it through the wooded area and to the building in the town centre where she and Blake had agreed to meet up if things went sideways. She just needed to shake the hunters off her back first.

Her elemental magic strained against the restraints she was trying to put in place. It wasn't enough that she could abnormally use all three strains – witch, mage, and elemental – but the latter was also her strongest and had the greatest urge to be released. The natural elements surrounding Kayla called out to her magic. And her magic was answering.

The past few months had seen her magic grow exponentially. Blake was worried, which annoyed her to no end, but he had a point; her magic scared her, too. Flare-ups and uncontrollable surges occurred at random, and she couldn't stop it when it wanted to be let out.

Like now.

Her magic pulsed and trees groaned unnaturally. The swell of energy sent her flying, then rolling, across the mossy floor. Power seeped from her hands where they braced themselves on the dirt-covered ground, calling to nature: the earth element. Roots from a gnarled old tree moaned and rattled. Her eyes widened with the understanding that they were searching for the source of power.

Her breathing came out in short, sharp pants. She knew the aura of her magic, the essence, was a beacon for the talented witch in the group chasing them. The witch could detect and follow magic, and Kayla was certain she was doing so now, tracking Kayla's outbursts. Panicking, she reached out to try and subdue the gnarled oak hands, but her elemental power surged. Recognising nature and connecting with it, she unintentionally sent another wave into the ground. The tree shook, its branches vibrating against each other. It would have been more discreet if she had held a neon sign above her head.

A burst of manic wind circled her and spiralled up into the sky, taking with it the debris of the wooded floor: dirt, twigs, moss.

Kayla covered her face with a quiet yelp, but when she heard fast approaching footsteps, she jumped up and froze. Her eyes darted around the area, hoping to locate the direction of the footfalls. To her left, the foliage shook and trembled as someone manoeuvred through the overgrowth.

Holding out her hands, she directed her magic as it built within her body, but she couldn't release it. Elemental magic danced along her skin. Goosebumps rose on her arms as a burst of power shot from her fingers, targeting the undergrowth. A strangled cry of surprise echoed through the air, followed by a dull thud.

"Blake?" she whispered, recognising his voice.

She'd only taken one step in his direction when someone raced towards her from the left. She turned and an unwelcome face appeared, thin lips tipping into a sneer. The fierce hunter knocked into her and sent her flying.

She landed awkwardly on her side, twisting her ankle in the process. The man advanced on her, and instinctively, she put her arm up to stop a blow. The hum intensified, as did the electric current racing all over her body, but she knew she had no control over it. The more she tried to reach for the reins, the further they slipped away from her.

Blake appeared and yanked the man away from her with a grunt. In his human form, Blake was physically bigger than the magic user, and with the surprise attack, Blake had the advantage. Wrapping his arm around the guy's neck, Blake's face strained as he struggled with the man in the crook of his arm.

"A little help," Blake grunted out.

Kayla slid the short distance, dragging her leg behind her. She reached her hand over to the guy's head and closed her eyes, desperately searching for her mage magic.

C'mon. C'mon. C'mon.

She grabbed at a thread. "Sleep."

The guy immediately went limp in Blake's arms, and Blake carefully let go of him but hovered close to make sure he was definitely out. When he was convinced that was the case, he sagged against a tree.

"Let's go," he whispered. He got to his feet but stayed low to the ground, surveying the immediate area.

"My ankle," she replied, trying to kneel and wincing at the effort.

Blake leaned forward and moved her jean leg up to look, holding her foot as he gently twisted. Kayla hissed and glared daggers at him.

"Sprained, I think. Common sports injury," Blake said, and Kayla believed him. She knew Blake was knowledgeable from growing up with a sports coach dad – his adopted dad.

Blake put his arm under her shoulders and bore most of her weight as he stood them up. Kayla limped heavily and leaned against him. Blake's height hadn't changed, but after his first shift, he'd started bulking up. Over the past six months they'd had to buy him three sets of clothes, but she was convinced he had stopped growing and was settling into his new body.

"Why aren't you in wolf form?"

He darted his eyes down to her as they moved. "I've told you. I think they track me better in wolf form like they do you when you use magic," he replied in a sharp tone.

Kayla knew there was more to it than that. They'd gone through quite a bit to get Blake to change for the first time, but ever since the night they escaped James and Oz – who had kidnapped them both and held Blake's family prisoner – Blake had trouble connecting with his wolf. Instead of allowing the shift, he fought it.

She suspected Blake was correct in his assumptions, but that didn't stop his wolf from being an asset. Blake had exceptional senses and was stronger and faster than the average human, but the added advantages his wolf gave him boosted those abilities. Plus, canine teeth were much more effective when they came up against human flesh.

But she knew his ability to do harm was the reason he resisted the change. After the kidnapping, Blake was forced to kill once more, and it had happened in his wolf form.

The sound of shouting behind them spurred them on. Blake pushed them down a short incline to hide.

"I'll leave a false trail." He concealed her within a patch of snarled greenery and raced up the path to cover their footsteps, leaving a few imprints going in the opposite direction. Afterwards, he circled back, sliding down beside Kayla.

His eyes grew concerned, and she suspected he could sense her magic.

"You have to control it. They're tracking you." She nodded tensely at him, breathing slow and deep, trying to push down the magic that sought release.

Her hands dug deep into the earth beside her. She pulled her knees up close to her chest and pressed her back against the mud, but she could feel the natural elements of the earth calling to her and knew her magic would respond.

She shook her head, face covered in a fine sheen of perspiration. "I can't," she whispered.

Blake pulled her in close, wrapping his arm around her shoulders to hold her against him. His familiar scent and the warmth of his skin overwhelmed her senses, and her magic responded immediately. The roaring desire for action quieted.

She tucked her hands under her chin and hoped her magic responded to the nature of the wolf rather than the elements around her. Closing her eyes, she listened to the sounds of magic hunters crashing through the forest, yelling commands to each other. They hadn't given up.

Blake wrapped his other arm around her, sealing her against him. He slowly and comfortingly stroked her dark locks, resting his cheek on the top of her head.

The embrace calmed her, soothed her magic, settled her anxious thoughts, and alleviated the rising mountain of panic she felt helpless against as her magic tried to take over her body.

Why was she always so . . . connected with Blake? Why was it him that offered the tranquillity she craved when her magic stormed to the surface?

She huddled closer and he squeezed her tighter. Their hearts thundered and the voices of the search party grew fainter as they followed the false trail.

Blake lifted his head, scenting. "All clear for now," he announced, turning his head to look at her. She lifted hers up, bringing their faces inches apart. Heavy breaths – and not from physical exertion – mingled, their lips separated by mere centimetres.

The tense moment they'd shared when locked away by Oz and James several months ago flashed into her mind. Their near kiss. They hadn't discussed it. They'd been too busy. And she was nervous. She didn't know what he thought, what he wanted, but it certainly couldn't be the unnatural freak of nature she was.

Shutting her eyes, she drew away from his stormy gaze. Her nerves regarding his feelings paled in comparison to her fear of the size of her own. She buried them deep. Again.

Blake looked away, clearing his throat and pulling her to her feet. She gave him a tight smile, grimacing at the pain in her ankle. "Let's get back to the car. Your ankle needs looking at."

They made it out of the woods unscathed, and Blake led her to where he'd stashed the car behind an old, seemingly abandoned building. He opened her door and lowered her into the seat as she gingerly pulled her leg inside. He shut the door and hopped over the bonnet, sliding across the dark blue metal.

She chuckled as he opened the driver's door. "What was that for?" she managed.

Blake shrugged, turning on the engine. "Just fancied doing it." He sounded nonchalant, but she heard the answering smile in his voice. "We need to find somewhere to stay for the night. You'll need to elevate your leg, and this car isn't practical."

Kayla sighed, knowing he was right. If she was being honest with herself, she craved a bed. For the past six months they'd slept in the car or in cheap hostels along the way, but whenever they napped in the vehicle, her back didn't thank her for it.

"Yeah, I agree. Just find a place along the motorway," she instructed. Blake pulled away from the town and merged onto a long stretch of road.

The car was silent as they each dealt with their own worries; she briefly wondered what he was thinking about but dismissed it. Dealing with the disappointment of the evening and an injured ankle – not to mention her uncontrollable magic – was enough for her.

CHAPTER TWO

BLAKE

HE PULLED UP BESIDE a budget hotel and ran inside to get them a room so Kayla wouldn't have to move about unnecessarily. At the front desk, he made sure to ask about an ice machine so he could help reduce the swelling.

He jogged back to the car and scooped her up, placing her firmly on her own feet when she started to protest.

"Don't you dare think about carrying me in, Blake!" she scolded.

"Wouldn't dream of it." He smiled as she clutched at him anyway.

They took a slightly longer route around the back of the building to use an exit into the hotel and then found the lift up to their floor. The building was clean and well-kept with a busy, dull-red carpet that matched the wooden panelling and cream walls. Their room was decorated in the same shades, boasting large windows, little floor space, and two beds placed almost side by side.

Blake left Kayla in a tub chair while he went back to the car for their packs and a few necessities. They'd learned the hard way how important it was to keep water, granola bars, and basic first aid supplies on hand. He grabbed the kit, thinking there might be something of use inside.

His dad was a sports instructor, managing a gym and training clients, so Blake was familiar with injuries of that ilk. Goodness knew how many sprained ankles his sports mad family had between them. A smile ghosted his lips as he thought of his adopted family. Finding out he'd escaped an assassination as a small child and was subsequently hidden so that others wouldn't find out his true identity as the last surviving heir to the shifter royal family, had been a shock to say the least.

He unlocked the door to their room and dumped the bags on the bed. Kayla had her arms on the side of the chair, one leg out straight before her, and she'd let her head fall back. She lifted her head to look at him as he came closer, holding up their small makeshift first aid kit.

"Shall we take a look at that ankle?"

She groaned. "Might as well get it over and done with."

Blake sat cross-legged on the floor and gently removed her shoe, rolling up the hem of her jeans. She winced when he tried to manipulate the ankle.

"Definitely sprained and swollen, but I don't think it's broken. That's good news."

"If you say so. What's the prognosis?"

"Not that you will, but I'd recommend a couple weeks of rest. Elevate your leg where possible. Ice, too."

Her eyes bugged out at him. "I'm not sitting on my butt for two weeks."

"I figured. Just rest it when you can. No driving, I'll do that part. And we need to avoid the magic hunters, so we do nothing that's high risk for a few days. You won't be in much of a state to run if they find us."

"Sounds like fun," Kayla deadpanned.

"We have a small supply of meds, you can take some to help with any pain."

"To be honest, it's not that bad right now." She sighed as she spoke, not meeting his eyes.

He kept his hands on her lower leg.

"Kayla," he began.

"I'm not sure I like that tone."

"I think we need some help. We're struggling here. We need more resources, more support."

"What happened tonight was because of those magic users! They lured us into thinking they had information about the original alliance!"

"Yes, but would we have fallen into that trap if we had more people helping us?" Kayla turned her head away, her face tight with tension. "It's not that I don't want to do this with you. I think we're a great team, but we can't do it alone."

When Kayla turned back to face him, her eyes glistened, and when she spoke, her voice wobbled. "But I don't want people to know about me."

"Your magic?"

She nodded. "I'm unnatural, Blake, and I'm . . . scared."

Blake let go of her leg and took her hands from where they gripped the side of the chair.

"What have I said about that?"

"That you wouldn't let anyone hurt me." Her voice wavered.

"And I mean it. What are we?"

A small smile grew on her face. "A team."

"Exactly. That won't change. Maybe telling others about your magic would help? People would see how powerful you are, and you do need to train with your magic."

Her hands tightened in his. "No. No, Blake, you can't. Magic users won't tolerate this. My mother used to tell me a story about the Creator and the very first magic user, a sorcerer. The Creator was willing to destroy people because they weren't what had been designed. If our own Creator would disown me and seek to annihilate me, what would everyone else say? You can't tell anyone, Blake. Promise me!"

"Okay, okay. I promise your secret is safe with me. But what about finding an elemental who can help you with that side of things? You weren't trained in that strain so finding a tutor would make sense."

"I can manage it."

Blake narrowed his eyes. "Can you? You keep having these pulses . . ."

"They're just . . . they're just surges of power. I can get it under control. I can."

Blake closed his eyes briefly, wondering how he was going to make her see what she refused to accept: they needed help. He knew she was worried about her magic, but surely the benefits outweighed the risks?

"And you know what happened to Ben; we can't let that happen to other people, your family," she continued, playing on his weakness. When they'd finally made contact with the person who Kayla's parents sent all their work to, they decided to meet. Ben was using her parents' files and research to help others in the supernatural community, hiding them when possible.

But something went wrong.

Ben never showed up at the meeting, and three days later they received a rushed call from Ben saying he had been discovered and barely got himself and the information he possessed out in time. He was in the process of setting up a more secure base, and they all agreed to cut ties as Ben's work was too important and couldn't be risked. Blake and Kayla also decided to cut ties with everyone else. Including Michael.

Michael was one of Kayla's acquaintances, and she had met him while searching for Blake's family. Michael helped the Collins after they escaped from Oz and James, and if someone got to Michael through them, he didn't know if he'd forgive himself.

"I know all that, but it's been six months. Maybe someone can help us at the very least with research. We need contacts – reliable contacts – to find someone who knows about the original alliance. How are we ever meant to replicate what my birth parents tried to do before they were killed without knowing what that was? I feel like we're just throwing sticks in the air and hoping one lands and points us in the right direction."

Kayla sighed, nodding as she wiped a hand across her eyes.

"I get all that, but we can't. We can't risk your family. We can't risk the work Ben is doing for innocent people. We can't risk anyone knowing about my magic."

Blake was quiet for a few long minutes, mulling everything over. He didn't want to let her down, didn't want to disappoint her, but he was worried their time was running out. One of these days, their luck was going to land them in a hole too deep to dig out of.

"Okay, we'll continue with the plan."

Kayla sagged. "Thank you."

Blake supported her as she hobbled into the bathroom to wash, and he ordered some food from the on-site restaurant. Goodness knew they needed a hot meal.

After they ate, he lifted her into bed so he could grab a shower. At least she was moving better than she had a few hours ago, which meant the pain medication was kicking in.

He faced the stream of water, welcoming the heat, and ran his hands through his collar length hair. Bracing his arms against the cool tiles of the shower cubicle, he sighed.

The magic hunters were catching up with them more often and becoming harder to shake. Of course he was worried about himself – they wanted to kill him, after all – but what he feared most was what they would do with Kayla. They wanted her magic. They knew what she could do, and he was convinced they'd go to extreme lengths to extract it out of her.

His heart still skipped a beat whenever he thought about the time they'd caught Kayla. Some sort of magical spell had begun by the time he was able to get to her and seeing her in the middle of the painted circle, writhing in agony, had brought his wolf out so fast he'd erupted there and then.

He injured several of their group and killed one before he was able to drag Kayla out of the circle.

He shook his head. The water turned cold, so he shut it off and got out. When he swiped a hand across the fogged-up mirror, he was once again struck with how different he looked.

For years he had coveted the muscle he so desperately tried to gain. Now he knew that he'd struggled because his shift had been delayed, a side effect of the decision his adoptive parents and Kayla's made to protect him. Ultimately, it had caused major difficulties with his first shift, as his wolf became too strong for the spell. He turned away from his reflection and the more defined face he saw there, struggling to match it to the boy he was before he'd met Kayla. There was nothing that would make him regret meeting her, but he struggled to make peace with how . . . unbothered his wolf was with taking lives, no matter how justified.

He pushed open the bathroom door. Kayla's deep breathing told him she was asleep, so he tiptoed across the room to check the locks.

As he put his dirty clothes in his pack, her heart rate soared and her breathing became rushed; he sensed her distress and moved over to her bed, sitting on the side.

She was having a nightmare again. They were fairly common over the past few months and he hated watching her go through it, knowing she was troubled by the deaths of her parents and the deaths of the shifters she'd caused. It didn't matter how many times he told her they deserved it and she'd done it to survive, the guilt still gripped her tight. Not that he was one to talk.

Sitting on the edge of the bed, he placed a hand on her shoulder, hoping to coax her out of the nightmare.

"Kayla? Kayla? Wake up, it's just a dream," he whispered, not wanting to shock her. She stopped breathing for a second and then sucked in a sharp gasp, sitting up lightning-fast and hitting her head against Blake's.

"Ow!" she exclaimed, and he flinched. He knew his head would be fine, being a shifter and all, but she'd probably develop a bruise from the knock.

"Sorry, I, err, you were having a bad dream again. I wanted to wake you up," he said, suddenly conscious of how close he was to her. She bowed her head to rub it, almost resting against his chest. He didn't say anything, but he didn't leave either, not while her heart was still hammering.

Eventually, she spoke. "Sorry."

"Don't be."

"I didn't mean to fall asleep."

"You need sleep. We had a busy night," he replied gently as he turned to move off her bed.

"Wait!" she blurted out. Her head snapped up and her wide eyes met his as she grabbed onto his arm. He stopped and looked down at her. "Um, don't . . . can you . . . stay?" she whispered, looking away as her cheeks bloomed bright red.

They'd been through the same routine dozens of times, and she was always nervous to ask him to sleep next to her. Normally, he just knew and neither protested; the fact that she was asking meant the nightmare had been bad.

"'Course, but my hair's still wet from the shower."

"It doesn't matter," she said.

He lifted up the thin duvet and clambered in as she scooted back to the edge. While the bed wasn't a single, it wasn't quite as wide as a double, and he was a shifter, so he was naturally larger than average. When they'd first started bunking together he worried about squishing her, but she'd admitted that she felt safer wedged beside him.

"They need to make bigger beds, don't they?" he asked, hyper-aware of how close she was. They lay on their sides facing each other; it was the only way they fit in the small bed with his size.

She sighed, and when she spoke, she sounded much more relaxed. "Thank you."

"You're welcome."

"You never ask me," she said, and he frowned, not sure where she was going. "You never push me to tell you about my dreams, the bad ones. You're just there . . . I also want to apologise for earlier. You're so patient with me, and I feel like you always have to do what I want. I'm just scared, Blake." She cast her eyes downward.

"I'm scared, too," he whispered. "I don't like hearing your heart beat that fast and I can – I'm not sure how to say this – I can smell your distress, which gets me agitated, so I'd rather you not re-live what you just went through for the sake of being nosey. All that matters is that you feel better again. I'm sorry I made you feel that way."

"It wasn't you, and I do. Feel safer that is. Your senses are coming along nicely. Makes me feel protected," she said snuggling a bit closer. She folded her hands under her cheek.

Blake chuckled. "I'm hardly going to be winning the shifter of the year award just because I'm in tune with you. We've spent an entire six months together. If I didn't pick up on things about you now, I'd be a shitty friend."

She'd been watching him closely, but her face clouded over, and he didn't know why.

"Friend," she said, sounding puzzled. Judging by her expression, she didn't even know why she was confused.

"Yeah, are we not?" he wondered, his heart the one now beating fast. What if she just saw him as the shifter Prince, a means to an end to fix the rift between the races?

"I like that better than acquaintances."

"I should hope we're better than acquaintances after everything we've been through," he replied in a low voice, and Kayla nodded, keeping her eyes on his.

One of his hands tucked under his head, mirroring Kayla. The other rested in the small space between their bodies. Her own hand moved next to his, but it took him a moment to notice he'd slowly been reaching his fingers over hers, covering her hand with his own. She glanced down at where their hands touched. Blinking in surprise, her heart rate began to climb again. Her eyes flashed back to his and they studied each other, neither ready for sleep but both content. It wasn't until he scented something different that he frowned.

"Are you okay? Your heart . . ."

Her eyes widened ever so slightly, but she nodded.

"Yes, I'm fine," she whispered, a little too high pitched. "We should sleep," she said, closing her eyes. He closed his, too, but he stayed awake while he listened to her pulse race. Gradually, it slowed to a steady beat. Her breathing levelled out, and he knew she was asleep. Once he was satisfied she wasn't having a bad dream, he drifted off.

CHAPTER THREE

KAYLA

Six months ago

"DANG IT!" BLAKE SHOUTED in frustration for the fiftieth time as he stalled the car – again. They'd managed to pick up the vehicle with cash a week after Blake's family had left them in the city to find somewhere safe to stay.

She knew his family was playing on his mind, but Michael said he'd contact them with news about their relocation the following week.

They'd purchased the car with the intention of driving where they needed to meet with people who claimed they knew about the original alliance. So far, they hadn't learned anything from the feelers they'd put out online, and they were still waiting to hear back from Ben.

"It's okay," she told him. "It's like, the fourth time you're driving." Luckily, they'd found an industrial estate to practise in, and as it was a Sunday, it was quiet. Blake had never driven before, and Kayla herself had only a few lessons from her father, but they both agreed Blake needed to learn in order to share the burden.

Getting them both a license, however, was proving to be tricky. She pushed it to the back of her mind; they were in no position to worry about that. It was a 'needs must' situation.

"I suck at this!"

"Well, I'm not exactly a driving instructor, am I? I've only had a few lessons from my dad myself! I think you're doing really well."

Blake leaned his forehead against the wheel and groaned.

"Can we call it quits for the day?"

Kayla sucked in a sharp breath in mock astonishment. "Absolutely not, Blake Collins! We do not give up! Plenty of daylight left. Let's get going."

She stared at him until he restarted the car and put it back into gear, and she smiled at him as he started manoeuvring the vehicle. He had this.

Four months ago

"HAPPY BIRTHDAY TO YOU! Happy birthday to you!" Kayla sang as she walked into their shared hostel room holding a tray of cupcakes she'd managed to buy without Blake knowing. Each one was lit with a candle.

Blake looked up from where he was lounging on the bottom bunk, surprise plastered all over his face.

"What's this?" he asked with a beaming smile.

"Oh c'mon, we're not letting your seventeenth go unmarked! Catching up to me now."

He rolled his eyes but sat up, clutching his side where he'd been hurt in a small scuffle the day before. They'd been followed by the same hunters for the past week or so, and when they had tried meeting a shifter who claimed to know about the Alliance, they were ambushed. They'd escaped, but the shifter thought he was being set up and attacked Blake, who hadn't been expecting it. Kayla's magic had immediately awakened the moment Blake was hurt, and she'd thrown the guy about twenty feet.

They high-tailed it out of there and they'd been lying low in the hostel ever since. The joint bathroom with everyone on the floor wasn't fun, but at least they had a room just to themselves.

"Are you going to make a wish?" she asked, holding the tray of store-bought cupcakes closer to his face. Blake obliged and closed his eyes before blowing out the candles. "What did you wish for?" Kayla asked as she bounced on her toes.

"I can't tell you! It wouldn't come true otherwise!"

Now it was Kayla's turn to roll her eyes. "Okay, superstitious boy." She handed him the tray of cupcakes and reached into her pack where she'd hidden his present. "Now, it isn't much, and it's not much of a gift at all, really, but I actually managed to find something for us for tonight."

Blake tried peering over shoulder, but she turned around with her hands hidden behind her back. "What is it?"

"You know that old piece of useless junk?" She bobbed her head in the direction of the all-in-one video TV.

"You mean the TV without an aerial and the ancient video player?"

Kayla nodded. "I managed to get us a video tape," she finished, pulling a rectangular box from behind her back.

"Is that an actual decades old video tape?" Blake asked in disbelief.

"Yep!" Kayla beamed. "It's not a modern movie, obviously, but I thought we could watch it as a birthday treat? I got popcorn, too, and there are a couple cans of lemonade stashed under the bottom bunk. They're probably warm now though . . ." she trailed off when she felt Blake fix his eyes on her. "What?" she asked.

He jumped up and hugged her, yanking her close and wrapping his arms around her middle, squishing her arms to his chest. "Thank you," he mumbled into her hair.

She relaxed into the tight embrace with a glowing smile. She'd been planning the surprise for a while, and it took a few deals with others in the hostel to get the video without Blake finding out. Spending the day without his family for the first time must've sucked, and she wanted to make him feel better.

"You're welcome. Ready to watch . . . *Dr. Dolittle?*"

"Sure!" Blake exclaimed, and when he pulled back, an excited, youthful look blossomed across his features. That had been her goal all along.

They grabbed the lukewarm drinks and the bag of popcorn and settled on the bottom bunk. Side-by-side, they watched the comedy about a man who could hear animals. It wasn't too bad actually, and they both needed the silly laughter and a carefree evening.

Kayla was peeling the paper away from another cupcake when Blake reached out and pushed the treat right into her face. Chocolate frosting went everywhere.

"I have frosting up my nose!" she spluttered, trying to frantically wipe it off her face. Any protests she made were drowned out by the deep, barking laughter pouring out of Blake. She grabbed a cupcake and smashed it against his cheek, catching the corner of his mouth. He froze, his laughter dying as he turned his head to face her. As he did, the stuck-on cupcake slowly slid down his cheek, leaving a trail of chocolate buttercream in its wake.

They stared at each other for mere seconds before they both doubled over in stitches.

"I can't believe you did that!" Blake managed between breaths.

"Me? You started it!"

"Tasted good though," he mumbled as he shoved the rest of it in his mouth.

"Well, I'm going for a shower," Kayla said as she got up from the bunk.

"Me too, but you go on ahead. I'll tidy this up for now."

"Are you sure? I can do that later?"

"Nah, you go while there might still be hot water left, because after I've been, there normally isn't."

Kayla smiled as she grabbed her shower things. "Too true. Okay, see you in a few."

She dashed out of the room and into the communal bathroom. A row of eight sinks sat under cheap mirrors to her right, and eight shower cubicles occupied her left. All four toilets lined the back wall. The sweaty, grimy smell made for an unwelcome greeting, and she grimaced. The boys never left it clean, and some of the girls weren't much better. At least with it empty she could get some peace and quiet. It had taken Blake far too long to feel comfortable with her going to the showers alone – not that she needed escorting anyway. She had her magic, and she was gaining more control with every week.

Sighing, she hung her towel and pyjamas on the hook inside one of the shower cubicles and stripped off her clothing. Dropping them in a puddle by the door, she turned the shower on and twisted the handle until it was swelteringly hot.

Steam curled its way around her aching body and she welcomed the heat, wanting to feel warm again. Since her parents died – and since she had taken a life when they'd found Blake's family – she was always cold. She only ever felt warm when she was near Blake, especially since his shifter heat was often ridiculous. Not that she was complaining. She actually enjoyed his heat. She enjoyed being near him, and that was something she would *never* admit to him unless the ground was going to open up and swallow her whole afterward.

Thinking of Blake, she couldn't help but notice how much he'd changed over the past couple of months. When he'd been injured by that shifter, she'd insisted on checking out his torso when he kept holding his side. She was half surprised her jaw didn't drop to the floor when he'd taken his shirt off. She'd frozen in her tracks. Unexpectedly stunned, she supposed. She knew he was getting bigger – buying new clothes had alerted her to that fact – but she hadn't quite realised how, well, *muscular* he was. He'd always been broad-shouldered, but now there was a well-defined 'V' shape to his body. It was the abs in particular that made her mouth go dry and her stomach flip. It had thrown her off guard and made her feel insanely self-conscious. He was growing stubble, too, which only made him look older than his seventeen years.

The attacks from both the magic hunters and the shifter who thought they were double crossing him, muddied her thoughts. She scrubbed her long chestnut-coloured hair clean, a scowl cutting across her face. No way was she letting her Blake go in blind to a new situation again if she could help it. She paused. *Her* Blake? What was she? A possessive wolf? She shook her head. Either way, he was too valuable to their mission for him to keep meeting strangers. Maybe she would have to meet them first and vet them, so to speak. She couldn't take the risk that someone was going to trick them or seek out Blake to kill him, not when Blake could be the key to uniting the races again.

She turned the water off and wrapped a striped towel around herself. Digging out flip-flops from her shower bag, she slipped them on and padded over to the sinks to brush her teeth. She wiped a hand over the fogged-up mirror and saw how unruly her hair was.

She finger-combed the waves and changed into her pyjamas, gathering her things to go back, but she stopped when she moved past the mirror and let out a long huff. It wasn't that she was nervous about going back to their room, but she was apprehensive. Her tired eyes and unruly hair were nothing to brag about. If only she could sneak in without Blake noticing.

Wait.

Why did she suddenly care what he thought she looked like?

She was being stupid. He was just Blake. Still the guy who brought light even in the darkest of their moments over the past few months. He was still just a teenage boy trying to figure out his path in life. He was still Blake.

But the almost kiss.

She closed her eyes and pushed the thought away. It had been two months. Surely it would have come up by now. It was probably just an 'in the moment' thing that he couldn't even remember because tensions had been so high. She shook her head.

As she opened their door, Blake looked her over, running his eyes down her body. It was a quick glance, nothing more than what he usually did to ensure she was okay, but his gaze made her shiver. Something deep inside her stomach clenched in response.

"You alright? Cold?" he asked, frowning.

"No, no, I'm good."

"If you're sure," he replied, his voice implying he didn't quite believe her.

She helped him finish clearing up before he decided to grab a shower for himself, and after checking that she was okay for the hundredth time, he left her on her own.

A sigh escaped her lips before she could stop it. What was she getting herself into?

Chapter Four

Blake

Present day

KAYLA'S ANKLE WAS MILES better after the previous week's attack, but the same couldn't be said for her mood. Being cooped up and 'useless,' as she'd mentioned a few times, was driving her crazy. She was going through her mother's journal, the one with spells, information, and contacts in it when he decided to go for a run.

"Hey, I'm going for a run. I need to use up some energy or something. Probably shouldn't have had that nap earlier."

"Or something," she repeated as she put the journal down. "You know you need to shift. I could find us somewhere safe and secluded . . ."

He shook his head. "Nope, not shifting."

"Gah! You're so frustrating. You have all this pent-up energy because you're not shifting regularly! You haven't shifted in like, four months! That's a long time for shifters to go without. Your poor wolf," she said, throwing up her hands in defeat.

"Leave my wolf alone. It's fine."

"He. Not it, he. And you forget that I know your wolf, sensed him when I removed the magic my dad placed on him. He wants to be out; why don't you let him? You seemed okay with the whole shifter thing, I thought."

"Yeah, well, that was when the stakes were pretty high."

"But the more you practise, the easier it will get."

"It still hurts, Kayla. The shift. I know that might still be the after-effects of what your dad did to me but . . ." He stopped himself, not wanting to voice his fear about the wolf and how easily it . . . killed. "I'll see you in a bit."

"Don't forget to–"

"Stay on the pre-approved routes, I know," he said softly as he shut the door.

The longer he ran, the clearer his mind became. He felt like he needed to do something, anything. Kayla would never admit it, but her magic was draining her faster than she could heal. He knew next to nothing about magic users, but his wolf sensed unbalance within her. Blake may not have been comfortable with his wolf, but he always agreed with the beast when it came to Kayla.

He ran a good few miles before starting to jog back, and while he did, he made a decision he hoped he wouldn't regret. They needed help. Specifically, Kayla needed magical help that he couldn't give.

Deciding on his course of action meant making sure he was out long enough for Kayla to fall asleep, so he ran all around the building they were staying in and even alongside the motorway before finally heading back.

The door moaned as he opened it, but he was relieved to see Kayla asleep under the covers. Quickly changing into clean clothes, he grabbed her mother's journal and then made his way back down to the lobby. The new receptionist was just starting the night shift.

"Hi!" he said brightly, and the older woman's face lit up.

"What can I help you with?" she asked in a pleasant voice.

"Just wondering if you had somewhere I could send an email?"

"Oh yes, not a problem. In the lounge area we have a few computers set up. They just need your room number to activate, and any charges can be settled up at checkout."

"Great, thanks," he replied when she beamed at him. He was just going to have to make sure he paid for the room when they left so Kayla didn't see the bill.

Blake made his way to the dimly lit lounge area, which was little more than a few couches and a TV. Along the far side of the room, a long bench with three computers glowed faintly in the dark. He made his way over and sat down at the furthest one. He wasn't entirely happy that his back was to the open room, but he hoped his senses would alert him to anything should they need to.

He flicked through the journal, landing on Michael's email address, and then created a new email account so he wasn't using Kayla's.

His fingers hovered over the keyboard. Was he really doing this? Was he really going against what Kayla wanted?

He started typing.

....

TO: Michael

SUBJECT: need a hand

MESSAGE:

Agreed upon secret phrase: wolfy boy. (I hate Kayla for that.)

Hi Michael, it's Blake. I know I'm using a different address, but I'm getting increasingly worried about Kayla. I think she needs an elemental's help with her magic; it's growing, and I don't think she has much control over it, but she would absolutely murder me if she knew I was messaging you.

We've been at this for six months now and nothing. We're no closer to finding out about the original alliance, and on top of that, we've managed to find ourselves the focus of a group of magic hunters who want to kill me and steal Kayla's magic.

I know we cut ties to protect you and the work you do, but is there anything you can do to help?

Blake

....

Blake folded his hands behind his head, puffing his cheeks out as he exhaled. His stomach churned viciously at the thought of Kayla finding out he'd asked for help, but it wasn't like he was telling Michael what she could really do – only that she needed help with her elemental magic, which Michael already knew about.

Ping.

He frowned. It was late. He hadn't been expecting a reply for hours.

....

TO: Blake

SUBJECT: re: need a hand

MESSAGE:

Blake! Thank goodness you're okay! Tell the Mrs it's not okay to just say you're cutting all ties and then disappear!

Agreed upon code phrase: Chester is the best.

As it happens, I know an elemental. He's pretty powerful, just incredibly annoying. I'll get a message out to him. He also works with a large group that has been steadily building relationships between the shifters and the magic users. He may be able to help, but he says there are issues within the organisation. He doesn't go into detail, and we keep mostly to business related matters. I'm not sure how safe it would be, but they're definitely on the side of an alliance, and I can ask him what kind of assistance he could offer. They have resources and manpower so they may be able to provide information about the original alliance.

And if her powers are becoming unpredictable, she needs training. Wyatt is the best I know. Unfortunately.

There is a powerful spell working on the both of you. I wasn't expecting to encounter such a protection spell, and I have no idea how you managed to find and convince a witch to do one, but at the moment, no one can track either of you. Are you able to disrupt it in any way so Wyatt can find you? It would be the safest way without sharing locations over potentially insecure lines.

I'll wait to hear from you.

Michael

....

Blake flexed his fingers and shot back a reply. He flipped through the pages of the journal, trying to find something he could use to interrupt the protection spell she'd done on them both. Little did Michael know that it was Kayla who had actually performed the spell in the first place.

He guessed the handwriting was her mother's, and on one page he read something about a pouch of herbs. He remembered that pouch. Kayla carried it in her pack. He also remembered when he had to give up some of his blood for it.

He shook his head as an unpleasant memory surfaced; he had a thing about his blood being used in spells – he couldn't explain it, but it gave him the heebie jeebies.

He just had to get rid of the contents of the bag, and then this Wyatt would be able to track them both.

Blake gulped. Kayla was one hundred percent going to kill him when she found out.

CHAPTER FIVE

BLAKE

TWO DAYS AFTER HE sent the email, he gave into Kayla's pestering, and they prepared to meet with a magic user claiming to know about the original alliance. Blake wasn't hopeful. It wasn't like any of their other leads had actually led to anything.

They sat outside a busy café after spending the morning roaming the area, scoping out places they could quickly escape to. They were meeting up with someone Kayla had found on a dark web chat for supernatural societies. He had yet to be convinced the whole web chat wasn't made up of questionably sane people.

Blake's leg bounced up and down; he wasn't too keen to be here after they were lured by the magic hunters last time, but it had been just over a week and Kayla was eager to carry on. She hadn't suspected Blake of anything yet, but he wasn't sure that made him feel any better.

The table they'd chosen was well-placed to look out for people approaching. Shoppers sauntered down the brick path between each row of shops, looking in windows at the large displays. Three different cafés lined the street, each with outdoor seating edged with hip height barriers advertising what goods their establishments had to offer. Kayla had picked a coffee shop to keep it casual.

A couple sat down at a nearby table, and he fought the urge to turn around and get a better look at them. High-traffic areas were good for disappearing into a crowd, but it also meant he was wary as hell.

"Why don't you use some of your shifter abilities?" Kayla asked, sipping her hot chocolate. Her words brought him out of his spiralling thoughts. "See if you can sense anyone heading towards us."

"I don't think I'm good enough for that yet."

"You can hear my heartbeat, though. Try it."

"I hear your heartbeat because I've been around you for a while. I know most of your–" He stopped abruptly. He couldn't believe he'd almost admitted that he knew most of her vital signs and scents. Kayla frowned but thankfully didn't press.

"Well, perhaps if you shifted more . . ."

"Kayla, please," he said. He wished she understood why he couldn't shift. He was too scared. What if he killed someone again, but this time, it was because his wolf liked it and not in self-defence? His wolf didn't seem to feel the same way he did about the casualties, and while Blake may not have been plagued by nightmares like Kayla, it didn't diminish the anxiety he felt. What if he shifted and hurt her?

"Okay, I'll stop pestering. I'm sorry," Kayla replied, holding her hands up.

They got to talking about other things and forgot, for a moment, that they were meant to be meeting someone who may have been at the Alliance when Blake was only a young boy. It wasn't until a new scent curled its way into Blake's nose that he stopped talking. Kayla immediately dropped her smile.

"What, Blake?"

"I can sense . . . I'm not sure. Magic's been used, but I can't tell which one. Like yours, but different."

"You can smell my magic?"

"Yours is pretty unique. This one smells like – maybe a witch?"

"A witch? The group that's after us?"

He sensed she was about to say more but a tall, broad-shouldered man joined their table. A thick scar ran across his cheek and his menacing leer pulled up on one side as he growled. A long battered brown coat did nothing to hide his intimidating stature. Blake had never seen him, but there was an air of familiarity about him.

"Waitin' for anyone?" the unknown man teased. Blake eyed the distance between the newcomer and Kayla. She leaned back, her face guarded.

"Depends on who you are," Kayla replied, flicking a quick glance towards Blake. He knew she didn't like the situation either.

"Well darlin', I'm not Richard. Unfortunately, he won't be joining us."

"Then we have no business with you," Kayla said curtly. She made to stand, but he clutched her arm, pinning it to the table. He must have been using some force, because Kayla winced and clenched her jaw.

"Shout, and I'll snap her neck. Lunge for me, and I'll snap her neck. Use magic, and I'll snap her neck." Blake growled involuntarily, low enough so others wouldn't hear but both the man and Kayla did. His eyes never left the threat. "Where did you get such a possessive wolf?" the man asked Kayla, jerking his head in Blake's direction.

"What do you want?" she whispered. Blake could hear the anger and the controlled fear just beneath her words – she wouldn't let the man know she was scared. That wasn't his Kayla.

"A little birdie told me that your wolf here might be the last in the Alastair line. That true?" He may have been asking, but Blake thought it was little more than wanting confirmation.

"Why do you care?" Blake spat. The man ignored him and kept his attention on Kayla. She tried to yank her arm out of his grasp, but he held on tighter, the skin going pale beneath his hand.

Blake sought to keep calm, but he could feel his wolf waking up, and this time, he wasn't sure if he wanted to force him back to sleep.

Kayla was in trouble.

Kayla needed protection.

The wolf's thoughts became his own.

"You ought to muzzle the dog," the man sneered, and Blake growled again. "Watch it, or I'll hurt her more."

Blake backed down, but the table groaned under the pressure of his grip.

"He's not a dog, and he's his own person."

The guy sniffed the air and blinked in surprise. "Well I'll be damned . . ." he muttered but then shook his head. "Enough of this. You'll both come with me. The wolf will walk ahead of us and listen to my instructions. The girl will walk by my side, and neither of you will do anything stupid because I'll snap her neck quicker than either of you can stop me. I know you haven't been with your powers for long and he just had his first shift, so let's not pretend you can get away. You can't. I'm stronger and faster."

He stood abruptly, pulling Kayla up with him. She stumbled into him, blinking against the pain, but when she looked at Blake, she shook her head. She wanted to play this out. Blake reluctantly moved ahead of them and followed the man's instructions. He hated not being able to see Kayla, but he listened to her heartbeat: fast, but consistent.

The man directed them out of the main street and towards an alley where they would be secluded. Blake couldn't see anybody else, and the noise of the crowd was vastly reduced – not that he could hear much over Kayla's racing heart. The path ahead was a dead end, so he turned around.

Kayla stood awkwardly next to the shifter who still had hold of her forearm, her face tight and pinched.

"When I heard what happened to my brother and nephew, I thought about finding those responsible and killing them," the man began, and both Blake and Kayla shared a similar look of uncertainty. "But then I was approached with a deal too good to pass up. Show me," the man ordered abruptly.

Blake frowned, not expecting the sudden command. "What?"

"I said show me – I want to see if you are the shifter Prince."

His mark. The man wanted to see his tattoo. Before Blake could decide what to do, the man's hand morphed and his fingers grew longer. Claws tore through flesh and dug into Kayla's skin. She gave a short cry of surprise as Blake watched her blood spill to the ground.

"Oh shit! You shouldn't have done that!" Kayla yelled as she turned to face Blake. Damn straight he shouldn't have done that.

Blake growled, pulling off his t-shirt and not taking his eyes off the man. Slowly, he turned around to show him his back. His wolf was straining to get out and protect Kayla, but Blake was trying to stay in control. While the man's grimy hands were still on Kayla, he wouldn't do anything to risk her, and letting his wolf out would lose him precious seconds while he shifted – seconds the man could use to snap her neck. He didn't doubt the promises the man made earlier.

"It's true," the man whispered. An element of awe climbed into his voice. Blake clenched his fists. The bastard was going to pay.

"What are you doing?" Kayla shrieked. Blake spun back to face them. The man was pulling a phone out of his pocket and typing in a number.

"Calling this in. I am going to get one heck of a bonus. Shame about you," he said towards Kayla. "You'd have been fun, but I'm hardly going to feel sorry for the low-life responsible for the deaths of Oz and James."

Blake reeled back in shock, but Kayla reached up and knocked the phone out of his hand. As she faced him, Blake shook off the revelation and let his wolf come forth. He was mid-change; faster than the last time he'd done it but still too slow. The man wrapped his free hand around Kayla's throat in obvious anger.

Twice now he'd let someone grab her neck.

Blake leapt towards the man in one bound. It was clear the other shifter let his anger get the better of him and momentarily forgot about Blake. That was all the opening Blake needed. Their attacker didn't have time to make a noise; Blake caught the man's arm in his jaws and tugged, hard. The two crashed to the floor as Blake tried to get his teeth around the man's throat.

Blake shook his head with the man's arm still locked in his jaw, but the man reached around and grabbed a fistful of Blake's fur. Using shifter strength, he yanked down, causing Blake to splutter and yelp. The man threw Blake off, sending him flying through the air. He rolled to a stop but sprung up to see the man coming towards him, the first signs of his shift evident. Distantly, he heard Kayla call out, and the guy flew sideways into the wall, sliding to the ground with a dazed expression.

Blake spun. Kayla looked at her hands, and he knew she'd used magic, but he wasn't sure what kind. He made a soft whine at the back of his throat to get her attention, and her head snapped up.

"I'm fine. We need to go." He noticed the tremor in her voice but let it go because she was right; they needed to get away from the scene as soon as possible.

CHAPTER SIX

KAYLA

KAYLA OPENED THE TINY window to their hotel room that overlooked the back of the property and wondered how Blake's wolf was going to get in. He hadn't changed back yet, and they couldn't exactly come into the room via the front door without scaring everyone in Blake's path. They were on the third storey, and Blake had to find a way up using the winding metal fire escape near their window. It hadn't been easy - she'd watched him to make sure he was okay, and he was finally perched just beyond their windowsill. He would have to take a leap to make it; the fire escape wasn't as close to their room window as she would have hoped.

She leant her head out. His white fur glowed in the moonlight.

"Blake!" she whispered. He stretched onto his hind legs, pawing at the window. His wolf eyes caught hers, and doubt flashed through them. "You can do this," she encouraged. He had to do this.

He crouched down again, huffed, and then sprung up, catching the ledge with his front paws, but his back legs scrambled at the brick wall.

"Blake!" she exclaimed as she reached forward and wrapped her arms around his hulking mass, yanking as hard as she could. Half his body squeezed in through the window with her arms tight around his furry neck. When he finally found purchase with his back legs, he pushed himself in. She fell backwards and he sprawled over her, furry limbs flying in odd directions.

His heavy wolf body knocked the breath out of her, but he quickly jumped up and checked her over, eyes alight with concern.

"That was close. You nearly fell!" she breathed.

He huffed.

"Are you going to shift back now?"

He continued to stare at her, his golden eyes so different from their normal colour, but he was the same Blake she knew.

"You can't, can you?" she asked softly, and he lowered his head. "Okay, well, let's not panic. Give it some time for the adrenaline to come down and then we'll see. You're not used to shifting frequently yet." She tried to sound confident, but she was worried, too. Blake wasn't shifting often, so of course he wasn't used to shifting back. That was it.

Blake sat back on his haunches, and she took that to mean he was going to try her suggestion.

She began tidying their room, which was already pretty spotless given their habit of leaving at a moment's notice.

"I can't wait till our lives are a bit more normal. When we can actually help people. I wonder if Ben's okay now?" She chattered away aimlessly. She stopped, realising she'd made the assumption that they'd still be working together after. And what exactly was 'after?' Who knew what that meant? She shook her head, not wanting to think about 'later' and glanced over at the wolf who sat with his head hung between his shoulders. His fast breathing made her own accelerate, and then he stretched uncomfortably, shifting from wolf to human.

Blake was crouching. He looked up, then glanced down at himself. He was wearing jeans, one shoe, and no top.

"Oh man!" he exclaimed.

"Nearly. Got a shoe this time."

"Can't wait until the effects of your dad's magic finally wear off," he said, standing up to his impressive height. He rubbed the back of his neck as he stared at the ceiling. She gulped, her gaze travelling across his broad shoulders, down his toned chest, and to his taut lower abs. She needed to snap out of it. He looked away from the ceiling, and her eyes jumped up to meet his straight away. "You okay?" he asked softly.

"Yeah, I will be. My dad could do telekinesis - move things with his mind. Not often. It was one of the last things he did before . . . well, just before. Guess I can do that now, too."

She looked down at her forearm and saw angry welts the size and shape of the man's fingers. The puncture marks from his claws were caked in dried blood. Blake came over and took her arm in a light grasp.

"Let's clean this up."

Blake led her to the bathroom and filled the sink with warm water. "Sit," he told her, gesturing to the side of the bath; she did as he said and held her arm out to him.

"It doesn't hurt that bad, honest."

"I know. You're too brave to admit anything else," he muttered. His eyes flashed to hers, filled with a knowing expression.

"Well, the marks will just match my other arm." As she said it, she pulled up her sleeves and studied the jagged scars running down the length of her arm. Blake's nostrils flared.

"James deserved worse than what he got," he said. Images of James and his father, Oz, swirled in her mind, and she had to tell herself they were both dead and gone.

She shrugged. "He's dead. That's good enough for me."

"He maimed you. Nothing will ever be good enough," Blake growled. She didn't like how it bothered him so much.

In truth, she, too, was bothered by the scarring, but she wasn't going to say that. Her arm was hideous. No one was going to look at it and find her attractive. She just had to accept that.

Blake finished wiping the dried blood away and inspected the marks.

"These aren't too bad. I imagine they will heal over time and won't leave a scar."

"Goody," she replied sarcastically, earning her a pointed stare. "What? It doesn't matter if anything else scars when I've got this monstrosity to deal with." She held up her scarred masterpiece.

"It doesn't matter what I say, does it? Nothing about you is a monstrosity, Kayla. Nothing."

He gently pushed her hair behind her ear and turned to clear the sink of the rust-coloured water. She didn't realise she was blinking back tears to begin with.

"When the shifter said nephew and brother, I wondered if he was, you know . . ." Kayla admitted, trying to push away the unfamiliar emotion tightening her chest.

"Related to James and Oz? Yeah, I couldn't believe it myself. I should have finished him off," he grumbled.

"You don't mean that."

"I do. He knows about us. He wants us dead, or at the very least you. I think someone was paying him to deliver me to them, or that's what it sounded like."

Kayla stood and placed her hand on his back as he cleaned the sink, offering comfort. "Regardless, we're not the monsters they are."

His eyes met hers in the reflection of the mirror, and a small smile pulled at his lips. "Wasn't I telling you the same thing not too long ago? That we aren't the monsters?"

Kayla rolled her eyes. "If you could listen to what I say and not what I do, that would be grand."

They both chuckled as they made their way into the bedroom.

"I've been thinking," she began. Blake glanced at her briefly to show he was listening while he rummaged through his pack to put on a spare t-shirt. "We were most definitely tricked. Whether it was the contact we were meeting, or Oz's brother, it doesn't really matter. I reckon we need Ben. I know I gave you such a hard time about it, and I'm sorry, but I've been thinking a lot and you're right. We need help. I feel like we're fumbling around in the dark and . . ."

"And?" Blake prompted quietly when Kayla stopped.

"My magic is too much. I was never trained in the elemental strain, and it's getting too big for me to manage. I'm scared of people finding out what I can do, scared of them wanting my head because I'm unnatural, but . . . I'm scared of the magic more." She bowed her head, ashamed and embarrassed at having finally admitted her biggest fears to him.

Blake engulfed her in a hug which she greedily accepted, leaning heavily against him, knowing he'd keep them both standing. Always.

When she leant back, she thought she saw a flash of guilt in his eyes before he blinked it away.

"I'll send a message to Ben tonight and see if he responds. We have that address to check out, too," she said. She was referring to one they got off another user on the dark web claiming her grandfather was at the Alliance.

"Why don't we check it out tomorrow, see if the guy there knows anything?"

Kayla nodded. "Yeah, sounds like a plan." The pair of them moved about, straightening up their small room in silence. "Hey, on the plus side you had some remarkable control over your wolf today, and you actually shifted. I'm proud."

Blake flashed her a shy smile. "Not amazing control."

"You won't shift in a public place. You proved that today. I've got faith enough in that."

"Unless–" he stopped short and began rummaging in his pack, she assumed so he could change out of his jeans.

"Unless what?" she asked curiously. Was that a blush on his face?

"Never mind. I'm changing. Turn around." She rolled her eyes but turned the armchair and sat in it, grabbing her mother's journal at the same time.

"Happy setting off early tomorrow? We'll need to check out of here first. The address is in a completely different county. It'll be several hours at least without traffic I'd say."

"No time like the present. We probably don't want to be around much longer in case Oz's brother comes looking again."

"Exactly my thoughts."

They shared a similar look of worry, and she didn't stop to wonder why Blake's was tinged with guilt.

CHAPTER SEVEN

BLAKE

THEY'D GONE TO BED early so they could get one more night's rest before leaving their brief safe haven. The slower pace they'd adopted while Kayla's ankle healed had been a welcome change and a stark contrast to their constant movement. He turned over in bed and sighed. He hadn't meant to wake up, and judging by the lack of natural light peeking out from around the blind, he guessed it was still night.

His eyes flew open. He couldn't hear Kayla's heartbeat or her rhythmic breathing as she slept.

"Kayla?" he asked, standing up, not seeing her in the other bed. She could easily just be using the bathroom, but something was causing his heartrate to accelerate.

He trusted his instincts.

He checked their en-suite before leaving the room, padding barefoot down the darkened hallway. He took the stairs towards the communal areas, and the old carpet helped to conceal his footsteps. There was no receptionist at the front desk, but even in the middle of the night, there was always someone on duty. Blake frowned. Muffled commotion greeted his ears the closer he got to the lounge. Running now, he threw open the door. Three large guys struggled in the room with Kayla. One had her pinned from behind, his hand over her mouth as they wrestled near the computer bench. His scarred face sneered at Blake when he entered. A blonde-haired man was trying to inject something into her arm. The last guy was trying to sit up, running a hand through his long brown hair, a dazed look in his unfocused eyes.

The blonde holding the syringe snapped his head towards Blake as the lounge door shut behind him; Kayla used the distraction to pour some power into him, pushing the needle away from her. It wasn't as strong as when she'd used the new power to slam their earlier attacker against the wall, but it was enough to force the guy away. Blake jumped on top of him. As the guy flew backwards, Blake was able to get him into a headlock, squeezing just enough to cause him to black out. Blake turned to the man Kayla was still violently grappling with, the would-be kidnapper struggling to keep a secure hold.

"Back away, wolf," the guy snapped breathlessly.

"That's not going to happen," Blake ground out, but Kayla's eyes went wide with alarm. The sharp click of a gun preparing for action made his stomach go cold.

"Gotcha now." The dazed guy from earlier pointed the gun at Blake. Kayla immediately stilled. "That's better, isn't it?"

"What sort of magic users need a gun?" Blake asked gruffly, scenting the air.

"We want her," Kayla's kidnapper said. "We thought grabbing her would make you more . . . acquiescent and that you'd come to us without a fuss."

Blake answered with a smirk, "Seems like you underestimated her then, didn't you?"

Both men barked with laughter, assuming they were the victors. Blake held Kayla's eye contact and then flicked his glance towards the water cooler to his right. Her brows drew together briefly and then understanding dawned. She closed her eyes and dropped one of her hands to her side. She flipped her palm towards the water cooler without either of the men noticing.

"Okay. What do you want to do now then?" Blake asked, trying to keep them busy and distracted while Kayla focused on her task. She'd been working hard on controlling her fire and water elemental powers. He just hoped she didn't let her magic pulse out.

"You're both going to come with us, no fuss, no noise."

"Or . . ."

"Really? Or I break her legs. That would stop her from running this time." The guy holding Kayla laughed and Blake couldn't help the growl that escaped his mouth. He clenched his fists, trying to curb his anger. That was twice in a short space of time someone had threatened to hurt Kayla. The guy's mouth made an 'o,' and then he laughed again. "I didn't know there was a possessive connection here. A magic user and a shifter? Pah, seen it all now."

Blake glared at him and sensed the change in Kayla's scent. It was subtle, but Blake noticed.

"There's just one thing," Blake said, bringing the guy's attention back to him. "She's stronger than you think."

Water broke free from the cooler and rushed into the air with force. Blake knew the gunman behind him was momentarily distracted and threw his elbow back. It connected with the guy's face, and the gun clattered to the floor. Spinning, Blake grabbed the gunman's head while he was stunned and slammed it against one of the sparse bookshelves behind him. The man went down, knocked out cold.

He turned to face Kayla but could only make out shapes through the watery curtain; he thrust his hand out, relying on instinct, and Kayla grabbed onto it. He pulled her forward and out of the room as water rained down around them. Shoving wet hair off his forehead, Blake slammed the door shut, but before he could run off, Kayla made a noise and hovered her hand over the lock. Familiar words met his ears as she spelled the door.

"Let's go," she said when she finished, moving water-logged strands of hair away from her face. As they turned down the corridor, two magic users appeared and made their way towards them. They recognised them as the hunters who'd been after them for weeks. "No, no, no!"

Without discussing anything, he tugged her hand and headed to the fire escape stairwell, but as they neared it, another user appeared from behind the door. Kayla barrelled into his side and they tumbled into their room. She spun on her heel to use the locking spell on the door but jumped back as fists pounded on it from the other side.

"We need to escape through the window," she said as she grabbed her pack.

"What?" he exclaimed. "I barely got in as a wolf!"

"Get changed, quickly. I'm not sure how long the spell will hold with other magic users trying to get through, and I'd rather not test it right now."

No longer caring about modesty, they stripped out of their sodden pyjamas and threw on clothes within seconds. Kayla lifted the blinds and opened the window, peering out.

"Looks clear, but you'll have to go first."

"Like hell. I'll go last in case they break down the door."

"But you'll be better getting to the platform below us to catch me, as there's no way I can make that jump on my own."

Blake knew she was right and clenched his fists in frustration. He didn't like it. "Fine," he muttered, snatching up the packs and swinging them out. They landed with a thud. He climbed onto the windowsill with his legs hanging over the edge. Kayla stood at his back.

"Be careful," she whispered. He nodded and pushed off just as more pounding thundered on their door. It distracted him, causing him to nearly miss the landing. "You okay?" she whisper-shouted. He put his thumbs up in response.

"Okay, now you," he told her. She climbed out like he had and sat on the ledge, legs dangling. She sucked in a deep breath.

"This is higher than I thought it would be."

"I know, but I got you," he reassured her, and they locked eyes. She took another breath and leaped off towards him.

He stretched out and grabbed her arm as she fell, pulling her into the shelter of his body. His arm circled her waist and held her tight, their breaths mingling, and the racing drum of her heart matched his own.

"You caught me," she whispered.

"Always," he replied breathlessly. The hammering grew louder, distracting him. "They're close. Let's go."

Blake led them down the winding metal fire escape and onto the concrete at the service entrance of the hotel.

With his enhanced senses, he breathed in the scents of several magic users in the area, searching for them. He took Kayla's hand, and she grabbed it without protest. They stayed low to the ground, skirting the edge of the building.

It was a clear path, and they wound their way to the car park, which, thankfully, was packed full. Their car was old and needed a key in the handle to unlock it; if it had been one of the modern ones that beeped, it would have alerted their attackers.

Kayla threw her bag in the backseat and climbed over the driver's side with Blake at her heels. Both hunkered down and were as still as possible. He blew out a breath, his hand on the key in the engine.

"You ready?" he whispered, knowing as soon as he turned the key, the car would roar to life and give away their position. She clicked her seatbelt on and nodded.

Blake twisted the key into action and revved the car, eager to get away. Shouts of alarm echoed through the lot. As they neared the exit of the hotel and the road to the motorway, Kayla flipped through her mother's journal. She twisted in her seat to look behind them and repeated words in the foreign magic language. Blake flicked a glance in his rear-view mirror, and as the magic users ran for their vehicles, the cars sunk.

"Did you deflate their tires?" he asked, swinging onto the motorway without being followed.

"Yeah," she replied weakly. He looked over at her, and under the lights of the road he saw the colour rapidly drain from her face. Her eyelids fluttered closed.

"Kayla? You okay?" he asked, worried, knowing he couldn't really afford to stop the car.

"I'll be okay, promise," she muttered, and then fell back against the seat, eyes firmly shut.

"KAYLA!"

His shifter abilities told him she was okay for the moment – unconscious but with a steady heartbeat – but part of him knew it was her magic. Something wasn't working, and it was eating away at her. If it wasn't the power surges, it was the drain of all her energy.

The guilt he felt at having contacted Michael was replaced by the hope that this Wyatt would find them soon and get her the help she needed. He didn't know what he would do without her.

CHAPTER EIGHT

BLAKE

HE DROVE ALL NIGHT and into the sunrise while Kayla slept. If it wasn't for his ability to keep tabs on her heartrate and breathing, he'd have stopped and forced her awake somehow, but he was trying to do what was best. Her body clearly needed sleep if she'd passed out, and they'd already planned to leave and make a stop at the address they had been given anyway.

Looking at her scribbles in the journal, he checked he was headed the right way, grabbing the map while he drove to make sure. His eyes darted from road to map and up to the road signs again in quick succession; he estimated about another hour or so and then he'd be in the right area.

His next debate was if he should wait for Kayla to wake up, or if he should meet the contact without her. In theory, the guy didn't know they were coming unless his granddaughter had alerted him that they might be on their way, but at least he didn't know when Blake and Kayla would be showing up. That put the ball in their court as far as he was concerned. But what if the guy was dangerous? Part of him wanted to keep Kayla away from any potential harm, but the other more practical side told him that having a powerful magic user with him – albeit one struggling to control her magic – would be better. Plus, she would absolutely kill him if he went without her, and he was already racking up a list of reasons she should.

Luckily, he didn't have to make the choice. A few miles later, she stirred beside him. He looked over as she stretched as much as one could in a car seat, and then she frowned, surveying the road before settling her gaze on him.

"How long was I out?" she mumbled sleepily.

Blake's sigh of relief was instant. "Just over four hours. It's nearly seven in the morning."

"Jeez, can't believe I was out of it for so long," she said. She sat up straight and looked at the journal and map on his knees. "You're driving us here?"

"Yeah, I figured we were going to be doing that anyway, and I didn't feel comfortable stopping to contact Ben, so this was the next best thing."

"Brilliant, thank you," she sighed, leaning her head back against the headrest. "How long left?"

"Maybe an hour or so. Was going to stop for breakfast soon and hope the smells enticed you awake."

Kayla's stomach chose that moment to rumble; she covered it with her arms, turning to look at him sheepishly.

"Breakfast sounds good!"

He pulled up at a popular chain restaurant to get something quick and easy. They both needed a stretch, so they went into the building to use the toilet facilities before ordering.

Blake stood in the queue, arms crossed over his chest, studying the menu options on the screens when Kayla joined him after using the bathroom. She did her usual quick inspection of the building and nodded, satisfied they weren't followed.

He was deciding between two options and was leaning towards a third option of just getting both when she moved closer, her body almost flush against his side.

"You okay?" he whispered, looking down. Her head was tipped towards the floor but she nodded, bumping into his arm. She pressed a hand against her forehead, which worried him. He unfolded his arms so he could comfort her, rubbing his hand across her shoulders. "Food and drink will do you good, replenish some energy," he said, hoping he was right. She nodded again but didn't look at him.

As the queue moved forward, he automatically reached down for her hand and gripped it to keep her close. She didn't protest, and if anything, clutched his hand a little harder.

He ordered way too much, hoping she just needed some decent calories in her, but as he went to pay, he picked up a subtle change in her scent. Magic. Her eyes closed as she breathed in deeply.

He grabbed their bag of takeaway breakfast and towed her outside, questioning her as soon as they were moving towards their car.

"What's wrong?"

"My magic. It built up while I was asleep and it needs releasing," she said. He opened the car door, but as he turned to face her, she climbed over the barrier and stumbled into the wooded area behind the restaurant.

"Kayla!"

She didn't stop. He cursed as he threw the food in the car and raced after her. It didn't take long to catch up. He grabbed her upper arm to stop her and turned her to face him. Her skin was pale and clammy. "What are you doing?"

"I need to release it. The surge. It's too big to keep it down!" A trickle of fear edged into her sharp tone.

"Okay, but don't run off to do it," he snapped, harsher than he meant to.

"I can't," she cried, trying to pull out of his grip, which was useless with his shifter strength. "Go back! I don't want to hurt you!"

"You won't. Just release it."

"No! Please, Blake! The surges are getting worse. I don't know what it'll do!"

"I'll be fine," he said as calmly as possible. She continued to panic and resist him.

Kayla shook her head. "Go away! I don't want to hurt you!" she screamed again, squeezing her eyes shut.

Blake reached out and framed her face in his hands, remembering the time he had to calm her down when they first went on the run.

"Kayla, your magic won't hurt me. I trust you. You just need help to control these outbursts, but you will not hurt me. Do you understand me? I trust you, and I'm not leaving you alone right now, so you have no other choice. Release the magic before it consumes you, Kayla. It's causing you pain to hold it in, isn't it?" he asked, and without opening her eyes she nodded. She gripped onto his wrists. "Then open your eyes and trust me, okay? You have this."

She breathed out and slowly opened her eyes, panic running rampant in them, but he gave her a small smile and nodded, trying to encourage her. It would do no good to admit he was a little worried about what would happen if she didn't release the magic. That thought overpowered any residual concerns he had for his own safety.

Kayla concentrated and breathed in and out. Her hands tightened on his wrists to keep him close, but he wasn't going anywhere. Absent-mindedly, his thumbs stroked along her cheeks where his hands rested on either side of her face.

She took one more deep breath in and released the magic. A wave of power flew from her and through him, disturbing the nature around them. He prepared for it and stood his ground as the magic washed through him. It took him a moment of concentration, but then it was over.

"Are you okay?" she asked breathlessly.

"Yes."

"Thank God," she replied, opening her eyes and watching him closely. "Did it . . . did it do anything to you?"

He smiled reassuringly at her. "No, I think it knew I meant no harm because it's an extension of you. You don't have to be afraid of it, Kayla. You just need some help learning how to control a powerful part of you, which is understandable. You were never trained in elemental magic, let alone how to wield all three."

"I know, I know," she whispered. "Thank you for staying with me."

"You know I'd never leave."

Kayla nodded and then pushed herself in close, wrapping her arms around his middle and pressing her head against his chest. He draped one arm around her shoulders and moved one to the back of her head, stroking her hair as she calmed. He tuned into her heartbeat and was relieved to hear it slowing down from its dangerously fast pace. He wondered if his would follow suit.

"I'm okay," Kayla mumbled against his chest. Did she hear his own racing heart?

They made their way back to the car, hand in hand, neither commenting on what had just happened. Blake's pulse had settled as Kayla's had, but it was still an adjustment getting used to being so . . . connected with someone else.

She flashed him a smile when they reached the car, and the trust she placed in his hands was a welcome burden. He knew he wouldn't let anything happen to her.

"Breakfast?" she queried, peering into the brown paper bag. Drool-worthy aromas wafted through the air and both their stomachs growled in anticipation. He reciprocated her smile.

"You bet," he replied, digging into pancakes as they reminisced about their first morning on the run together, eating the same meal.

CHAPTER NINE

KAYLA

DAYLIGHT SURROUNDED THEM, FOR which she was grateful, because the dark, gothic-looking house that sat before them in the middle of nowhere gave her some serious haunted vibes.

"Are you afraid of ghosts?" Blake asked, mirroring her thoughts like he so often did.

"Um, I wasn't," she replied, wrapping her zip-up jacket tighter around her body.

"Reckon my wolf can sense, you know, spirits?"

Kayla shrugged. "Ready?"

"Yeah, why not? Just walk up to the freaky looking haunted house and ask some old dude some questions about a massacre twelve years ago. Totally normal thing to do on a sunny morning."

Kayla smiled at his commentary as they climbed the five steps to the door. The front windows had thick curtains hiding the inside of the house from view. Blake went to knock on the peeling door, but as he did, it creaked open.

"Oh man! Did it have to whine?" Blake muttered, peering inside. He was probably able to see further than she could with his wolf abilities. It was so dark in there.

"Mr. Renolds?" she called out in what she hoped was her most welcoming, cheery, non-threatening voice. She shared a glance with Blake. "Do we go in?"

"I don't want this to be a wasted trip, so we should go inside, but . . ."

"But what?"

"Stick by me? We need to be able to protect each other or leg it if we need to."

She nodded. "Wasn't going to suggest splitting up in there," she said, a shiver tearing through her body.

Blake stepped over the threshold and called out for Mr. Renolds once again. Kayla followed, staying close to Blake.

The musty scent of dust and stale aftershave wound its way up her nose, the kind a grandfather might have bought fifty years ago. As she stepped into the entry, she could make out oval frames fixed on the floral papered walls and a dresser with a crocheted mat on top. Silverware was arranged on a tray in the middle, unused. For decorative purposes, she imagined.

"Do you detect anyone here?" she whispered at Blake's back as he tipped his head, listening.

"No, but . . . my wolf thinks there is," he replied, frowning. "Could magic be blocking his presence?"

"Would be pretty powerful to block a shifter's senses."

"Yeah, that's what I'm worried about. I don't hear anything, but my wolf is really agitated, pacing. I think someone is through the door."

Kayla nodded at him and he slowly entered the room.

The open space in front of them spanned the width of the house, and the small kitchen was brighter than the entryway thanks to a pair of large windows looking out on a back garden. She still couldn't see much of the outdoors as the glass was caked in grime, and overgrown foliage crept around the cracks in the panes.

The room swept out to the left into a conservatory of sorts with wicker furniture and large windows that were equally hard to see through. The large patio door was open, and as they moved towards it, she heard muttering.

"Quiet! No, I said three. Not two!" a deep scratchy voice said. "What do you mean? The cat is always green."

Kayla frowned. A grey-haired man hobbled back and forth using his wooden crutch for support. A baggy cardigan hung off his small frame. He held out his hand, pinching his thumb and forefinger together repeatedly as he shook his head.

"No, no. That won't do. Let's get you in the basket," he continued, making no sense whatsoever and certainly not speaking to anyone.

Blake cleared his throat in the doorway and the old man looked to them both, a frown etched deep into his weathered face.

"Can I help you?" he asked, seemingly un-phased by their presence in his house.

"Um, we're sorry. The door was unlocked and we wanted to speak with you, if that's okay?" Blake asked, trying to hold his body in the least threatening way he could, which was quite a feat considering his muscle. Luckily, the jacket he wore hid a lot.

The man's face lit up. "Jolly yes! Let me make you some tea! Come! Come!" he called as he bustled past them and into the kitchen.

He brought over a tray with three teacups, placing it on the small coffee table in the middle of the wicker furniture. He took a single armchair while Kayla and Blake chose a double sofa. Kayla was still wary; the man seemed to accept his unexpected guests without question.

The man gestured at the tea, nodding his head eagerly, so Kayla leaned forward and grabbed a cup. She paused as she lifted it to her mouth. Just as she thought: It was empty.

"It's good tea, yes?" the man asked, eyes bright.

"Oh, yes, thank you," she replied, unsure of how to respond. Blake frowned into his cup but smiled at the man in thanks. "We were sent here by your granddaughter actually."

The man's face quickly soured at that. If it wasn't for the man's obvious age, Kayla would say his expression closely resembled a toddler's.

"What does she want? She is no good. No good. Do you know what she tried to do last time she was here?" he asked and waited for them to guess. Blake shook his head. "She wanted to move my things! Wanted to get a professional cleaner in! But that's not nice for Molly, is it? How rude!"

"Who's Molly?" Kayla felt compelled to ask.

"Shh. She knows who you are, my sweet," the man said, gazing into the corner of the room.

Blake and Kayla shared a tense look. She wanted to move this along.

"Look, Mr. Renolds, we were hoping you might have some information about an event that happened twelve years ago. Your granddaughter claims you were at the original alliance?"

Mr. Renolds froze, his face screwing up in anger.

"Get out," he said quietly.

"So, were you there?" Kayla pressed and Mr. Renolds jumped up with more agility than she was expecting. Both Blake and Kayla followed suit.

"Get out!" he shouted. "We don't speak of it! Don't come here talking to me! They'll find us! You hear me? They'll find us!"

He hobbled closer to them, stopping with a frown.

"Okay, well thank you, Mr. Renolds. It was great talking with you," Blake hurriedly mumbled as he reached for Kayla's hand. As soon as he did, the old man gasped, clutching at his chest.

"You!" he cried, pointing at Blake. "You're the heir! You're the heir! You'll get us all killed!"

"We're sorry to have bothered you."

Kayla tried to stay put. "Yes! He is! He is the Alastair prince. What happened at the original alliance? We need to know."

The man's eyes moved to her face, and he squinted before taking a step back. "What are you?" he screeched.

"I'm a magic user, like you."

"No! You're – you're not right. All of it. All the magic inside you, crushing you. Crushing you dead! Your magic should be abolished. Kill her! Kill the unnatural!" he screamed and moved for them again.

She froze, unsure of what to do, but Blake pulled her back. The man whispered some foreign words and sparks flew in the room. Kayla yelped, covering her face with her hands.

A bolt of lightning struck the bookcase behind her, sending splinters of wood raining down on them both. The acrid smell of burnt paper singed her nostrils as another bolt sped for her face. Blake yanked her aside just in time, tucking them behind one of the useless wicker chairs.

"A little help here, Kayla!" he moaned at her. She looked at her hands.

"He's an old man. I could kill him."

Blake waved his hands manically as his face took on a look of shock.

"Duh! He's shooting lightning bolts at us! Now is not the time to worry about hurting him!" Kayla growled as she closed her eyes and tried calling on her magic. "Not too much," he added unhelpfully. She shook off his comment and drew on her mage magic, specifically the telekinesis she must have inherited from her dad. Or at least, she thought she was pulling from the mage well.

"It's not mage," she whispered. Blake put his hand on her shoulder and pushed her down further when sparks flew overhead.

"What?" he asked, rolling his shoulders back.

"Don't shift! The magic might attack!" she ordered, letting the magic free. The taps in the sink rumbled and water jetted high into the air. The man yelled and cursed, stumbling wildly before he screamed. Chaos reigned as he shot lightning around the room.

"What have I just walked into?" a strange male voice asked. Kayla peeked around the corner of the furniture. A familiar blonde magic user stared at the pandemonium and tracked the mess back to Mr. Renolds. A younger woman stood next to Wyatt, her short dark hair gelled back. She elbowed him and pointed at the old man.

"Witch. Powerful one."

"Wyatt?" Kayla muttered, and Blake peered around her shoulder to see.

"You know Wyatt?" he asked. She frowned.

"Do you?"

"Abomination!" the old man cried. He whispered more foreign words, but Wyatt directed the water cascading from the taps at the man. At the same time, the woman behind him mumbled a spell and the man stopped in his tracks, falling to the ground in an unconscious heap.

Kayla and Blake slowly got to their feet, with Blake angled slightly in front of her.

"You Wyatt?" he asked.

Wyatt looked at the dishevelled pair and his eyes went wide. His mouth dropped open, earning him another elbow from his companion.

"What's up?" she asked, eyeing them suspiciously.

Blake turned his head to Kayla when Wyatt made no move to speak. "You know him? How?"

"How do you?"

"I don't, he–"

"Killian?" Wyatt stammered. Shock slackened his companion's face.

Kayla readied her magic, no longer worrying what strain she managed to grab onto.

"How do you know that name?" Blake asked warily, and Kayla was glad he didn't outright confirm his identity.

"You're Killian," Wyatt responded, running his hands through his hair. He let out a laugh that turned into a whoop of joy. "Jesus, Mia, this is Killian!"

"I heard you the first time but . . . this dude?" She frowned, throwing her thumb in Blake's direction. "Really?"

"Hey!" Blake retorted.

"Blake, shush!" Kayla snapped. Mia narrowed her dark brown eyes.

"You called him Blake."

Wyatt threw his arms out, a massive smile plastered on his face. "Well, of course, he's hardly going to use his birth name, is he? I cannot believe this!" He grinned, but his smile fell a moment later. He leaned over, hands on his knees, and groaned. "Oh, I can't believe this. What did Michael get me into?"

"Michael? What's Michael got to do with anything?" Kayla questioned.

Wyatt stood back up. "Michael asked me to track you guys because you needed help. I knew it was you, Kayla, but I didn't know he also meant Killian of all people," he answered, gesturing to Blake. Kayla frowned.

"How did Michael know to send you? How did you get over my mother's protection spell?" she asked, her mind working overtime. She glanced over at Blake, who refused to meet her eyes. "Blake?"

"Who's this?" Blake asked, pointing to Mia and ignoring Kayla.

"Hey!" Mia exclaimed. "I'm the witch who tracked your asses and helped out with your little problem." She smiled curtly, tipping her head at the unconscious old man.

Kayla wrapped her arms around her middle. Her magic swirled, reacting to the emotions she felt churning alongside the power.

"I'm confused," she muttered. "That spell is water-tight, powerful."

Wyatt didn't respond. Kayla closed her eyes, fearing that when she looked at Blake, she'd see guilt. Blake placed a hand on her elbow, trying to turn her to face him, but she stayed firm. Thankfully he didn't use his shifter strength.

"Kayla, you know we needed help. You even admitted so yourself!" he tried to justify.

"And that would have been a decision we made together. This was you deciding for me. We said we were going to . . ." she stopped just before she mentioned Ben, but she knew Blake would understand.

"I'm sorry. I thought I was doing what was best," he replied, his voice low and strained. She didn't dare look into his eyes.

Wyatt clapped his hands. "So look, this sort of complicates things a little. Mia and I work together a lot on Michael's cases, but bringing you to the compound probably isn't a wise option."

"Too right," Mia confirmed, and Kayla frowned.

"I thought Michael sent you because you help both sides?" Blake questioned.

"Yeah, we do, but you're Killian."

"What?" Kayla asked. "Why does that matter? What do you know?"

"Kayla," Wyatt began, but Mia's phone rang and she stepped out to answer it. "Look, Kayla, I didn't know you were with Killian, I never did. Michael didn't shared that information with me."

"He didn't exactly know who Blake was in the first place," she answered.

"Well, that explains that. I was gonna be having his ass for keeping that major detail from me," he said, smiling. She responded in kind. She'd forgotten about Wyatt's humour. They'd crossed paths months ago at Michael's, when she'd gone looking for information on where Blake's adoptive family had been taken.

Blake coughed, drawing her attention back to the conversation at hand. "So we've established that I called this in, but how do you two know each other?" The slight edge of pain to his tone hurt her, but she was glad he, too, felt like she had kept something from him.

She finally allowed their gazes to collide. "I met Wyatt at Michael's."

"You didn't tell me."

"Not nice, is it?" she responded, harsher than she intended. His eyes softened, but she stepped back. "It wasn't important at the time; we were busy being kidnapped if you remember? And after that, I just forgot. Unlike some people, I didn't deliberately keep it a secret."

Wyatt gasped dramatically. "I'm forgettable?"

Mia walked in and smirked. "And then some." He turned to her and laughed.

"What's up?" he asked, motioning to the phone she still held in her hand.

"The taskforce is calling me back. We need to make a call on what to do."

"Taskforce?" Blake asked.

"Probably not the time to go into that right now, Killian."

"It's Blake," he said tersely.

"Sorry, Blake," Wyatt corrected. "Well, we were called because Kayla needed help with her elemental magic."

"Yeah, she was never trained in it."

"Interesting. I had a feeling she was quite strong when I first met her. She actually created fire."

Mia gasped, turning to face Kayla. "No way! Dude, that's impressive! Oh. But Marcus?"

Wyatt scratched his chin. "My original idea was to bring her in and help her without Marcus finding out. I didn't want him knowing about her skills."

"Marcus?" Blake interrupted.

"Our leader," both Mia and Wyatt blurted out as they continued their conversation.

Kayla's thoughts tumbled haphazardly. People knew about her. Earlier that morning it was just her and Blake, but now she had Michael and Wyatt and Mia and this Marcus to worry about. Too many variables. Too many people who could find out about her magic.

Power roiled within her, swirling like a violent vortex as she struggled to grapple with her emotions. Betrayed. Out of control. Her mind spun and her magic grew wilder, demanding to be let loose. She winced, and Blake immediately turned to her.

"Kayla?" he asked, voice full of concern as he forcibly turned her to face him. "Magic?" She nodded.

"What's happening to her?" Mia asked.

"Um, part of the reason I asked for help. She's powerful, but she doesn't know how to control it yet."

Kayla groaned and put a hand to her head, rubbing her temples.

"How does it feel?" Wyatt asked as he came closer. He stopped when he looked at Blake. "Can you describe it, Kayla?"

"My head feels like it's going to explode. The magic . . . it's deep in here," Kayla answered, placing a fist over her middle.

A growl in the doorway had all of them spinning to the kitchen. The shifter who attacked them earlier, Oz's brother, stood in the doorway, a maniacal grin on his face.

CHAPTER TEN

BLAKE

"OVER HERE!" THE SHIFTER shouted over his shoulder. "Look what I found!"

Wyatt forced the water jetting out of the tap into the shifter's face, and while he spluttered, Mia kicked him in the stomach. He flew backwards and she slammed the door shut, muttering a quick incantation over the lock.

"Out the back, now!" she ordered.

Blake placed an arm around Kayla's waist and followed Wyatt, with Mia right on their heels.

They skidded to a stop when they burst onto the driveway and saw four shifters.

"Nige! Here!" one called out to Oz's brother.

"How many can you take?" Wyatt asked under his breath.

"Without my weapons? I'll still take my chances," Mia responded, clearly not afraid of a challenge.

"Can't you make them sleep like you did to the man in there?" Blake asked.

"Unfortunately, doesn't work on wolves."

"Helpful."

"Quite."

Kayla moaned and tried to bend over, but Blake held her up.

"She really is struggling, isn't she?" Mia questioned. Blake nodded.

"Alrighty then, fight it is," Wyatt murmured, rolling up his sleeves and cracking his neck. "Blake, you stay back and protect Kayla, okay?" And then Wyatt whirled his hands around to attack as one of the shifters shed his human skin. Mia raced forward, muttering a spell under her breath.

Blake pulled Kayla to one side, knowing his shifter strength would help Wyatt and Mia. Kayla paled beside him, her eyelids drooping.

"Kayla? I've got to join the fight. Can you stay here?" he asked quickly.

She nodded as she moved to the lamppost, resting her head against the cool metal.

"Go, help them," she whispered. He reluctantly stepped away and shifted, clashing with one of the wolves. He was certain it wasn't 'Nige,' but he threw his weight into the shoulder of the tan wolf approaching Wyatt, bringing him down easily. Coppery liquid burst into his mouth when he clamped down on the wolf's shoulder. Mia had already taken one to the ground, so that left . . . a scream punctured the air.

Blake looked over and growled as Nige grappled with Kayla in his human skin. Blake's wolf stood up, hackles raised. He padded closer with Wyatt and Mia not far behind him. Nige said something, and even though his wolf wasn't paying attention to the words, he heard the tone.

Deciding he couldn't help Kayla with growls, he shifted back, standing tall as his glowing eyes focused on the threat.

"What do you want?" he ground out, his voice still rough and raw.

"I already told you. Revenge for my brother and nephew – justice!" Nige spat.

"Where was the justice in what they did?" Blake asked.

"They were following orders. It's the natural way of things. What you're doing here? Working with magic users," Nige sneered the word. "It's abhorrent. Unnatural."

Kayla's breathing hastened, and for a brief moment her eyes flashed silver; he wondered if he'd imagined it, but Kayla screamed, forcing Nige's arm off her. His eyes grew wide and his mouth gaped open as Kayla turned her back on Blake. She grabbed at Nige's clothing and shoved him hard, but instead of tumbling to the ground, he flew backwards and hit the base of a tree that lined the opposite side of the road.

Kayla crushed her hands to her head and turned back to Blake, her face screwed up in pain.

"Blake," she whispered. He moved forward, but her eyes snapped open. "Stay back!"

"Get back!" he yelled to a confused Wyatt and Mia, but he was too late. Kayla expelled the force that had been building inside of her. Nige's body erupted in flames, and Blake saw Wyatt and Mia stumble backwards and hit the ground, but they were otherwise okay. He gritted his teeth as he pushed against the force trying to take him down, and he was just able to stay on his feet when the pulse subsided.

Kayla swayed.

"What was that?" Wyatt exclaimed. Blake wasted no time, using his shifter speed to reach Kayla as she swayed dangerously. He opened his arms as her knees buckled, catching her and lowering them both to the ground. He made sure Kayla was secure in his embrace, and he brushed the hair from her clammy forehead as he took in her pale face and shallow breathing. Her eyes darted from side to side under her eyelids.

Wyatt and Mia's footsteps pounded on the concrete.

"Is she okay?" Mia asked, breathlessly.

"I don't know. I think this is the worst I've seen her."

Wyatt moved to place a hand on her forehead, but he froze a few inches away. "I'm just checking her over," he said slowly, and it took Blake a moment to realise he'd growled.

"Sorry, I . . ."

"No need to apologise," Wyatt said as he completed his assessment.

Mia blew out a breath. "She set the shifter on fire and knocked us on our asses. How did you stay standing?"

"Not without difficulty, but I think . . ."

"Think what, Blake? It could help us with her," Wyatt urged.

"I think her magic somehow recognises me, or recognises my wolf. I don't know. The closer I am to her, the better I'm able to help."

Mia and Wyatt shared a quick look.

"Interesting," Wyatt murmured. "I think we should bring her back with us, to the compound. We have healers, and I can train her in elemental magic – I know she needs that."

"I sense a 'but' coming."

"Marcus isn't right in the head. We've been working around him, worried about how he leads. I don't think it would be safe for you, especially knowing that you're Killian, as he's been looking for you for ages. He wants to complete the original alliance."

"Wait. He knows about the original alliance?"

"This is dangerous. For both of you. Do you know what he would do to Kayla if he found out how powerful she is and how . . .?" He trailed off.

"What? How what?" Blake prompted, but Wyatt and Mia shared another look. "What are you guys hiding from me?"

Wyatt shook his head. "Now isn't the time. We need to figure out a plan for Kayla. She needs a healer before I can help her. Mia, do we have a healer with us?"

"No. We nearly have Heidi, but it's taking time."

Blake frowned in confusion. "You're not making any sense. Kayla and I have been searching for information on the original alliance so that we could try and replicate it somehow. If this Marcus has that information, and you have people there who can help Kayla, then surely it's a win-win situation?"

"No, it's not that simple. The original alliance is what will put Kayla in danger. Now that I've seen . . ." he stilled, looking to Mia. "Now that I've seen what I've seen, I think taking her there is too dangerous."

Before Blake could argue and question more, Kayla moaned and arched her back, her breath coming out in short pants. He clutched her closer.

"What's happening to her?"

"The magic is eating away at her control, her mind. Magic is good, but it needs training. She needs a healer to soothe her mind long enough for me to teach her control. I'm one of the best elementals you'll meet, so I can help her, but we need a healer first."

Kayla cried out and gripped onto Blake's shirt.

"You say it's dangerous, but what happens if we don't go?"

Wyatt's eyes dulled. "The magic will consume her completely."

Blake didn't need him to clarify what that meant as he held her close.

"It's worth the risk; we'll be careful. Can you help hide how powerful she is from Marcus? If that's causing some of the concern, can we conceal it? Protect her?"

"We can try. We have Heidi. Hopefully she can help us with that," he replied, looking for confirmation from Mia.

"She's certainly our only hope of keeping Kayla's power quiet. I'll speak with her."

Blake lifted Kayla and carried her to Wyatt's car, which looked just as old as their own. Mia offered to drive theirs behind them. Questions about the Alliance and Marcus sat on the tip of his tongue, but he didn't dare ask them. He was close to answers, and those answers worried him. More than that was the overwhelming sense that a change was coming – a change he wasn't sure he was ready for. He looked down at Kayla sleeping restlessly in his arms and he knew whatever they were about to head into was worth it. If it meant he could help Kayla, like she did for him, he'd do it. He'd give the world to her if he could, and that . . . that was the thought that terrified him the most.

CHAPTER ELEVEN

KAYLA

GREY MIST MOVED AROUND her in an elegant dance, bringing comfort to the infinite darkness.

"Hello?" she called out. No response, yet again. Kayla huffed. She certainly didn't feel threatened, but she wasn't a fan of her current environment, either. Something told her she was dreaming, but how could she be so lucid in a dream about nothing?

Light seeped into the dark, and as she looked up, an image emerged. A luscious green forest. A cottage with a thatched roof nestled between protective trees. A swept path winding through the woods, deeper than Kayla could see.

She stepped toward it, and the darkness behind her receded. Tranquil music trickled through the air: birds chirping happily, water running, light laughter. Kayla followed the sounds around the back of the cottage. A young woman laughed at the antics of a man in simple woven trousers and a tunic as he danced around a small vegetable patch like a fool. He looked only a few years older than she; his face suggested he only danced for her smile, his eyes bright with wonder and love.

The woman pulled up her long woollen skirts to kneel while her sparkling blue eyes continued to laugh. She tucked long blonde hair behind her ear and shook her head as she pulled carrots from the ground. Her tanned skin suggested she was often outside, tending the garden.

"Oh Edmund, you silly fool. You'll trample the leaves!" the woman's lilting voice sang. Kayla smiled at the carefree nature of their attitudes.

"Pfff. I can easily grow some more for you, my love," he replied, kneeling in the patch he had stepped over. He hovered a hand over the crushed pile, and Kayla witnessed the leaves healing and growing. The woman smiled warmly. The man must be an elemental.

"Sometimes it's nice to do things the long way. You learn more."

The man flashed her a brilliant smile as he lifted her basket of carrots. "The magic flows through me as natural as my breath." He kissed her lightly on the lips and followed her towards the back door. Just before they entered the cottage, a long, drawn-out meow drew their attention.

Hopping around the side of the one storey building was a grey tabby, holding up its small front paw. The man, Edmund, immediately went to the cat's aid, swooping the feline up as he examined his injury. The woman cooed and fussed over the creature while Edmund held the paw in one hand, uttering a spell.

Kayla gasped, "He's a witch too!" It took her a moment to realise she'd said it out loud but neither turned to look at her.

"Yes, he is," a regal tone announced. Kayla jumped as a woman appeared beside her, her honey-coloured skin in stark contrast to her bright silver eyes. A cool shiver traced down Kayla's back as she froze in place. No physical force was exerted upon her, but she felt the opposing push and pull of the unknown woman. "Who am I?" the woman questioned as if Kayla had spoken from her lips. "I'm nobody and everybody."

"What's that supposed to mean?" she asked, but the woman simply smiled at her and then turned her attention to the couple as they fussed over the affectionate cat. Kayla couldn't put a finger on the woman's age. She looked young and old at the same time. How was that possible?

"Oh, everything is possible," the woman said with a glint in her impossibly silver eyes.

"How are you reading what I'm thinking? Is that mage magic?"

The woman snorted in disdain. "Please, Kayla," she lightly chastised.

"How am I not surprised you know my name?"

"Because you learn, and you do so quickly. Observe. Tell me what you see," the woman commanded with a wave of her arm. Kayla had never felt such desire to follow an order, even as she knew she was being judged.

"I see a man and a woman. It looks like the past?"

The woman nodded as she spoke. "No questions. Just tell me statements. Facts."

"Okay. We *are* in the past, and there is a man who can do at least the elemental and witch strains of magic. I'd wager he can do all three."

"You'd guess? Or you know?" the woman prompted, a little infuriatingly.

Kayla blew out a breath. "How could I know? You know what? Yes. He can do all three."

"Familiar?"

Kayla froze.

How could the woman know that?

Of course she knew. She knew everything else.

"Afraid?"

Kayla gulped. "No," she lied.

The woman smiled. "Good. Now watch."

The scene changed to the inside of the one room cottage. A fireplace simmered gently and a rudimentary bed of wooden slats, straw, and linen blankets lay near the flames. A wooden table and chairs sat next to a work bench, which held many of the vegetables Kayla had seen earlier. The woman was weeping in front of the fire as the man argued with an unseen force. If anything, he appeared to be looking where they stood.

"Don't worry. He can't see us here now."

"What are they upset about?" Kayla asked, unable to focus on anything but the fear and sadness in the room.

The woman beside her said nothing, but when the man fell to his knees, hands clasped tightly together, Kayla knew he was begging. But for what? He gestured wildly at his partner as she wept by the fire, rocking back and forth.

Kayla gasped. "He's the first sorcerer. This is when he begs the Creator to let him keep his child – a child he wasn't supposed to have. He ended up with three. Each child had a strain of his magic."

"You know the story," the silver-eyed woman stated.

"Why am I being shown this?"

The woman waved her hand, and the scene drifted away in the wind; Kayla found herself in darkness once again. Grey mist snaked around her feet as the woman focused her attention on Kayla. Kayla turned to face her, mesmerized by her striking eyes.

"What do you believe about the Creator?"

"Um," Kayla blinked in surprise at the question. "That they made a mistake. Something unnatural happened, and the Creator had to alter it, change it, so it could continue to support our way in the world."

"And what is that 'way in the world'?"

Kayla drew her eyebrows together. "To look after it? To protect the weak?"

"There you have it. Your answers to everything."

"My answers to what now?"

"Everything can be answered by what you have just said. Let me ask you something else. Do you think the Creator is weak?" The weight of her eyes bore down on Kayla. She gulped and shook her head. "So why do you question so often? Is your magic a curse?"

Kayla shrugged and mumbled, "Sometimes."

"You'd wish it away?"

Kayla thought for a moment. "No," she said, feeling more confident.

Ice-grey eyes smiled down on her. "Tell me, why is your magic a gift?"

"Because without it I wouldn't have met Blake, wouldn't have the opportunity to help him and the supernatural community."

"And this Blake, he's important to you?" the woman asked, a small knowing grin skirting the edges of her lips.

"Incredibly," Kayla answered. "To everyone, that is," she clarified.

"But everything requires balance. If this Blake is important as a shifter," she explained, giving Kayla a quick glance, "then there must be an equally important force in a magic user." Kayla frowned.

"If you mean me . . ." she trailed off.

"Can anyone else do what you can?"

"The sorcerer can. And look what happened to him! He had to beg the Creator for forgiveness – for love! I'm not meant to be. The powers were divided for a reason."

"And they are combined for a reason. Ever thought of that?"

"But why? Why me?"

"Why anybody, Kayla? Why Blake?"

Kayla growled, much like Blake would. "You are incredibly frustrating!"

The woman laughed. "As I intend to be. Nothing is worth it if it is easy. The Creator knows that the path, the journey, is just as important as the end."

"Well, the path we're on is certainly not easy. You seem to know everything. Can you tell me what the original alliance was about? Can you show me? We don't know how to build a bridge between the two sides; if we knew what the original alliance was, maybe we could recreate it."

The woman glanced away, and when she looked back, her eyes were clouded. "No. I cannot show you. You are not ready."

"How is that fair?" Kayla shouted.

"You have to understand. The Creator 'creates' and sets things in motion, but how they fly, how they grow and manifest? That's entirely up to you: the shifters and the magic users."

"But if the Creator is so powerful–"

"Powerful enough to respect free will, Kayla," she replied sternly.

Something her mum once said came back to her. *"What if the Creator gets it wrong again?"* She'd asked her mum.

"Do you want to know a secret? I think the Creator knew exactly what they were doing all along."

"Why?"

"Free will. I'll explain it to you one day, but free will is so important to humans."

"But Mummy, we're magical, not human!"

Her mum chuckled again.

"My mum once spoke about free will," Kayla murmured to herself.

"Wise woman."

Kayla was quiet for a moment. "Why are you here? In this dream?"

"Because you were losing your way faster than others could help you find it again," the woman replied, in the softest tone she'd used yet. "And like I said, you are as important as Blake. You have a role. A purpose, and I want you to find your way there. I can't show you. I can't take you there. I can only guide you."

"Free will?"

"Free choices."

Kayla nodded but frowned as voices entered the atmosphere. "What's happening?"

"Healers. You'll be pulled from this deep part of your subconscious soon, but just remember: You are important. You are here for a reason, but you also have choices. I trust you'll make the best ones you can."

The darkness began to lift, the mist fading.

"Wait!" Kayla called out as the woman drifted into the darkness. "Who are you?"

Her silver eyes smiled as she chuckled. "You already know."

Kayla blinked as strange artificial strip lighting flashed above her. A face swam into view: Wyatt? And then an older female with light hair leaned over her, frowning as she checked Kayla's pupil responses. Somewhere in the distance, she swore she heard Blake's gruff voice. She fisted her hands and found them full of soft linen. Was she lying on a mattress?

"Bluh shif ooh?" Wait. Did she just say that?

"Come again?" the older woman asked, squinting brown eyes at her.

Kayla coughed. "Blake?" she tried again, opting for a singular word.

Blake's worried face appeared above her, eyes searching hers. He finally gave her a small smile.

"Hey," he said softly.

"Where?" Kayla asked, keeping to singular words while her brain tried to catch up.

"Wyatt bought us to the compound so a healer could help you. Wyatt said he'd train you in elemental magic so you can control it better. You scared us," he admitted quietly.

"I did?"

Blake nodded. "Passed out and wouldn't wake up."

"I'm sorry."

"Don't be. You feel better?"

Kayla frowned and searched for the answer. She didn't feel as overwhelmed, that was for sure, and while she felt foggy, like she was struggling to wake up, her mind was clearer than it had been for ages. She sighed.

"Much."

A door banged open as someone rushed into the room.

"Hate to break up the party, but Marcus is coming," Mia rushed to say as she came to stand by the bed.

Kayla reached for Blake's arm and pulled herself into a sitting position. Her body felt weak, but she was happier, more at peace. They were in some sort of medical bay, a curtain cutting off the vast majority of the room. Four concerned faces watched her.

"What? What is it?"

Wyatt gulped. "Marcus isn't the best person for us to be around. I was hoping we could avoid him knowing I was back. Damn it!" he quietly cursed, rubbing the back of his neck. "Heidi, thank you for your help. Don't worry about him. I'll take this, okay?"

The older woman smiled tensely and nodded as she wrung her hands together.

Kayla turned her head to face Blake and had to look up so she wasn't talking to his chest; he'd moved closer when Mia barged in. "What's going on?" she whispered.

"Um, I made a decision for us and I'm sorry, but I had to get you help. Just stick by me and we'll be fine. Wyatt says Marcus is dangerous and we cannot trust him, but he may have information we need."

Kayla nodded, trying to absorb what she could.

"Remember," Wyatt instructed. "Kayla needed help because she is untrained. No mention of how powerful she is." He looked to Heidi, whose face was uncertain, but she nodded as a man entered the room.

CHAPTER TWELVE

BLAKE

THE GUY WAS BUILT, with dark brown hair cropped close to his head and a serious frown on his face. Blake guessed he was in his early thirties. The man stared at Blake wide-eyed before lowering his gaze.

"Luke!" Wyatt exclaimed, his tone loud and unsure.

"Marcus wants to meet you and the newcomers in the lounge area," he told them, his voice gruff. He turned and exited the room.

"The lounge area?" Kayla questioned.

Wyatt sighed and turned to Heidi. "I think you're off the hook, but be careful," he told her. Heidi left the room with eager steps. "You didn't see when we brought you in, but this compound is actually a repurposed hotel. Meets all our needs with large communal rooms like the lounge and dining area, plus lots of accommodations and rooms we can convert to offices. We work here side by side with shifters, supporting our community, looking for an alliance." Kayla shot Blake a look, and he fought the urge to squirm. What wasn't Wyatt saying?

"Okay then, let's go," Kayla announced, sliding off the bed.

"Woah there. Let's take it slow, okay?" he said to her.

"If he has answers, let's go get them."

"No!" Mia and Wyatt answered in unison.

"What? Why? I'm fed up with this!"

Wyatt rubbed the back of his neck as he huffed. "Please do not push Marcus. We're not sure how far he'll go if he recognises certain things, and you absolutely cannot tell him about your magic. You need to maintain that you are just an untrained elemental who I happened to come across. He cannot know we met months ago."

"If he's so dangerous, why do you stay?"

"I have my reasons, one of them being that we can do good work here by bridging the gap between our communities."

Kayla sighed. "Fine. Fine. I'll follow your lead."

Blake put his arm around her back and was both surprised and relieved she didn't shrug him off. Mia grabbed their packs and followed them out of the room.

The group made their way down a short corridor and into a lobby. As it was night, it was quiet and empty. Dim night lights, placed strategically around the large space, cast a delicate golden glow. Blake could just make out wide circular disks on the ceiling – he assumed those lights would be brighter if they were on.

Narrow hallways branched off the main room and an unused reception desk was littered with leaflets and flyers, but the great expanse of the pale lobby held no other furniture.

Wyatt led them across the marble floor and through a set of double doors to a bar.

Even though Wyatt said it was a hotel, Blake hadn't expected their base of operations to look so . . . hotel-like. Kayla swivelled her head as much as Blake's arm would allow, no doubt checking for potential exits.

A bar stretched along one side of the room, and sofas and coffee tables were scattered throughout. The sofas sat opposite each other or curved in 'U' shapes, giving the bar a somewhat homely appeal, which surprised him. The only lighting came from the bar area, which had a blue strip light running along the back cabinets and small touch lamps glowing softly on the tables. As they made their way towards one set of sofas, the doors opened behind them and two men and a girl around his age entered the room. One of the men was Luke, the guy who told them to meet there in the first place.

"Wyatt, you did it!" the other man gushed, his eager green eyes standing out against his dark skin. He stepped forward and clapped a hand on Wyatt's shoulder. Luke stood behind them, crossing his hands in front of him with his feet slightly apart. Was he another guard? Blake had seen a fair few when they'd come in earlier, but Wyatt had taken him in another entrance to avoid seeing too many people.

Blake kept his arm around Kayla's back as she tucked in close. She looked better and definitely had more colour, but he was eager to have her sitting again as she continued to gain strength.

"Still alive I see," the young girl with Luke and the man Blake guessed to be Marcus quipped towards Wyatt. Athletically built and nearly as tall as Wyatt, she shared a familiar resemblance to the man who spoke. Her green eyes sparked with anxiety.

Her thin joggers, baggy shirt, and messy ponytail indicated she'd been dragged out of bed with little notice.

"Still annoying I see," Wyatt snapped back in the same tone.

"Children!" the man shouted, his exasperation clear. "Please!" He shook his head and the wide smile returned. "I'm Marcus. It's nice to see you again, Killian." He smiled as he stepped forward, extending his hand.

Blake frowned. "How do you know Killian?"

Marcus retracted his hand. "I recognised you of course, and we've been looking for you for years."

"Shall we sit? Kayla still needs rest," Wyatt interjected, and Marcus frowned.

"Oh. I'm sorry. Do you need any medical care?"

Before Kayla could answer, Wyatt jumped in. "No, no, I was able to grab a healer to help her. She just needs some more formal training in her elemental abilities."

Kayla smiled apprehensively as Marcus studied her. Blake's arm tightened around her back, his wolf whining at the way Marcus assessed her.

"It's Blake, by the way," he announced, taking Marcus's attention off Kayla. Marcus raised his brows. "And this is Kayla," Blake continued.

"Ah yes, Kayla, you must be the girl we've heard about, the one staying with . . . Blake."

"The one and only," she remarked, and for a moment, it reminded Blake of the attitude she'd displayed to him and Josh at school when they first met.

"Mmmm, shall we sit then?" Marcus gestured to the plush chairs. Blake helped Kayla to the sofa and glued himself to her side, their bodies touching. Good. While he didn't sense immediate danger, he was wary of new people and wanted her close in case they needed to scram. His wolf approved of the contact regardless of any danger they might have been in.

Marcus and the girl sat across from them. Wyatt perched casually on the arm of the sofa and Luke, who'd yet to speak, stood behind him.

The girl scowled at Wyatt and then scooted over as much as the space would allow, composing herself by crossing her legs and resting her hands on her knees.

"This is my daughter, Imogen," Marcus began, which explained the similarities between the two.

"Hi," she said. She quickly glanced at Kayla, but then focussed her gaze on Blake. It made him feel uncomfortable. He didn't like being the centre of attention. Put him on the field to captain a team, fine. But here? Not so much.

"My daughter and I, along with Wyatt, have spent years looking for you because we want to end this war between the shifters and the magic users."

Blake shifted, pressing his leg against Kayla's. "I know people think I can. Even Kayla thinks I can, but what is it that I'm supposed to do? I'm just one person." He didn't want to outright ask him what the Alliance was, as he trusted Wyatt's opinion of Marcus more than ever. His wolf had been on high alert since meeting the guy.

"You're so much more than one person, Blake. You're the last of the Alastair royal bloodline – a very powerful bloodline. Why don't we get some sleep? It's late, and you need to heal. We can discuss our next steps tomorrow. You will stay with us, won't you?" Marcus asked, and Blake turned to face Kayla. She was the one who came up with the plans, and he'd made enough decisions for them both the past couple of days. She studied him closely for a few moments before nodding.

"Yes, we'll stay. We want to do our part," Blake said. Marcus's grin spread across his face, but Blake swore a hint of sadness and disappointment flashed across Imogen's.

"Fantastic! We'll get you set up in your rooms within the hotel. Luke? Are they ready?" He addressed Luke behind him while Blake helped

Kayla to her feet.

"Yes," was the one-word reply as they made their way out of the lounge towards a lift. They all piled into the small, crowded space and moved to the penultimate floor.

Wyatt seemed bored, and Blake wondered if it was an act. Kayla shot him a worried glance. Did she sense the same tension he did?

"All of our guests stay on this floor, just as a precaution. There are more people for them to pass if they mean us harm, but more of us to help protect our guests should they need it," Marcus explained when Kayla studied the floor number. Blake was more concerned with how unusually quiet she was. As the lift rose higher, Imogen and Wyatt spat angry, juvenile insults back and forth.

They stepped out onto the floor and walked only a short way before stopping. The walls had more colour up here: beige with flecks of gold. The carpet was patterned, beige again with green leaves woven into the design. It was clearly old.

"Here are your rooms," Marcus said, gesturing to the two rooms opposite each other. Kayla's body tensed beside his. "You can lock them from the inside. Luke is your go-to guy if you need anything. He's also on this floor; his number will be next to the phones in your room, but please note, for safety, that the phones only go to other rooms in the hotel – you can't dial out."

"I'm sorry, Marcus, but Kayla and I will be sharing a room," Blake said confidently. Marcus spluttered.

Wyatt stepped in. "They have just spent six months working together, Marcus. Let them acclimatise."

"It's a safety thing," Blake explained, using Marcus's earlier excuse.

"They can share." Luke spoke properly for the first time, and Blake wondered why the guy had suddenly found his voice. Marcus looked bewildered, but after a nudge from his daughter, he nodded.

"Yes, yes, I suppose that's okay for now. The rooms are twins."

"Have fun!" Mia saluted, handing both backpacks to Blake.

Marcus let them in, and Luke moved to the lift as Kayla turned to shut the door. Enclosed in their room, Blake squeezed next to Kayla to rest an ear against the wood. The voices were muffled, but he closed his eyes to focus his shifter hearing.

"Well, what did you think, Marcus? It wasn't exactly a bonded pairing, was it?" Wyatt accused.

"Shut up, Wyatt," Imogen snapped. Marcus mumbled his response as they got into the lift.

Kayla left him by the door to listen, and when the voices faded, he shuffled past the bathroom and into the main room. The walls were a plain, off-white colour, and the dark grey carpet looked cheap. There were two single beds, a desk, a TV, and a coffee making station complete with a mini kettle that wouldn't have been out of place in an actual hotel.

Kayla sat on one of the white beds.

"Thanks," Kayla said when Blake joined her.

"Wasn't going to let them split us up," he answered, dumping their packs on the floor between them. He fell onto the other bed and groaned. "Okay, these beds are far superior to any we've ever slept on!" Kayla was quiet, and he turned his head to study her as she sat deep in thought. "Penny for your thoughts?"

"I was just . . ." She stroked the covers and threw herself back, settling into her pillows. "Yep, you're right. These are *much* better!"

CHAPTER THIRTEEN

KAYLA

KAYLA WOKE UP THE next morning to the sound of the shower running. She rolled onto her back and raised her arms above her head. The past couple of days had been one heck of an emotional rollercoaster ride. Escaping the hunters who were after them, passing out because of her magic, losing her grip on her magic *again*, having the old man call her unnatural, Wyatt, the dream she'd had – it was all too much. Had she really met the Creator? She was struggling to process it all, and she'd be lying if she said she wasn't confused.

Wyatt wasn't sure about Marcus, but he probably had the answers they were searching for. She would continue to hide her magic from the others so she wouldn't be a threat, but she didn't know what Marcus's problem would be. She wasn't entirely upset, though; hiding what she could do with her magic was the best scenario. The less people knew about her abilities, the better. The woman from her dream came back to her, bright silver eyes chastising her with a single look.

Kayla sighed. How was she meant to be important if she couldn't even control the magic she was given – assuming the Creator had given her all three strains of magic in the first place and she wasn't just some freak of nature. Could she really help Blake more if she opened herself to her power? What if people turned her away, cast her and her unnatural magic aside?

Kayla shook her head. No. Hiding her power was the best thing to do. Wyatt's reasons may have been different from her own, but the result was still the same. Besides, the compound was surely the best place for Blake to be. There was a whole faction of people there dedicated to bringing the supernatural races together. If Marcus had knowledge of the original alliance, then they could act. They could bring about another alliance and work together with the groups who wanted peace. This could work. With or without her.

So why did she feel so hollow inside?

When Blake had insisted on them not being separated, the strength of her relief surprised her. She hadn't realized how much it would hurt to lose him, even for the evening. They were finding out what their roles would be later that day, and she was terrified. Was it because she didn't want to leave Blake?

As she contemplated why her heart was racing at the thought of no longer seeing him, which was puzzling enough as it was, Blake stepped out of the small bathroom with just a towel around his waist. Water ran in rivulets down his broad, muscular chest – muscle she knew he'd worked hard to achieve before his first shift had given it to him naturally – and his hair flopped over his forehead into his eyes. The thick, water-logged strands were almost black in the low light. He pushed his hair back, squeezing out the water, and the motion made his arm muscles flex. She gulped, thankful for the duvet covering her face.

What. The. Actual. Hell.

Was she developing a crush?

They'd never really discussed the near kiss they'd shared when they were captured six months ago; she just thought it was because it was a spur of the moment thing and they'd been busy since. But now, she was beginning to wonder if she'd deliberately pushed it to the back of her mind. He probably didn't feel the same way she did, otherwise he would have brought it up. Surely? Did he feel like she was a burden? What could she offer him now that Marcus couldn't? Doubt consumed her.

"Kayla? Your heart is . . ." He didn't finish, but she knew it was racing. She took a few deep, calming breaths and tried to push her worries to one side. They had to figure out what they could do for the Alliance.

That was the focus for today. Where she would be after that? She'd worry about it tomorrow.

"Yeah, I'm fine. It's just been a crazy couple of days." She sat up in bed, feeling calmer. She hoped her heart rate didn't betray her.

"Good." Blake smiled, reaching for another towel in the wardrobe to dry his hair with. She giggled at the shaggy dog look, which drew a wider smile from him in response. "You look better."

She stretched. "Feel it. Whatever that healer did, it was magic." He stopped and stared at her, and she laughed. "Yes, yes, I know it was actual magic." She rolled her eyes.

Blake grew serious. "We just have to watch your magic around the others while we get what information we need and judge if the people here can help us. We won't stay if it puts you in danger. If you feel your magic building again, get to Wyatt so he can help before the others find out . . ."

"You didn't tell Wyatt?" she asked, her voice going small.

"No. I'd never do that. But I think, if we need, we can trust him. He knows how powerful the elemental side is in you and he can help control that side at least." He was so honest, and as he looked her straight in the eyes, her stomach tightened. She jumped up and grabbed some clothes from her pack. "I'll go get showered and dressed, and then we can figure out where we get breakfast." She left quickly, brushing past a half-naked Blake to get into the bathroom. They'd been in small spaces before, why was it hard to breathe in one now?

When they left the room a short while later, Luke was exiting his own room down the hall. He moved towards them and even gave a small smile, which was a marked difference from the seriousness of last night.

"Everything okay, Prince Killian? Kayla?" he asked. She was shocked that he both remembered her name and called Blake 'Prince Killian.' Blake shifted uncomfortably.

"It's Blake, please, and yes. Thank you. We were just looking for some food."

"Forgive me, and yes, of course. Follow me." He turned tail and called the lift.

The lift doors opened to reveal another shifter; both Luke and the newcomer shared nods as the three of them entered the lift and Luke pressed the ground floor button.

"This is Mal," Luke said, introducing the second shifter. He was impressively tall, like many shifters were. Unlike Luke, Mal's hair was straw-coloured and long, tied up high in a bun. Blake nodded in Mal's direction, and he returned it with a grin.

"Thanks for supporting us last night," Blake said to Luke, filling the silence. "We just feel safer this way."

"It's all right. I could tell there was a bond here and we don't mess with them."

"Bond?" Kayla squeaked. The shifters stared at her quizzically.

"I don't mean to offend. I just meant that you looked like you needed to stay together," Luke said slowly, a frown on his face.

Kayla shook her head and smiled. "Sorry, yeah, it was just a long night. I think I'm still tired." Luke's lips turned up at the edges, but then his nostrils flared. "Are you sniffing me?" she asked, amused.

A soft growl came from Blake, and when he spoke, his voice was rougher than normal. "He better not be."

Luke immediately stepped closer to Mal, who looked just as wary as Luke did.

"It's fine, Blake. He doesn't mean us any harm." She was surprised at how convinced she was of this fact.

"I'm sorry Prin–Blake. I thought I detected she was a witch, but I also thought elemental, and I was merely curious. I shouldn't have tried scenting her." His eyes were downcast, and it wasn't until Kayla glared a hole in the side of Blake's face that he turned to look at her. She raised her brows and gave him her 'you need to apologise' look. Blake rolled his eyes.

"It's fine. Sorry, Luke. I've had a rough few days with everyone threatening to snap her neck. Can't help it."

Kayla was taken aback. Did he really feel worked up over her safety?

"Understandable, and we want you to know that Mal and I will help you with whatever you want or need," Luke said, and Mal nodded in agreement. "Before we stop, we just want you to know that whatever happens with this alliance, we'll support you and you can count on us."

Both Luke and Mal placed a fist over their chests, just below their left shoulders. Were they pledging their loyalty?

"Um, thanks?" Blake said, looking entirely uneasy with the display.

"You can scent the type of magic a user wields?" Kayla asked, wary again.

"Sometimes. It's certainly one of my strengths, but I'm not always accurate."

"Blake can, too, or he's starting to." Blake looked at her. "What? He might be able to teach you or something!"

Luke and Mal chuckled. The doors opened and they all stepped out, Blake giving her a questioning look as they moved across the foyer. There was a dining room ahead of them, and the delicious scents of a full English became thicker the closer they got; it made her stomach rumble in anticipation.

CHAPTER FOURTEEN

KAYLA

THEY WALKED IN BEHIND Luke and Mal, and Kayla's eyes went wide as she drooled over the long buffet table down the length of the room. It was covered in cold breakfast items such as cereal and fruit, but there was also a selection of hot items like bacon, eggs, beans and toast. She looked up at Blake, whose face mirrored her excitement. They hadn't eaten that well in months.

Luke led them to the start of the queue, and they moved around the spread, piling their plates high. Even as a non-shifter her plate was excessive, but she didn't much care what anyone thought. She smiled when Blake started layering up bacon and toast like Jenga; he shrugged when she inspected his handiwork but there was a boyish grin on his face.

When their plates couldn't fit another bite, Luke took them over to where Marcus sat with Imogen. Wyatt sat at the next table over, and Luke and Mal grabbed a chair next to him; Marcus gestured for Kayla and Blake to join his table.

"Good morning!" Marcus beamed at them. He was overly cheerful, and she wondered what he was compensating for. "I trust you slept well?"

Blake glanced at Kayla and then responded, "Very well, thanks." Kayla decided she wouldn't let anyone spoil her breakfast and went to tuck in. Before she even realised she'd forgotten cutlery, Blake handed her one of the two sets he'd picked up. She smiled in thanks, and he winked. He'd winked at her. Winked! What did that mean? She shook her head and focused on her food; there was no need to dissect every little thing he did. Absolutely no need.

She barely registered Marcus's words to Blake. "Good, good. I wanted to discuss what we could do today, and I was hoping, Blake, that you might join myself and Imogen for some training of sorts?" Kayla stilled, fork halfway to her mouth. And so it started.

"I don't mean to be rude, but you're magic users and I'm a shifter."

"Oh, there is plenty of stuff we can look at together. I insist!"

"And Kayla?" Blake asked. Marcus looked at her, as if just then noticing someone other than Marcus, Imogen, and Blake existed.

Marcus's lips pressed together in a thin line before he answered. "I've been informed that she might be an untrained elemental user? Wyatt is one of the best elemental users you'll find." Imogen snorted, but quickly covered it up with a cough when her father gave her a pointed look. "I thought perhaps they could do some training together today, as she's clearly not been trained up till now? Of course, it won't be as beneficial as it would be if she was younger, but what can we do? I'm sure she'll catch up."

Kayla tried to ignore the thinly veiled dig and patronising tone as Wyatt leaned across the gap between their tables.

"What do you think, Kayla? Fancy doing some magic with me? I don't get a partner very often – at least not with someone of my own magic." When he spoke, Imogen, who had been mostly silent, opened her mouth, but she snapped it shut and turned her body ever so slightly so that more of her back was facing Wyatt.

Kayla needed Blake to confirm that this was what he wanted. No matter what she thought – or felt – he was the one the Alliance needed, not her.

Blake blew out a long breath and agreed, so she nodded to Wyatt, indicating that she'd join him. She would just have to trust that Blake would get the information they needed while being careful around Marcus. She didn't like the way he watched Blake.

"Wonderful! I think we should start right away, as soon as we finish breakfast, perhaps? Imogen?" Marcus asked.

"Sure, Dad. Why wait, right?" It was a small eye roll, but it was there, and Kayla wondered what Imogen's deal was.

She hoped Blake could find out more during his so-called 'training session' with them. It did *not* take a genius to figure out that Marcus just wanted her out of the picture.

Wyatt got up from his table after he finished and came over to Kayla's side. As he did, a commotion out in the lobby caught their attention. A group of individuals outfitted in black combat trousers, black long-sleeved t-shirts, and black boots walked by. All were carrying small packs or fixing belts that held guns as they passed the open double doors of the dining room. Kayla recognised Mia as she looked in the room and waved at them. Some of the other guys in the group nodded in their direction, mostly towards Luke, as they strode down the hall. Mia left with another female about her height and build with a long braid spilling down her back. Mia's was gelled, much like the first time they'd met.

"What are they doing?" Kayla asked the table.

"That's our small taskforce group, which is a mix of shifters and magic users. They're the best fighters we have. They go out to physically help those in need and thwart assassination attempts and attacks where possible. They've done a few rescue missions, too," Wyatt replied.

She found Marcus studying her. "The taskforce is an elite group of individuals, supporting the unison of both our sides," he added.

Kayla stayed quiet. Wyatt held his arm out to her like a gentleman did in old movies.

"Shall we, my lady?" he asked dramatically, and she couldn't help but smile at him. As she left her seat, Blake scowled, but Imogen leaned over and placed a hand on his clenched fist. It was at that point Kayla turned away and focused on Wyatt.

"Don't worry. It gets easier," Wyatt said as they left the dining room. He took her further into the hotel, and they passed more rooms, offices, and even a gym.

"What does?"

"Marcus being very clear on who his favourites are."

"Like his daughter? And now Blake?"

"Yep. Here's a fact for you. I'm actually Marcus's ward and have been since before I can remember."

"Really?" she asked. That explained his earlier comment; Marcus didn't appear to treat Wyatt like he had raised him.

"Oh yeah. He took me on as an obligation to my parents. I don't know much about them, and he doesn't talk about them. Just a fact of life. Marcus is, for all intents and purposes, my father, but he'll never treat me like his son."

"Because of Imogen?"

"Because of Imogen," he replied sourly.

"So, you two aren't like siblings. You don't get on?"

"Ha! Me and Imogen? Absolutely not. She has been a pain in my side since, well, since the day we met. They're the only family I have, but they just treat me as a means to an end. If it wasn't for the fact that he genuinely realises how powerful I am, I'd be of no more use to him now that I've found Blake."

She studied his profile as they walked and felt inexplicably sad for him. He didn't know the love of his parents like she had. Sure, after their deaths she'd discovered that they'd used magic on her and kept things hidden from her all her life, but they'd still loved her. Had Wyatt ever known that? Despite the difference in their upbringings, she felt a strange affinity with him that she didn't understand yet, like she was connected to him in some way.

"Don't get me wrong. He's done all this for the sake of uniting both races, but he's an extremely sucky father figure."

"Mia looks happy in the taskforce," she commented, trying to change the subject. She wasn't sure how else she should respond.

"Yeah, she loves it. Loves the adrenaline I think."

"But she's working with you to . . . what exactly are you two doing?"

Wyatt shifted uneasily as they continued down the corridor.

"There are a few of us who are starting to suspect Marcus and his more dubious ventures. We want both of our sides to be working together, in peace, but Marcus . . . I think he's doing dangerous acts to achieve some things he personally wants for very selfish reasons. I'm not sure everything he has us doing is for the good of all. Mia and I, along with a few others, are working behind Marcus's back to fix his mistakes and protect those weaker than him."

"Why not just leave him?"

"Good question, and it comes with many answers, but one I'm sure you'll appreciate is that here we can monitor him and gain the same information he does."

They stopped in front of a nondescript door with no windows looking in on the room. Wyatt directed her inside, but before he shut the door behind them, he flicked the sign on the front that read 'in use.'

The room was a fairly blank canvas, just four walls and the door they'd come in through. The paint was a cream colour, and the carpet was dark. But what was most interesting was in the middle of the room: A table sat with objects hidden beneath a cloth. She eyed the table, as it was the only thing that drew her focus.

"I use this room when I train with other elementals," Wyatt said, walking over to stand next to her.

"You've trained others?"

"Well, don't act so surprised. How many times do people have to tell you I'm good before you believe them?"

"It's just . . . you're so young. You look like my age."

"I'm a couple years older than Immy, and she's the same age as Blake and you."

"Firstly, Immy?" Kayla asked, trying to hold back a smile.

"Oh, she hates it. Please, please use it."

"I'll file it in here," she noted, pointing to her head, "and yes, I'm about six months older than Blake."

"Ah, interesting . . ." he trailed off, stroking an imaginary beard. He gave her a mischievous wink and she giggled.

"What's interesting then?" she queried, enjoying his playful nature.

"Nothing, nothing. I'm messing with you. Shall we start?" he asked, pointing at the objects. She nodded enthusiastically as he whipped the sheet off the table. An empty metal bowl, a porcelain bowl full of water, a small desk fan, and a small plant pot with a seedling were placed on its surface. "So, you know the four elements I take it? Your parents taught you that much?"

"Yeah," she commented, not wanting to go much further than that. He already knew that her parents weren't elementals from when'd they met at Michael's.

"I've not told anyone that you can create elements from nothing, Kayla. You can trust me," he said sincerely, and she believed him. "We have earth," he pointed to the seedling, and then pointed at all the other objects in turn, "air, water and lastly fire." He stood in front of the metal bowl. "Fire first? We know that's your strongest." She remembered back to when they'd first met, and she'd created more fire within the fireplace.

"I think it is, yes."

"Good stuff! Do you want to see if you can conjure any fire? I have the matches and kindling here, but it would be good to assess that skill of yours." As he spoke, she nodded. She'd been practising regularly when she had time over the past few months, at least until her power started surging. She felt more confident with Wyatt by her side.

She held her hands over the metal bowl and closed her eyes, focusing her energy on fire. She visualised it in her head, asking her magic to bring the image alive, and power hummed within her body. It was all about control. Control the magic. Don't let it control her. She repeated the mantra inside her mind as she slowly welcomed the magic.

"Amazing," Wyatt whispered. She opened her eyes to see the kindling in the metal bowl alight. "I still don't know of any elemental who can do that!"

"And I'd still really appreciate it if you didn't tell anyone," she said, chewing her lip.

"Honestly, it's not a worry. Your secret is safe with me." He placed a hand on her shoulder as he spoke, and she tried not to dwell on the fact that there was more secrecy surrounding her magic. She trusted him, but she'd have to work up to telling him all of it.

Wyatt waved his hand over the fire and it danced, leaning one way and then the other.

"Is everything okay with it?"

"Yes. I just wanted to see if I could still manipulate the fire that you conjured. And yes, I can!" She couldn't help but grin at his enthusiasm; it was infectious.

"Can I see you work with water? You said that was your speciality, right?"

"Sure!"

Wyatt grinned at her as he swirled his hand over the basin. The water followed the motion as he hovered his fingers over the surface.

"Don't you like, have to concentrate? Close your eyes?"

"No, I've been at this a while and I'm–"

"Good," she finished, and he winked again.

"Yep! What I'm doing is just forging a link with the water, slowly building the strength of the connection so it'll do what I want."

"You talk like it's a living thing. Like you're building a relationship?"

"Yeah, we are. The elements are living entities, Kayla. We are the lucky ones who get to tap into that."

"Why are we lucky? The elements aren't seen as the most powerful magic to have."

Wyatt rolled his eyes at her. "You've not had much information about the elemental magic strain, have you?" She shook her head. She was primed for being either a witch or a mage – both of which she could actually tap into – but she didn't tell Wyatt that particular secret. He continued, "For me, I am more powerful than the average mage as long as there are elements around for me to use. I'm assuming you agree that mages are considered the most powerful in the right circumstances?"

"Yeah, but again, depends on the level of the magic user, doesn't it?"

"Absolutely. If I had access to water and was duelling with Marcus, I would win. Hands down. However, put me in a room with nothing, or, say, on top of a roof in the still night, and I've not got much to offer, or it takes me much longer to work with what I can."

"Is that why you learned to fight? I didn't catch all of it, but when you and Mia took on Nige and his men, you were physically fighting. Are you part of the taskforce, too?"

Wyatt laughed. "Ha! No. Can you imagine? I don't know if you noticed, but they're all bad assess. Hence why Mia is part of the team. Can you imagine me in that group?" he asked, sweeping his hands out away from his bright blue jeans and mustard coloured jumper. Wyatt did give off a careless and jovial vibe, but underneath, Kayla could see the dedication to his cause – the concern and care he had for others.

"Mmm, I think you'd fit right in."

"If you say so, but to answer your earlier question: yes. Marcus insisted on both Imogen and I learning to fight, and we have plenty of shifters here who helped train us. I can't beat Luke, though. That's why he's one of our most formidable shifters."

She soaked up the information. "So, about this connection with the elements?"

"Oh, yes. Even the weaker elemental users all say that being able to connect with the elements is far more gratifying than any spell or any magic cast by a mage."

"But how would they know if they're not a witch or a mage, too?"

"It's all in the statistics. On average, elementals live the longest. They report higher levels of satisfaction, love, and . . . pleasure."

"Being an elemental does all that?"

"We're more in tune with nature. It's within our very souls. How can we not love more and be freer?"

She wondered if she'd ever felt a difference when she'd used elemental magic compared to witch or mage magic. She couldn't say for certain, as she was mostly running on adrenaline and using magic to stay alive, but when she tried practising while with Blake, it was her elemental magic she leaned towards. She always assumed it was because she wasn't trained in that strain of magic, but there was a sense of 'rightness' when she used it. Was that what Wyatt was referring to?

Wyatt spoke, drawing her from her thoughts. "We aim to ask, not take."

She paused and considered what he was telling her. "I've never worked with the earth element," she said, gently touching the small green leaves on the sapling.

"Shall we then?" He moved closer to the plant and smiled. He took her hand in his and held it over the plant, too. "Try and connect with your magic and extend it to the plant. Offer your help, and you'll develop a connection."

"Can I . . . can I close my eyes? It helps me concentrate," she whispered. He nodded, so she allowed them to fall shut, taking the deep, calming breaths she'd learned to do when she tried to control her magic.

Wyatt murmured words of encouragement as she felt the first hints of the connection. She relaxed, and a peaceful feeling washed over her. She wanted to help the plant grow, and she sent a little of her magic towards it.

"Careful, Kayla. You're pouring too much magic into the room," Wyatt warned, but Kayla was too busy focusing on the plant and encouraging it to flourish. She wished for the earth to provide the nutrients the sapling needed so she could amplify the effects. It was only when Wyatt yelped that she realised she couldn't turn the magic off, and it poured out of her readily, infecting the water, fuelling the fire.

"I can't stop it," she panicked.

"Um, okay, let's not panic. I'm going to try and do something that my mentors did with me, all right? I'm going to place my hand on your shoulder and try to connect with your magic, help you steer it."

"Will that work?"

"Sure? Why not?"

"You don't sound so sure . . ."

"It'll be fine. I've just never done this before."

She felt his hand on her shoulder like he'd said, but something went wrong. Her magic got excited, sensing his nearby, and her mage magic rushed up – at least, that's what it felt like.

The room rumbled as the fire she'd started spread to the vortex of wind that circled them. Before she could even think about what to do, Wyatt's arms wrapped around her, drawing her body close to his. His shout was lost in the explosion that followed.

CHAPTER FIFTEEN

BLAKE

BLAKE SCOWLED AS KAYLA left the dining room on Wyatt's arm. It was only after they'd exited that he realised Imogen had her hand over his fist. He unclenched his hand and glared at her, and she pulled back immediately. A surge of guilt rushed through him as she flinched, but he continued to scowl at Marcus. The guy clearly didn't want Kayla around today, and after Wyatt's warnings, his wolf was agitated.

"Can we get this over with?" Blake asked harshly, and Marcus, not letting Blake's mood deter him, smiled widely.

"Of course! Let's go," he replied, standing up. The three of them moved towards the exit, Luke following close behind.

"Does Luke always join you?"

"Yes, he's responsible for my safety. Excellent at his job."

Blake looked behind him at the tall shifter. "He could walk with us rather than behind us." It was barely noticeable, but one side of Luke's mouth quirked up.

Marcus made a noncommittal sound as they entered a well-manicured garden the size of a football pitch. Flowers blossomed along the edges of the large expanses of verdant green grass, and there were several patches placed around the garden that Blake recognised as vegetables, like sweet peas and tomatoes.

"What do you know of the Alliance, Blake?"

"Just that my birth parents tried to arrange one, but they were assassinated before that could happen. I wasn't really aware of my heritage until about six months ago."

"And that's when you met Kayla?"

Blake didn't like that tone from Marcus. "Yes."

"And is she . . . more than a friend?"

"Err," Blake began, not knowing what to say. "We're close friends, yes."

"That's good, that's good."

Blake frowned. "I don't see how my . . . connection with Kayla matters." He controlled his words, not wanting to give Marcus any reason to see Kayla as a threat. Wyatt's warning screamed in his head to watch where he treaded, but at the same time, Marcus held answers both he and Kayla were trying to find.

"It matters a great deal because the Alliance was formed by your parents and me. For *our* children."

"I'm not following." Blake looked to Imogen as she stood to the side, her face pinched.

"My daughter, Imogen, and you have been declared *the* shifter and magic user who will unite the bloodlines."

"As in . . ." Blake asked, not liking where this was going at all.

"Children," Imogen said. "Our children will have shifter blood and magic blood."

"Will have? As in, there is no choice in the matter? The great Alliance rests on the two us having kids?"

"Your parents and I thought that by joining the bloodlines, it would create a unity that couldn't be broken; a perfect mix of supernatural offspring."

"You mean choosing your daughter's future, taking away the decisions she should be making about who she loves and has children with. I can't believe my birth parents agreed to this!"

"It's not about her choices! It's about her duty, and you would do well to think the same way!" Marcus argued, anger seeping into his words.

"How do you feel about this, Imogen?" Blake asked. Her brows drew together.

"Me?"

"Yes. Surely you have an opinion?"

"To be frank, I'm not thrilled with the idea of being reduced to a brood mare, essentially."

"Imogen!" Marcus chastised, but she quickly continued.

"Neither do I like the idea of an arranged marriage, but I don't want this war between us anymore. Too many have died," she finished, raising her shoulders in a shrug, as if she was just accepting her fate.

"An arranged marriage? You want us to marry, too?" he asked Marcus.

"Well, yes. We can't have illegitimate children to the royal shifter line!"

"That's why I'm important? Because I'm a royal? That's how I'm useful?"

"What did you think was going to happen?"

Blake scoffed because he actually didn't know, and he certainly wasn't doing a good job of hiding his feelings.

"For what it's worth, I'm sorry you weren't brought up knowing about the supernatural world or what the Alliance entailed. It wasn't your parents' or my own intentions. We thought if you both grew up beside one another, knowing this was your path, then it would be easier to accept because it was all you would have known. Alas, that didn't happen."

"Dad, maybe we should let Blake have some time to himself, let him think things through?" Imogen offered, and he was grateful for the reprieve. She'd grown up knowing about this. He hadn't.

"What's there to think about, Imogen? His parents signed the contract! And it's more than a contract: It's duty." Marcus left the words hanging in the air, and the full impact hit him square in the stomach.

"Still, it's a lot to take in," she finished, and Blake tried to give her grateful smile.

Could he do it? What would Kayla think? Oh God, Kayla. She'd helped him get this far – kept him alive, no less – and the thought of her finding out had his stomach twisting in knots.

"What about Kayla?" he asked Marcus. It was clear the guy didn't like her, but she was an important part of his life. Marcus frowned.

"Nothing. She's not important anymore. You must focus your time and energy on Imogen. The people must see you both as a consenting item."

"Oh, so not like we're being forced into this? Why us? Could it not be *any* shifter? *Any* magic user?"

"You're the shifter Prince, the last of the Alastair bloodline, the most powerful shifter blood there is–"

"Okay, okay! I get me, but why specifically Imogen," he asked. He turned to Imogen and rushed to add, "Not meaning any offense to you, of course." He was relieved when she shook her head.

"Because Imogen is from a pure mage line – the most powerful strain of magic – and the daughter of one of the magic user councillors. At least, we were a council before shifters came in and tore us apart. We were left standing, Imogen and I, although I am sure there are other witches and elemental users who could join us and form a council again. It is something I hope to do when the Alliance has been formed and the royal shifter line has been established once more. Anything other than a pure, well-respected mage bloodline would not meet the parameters of the Alliance set out by the old magic user council and your parents. This was carefully thought out and reasoned. You need to trust that your parents knew what they were doing."

Blake ran his hands through his hair and then crossed his arms over his chest. There was a lot to process, and he couldn't do it all at once. He somehow had to tell Kayla, and that filled him with more dread than he thought possible. If it filled him with dread, he knew he was taking this seriously and contemplating going through with it.

Imogen stood by her father. She was pretty enough, and she seemed nice, so it wasn't the worst pairing he could imagine. He felt sorry for her that she'd been brought up with this burden alone. She probably needed a supportive partner in this, too. She'd had her whole life to worry about who he would be, who she would be forced to marry and have children with. At least he thought they could be friends. Could friends marry? Have children? Could he learn to love her in more than just a platonic way? He shook his head. There was too much to think about.

"I'm happy to talk with you at some point, alone," Imogen said pointedly, "but for now–" She was cut short by a small explosion and shouts of distress. Something detonated within the hotel. An alarm sounded, and Blake knew Kayla was involved.

"Where's Kayla?" Blake asked Marcus.

Marcus waved his hand nonchalantly in the air. "I'm sure she's fine. I have people who deal with this sort of thing. Magic user training can get a bit messy at times. She's with Wyatt, he'll look after her." He spoke as if even discussing Kayla was giving him a headache. Blake whirled on him.

"Marcus! Where. Is. Kayla?" he shouted, feeling his wolf's agitation. Marcus sputtered in surprise at Blake's anger. Blake turned and marched to Luke, who stared at the building in concern. "Luke? I know Kayla's involved. I can feel her heart racing, take me to her." He didn't plead with Luke, but his voice was less hostile than it had been with Marcus.

The moment Blake heard the explosion, he'd automatically tuned into her heartbeat; it must have been habit after being with her for so long. He didn't think he could hear her pulse from where he was, but he could feel it, and it was far too panicked for his liking.

Luke nodded and led Blake away from Marcus, who shouted at their retreating backs. He argued that Kayla didn't matter and demanded they let others deal with it. The shifter beside him gave Blake a sideways glance when Blake growled under his breath.

"They'll be in Wyatt's training room," Luke ground out as they picked up the pace. He clearly wasn't impressed with Marcus either.

A crowd of people stood in the foyer, gasping as smoke and dust billowed out of one hallway. They ran down the long, murky corridor, and as the dust started to settle, Blake saw a door hanging off its hinges. Both Luke and Blake dove inside. The ceiling had collapsed from the room above, and electrical wires were draped over piles of plaster like vipers waiting to attack.

Blake's attention, however, was drawn to the two people in the middle of the chaos. Kayla stood in the shelter of Wyatt's arms as he held one hand up, protecting them from most of the debris with a shield of water.

Wyatt slowly moved his hand, and the body of water fell to the floor with a splash. Kayla looked up at Wyatt and giggled as she tried to wipe herself down.

"What's going on, Wyatt?" Luke commanded. Kayla's head popped up and she noticed the two shifters in the doorway. Her carefree smile reached her eyes, which only added to the knots in Blake's stomach.

"Oh, you know, just a bit of elemental magic. I hadn't quite accounted for how powerful Kayla was," Wyatt said, but his smile fell as Marcus and

Imogen crashed into the room. They took in the destruction with wide eyes.

"What in God's name, Wyatt?" Marcus chastised.

Wyatt sighed. "Just a mistake. I tried doing something to alleviate the magic she was building – just as my mentors did for me when you sent me away – but I've not had to do it on someone else before. I know what I have to do next time."

"I don't think there should be a next time!" Marcus shouted, and Blake thought he detected a hint of apprehension coming from the man.

"What do you mean by that?" Kayla asked warily.

"I don't want that kind of magic practised here. It puts us at too much risk! You put us at risk!"

"But Marcus, she can be an asset. I know what I did wrong. It was me, not her. Magic like hers – mine – needs practise and someone willing to help. I can do it, Marcus, you know I can," Wyatt pleaded.

"NO! We can't have untrained elementals around here. Think about the alliance. Her magic is better off elsewhere!"

Blake growled and approached Marcus and Imogen, his chest rising and falling as his fists curled inwards. When Imogen took a step back, he sensed his eyes had changed as the wolf fought to the surface.

"Do not threaten her," he ground out.

Marcus met his glare with one of his own; the directness of it made his wolf's hackles rise.

"Blake," Kayla warned from behind him, and his wolf yielded.

Marcus backed away. "No more magic. These are my orders. You'd all do well to remember who's in charge here," he declared, looking around at the quiet faces.

He turned and marched out of the room, leaving the stunned group in his wake.

Luke cleared his throat. "Lunch will be on shortly. Perhaps you'd like to go and clean yourself up, Kayla? I will stay and sweep the rubble."

"Oh no, that's fine. I'll help. It was me, after all," she said, waving her hand as if it was no trouble.

"Please, let me help," Luke asked, and she nodded, sensing the same thing Blake did. For some reason, Luke needed to do this. Luke walked further into the room and stood next to Wyatt.

"Thanks buddy," Wyatt said. Luke nodded, back to communicating without words.

"I'll help you clean up, Kayla," Imogen offered, and the girls left.

"Marcus told you, hasn't he?" Wyatt asked Blake, pulling his focus away from Kayla. She looked unharmed, at least.

"You knew?"

"Yep."

"And what about you?" Blake asked Luke.

"I'm not an advisor. It isn't my place."

"But you're a shifter, and I want your opinion. I don't know many shifters. I wasn't brought up as one."

"I . . ." Luke looked towards Wyatt, who shrugged indifferently.

"You know I'm not going to run to Marcus if you disagree with him."

Luke took a few seconds to gather his thoughts before he spoke. "I think more people should be involved in the decision-making process. I appreciate that this is the contract your parents signed, but they're not here anymore, and a new Alliance – one that works for the here and now – needs to happen. If people saw strong and respected magic users and shifters working together, more would follow. As for any extremists . . ." he shrugged. "They're just out for themselves, anyway."

"So you think I shouldn't agree to this? Marrying Imogen?" Blake couldn't believe he'd said those words out loud.

"I'm not saying you should completely dismiss a relationship with a magic user. I'm just saying that . . . it's unnatural for shifters to be with someone who we don't love. You may end up caring for Imogen, but if that's not where your heart truly lies, it'll eventually affect your wolf. We mate for life if we find the right person. You and your wolf will be in a constant struggle."

"Have there been any shifter-magic user pairings before?" They shook their heads. "So it's unlikely I'll find someone who's not a shifter," he stated, feeling deflated.

"It's not my place, but I think you've already formed a connection with a magic user, and you should be careful about it," Luke said quietly. He hung his head.

"Luke, I'm not Marcus," Wyatt said softly. "I certainly don't think the same way as him. I only stay because, well . . . never mind."

Worry burrowed itself deep into Blake's head. "What do you mean,

Luke?" Blake asked.

"Marcus won't be happy – he's not happy – with Kayla."

"We're . . . we're just friends."

"Sure, but Marcus still sees her as a threat," Wyatt said.

"Because he senses her power?" Blake didn't feel so happy with Kayla being apart from him.

"And because the Alastair family has a lot of money. Marrying his daughter to you would make him rich, and the prestige doesn't hurt, either. He's gotten more obsessed as the years have gone by."

"Even if I were to agree to this, I'm barely seventeen! And I certainly don't have any money."

"Your money is locked away in assets and accounts. I've located some but can't get access, obviously. And age doesn't matter to him. If he'd found you a few years ago, I'm sure he would've pushed Imogen and you to start having children right away," Wyatt sneered.

"But that's his daughter he's talking about!" Blake shouted in disgust.

"I know. As I said, he's become obsessed with marrying into the admired – and more importantly, lucrative – Alastair line."

"You need to protect Kayla," Luke advised.

"Is it still safe to stay here?"

Wyatt answered him. "If you'd asked me that eight years ago, I would have said yes, but now? I'd say to watch out for Kayla, no matter what you think your relationship is with her. I've seen how . . . crazed Marcus looks when he watches her."

The guys began cleaning up, but Blake's head spun. Too much information. Too much change. He realised the one person he wanted to speak to about everything was probably the one person he shouldn't confide in.

CHAPTER SIXTEEN

KAYLA

KAYLA FOLLOWED IMOGEN DOWN the hall and up one flight of stairs.

"There are some toilets on this floor," Imogen said, pushing open a swing-through door. A row of cubicles sat on one side with sinks and mirrors fixed to the pale peach-coloured walls on the other.

Kayla grabbed some toilet paper and wet it before patting herself free of any dust debris. Imogen handed her a stack of paper towels.

"Thanks," Kayla muttered, not sure why Imogen was so eager to help. She knew the girl wanted to ask her something, but she was holding back. "Let's hear it," Kayla sighed, resigned. She shook out her hair and ran her fingers through the tangles.

"What's the deal with you and Blake?" Imogen asked, avoiding Kayla's eyes.

"Me and Blake?" Kayla repeated robotically.

"Are you . . . are you guys in a relationship?"

"Relationship!" she squeaked. "Um no, we're just close. You would be close with someone you spent an entire six months with, right?"

"Sure." Imogen nodded.

"And we've been through some stuff together . . ." She slowly trailed off. Damn her traitorous thoughts for bringing their near kiss to the forefront of her mind. Thank God Imogen wasn't a shifter, and thank God Blake wasn't nearby, because her heart was racing. As it was, she hid her face – and the rising heat she felt creeping across her cheeks – from view. She grabbed another paper towel and wiped at her neck.

"That's good that you had each other. It can be lonely here, so I'm glad he was with you."

"Didn't you have Wyatt though?"

"Hmm, yes. The boy that hates me," Imogen bit out. Kayla heard the sadness buried in her tone.

"I don't think he does. He talked about you in our training session, you know."

"He did?" Imogen's voice rose and her head snapped up.

"Yeah, I don't think you're quite as alone as you think you are. But he did tell me to call you Immy."

Imogen snorted. "Please don't listen to that advice!"

"I wasn't planning on it. I feel like Immy is a name that only someone who's known you forever can call you."

"Ugh, he has known me forever . . . unfortunately." The girls went quiet as Kayla plaited the hair off her face. "He'll need you." Imogen spoke so quietly that Kayla nearly missed it over the running tap.

"What?"

"Blake. He'll need your support, with the Alliance and everything else. I can tell he respects you. I think he'd be heartbroken if you didn't stay."

"Why wouldn't I stay? It was my mum who told me to find him in the first place, and I'm not going to break my promises. I said I'd help him, and I will."

"Good. Good."

"What's this about, Imogen? What do I not know?"

Imogen flinched and looked at her watch, avoiding Kayla's eyes.

"Oh, it's lunchtime. Shall we go down to the dining room?" she asked. Kayla nodded and finished wiping herself down. She wanted to trust Imogen, but the girl was Marcus's daughter, and Wyatt's warnings were clear about him.

She didn't know Imogen very well, but she knew when something was being kept from her.

As they left the room, Marcus appeared out of nowhere and stopped in front of her.

"Can I have a word with Kayla, please?" he asked, but his tone suggested it was more of a command. Imogen nodded uncertainly but moved away regardless. Kayla pulled her shoulders back and faced Marcus, who dropped the act as soon as Imogen was out of view. "You don't belong here," he hissed.

"I've helped Blake get this far. Surely that deserves some respect," Kayla shot back.

"That's the only reason I haven't sent you away. You need to leave before you ruin everything. You're not important. Blake is," he said, mirroring her earlier thoughts. "Your magic is untrained, I can see that. But don't think I don't recognise what you are."

"What I am?" she questioned. She wanted to step away from him but she refused to back down.

"Powerful. It's your magic that has drawn others to you both, isn't it?"

Kayla's head jerked back. "How do you know about that?"

Marcus smirked. "I have my ways. You need to leave Blake alone so he can focus on his role. Take your magic and support the alliance where you won't be a distraction and a danger to us all." Kayla was quiet, and Marcus smiled triumphantly. "You think the same. It would be wise to listen before something . . . unpleasant happens."

Marcus walked away and Kayla fled down the stairs on shaky legs. Imogen joined her on the next floor.

"You okay?" she asked, furrowing her brow.

"Yeah," Kayla breathed, not sure what else to say. If she mentioned something and it got back to Blake, he'd lose it, and they couldn't afford that – not with the resources and manpower Marcus was offering.

"I'm sorry about my father. He can be a bit direct."

"So it seems."

"I hate talking about the alliance and I don't have many girl friends here, so tell me more about you. Like, I don't know, where are you from, what do your parents do, what do you want to do after the alliance?" Imogen asked cheerfully, genuinely eager to hear what Kayla had to say. It took Kayla a moment to gather her thoughts.

"Um, well I suppose I'll do what my parents did. They worked to protect shifters and magic users from attacks. Maybe I can help reunite people with loved ones who had to go into hiding. It would be good to continue what they started now that they're no longer here, but it depends on the Alliance, of course." And Blake, but she didn't elaborate on that.

"I'm sorry to hear about your parents, but it sounds like something they'd be proud to see you do. I think you're a good person, Kayla."

Kayla barely knew the girl, but she felt obliged to say something in return – she just couldn't find the words.

"What about you? Any future plans?" she asked instead, and Imogen went quiet.

"I think my future has been chosen for me," she whispered as they entered the dining room. Kayla blinked in surprise. What about Imogen's future had already been decided?

Imogen took her to the buffet set-up again. This time, salads, meats, and sandwiches lined the table. Kayla piled her plate high and tucked in as Blake placed his even larger meal next to hers. Imogen sat across from her, and Wyatt sat opposite Blake. She smiled at Luke as he slid into a seat at the next table with Mal and what looked like a couple of other shifters. She tried not to let her conversation with Marcus get to her, knowing she couldn't tell Blake about it. She knew Blake would be angry, and as much as it pained her, she could see the truth in Marcus's words.

Kayla studied Blake as he stuffed his face, rolling her eyes inwardly – shifters and their appetites. She noticed Blake flicking glances her way and wondered if he'd always checked on her or if it was something new.

He took another look at her and then reached for the jug, pouring them both a drink. How did he know she was thirsty before she did? When had that started happening?

Imogen watched them as Blake handed Kayla the water, a wistful, faraway look in her eyes.

"Earth to Immy," Wyatt said, snapping his fingers. She shook her head and frowned at Wyatt.

"What?" she barked.

"You zoned out. What were you thinking about?" he asked, trying to sound indifferent.

Imogen locked eyes with Blake. He coughed, spluttering on his water, which only intensified Kayla's belief that something was going on – something that she wasn't being told about.

"Nothing, nothing," Imogen swiftly replied.

Luke's phone rang, pausing the group's conversation. As he answered it, they all listened in. Knowing Blake would be able to hear if he concentrated, she watched as his eyebrows raised then gathered in a scowl. Luke ended the call, and an unspoken exchange passed between him and Blake.

"You know that isn't happening," Blake said first, and Luke nodded in agreement.

"I am aware."

"What? What's going on?" Wyatt asked nosily – he clearly wasn't self-conscious about butting in. She was beginning to like that about the guy.

"Marcus is being kept busy with something and asked me to take Imogen and Blake to the meeting he set up in town. It's only a short ride."

"Oh, a meeting," Wyatt repeated, and something in his tone suggested he knew its purpose.

"What kind of meeting?" Kayla asked.

"One that could get more shifters and magic users on our side. We were hoping Blake would agree to go and prove who he is . . . for the Alliance," Imogen said, aiming her words at Blake. He visibly flinched.

"That doesn't sound so bad. It's a good thing, right?"

All of them looked at Kayla as if she had suddenly sprouted horns.

"I'll go, but Kayla's coming, too," Blake argued, as if it had been previously discussed without her. Imogen opened her mouth and spun to Luke who shrugged. Clearly Luke was going to do whatever Blake wanted.

"Are you sure, Blake?" Wyatt asked, and for the first time since she'd know him, he looked uncertain.

"Well, I'm hardly going to leave her here, am I?" he shot back quietly, and Wyatt glanced away, refusing to make eye contact with Kayla.

"But . . ." Imogen started.

"It'll be fine. They just want to see I exist, right? And then they'll join us."

"Sure," Imogen agreed eventually, and the group went quiet again. Wyatt leaned over to Luke.

"Luke, is Mal okay to run . . . interference while we're gone?"

"Yes, on it already," Luke said. He nodded at Mal, who cast a quick glance at Kayla. What was going on? She was positively paranoid now. She needed to speak to Blake on his own.

Blake must have sensed her unease because he turned his broad upper body towards her and leaned in close, effectively blocking everyone else from view.

"Don't worry. We're sticking together. Promise?" She was surprised to hear a hint of pleading in his tone.

"Course. We have our list to complete," she said, smiling. She wanted to comfort him, but she didn't much like the effect the table's discussion was having on her insides.

"Our list," he agreed.

THE CAR RIDE WAS TENSE, filled with unspoken conversations that Kayla didn't understand. Luke drove with Wyatt in the passenger seat, which meant that she, Blake, and Imogen were all squashed into the back. Blake sat in the middle. She knew they were keeping something from her, perhaps about the alliance, but it was Blake's silence that upset her the most. They were meant to be in this together.

She couldn't focus on anything when she sat so close to Blake. Each time their bodies jostled together, electric currents ran over her skin, and her magic buzzed through her veins. It was as if her magic was happy being this close to him and wanted to be let out.

This, of course, made her more nervous, which in turn drew Blake's attention. He kept a close eye on her, shooting her glances as they listened to Wyatt and Imogen bicker over the radio station. At one point, Luke reached out and switched the whole thing off, and after a quick growl from the driver, the pair ceased their constant squabbling.

"So, who are these people we're meeting?" Kayla asked, breaking the silence. On the other side of Blake, Imogen stared out the window.

Wyatt answered, twisting around in his seat to face Kayla. "A group of magic users and shifters who are reluctant to join, out of fear mostly, but who have all expressed interest in supporting us. We've reached out multiple times and helped them with issues in the past, and they're beginning to break down the walls between themselves. They've all lived in the same general area for the past year or so, I would say, so they're doing well. Some are concerned about their safety – which is understandable – and some are still wary of each other. I think the shifters of the group want to see you, Blake, and the magic users are just curious about how we could be working together now. The original Alliance pact was kept secret, mostly because nearly everyone there died, so all that's left is speculation."

"Why have you not told them? And what was the original Alliance pact? Do you know? That's all Blake and I have been trying to find out these past few months." Beside her, Blake's body tensed.

Wyatt nodded his head. "Yeah, we were there."

"We?"

"Myself and Imogen."

"What was it then? Is it something you've been working on? Did Marcus tell you?" she asked Blake, and a heavy feeling sank in her gut.

Wyatt said, "Marcus thought it best not to release the details, mostly for protection . . ."

"Protection? To protect Blake?"

"Yes and no. We didn't know Blake was alive back then, and if there were some distant relative who could have taken his place, we didn't want to add a higher bounty to his head. But Marcus was worried about Imogen. That's why he sent me away to train with the best academy of elementals there is."

"Why was he–"

"Company," Luke snapped, interrupting Kayla as they looked behind them. A van raced up towards their car.

"Are we being followed?" Imogen finally asked, sitting up straight.

Luke switched his focus between the road and the mirror. "Yes, for a few miles now. I was hoping it was a coincidence, but they're starting to weave in and out of traffic to catch up to us."

Kayla twisted in her seat to look out the back window at the dark van creeping closer. The memory of being taken in a van all those months ago flashed through her mind. Swallowing hard at the quick jolt of pain, she tried to squash it down. Blake placed his warm hand on her leg, and judging from the look of his pinched features, he was remembering it, too.

Luke sped off the main road and took them on a rapid, winding journey through the countryside. Trees and wide expanses of field greeted them – and, thankfully, fewer cars – but the black van gave chase, disrupting the natural harmony of their surroundings.

She heard the low hum of their car's engine as it struggled to gather speed with full occupancy, and she was jolted forward when the van nudged them from behind. Luke got the car under control again, but she heard him swear viciously, which was very unlike the Luke she knew. The next hit came from behind again, and it was much more jarring. She yelped, as did the others.

"Kayla, your magic," Blake whispered as he turned to her, eyes wide. She knew he was wondering if she could use her magic like she'd done to their attackers the week before, but she didn't know if she could. She didn't have the spell book on her.

"I haven't got the spell book, and last time my magic was too much. I lost control," she whispered back, shaking her head. Yes, she was always anxious about others finding out she could do more than one strain of magic, but it didn't seem to matter at the moment.

"This car isn't going to take another knock like that!" Luke ground out as he struggled to keep the wheel straight. The jerky movements of the vehicle knocked her and Blake together.

"What are you doing, Wyatt?" Imogen shrieked as his fingers flew over his phone.

"Jesus, what's with the judgy attitude, Immy? I'm trying to find our co-ordinates and send them to Mal for backup!" he answered sharply, but his words ended with an 'omf' as Luke jerked the car away from another hit.

The van lined up next to Kayla's window and profanity spewed from Wyatt's mouth. She recognised the driver of the van as Luke grunted in anger.

"It's them, Blake!" she yelled, fear clawing up her throat. The magic hunters had found them again.

"Who's them?" Wyatt shouted.

Kayla closed her eyes, drawing on her magic; she would just have to use instinct rather than a spell and hope the healer had done enough to protect her from another burnout. She felt her power swell, though she was unsure what kind it was, and released it. Their car jerked, but Luke held control as the wave of magic raced towards the van.

"They have a shield with them," Wyatt whispered in shock as the wave of magic bounced against the van, leaving it untouched, and the energy rushed back at their car.

It was a painful realisation.

She braced for the impact.

Blake's gasp was the last clear sound she could distinguish before everything was muffled by the crunch of metal. Crumpling steel creaked all around her as the car flipped, and she was momentarily suspended upside down in the air.

Imogen screamed.

Gravity pulled them from the sky like a cruel tormenter.

CHAPTER SEVENTEEN

KAYLA

LOUD METALLIC GROANS AND clicks accosted her ears when she came to, and the stench of burning rubber curled through the air. In the distance, she heard muffled grunts and shouts as if she were listening to the fight from underwater.

Opening her eyes, she wondered how they hadn't landed upside down; she was sure the car had been falling that way. Groans of frustration infiltrated her mind and drew her back to the present.

Wyatt, Imogen, and Blake were outside the car, engaging with several magic-users. She sucked in a painful breath, her body struggling to let go of the paralysing fear the hunters ignited.

Blake tackled the man who'd caused her ankle injury not long ago, stopping him from using his magic as they tumbled to the ground. Blake had the upper hand, and he punched him hard in the face. Her heart raced; they'd been trying to kill Blake for months, and he was fighting without her!

Kayla leaned forward, trying to rotate her arm. Her shoulder had hit the side of the car with some force when the van rammed into them. Her seatbelt had kept her locked in place but now it was stuck, refusing to budge as she tried to undo it. Luke was still strapped into the front seat, but animalistic murmurs made her pulse stutter.

"Luke?" she asked, worried about drawing attention while the others were fighting. The car sat across both lanes of the empty road, with Luke and Kayla's side facing away from the brawl. She allowed herself one last glimpse of the fight – of Blake – before she turned back to the shifter in front.

"Stuck," he panted, pain lacing his voice.

"How? Are you okay?"

"My door and the foot well . . . twisted around me."

"Gah!" she muttered as she tugged at her seatbelt. Her frustration grew as she wiggled, trying to free herself. She knew she had to get out from her belt, but the fabric was caught and refused to budge. For a moment, she contemplated using magic, but she decided against it. If the magic distracted the others, or their attackers sensed it and came over, they'd be screwed. Using her magic hadn't exactly worked well for them last time.

Luke's breathing quickened, and he began to wheeze. "Seriously, Luke, talk to me," she begged as she tried to twist the belt some more.

"Window screen . . . impaled."

She froze as his words sank in. Her heart dropped.

"What?" she barely whispered.

"You need to get out and . . . save Blake."

"God, even in pain you put someone else first. How about we help you, yeah?" she asked, hoping that by talking, he would stay focused. "Can you shift?"

"No . . . too risky. Small space . . . cause more damage."

"Okay, so we need to get you out and then you can shift to fix the holes?" This time, instead of fighting with the buckle, she slowly started pulling the belt through from the top to give herself more space. If she went too fast, the belt would lock and trap her once more.

"Muh . . ." Luke mumbled, and she knew he was far from okay.

"Luke! Hey Luke! Listen to me, we'll get you out," she rambled, pulling her legs up to loop the belt around her feet. It was hard work, especially considering how sore she was from the impact. How on earth were the other three standing so confidently, let alone fighting? "I'm just trying to climb out of my seatbelt and then I can help. Why don't you talk to me? Tell me more about yourself?"

"It's. Been. Honour."

"Honour? What's an honour?" she asked as she untangled herself. She tried to keep her movements as minimal as possible. She had to keep the attention off them both until Luke was out.

"Prince Blake, you . . ."

"Me?" That stopped her, but when she didn't hear him continue, she leaned forward, careful not to be seen.

Luke was slumped against his seat, and the blood pooling in his lap reminded her of Gaby's tortured body left as a warning months ago. Protruding from Luke was a wide, sharp piece of glass about the size of a textbook. Blood soaked his shirt and dripped down his arms from where he'd tried to free himself. She couldn't quite see his legs from her angle, but the metal of the car had clearly caved in. She'd have to leave the confines of the vehicle to get a better look.

She moved back to her seat and tried opening her door, but it wouldn't budge. It was caught on something, so she swung her leg back to kick it. The impact jarred her injuries and rippled up her legs. She wasn't worried about their attackers discovering her; she had to get out and help Luke before it was too late. She prayed the others would keep the hunters busy.

Leaning back on her elbows, she used both feet to hit her door again and heard another guttural groan coming from the front.

"Hold on, Luke, I'm coming," she said just before she kicked again, this time channelling a small trickle of her power. The door swung open. Seeing nothing on their side of the road, she scrambled to slide out. Her back twinged, but she knew her pain was nothing compared to Luke's.

The blood rushed to her head as she clambered to her feet, but it soon passed and she moved to Luke's door. She quickly surveyed the fight on the other side of the vehicle and thought her friends were gaining the upper hand against the magic users, but she wasn't brave enough to look closer. She wasn't brave enough to see if Blake was okay.

Luke's door was riddled with dents. It was as if the metal had moulded itself to his side – probably because shifters tended to be quite strong – but for this to happen . . . was Luke made of metal himself? One look inside confirmed he wasn't. Almost every surface was painted crimson.

His head leaned back against the headrest as the windshield pinned him to the seat. Soon, it wouldn't even matter if she got him out or not – he was losing too much blood.

Most of the glass from his side window had shattered on impact, and she warned him to turn his face while she cleared it. He followed her instructions, which she took as a good sign. He could still hear, at least. She shrugged off her thick jacket, wrapped it around her hand, and proceeded to break away the rest of the glass, clearing the way to Luke. When most of the shards had been swept away, she draped the jacket over the open window to give her some protection as she leaned in.

"Luke? You okay, Luke?" she asked, her heart faltering when he didn't respond. She felt for his pulse and released a shaky breath when it thumped weakly in his neck. "Okay, Kayla, what do we have?" she mumbled to herself, looking inside to see where the metal was. She wondered if she could move the door with her magic and wake Luke up. If so, would he be able to help pull himself out?

She was contemplating what to do about the glass shard in his stomach when footsteps sped towards her from behind. She whirled to find one of the magic hunters closing in on her.

"You're coming with us!" he hissed, but he let out a garbled cry when someone slammed him into the side of the car. Blake.

Her heart thundered and her stomach flipped over at the sight of Blake fighting back against the magic user. She turned away. The distraction would affect both of them if she wasn't careful.

Trusting Blake with the magic user, Kayla turned her attention back to Luke and placed her hands on the door, hoping to use some of the telekinesis power she'd developed. She breathed in and out, slow and controlled, and called that part of her magic forward.

It flowed beneath her skin, but not enough of it, and her shoulders slumped in defeat. Blake slid to her side, pressing his heat against her as he peered into the car.

"Luke?" he panted heavily.

"He's stuck. He can't shift to heal the wounds until he's out," she relayed. Blake nodded at her. A tremble rippled through her body, and Blake placed his hands on her shoulders, turning her to face him.

"Hey," he said softly, cupping her cheek in his palm, "we'll get him out, but we might need to work together." She nodded at him. "Can you try using your power as I use my strength?"

"I'm ready," she said, trying to shed doubt that crept into her mind.

The pair worked together in silence, and she recognised how natural it was to combine their efforts. Kayla laid her hand on the door to channel her magic and Blake gripped the window frame. She could tell he was using his shifter strength when the muscles in his arms bunched. She took a slow, steadying breath – not for the sake of her magic – and concentrated on her power.

The metal began to groan and creak, and then a pop reverberated through the air. The door was off the hinges. Blake put it down and reached for Luke, dragging him onto the grassy verge near the car wreckage. Wyatt and Imogen joined them, and Imogen gasped when she saw Luke, one hand flying to her mouth as the other grabbed onto Wyatt's back.

"Is he okay?" Wyatt asked, visibly shaken.

"He needed to get out of the car before he could shift. I know it's risky, but if he doesn't shift, he'll lose too much blood anyway! The magic users?" Kayla asked. She scanned the group and noted that both Wyatt and Imogen seemed uninjured.

Wyatt nodded, but he didn't take his eyes off Luke. "Taken care of."

Imogen sucked in a breath. "I'm sorry. I–I didn't have time. It all happened so fast, I couldn't think." Her arms hung by her side, limp. Wyatt grabbed her hand and squeezed.

"It's not your fault, Immy. Don't blame yourself."

Kayla frowned. "What do you mean?" she asked him sharply.

"Immy has shield magic. She touched me and Blake as we were hit so we were protected from the impact," Wyatt explained. Guilt flashed across his face, despite what he'd told Imogen.

"Aghhh!" Luke gurgled. Blake knelt next to Luke, holding the large glass shard in his hand.

"Shift, Luke," Blake said, casting the glass away.

Wyatt and Imogen came closer as Kayla stood beside Blake's kneeling form, her hand resting on his shoulder – for her comfort or his, she couldn't tell. Blake rose with a wince, and the backs of their hands brushed together. A strange surge of electricity caressed her skin where they touched. She didn't have time to question it; Luke hadn't shifted like she expected him to.

"Shift," Blake commanded.

A heavy silence hung over them as Luke remained human, and Kayla wondered if they were too late.

"Shift!" Blake roared, and something moved through the air – a power that hadn't come from the magic users. Blake's eyes turned golden as he exerted his Alpha influence. She didn't even know he could do that, but it worked. When the wave of power crested, Luke shifted, and within seconds a large brown wolf lay on the ground, panting heavily. Imogen dropped down beside Luke and apologised with tears in her eyes.

There was commotion among the group as Luke healed his major injuries, but there was an unnerving stillness to the side of her. Placing a hand over her stomach, she looked at Blake, noticing the faint covering of sweat over his brow and the pale, clammy appearance to his skin.

"Blake," she whispered. Something inside of her sounded off in warning. Blake swayed ever so slightly, and he fell to his knees with a moan. She crouched in front of him and pressed her hands against his chest, wondering if the Alpha influence had been too hard on his body. "Blake? What's wrong?" She glanced down and her blood ran cold as he clutched the side of his stomach.

A sense of dread filled her. Her mouth went dry. She moved her trembling hand to his and gently pried his hand away from the t-shirt, and his red-stained palm stared back at her. She lifted the hem of his shirt and found a puncture wound dripping with blood. She frowned. There wasn't enough blood to explain his reaction to the injury.

"Wyatt!" she shouted. The others paused their celebration and rushed over. Wyatt inspected the wound and Blake wavered on his knees, eyes bleary and unfocused.

"Look for a weapon, Immy," Wyatt instructed. Luke's wolf stumbled over, not quite fully healed.

"What's wrong, Wyatt? He shouldn't be like this. His body should be trying to heal!" Kayla cried and Wyatt frowned, worry creasing his brow.

"I know, I know," he said as Blake slumped forward, crashing into Kayla's shoulder. She did her best to support him and keep him upright.

"C'mon, Blake, what's up? What are you feeling? Talk to me," she pleaded softly. She couldn't make out his inaudible whisper.

"Wyatt," Imogen called, picking up a pocketknife from beside the man Blake tackled. Imogen's voice trembled. "It's silver."

Wyatt sucked in a sharp breath as Luke whined and shifted back, human again and on his knees, face pale as ice.

"My prince," he croaked.

"Luke, can you sense anything on the knife?" Wyatt snapped, working something out as his eyes clouded with worry and calculation. Imogen brought it over for Luke. He didn't take the knife but sniffed it.

"It's been spelled." He slumped, and Kayla could tell by his complexion that he was still doing some major internal healing.

"Spelled? Spelled how?" Kayla spat out to no one in particular.

Wyatt scrunched his face up in concentration. "Maybe. . . ahh! I don't know! Maybe to make the silver poisoning work quicker on a wolf?"

"But he was fine! He healed Luke!"

"Adrenaline . . . his alpha abilities? I don't know, Kayla!" Wyatt snapped.

"What do we do?"

"Both the vehicles are out," Luke stated as smoke rose from the van that had crashed into them. Their own vehicle was a mangled mess. "We need to get away from the open road. If they send more people after us . . ." Luke scanned their surroundings, his protective instincts coming back online.

Wyatt and Kayla lifted Blake to his feet between them, putting an arm around each of their shoulders. Blake moaned and hung his head, like it was too much to even keep it up. Kayla choked back a sob – it wasn't the time to lose it.

Luke started walking, stumbling slightly. "Come on, this way."

Imogen stayed close to Luke because the shifter was still healing, and every now and then he needed her help. Even though it had only been a few minutes, the walk through the country was taking its toll.

"What's wrong with Blake?" Kayla asked as they moved.

"A spelled silver knife. Silver is poisonous to shifters. They can't heal from it without major intervention," Wyatt answered.

"But we can help him, right? As soon as we get somewhere safe?" Panic gripped her when no one answered her.

CHAPTER EIGHTEEN

KAYLA

THEY STAGGERED THROUGH A field, dark clouds blocking out the sun and stealing the warmth from their backs. Kayla and Wyatt shouldered most of Blake's weight as they followed Luke and Imogen. The further they got, the stronger Luke appeared to be getting, and it wasn't long before a barn popped up in the distance. They were surrounded by fields and farmland, so it made sense for there to be some structures for storage; she just hoped nobody was in it.

Luke and Imogen pushed open one of the heavy wooden doors so she and Wyatt could come through with Blake, his feet dragging behind them. The barn was tall, with high beams criss-crossing above them. As the door shut, she looked around and motioned for one of the hay bales. Luke pulled it down, a grunt of effort escaping his lips, and Wyatt helped her lay Blake on top of the makeshift bed.

Kayla fought back tears when his pale face took on a grey pallor, his breathing shallow. Throwing herself into action, she used the hole the knife had made to rip open his shirt, exposing his bare stomach. The wound wasn't horrendous; his body should have been able to handle it.

"Is anyone going to tell me how we heal this?" she asked, sounding far stronger than she felt. Her three companions exchanged glances.

"Tell me!" she commanded, a little of the hysteria that threatened to overwhelm her leaking into her voice.

"Silver poisoning . . ." Wyatt began, looking at Blake's body. "It's a tricky one to beat. He needs a shifter blood transfusion. That's the only chance shifters have when they're infected with silver."

At first, she didn't know what to say. Surely they just had to find equipment for Luke to give some blood to him? But the way they continued to avoid her eyes made her stomach fall.

Luke stepped forward. "I'll do it. If we search for something we can use, I'll do it." Imogen's mouth dropped open.

"But Luke . . ." Imogen started.

Kayla snapped. "What? Spit it out guys!"

Wyatt met her head on. "We have a stockpile of donated shifter blood. It doesn't really matter what type, as shifter bodies process it the same, but he would need about half the amount of blood he has inside of him. The other half would have to be drained to give him the best chance of washing away the poisoning. Even if we could somehow fashion a system here, that would mean Luke giving up over half of his blood." Kayla swallowed the lump in her throat. "No one can lose that much blood at once. Luke's body wouldn't have time to replenish itself, even as a shifter."

"I know this. I will gladly give my life for him," Luke said stoically. Kayla looked down at Blake, grabbing his hand and wrapping hers around it for stability. Blake wouldn't want that. She knew it down to her very bones.

"No."

"I'm prepared, Kayla," Luke argued.

"No. He wouldn't want this. He wouldn't want you to exchange your life for his. I won't let you do this. We have to find another way. How far away are we from the hotel?"

"Too far, especially on foot," Wyatt answered.

"What about Mal?" Imogen asked, and Kayla glanced at Wyatt again.

"I assume he got my message, but my phone was destroyed in the car. We drove for a couple miles after I sent that message, and then we walked here. Hopefully he'll be able to scent us, but . . ."

He didn't have to say it. She could see on his face that he wasn't counting on Mal finding them in time to get them back to the hotel.

They were on their own, and the silver was poisoning Blake too fast.

Damn the witch who accelerated the poison. If Blake hadn't attacked the witch himself, Kayla would have made sure they were in a world of pain. Even then, it wouldn't compare to the anguish she felt as fear tumbled through her entire body.

She needed to focus. She needed Blake to heal.

She needed Blake.

Shoving those thoughts away for the moment, she asked the others to explain more about silver poisoning. She knew some from her parents' work but not everything. Closing her eyes, hand still clutching Blake's, she listened to Wyatt explain how silver infiltrates the wolf, slowly killing the animal and thus, the human, too.

"Stop," she said in the middle of Wyatt's explanation. "I have an idea."

Imogen jumped up from where she'd been resting, her shoulders hunched.

"The wolf. The silver affects the wolf, right?"

Wyatt nodded. "Yes."

"So if I can contain the wolf, perhaps we can treat the poison. Extract it somehow." She rushed through her idea, growing hopeful.

"How can you contain a wolf? We're one and the same," Luke said, frowning at her. Not in disbelief, but in confusion about the prospect.

"My dad, he was a mage. He pushed back and trapped Blake's wolf. That's why Blake couldn't shift for all those years, because his brain was duped into thinking he wasn't a shifter. I was able to use some of my own magic to help release his wolf, and that's how he shifted for the first time!"

The three of them stared at her in shock, mouths wide open.

"You have mage magic?" Imogen said, startled, and Kayla realised she'd just exposed herself. There was no point in hiding it, not if they could save Blake.

"Yes, and my mother was a witch. I can also perform spells."

"You can do all three strains of magic?" Wyatt asked, and she nodded. "I knew you were powerful," he said with a whistle. That was all he said. No judgement. No fear.

"If I can subdue the wolf, hide him behind a spell or use mage magic, then maybe I can use my elemental power to draw out the silver. Can you help me, Wyatt?"

"I'll do what I can, but silver isn't an element," he stated.

"But it's of the earth, and that's something we have power in."

Wyatt nodded thoughtfully. "It's worth a try, isn't it?" he replied with a mischievous glint in his eye. She knew he liked to experiment, and he was willing to do anything for Blake, just like she was. She looked down at Blake's lifeless face and wished for nothing more than to see his eyes fill with emotion again.

She'd been afraid of how much she had to say, that the words weren't right or it wasn't the time, but now she was afraid she'd never get to say it at all.

"Yes," she answered, her heart hammering.

"You can't!" Imogen yelled.

Kayla sputtered, "What?"

"That's . . . that's . . . what if you do more harm with your . . . *magic*?"

Kayla wasn't sure if Imogen had meant it, but the tone of accusation made Kayla wince.

"Anything is better than nothing," Luke told Imogen. He turned to Kayla. "Do it."

Wyatt moved over to Imogen, gently taking her elbow and whispering into her ear. Imogen listened carefully. Kayla couldn't hear them, and she doubted even Luke would be able to with how close Wyatt was to Imogen. Wyatt held her focus as she watched him closely. He stroked his thumb on her arm, holding her elbow in a light grip, and when he straightened, Kayla couldn't decipher the look on his face. Something passed between them, something unspoken, and Imogen nodded.

"Okay," she whispered, looking briefly to Kayla before dropping her gaze again. This time, not as much fear was evident in her eyes; whatever Wyatt had said to calm her worked. Wyatt moved back to where Blake was laid out on the hay, opposite Kayla.

"What do you need me to do?" he asked. He was putting his trust in her.

"First, I'll see if I can replicate what my father did to him. I might have to use a spell to strengthen it because he can shift now. But I know his wolf. If I ask, he'll do what I say."

"You spoke to his wolf?" Luke asked, eyebrows shooting towards his hairline.

"Yes, when I helped the wolf break free of my father's magic," she answered. Luke frowned pensively. She couldn't dwell on it, she had to focus.

She opened herself to her magic and placed a hand on his forehead, fighting back tears when she realised how cold he was to the touch.

"Blake?" she whispered, her words intended for him only. "Let me in."

WHEN SHE OPENED HER EYES, she was in Blake's mind again, but it wasn't like before. It was still dark – dark walls, dark floor, dark ceiling – but the TV screens that held memories cycled through images too quickly for her to keep up with. They spilled out in front of her, like ghostly apparitions. As she moved through them, searching for his wolf, the memories scattered like mist. Playing with his younger brother, Charlie, as kids. Laughing with his adoptive parents, their love for him shining through their eyes. She even saw herself a few times in the moments they'd shared over the past six months. Memory after memory played out in no discernible order.

She spun when she heard a pained whine curl through the air.

"Where are you?" she asked, searching through the memories. They dispersed as she moved through them, but another memory always took its place.

And then she saw him. His wolf. His belly and head were pressed to the floor, and pain flashed through his golden eyes. She fell to her knees beside him and ran her hands over his ice-white fur, taking solace in his presence. She didn't know why, but she knew her touch calmed him, and providing comfort gave her a sense of peace.

"You're okay. I'm here to help. I need to use my mage magic on you. I don't know if it'll work, but if I can secure your wolf somewhere safe, I might be able to draw out the poison. It's a wild guess, a complete stab in the dark, but I can't . . . I can't just let you go without trying." He bumped his muzzle against her leg and she knew he understood. "Thank you," she breathed.

She pulled her mage magic forward, feeling for it like she had when she'd first helped him and his wolf. The power rushed forth, and she silently thanked the healer for the work she did on her. Kayla directed the power to the wolf and willed him to sleep, preventing his shifting ability. When she sensed the wolf was unconscious, she called on more of her magic and instructed it to protect him. Her parents always said the most powerful magic was strengthened with intentions, and right then, there was nothing stronger than her will to keep him alive.

"I know you're there. You've always been there," she whispered to the magic that resided within her. It wasn't a spell, per se, but her words held power. "You were late coming to me, but I had faith. I had faith that what was meant to happen would. I know it didn't always seem like it, but you never stopped guiding me, and you've gifted me with more magic than I deserve. I'm asking you to help me. Protect him, protect him, protect him . . ." she trailed off and sat back as a shield rose up from the dark, nondescript floor. The bubble-like structure moulded itself to Blake's slumbering wolf. The shield emitted a faint hum, and it told her there was magic at work. She pulled her hands back as it sealed shut, and she knew Blake was safe for now, cocooned within her magic. She nodded and thanked her magic as she stood.

"I'll release you soon. I'm sorry you're caged again but it's for the best," she said to the wolf, but the words fell on deaf ears as he slept.

Marcus's voice yanked her from her thoughts. She spun, surprised and wary, but she relaxed when she saw it was coming from one of Blake's ghostly memories. The likeness of Marcus wavered slightly as the image strengthened. Pale imitations of Imogen and Blake joined the memory, too. She didn't know what drew her to the scene, only that she moved closer to hear what was going on.

"My daughter, Imogen, and you have been declared the shifter and magic user who will unite the bloodlines."

"As in . . ." Blake asked.

"Children," Imogen said. "Our children will have shifter blood and magic blood."

"Will have? As in, there is no choice in the matter? The great Alliance rests on the two us having kids?"

At first, she didn't understand, but then everything clicked into place.

"An arranged marriage?" Blake's voice rang out.

"Well, yes. We can't have illegitimate children to the royal shifter line!"

And her heart broke into more pieces than she'd ever thought possible.

CHAPTER NINETEEN

BLAKE

THE KNIFE PIERCED HIS flesh, sharp pain sinking into his abdomen, but he'd have to worry about it later; Kayla and Luke needed him. He tossed the witch's body to the ground, knowing he'd regret giving the man a quick death. After everything those hunters had done to Kayla and him, he held no remorse.

He turned to Kayla, and fear and worry swirled in her eyes. He wanted to take it away, but Luke was in trouble.

Working with Kayla was as easy as breathing, and together they managed to free Luke, but when the shifter was removed from the car, Blake could sense his life force seeping away.

He wouldn't let Luke die.

"Shift," he encouraged him, but Luke must have been too far gone. He stayed as he was, moaning. The wound was wide and deep, but all Luke needed to do was shift and the magic would heal his injuries, even if it took time.

When nothing happened, some primal part of Blake awoke. Something clicked into place. A rush of adrenaline, a rush of *something*, ran through his veins.

"Shift!" This time, he put power behind the word, and he commanded Luke – Luke's wolf – to take over. It worked, but the price was the effect on his own body. He hadn't realised how weak he was until he fell to his knees, and Kayla crouched in front of him to touch his stomach. He winced when she came near his wound, and he couldn't string together a coherent thought. He should be healing. It was a stab wound, but not a major one. His shifting abilities should be kicking in. Should be.

He fell forward against Kayla. His wolf whimpered inside, craving her touch. She'd always helped him before. He trusted her.

Wait.

What was happening?

He didn't know when he'd been hoisted up, but he knew he was being dragged, held upright by Wyatt and Kayla. Kayla. Was she okay? He couldn't look. His head was heavy. His feet uncooperative. Kayla.

The world was dark, but her voice was clear. His eyes wouldn't open. A hand touched his, held it tightly. It was Kayla. He tried reaching for her, but nothing worked.

That's when the pain began.

Fire scorched his veins.

Words penetrated the pain, but he couldn't make out whole sentences. He didn't know what they were saying. Bits and pieces made it through the fog, and he heard Kayla admit her magic out loud. He feared what the others would do to her. Then she placed a hand on his head, and her presence pulsed nearby.

He basked in the calming sensation that swept over him.

"Let me in," she said. He had no worries, no doubts, only acceptance.

The moment she connected with his mind, he sighed. His relief tasted sweet even as he struggled to make sense of what was happening to him.

He heard her talking, felt her delicate hands on his wolf. How did she do this? How did she see his wolf in his mind? The words weren't clear, but her voice was enough.

He sensed when his wolf began to slumber and his thoughts quieted. He'd lost something, a piece of him, but then her voice echoed through his head, and he was more at peace. A part of him was missing, but his light was still there.

It wasn't until he heard the light again, his saviour, that he realised she was crying.

"Why didn't . . . tell me!" he thought he heard. Only parts of the whole were getting through to him. Other voices murmured, but only hers reached him. She was the only one he cared about. She was the only one he wished he could comfort, but instead he remained paralysed, his body a prison.

"How . . . agree?" she said, and then he heard a male voice. Blake wanted to growl. The man sounded like he was close with her. Blake strained against his bonds, but nothing moved; a small groan reached his ears.

"We have . . . of course I will . . . must hurry . . . for the . . ." He wanted to howl for her. Her pain was his pain.

Lost in a haze of agony in both his body and his heart, he called out for his wolf, but the familiar presence was gone. The wolf was part of him, two halves of the same whole. Why had he only just come to this conclusion?

He screamed. Fire raced through his veins, gleefully infecting every aspect of his being, but she followed. He knew she did. She was coming after it, calling the monster away, taming the beast, draining the poison. He heard her voice and concentrated on the melody.

He was drained but free.

The fire was gone.

"It's done," the voice said again, but it sounded wrong, hollow. He tried reaching out, but his limbs were heavy. He called for his wolf, but as the bonds that protected the furry animal receded, he knew the wolf was deep in sleep.

He was alone.

BLAKE BLINKED OPEN HIS eyes, finding wooden rafters above him. The scent of grass, field, and hay reached his nose, and something scratched at his back. He turned his head and Imogen jumped up from where she sat with a loud gasp.

"Wyatt!" she shouted.

Blake tried to speak but coughed instead. His body ached like he'd been hit by a freight train.

Wyatt came over with a big smile on his face. "You're awake! We were just discussing how to get you back! Man, you worried us!"

Blake glanced between them. While relief was evident in their eyes, something else hovered close to the surface.

"Luke? Kayla?" The last he remembered – coherently – Luke was shifting from his injuries.

"Luke's fine, thanks to your command. I never thought I'd see something as powerful as the Alpha display. It sure was something!" Wyatt whooped.

"And Kayla?" Blake asked again, turning his head toward the open barn. Hay bales were stacked in each of the corners, and he figured it was what he was lying on. He didn't see Kayla anywhere. Wyatt and Imogen exchanged looks, and his heart sped up. "Guys, where is she?"

Wyatt rubbed a hand on the back of his neck as he spoke. "Mal arrived. He got my co-ordinates. It just took a bit of time to gather a team and get here. He thought the worst when he saw the car wrecks, but he followed our tracks here."

Imogen continued when Wyatt stopped talking. "And then because Luke had been injured, we decided it was best if he went back with Mal. They only had one vehicle with them, and we didn't know how long you'd be out for. Three guards are stationed outside, waiting for Mal to return." None of this told him about Kayla.

Blake sat up, ignoring the wave of dizziness as a growl climbed up his throat.

"Kayla!" he demanded, and both Wyatt and Imogen gulped.

"Kayla . . ." Wyatt began.

"Knows that it was meant to be you and me coming together for the Alliance," Imogen said, and Blake froze.

"How?" he breathed. He needed to explain – she had to let him explain.

"When she was in your head, she saw your memory. She finished using her magic – the elemental strain, that is – to draw out the silver poisoning, but then she left with Mal and Luke."

He couldn't even dwell on the fact that they knew Kayla possessed more than just elemental magic, nor did he acknowledge that she'd undoubtedly saved him using her unique power. All he could think of was how he hadn't had a chance to explain. How he just knew she was hurting, and it was because of him.

"I need to talk to her," he said, making a move to stand up, but Wyatt placed a hand on his shoulder.

"Blake, I wouldn't. I'd give her time to deal with this."

Before Blake could answer, the rumble of a vehicle interrupted their conversation. The engine ceased, and Mal walked into the barn. Relief flooded his face when he saw Blake sitting up.

"My Prince," he said, coming up to them and placing his left fist on his right shoulder, bowing slightly. Blake didn't miss the way Imogen's brows rose.

"Kayla? How is she?" Blake asked Mal, and he dropped his eyes to his feet before meeting Blake's gaze again.

"She is safe with Luke at the hotel," he answered. The distinction Mal made about Kayla being 'safe' didn't sit well with him.

"We need to get back."

"Of course. Marcus is waiting for a debrief from you all."

Mal turned to leave, and Imogen hung her head.

"Not what we need," she muttered. Wyatt moved to place his hand on her back but thought better of it.

"Well, the quicker we move, the quicker this debrief is over with."

Wyatt helped Blake stand up, as his legs weren't quite as stable as they should've been. He only wished that Kayla was the one beside him. All he wanted was to see her, thank her, and explain. But he didn't know what words to say. The Alliance was exactly as she saw it in his head. How else could he put it?

He was being selfish. He wanted to discuss it with her and understand what he should be doing, but after all this time with him, she'd found out that she was being replaced – not that he had a choice. He was such an idiot. None of that mattered. She mattered. He didn't want this Alliance with Imogen. He wanted Kayla.

The revelation shocked him as they drove back to the hotel, and it took all he had not to jump out of the car to find her when they arrived. He knew Marcus didn't like Kayla, and if he knew Blake's intentions . . . he worried for Kayla's safety.

The man in question stood in the main entrance of the hotel when they arrived. Blake was able to walk on his own now, but he was still slow. He was in no shape to fight if he needed to, so he had to keep his cards close to his chest.

Marcus looked indecisive, as if he couldn't decide whether to yell at them or ask if they were okay. He did neither, turning around swiftly to march inside. Wyatt paused next to Blake.

"He means for us to follow," Wyatt mumbled and strode after Imogen into the building. Blake trailed them both into what must have been Marcus's office. A large wooden table sat in the middle of the room with two small armchairs in front of the door. Marcus went behind his desk, sitting in his office chair. Papers neatly filed on the desk next to a computer monitor. Apart from one bookcase and a metal filing cabinet, the room was bare.

He knew Kayla was in the room without even needing to look; he sensed her presence so acutely – how had he not realised it before? Hers was the only presence he searched for.

She was in a chair, one leg crossed over the other, adamantly ignoring him. Luke stood to one side, looking better than when Blake had last seen him. Imogen and Wyatt stopped near Kayla's chair but neither sat. The only other seat was next to Luke.

Marcus's face twitched as he struggled to hold his mask of calm.

"Please, sit, Blake," Marcus suggested, but from his tone, it was an order. The man took a deep breath, his nostrils flaring. "So, Luke tells me there was a little incident?" He may have asked the question, but it was obvious he already knew the answer. However, Blake wasn't sure if he knew about Kayla's magic. She refused to make eye contact with Blake and kept tucking and untucking hair behind her ear.

"I've already explained," Luke began as Wyatt and Imogen opened their mouths like goldfish, no words coming out. "We were ambushed. I was injured in the car, but Blake and Kayla got me out. I shifted to heal, and then Blake was stabbed. We took him to a barn so we were out of sight and waited for Mal's team to find us. Kayla was able to use elemental magic to draw the poison out of Blake."

Marcus pinched the bridge of his nose. "But that is not elemental magic! Why don't you tell me what happened, Blake?" he asked, trying to tone down the volume as he spoke.

"It's true, but I also wasn't very conscious. Without Kayla, though, I would have died," he said. He tried glancing at her, but she stared straight ahead, looking at nothing.

"That doesn't explain the unnatural nature of Kayla's . . . magic,"

Marcus spat, and Blake noted the tiny flinch from Kayla. A grumble rose up from the back of Blake's throat, but he was able to squash it down. Instead, Wyatt spoke.

"We experimented, Marcus. We thought that since silver is an element of the earth, and we wield the earth power, we might be able to summon the silver. It was pure luck, but we did base it on sound theory."

"It's true, Dad," Imogen finished, and Blake sagged ever so slightly in relief. They were keeping Kayla's magic a secret. At least for now.

"And what do you have to say for yourself?" Marcus demanded of Kayla; Blake felt a pang of pride when she coolly turned her head to meet his stare.

"I helped save Luke and your prized possession. Problem?"

Blake held in a wince. Marcus's eye twitched, and Blake's body tensed.

"I will deal with you later," Marcus said to Kayla. "You are also dismissed," he said to Wyatt, flicking his wrist as if he couldn't care less. "Blake and Imogen, you will stay. We have much to discuss."

Blake noted that Luke wasn't included, but he guessed the wolf was always around Marcus anyway. He tried catching Kayla's eye as she left, but she hurried out with Wyatt.

Imogen took Kayla's seat and they shared a similar look of dread as Marcus turned to them.

THEY SAT IN THE room for a little over two hours before Marcus dismissed them, and he spent the entire time thinking about Kayla. He had to pretend he was taking the Alliance and the proposition seriously so that Marcus wouldn't see Kayla as a threat. The more he was around Marcus, the more he understood Wyatt and Luke's warning. There was a slightly unhinged look about the man when he spoke about joining bloodlines. It was as if he wasn't discussing marrying off his daughter to breed children – a phrase he actually used more than once. Imogen shrunk inward every time he reduced her to a means to an end, and Blake felt sorry for her. She deserved this no less than he did.

He wanted to discuss it with Kayla, to see if there was a way to help Imogen. It worried him that Kayla wouldn't even look in his direction, but when Marcus dismissed them, Imogen went to her floor and Blake rushed to his. Luke stayed behind again.

As he stepped onto their floor, he spotted Wyatt leaning against his door. Wyatt stood up, shoving his hands in his pockets.

"You okay?" Wyatt asked, concerned.

"Yeah, just about. I don't mean to be rude, but why are you here?"

At least Wyatt had the good sense to look guilty when he spoke.

"She asked me to tell you that she was staying in the other room tonight," he said, nodding his head towards the opposite door.

"What? Why?"

"She needs some time to think, and she can't do that around you."

"Are you like, her personal messenger now?"

"No." Wyatt bristled slightly. "I just know how she feels, in a way."

"And how's that?" he asked, thinking it was the only insight he might be able to get that evening.

"Redundant, for a start. Look, mate, she did some pretty epic stuff for you today. She saved your freaking life."

"Do you think I don't know that? I just want to . . . thank her."

"She likes you a lot. It's pretty darn evident, Blake, to everyone but you, apparently. Just think about it. If the one thing you wanted in the world – the person you worked hard to protect – had to be with someone else, how would you feel?" Blake couldn't help the animalistic snarl that escaped. "Precisely. You both have a lot to work out, and I don't know what the right answer is. I sure as hell know Imogen doesn't want this, but I'm not the one pledged to a contract. Get some sleep, give Kayla some space tonight, and decide your priorities. But just so you know, what you decide affects all of us."

"You say that as if I should just go along with what Marcus wants."

Wyatt gave a small, sad chuckle. "That would be easier, and safer for Kayla, but is that what you want?"

"What if I don't have a choice? What if Kayla's safety is too important to risk?" he asked quietly. He knew Wyatt was taken aback by the question, as if he hadn't expected Blake to ask for his council.

"Then I think you're underestimating what she can do and what she would fight for."

Wyatt walked towards the lift, leaving Blake alone with his warring thoughts.

CHAPTER TWENTY

KAYLA

KAYLA WOKE AFTER A night of disturbed, agitated sleep. She knew Blake was across the hall, and more than once she'd wanted to crawl over there and bury herself next to him, to feed off his warmth and comfort. But then she reminded herself that he was promised to another – and had kept it from her. Everyone had kept it from her. But it was Blake and his secrecy that cut the deepest. They shared everything, or so she had thought.

Last night, Marcus had told her he had a spot opening in the taskforce that she could join. She would be able to learn how to control her magic and still support an alliance while helping others. He hadn't shouted or commanded, and she wondered if it could be her best option. He left her with her thoughts, and they'd plagued her all night.

She sat up in her cold bed, wrapping her arms around her middle. She'd not fetched anything from their room last night because she hadn't wanted to go into the space. It may have just been a room that they shared, but it was one which he had fought for them to stay in together.

Sighing, she threw her head back and stared at the ceiling. She needed a shower. She needed clothes. She needed to get her pack. Resigning herself to seeing Blake, she knew she had to come up with a plan on how to approach him. Clearly, he didn't regard her in the same way she did him, otherwise he would have told her about the arrangement as soon as he learned of it.

Her feelings were her own, and she would have to bear them alone. A sob threatened to bubble up, but she fought it back down. She couldn't let it win, not if she was about to see him. She thought they'd shared . . . something, but she was realising just how foolish she was. He'd been her constant since her parents died – since her world was thrown into chaos – and the thought of not being near him brought about a deep-seated sadness she didn't know existed. It was as if her very essence – her magic – was grieving, too.

At some point during the night, she'd made the decision to take Marcus up on his offer. It would get her away from the guy and allow her to support the alliance from afar. She couldn't be at the hotel, watching them. If the taskforce didn't work out, she would join Ben and help him with her parents' work. If all went to plan, their society would grow more peaceful, and she wanted to unite the people that her parents had hidden. Despite the lies and secrets her parents had withheld from her, they had done good things for the people of both races.

Before she lost the small amount of courage she'd built, she crossed the hall and stood outside the room she'd shared with Blake. It was now or never. She would grab her things and calmly explain to him that she was leaving. It wasn't like she was abandoning the Alliance, she was just supporting it elsewhere now that he had people who would help him more than she could. That was all.

A quick pang of guilt shot through her, but she squashed it down; yes, her mum had asked her to find Blake because he was the key –*her* key – but that didn't mean her mum was right. Her mum could easily have meant Imogen, and now Kayla was leaving him in capable hands.

She justified her choices to herself and raised a hand to knock, certainly not feeling comfortable enough to just walk in, and the door opened wide. Luke answered and gave her a small smile.

"Kayla, how are you?" he asked with genuine concern.

"Um, yeah. I just needed to get a few of my things. Is everything all right?"

"Of course. I was just explaining to Blake what Marcus wanted him to do today."

"Riiiight," she stretched the word out. She knew she wouldn't be receiving instructions because Marcus just wanted her gone. He'd said as much last night. She sighed. She should be relieved, considering it meant she could leave without a fuss.

"I'll see you later," Luke said as he moved out of the doorway and down towards the lift.

Kayla watched Luke leave because she knew Blake was studying her from inside the room. Truthfully, she needed a moment to compose herself.

When she turned her head, her breath nearly left her. Blake leaned one shoulder against the wall in their room. He would have been right behind Luke when they'd had their conversation, not that it mattered with his shifter hearing. Blake's head hung low, but his eyes were focused on her. Sadness shone in their depths, but it was the glimmer of pain that made her look away. Blake put his hands in his pockets and straightened.

She walked in, closing the door behind her. She tried not to look him in the eye again as she moved about the room, gathering her things.

"What are you doing?" he asked softly.

"I'm getting my things together." She pressed her lips together in a hard line. She could do this.

"Are you not coming back to stay in here with me?"

The vulnerable way he said it had her heart clenching tightly. No. No, she couldn't, not when he was promised to another. He may have wanted her as a friend and confidant, as they had been to each other the past few months, but now that she realised the true extent of her feelings, she simply couldn't stay with him.

"No, Blake, I'm not." She didn't mean to sound harsh. After she shoved the last of the clothes in her bag, she turned around. He was much closer than she expected, and she flinched at his proximity. Hurt marred his features as he stepped back.

"Please don't go anywhere. I'm sorry I didn't tell you. I . . ." He trailed off, running a hand through his long hair. He followed her into the bathroom as she grabbed her toiletries.

"But you didn't tell me, Blake, and that's okay. I shouldn't expect you to tell me everything."

"But you should! We've been in each other's pockets for so long. We have been telling each other everything. I should have come to you straight away. I wanted to . . ."

He stood in the doorway, taking up the whole space; she had to brush past him to get into the room. She tried not to dwell on the familiarity of his warmth, his body, as she did. She gulped down the sob that threatened to choke her. She would not show weakness. He had made his choices. So would she.

"Please don't, Blake. The Alliance was never about me. It was always about you. I did what my mum asked. I found you. And now you're here with others who have dedicated their lives to the Alliance. I won't stand in the way of that."

Blake's head snapped up, a deep crease between his brows. "What do you mean, 'you won't stand in the way of that'?" he asked, stepping closer. She tucked the toiletries inside her bag and zipped it up.

"It doesn't matter now," she breathed. When she turned, Blake was even closer, and she fought the urge to step forward. Instead, she moved back. A small scowl formed on Blake's face. Good. She could deal with annoyed Blake. She couldn't deal with hurt Blake.

"Yes, it does. I think it matters a whole lot now."

Angrily tucking hair behind her ear, she glared back at him. It didn't escape her that he'd placed himself between her and the door.

"The only thing that matters is the Alliance, Blake. You know that."

She pushed past him and reached for the door but she felt him at her back. He grabbed her arms and spun her around. He was stupidly close, a dangerous, panicked glint in his eyes.

"No, it isn't the only thing that matters, Kayla. You matter. You matter to me. You're part of my pack. I know it as sure as I know anything. My wolf accepted you as ours long before I knew what that meant. I cannot do this without you, and I will not do it without you, because I should have said something, done something, long ago." He finished his passionate speech, breathing heavily. She couldn't form words; she could barely breathe. Her eyes found his, so close to her own. Their breaths mingled, and it would only take one of them tilting their face forward ever so slightly for their lips to meet. She didn't know if she'd ever wanted something so badly before.

She froze in place. She couldn't pull away from him, but she couldn't lean in, either. The moment his intention became clear, she didn't stop him. He lowered his head the inch he needed to, and their lips met.

They were soft at first, questioning, but when she didn't pull away, he slanted his lips over hers and she melted against him. She was powerless to her hormones and true desires. His warm hands moved up her arms, leaving trails of electricity dancing across her skin. He brushed over her shoulders, caressing her neck before cupping her face protectively. He angled her chin and deepened the kiss. She dropped her pack and gripped onto his strong hips for support before her weak knees betrayed her.

As one of his hands tangled in her hair, keeping her close, the other gently stroked down her body, leaving trembling sparks in its wake. He smiled against her lips, and she couldn't help but answer with her own.

When his hand rounded her hip, she gasped, her lips parting in surprise at the touch. He used the moment to gently taste her with his tongue, asking permission, and she moaned in answer. He took encouragement from the sound, and she met him just as hungrily. A low rumble vibrated through his chest as he pulled her flush against him, but it wasn't enough for her.

More. Closer. She moved her hands up to his biceps, caressing the smooth, hard skin, and was satisfied when his muscles jumped at her touch. It made her happy that he was just as affected by her as she was by him. A small, possessive growl emerged from his throat. Her eyes flashed up to his, momentarily breaking from the kiss to find them glowing, their golden colour intense with unsaid emotion.

"Your eyes . . . your wolf," she breathed, not afraid, but in awe.

"Wants you as much as I do," he said gruffly, his wolf close to the surface. Muscles rippled beneath her hands and sent sparks of excitement through her body. All coherent, sensible thought was banished as her focus narrowed. She only saw him.

He pushed her back against the door, pressing his body as close as possible. Their mouths met in hunger, and it was like she was able to breathe properly for the first time – as if it was always meant to happen, but it still wasn't enough. She pulled at his shirt, pushing her body up against his and yelping when he picked her up. He placed a strong hand on each hip, holding her close. Her arms circled his neck, legs wrapping tight around his middle, and she looked down at him from her perch. She bent her head, meeting his plump lips again, and kissed him as she leaned heavily against his solid body. One of his arms moved to support her weight as he walked backwards, towards one of the beds.

She couldn't quite get her brain to figure out what was going on, but she knew as long as they stayed connected, everything would be all right. When he gently laid her on the bed, never breaking their kiss, she sighed against his lips. His heat, his scent, surrounded her. She felt cocooned. She felt safe. She felt wanted.

"Kayla . . ." he moaned into her ear as he trailed soft kisses along her jaw and down her neck. One of his arms rested next to her head, propping him up just enough to kiss her. His other hand stroked down her body and entwined his fingers with hers. Even through her clothes, the heat of his touch etched into her skin.

His groan was a delight to her ears. His mouth found hers again and there was desperation there, both of them wanting more and more. Her free hand found his face and she stroked his cheek, stubble tickling her palm. She slid her hand to the base of his strong neck and pulled him closer still. His desire for her was evident, and when she met his eyes again, she tumbled into the depths of his emotion.

A loud knock jolted them from their passion, and his lips stilled against hers. They panted heavily, their breaths twining together as they stayed frozen, neither daring to move.

"Is . . . is someone out there?" Her lips touched against his as she whispered, her voice trembling. Blake nodded, his nose brushing tenderly against her face.

"At your door. It's Wyatt," he replied.

With those few words, the weight of what they'd done pressed down on her, and her brain started functioning again.

"Blake, I . . ."

"Please don't. Don't say anything, please. Let us have this," he begged, placing his forehead against hers as she tried to get her breathing back to normal. His thumb stroked circles on her hand, and his breath tickled her neck. It was hard to think.

"We, um . . . this shouldn't have happened," she finally managed. He stilled, his body going rigid when she spoke.

"Kayla . . ." He said her name with a low, pained groan.

"No. Don't. I'm finding this hard to get out, to say. I can't stop . . . this . . . on my own. One of us has to be stronger. We cannot do this. The Alliance . . ." she trailed off, not sure if her voice would stay whole.

"Fuck the Alliance!" Blake growled, but Kayla wasn't afraid of him.

She never could be.

"You don't mean that, Blake." Tears gathered in her eyes, and his gaze softened. His free hand brushed her hair back from her face and caressed her cheek. She closed her eyes as he rested his forehead on her shoulder.

A louder knock at the door made her jump.

"We should . . ." she began, wanting to end the moment for the right reasons but afraid it would be the first and last time they could ever give in to their emotions. Blake nodded and slowly, reluctantly, eased himself away from her. As soon as the heat of his body left her, she felt cold. It was more than simply not having him nearby, she missed his presence already. She had to leave. She couldn't be around him and not want it.

Gulping down a new wave of grief, she walked over to the door on unsteady legs and picked up her bag where she'd dropped it earlier. She didn't turn around to face him.

"It doesn't matter if you did something earlier or not. The end result would have always been the same," she whispered, trying hard to keep her tears at bay. She didn't let him answer. She opened the door and found Wyatt with his fist raised, ready to knock again.

"Oh! Kayla! I was just looking for you . . . did you decide to move back in here?" he asked, frowning at her. He looked over her head towards Blake. Wyatt wasn't a shifter, but she didn't think he missed the tension pulsing in the room.

"No, I was just getting my things. Why were you looking for me?"

"Luke told me that he was leaving with Blake and Imogen to go to the meeting we should have been at yesterday, He asked me to stay with you . . . for company."

"That makes sense," she said, moving past Wyatt.

"Kayla, wait!" Blake suddenly blurted out, following her into the hallway. "It's just a meeting to show them I'm alive. I asked Luke to make sure you'd be okay while we're gone as Marcus insisted on only us three going," he rambled at her.

"It's okay, Blake. I knew this was going to happen. You have your duties to take care of, and I have mine."

She'd only taken a few steps towards the other door when Blake's hand caught hers and spun her around to face him. He was careful not to bring their bodies too close, and for that, she was grateful.

"Please don't make any decisions before I'm back . . . I just . . . I just need time to think, to work everything out. Please," he begged. She knew she couldn't lie to him, so she didn't say anything about leaving.

"There's nothing to work out, Blake. You stay safe, okay?" she said.

Luke exited his room and beckoned Blake over. Blake gave her one last scorching look – one she couldn't quite decipher – and disappeared into the lift with the other shifter.

"Want to talk about it?" Wyatt asked when they were on their own in the hallway.

"Not really."

"Want breakfast?"

"I'm not hungry." At least, not for food. "I know you were told to keep me company, but I'd rather have some time on my own, if that's all right?"

Wyatt's face pinched in thought. "Um, Kayla . . ."

"I'll be safe in my room if that's what you're worried about. Marcus doesn't care about me. I'm not a threat to the plan. I'm making sure of it."

"What does that mean?"

"Nothing, nothing. I just need some time on my own, please?"

"I'll come back to check on you after breakfast, okay?"

"Yeah, sure."

Wyatt walked to the lift and pressed the call button. She waved as he stepped inside, and then she was on her own. Just like she'd asked to be. Just like she had to be.

Tears gathered on her lashes, and she didn't stop them as they fell.

CHAPTER TWENTY-ONE

BLAKE

HE HATED LEAVING HER, especially with that broken look in her eyes, but he had to keep up pretences with Marcus. He also needed to speak to Imogen. He didn't want to go to the meeting, but he knew they needed as many people on their side as possible, otherwise, the Alliance opposers would crush them. They were fighting a war they could only win with support.

Following Luke out of the lift, he spotted Imogen standing by her father. Their pinched features, drawn brows, and thin lips indicated they were having a hushed argument. Luke and Blake made their way over, but the pair stopped speaking when the two shifters were in earshot. The lobby was busy, so it was hard to pick out their specific conversation, anyway.

"Blake. Luke," Marcus addressed them. "Thank you for agreeing to meet with these people again. They were saddened to hear what happened, but I assured them you were making a quick recovery."

"But you didn't tell them who saved him, did you?" Imogen sneered, and it was the first time Blake truly heard her anger directed at the man. Sure, he knew she didn't like what he'd planned for her, but she'd been quietly accepting it. The tone of her voice and her words spoke volumes.

"Imogen, you will *not* question my judgement. You hear me?" he chastised quietly. Somehow, the softly spoken words caused more worry to settle in his gut than if he had shouted.

Imogen scowled.

Luke interjected, as keen as he was to get the meeting over and done with. "Shall we?"

"Yes, go. Prove to them you're Prince Alastair, and then we'll discuss more tonight – just the three of us," Marcus concluded. Imogen rolled her eyes.

Blake and Luke followed Imogen outside, and Luke directed them to the four-by-four vehicle they were taking. Luke climbed into the driver's seat and Imogen pointed to the front passenger door, telling Blake to get in.

When they were settled in the car and on the way, Blake couldn't stop checking his side mirror. He knew Luke was being extra vigilant, but it wouldn't hurt to have both of them on the lookout. Imogen leaned forward in her seat, bracing her elbows on the centre console.

"How's Kayla?" she asked innocently, but Blake jumped, wondering if she knew they'd had a major make-out session. "Blake, you all right?"

"Um, yeah. And I think she is."

"'Cos that magic yesterday . . . I'm sorry I wasn't so cool to begin with . . ."

"I was unconscious. I don't really know what happened. All I know is that you covered for her with Marcus, so thank you for that."

"My dad wants me to announce to these people that we're together – as part of the Alliance," she said. Luke's knuckles tightened on the steering wheel as Blake's mind spun. He thought the meeting was just about introducing himself, but of course Marcus was trying to direct things again. "It's what we were arguing about. I said it was too soon."

"Why would you say that?" Blake asked, genuinely wondering. Would Imogen agree to help him?

"Because I have eyes. I saw what happened yesterday."

"You mean me getting poisoned?"

"About Kayla."

"What do you mean by that?" he questioned, more guarded than before.

"Bonds aren't that common anymore, and you have one." She turned to Luke. "I'm right, aren't I, Luke?"

"Yup," Luke replied, and Imogen smiled triumphantly.

"You have one with Kayla. We can all tell, especially Luke as he's a shifter. Am I right again?"

Luke nodded his confirmation.

"Hang on–" Blake began.

"No, shut up for a moment while I still have the courage to go against my father," Imogen interrupted. She huffed. "I was brought up knowing that this was my fate, and I resigned myself to it. Then you appeared, and I thought to myself, 'I can do this. He's all right. At least he doesn't seem like a douche'." She paused, and Blake blinked at her candidness. He'd always thought she was quiet, and here she was using words like 'douche.' "But then I saw Kayla, and I couldn't ignore the way you two acted around each other. At first, I continued with what my father wanted because, well to be honest, I was scared of what he would do if I didn't. But after yesterday . . . a bond like yours shouldn't be messed with. That sort of bond, between a shifter and a magic user? That hasn't been seen before. What if *that's* the Alliance we all need?"

"What about what your dad said about being 'pure'?"

"I'm from a powerful and influential mage family, yes, but I couldn't have pulled off what Kayla did yesterday. That took skill . . . and a deep connection with you."

"Are you really suggesting we don't go through with this Alliance?" he asked, his tone rising with a smidge of disbelief. She flashed him a small grin.

"Forcing two people together isn't what the alliance should be about. Plus, I'd like to choose my own future. This is the start of that."

Blake didn't know what to say. He opened his mouth several times, but nothing came out.

"I'm not a bad person, you know," Imogen said quietly.

"I know. You've been put in a horrible situation, by your own father no less."

"What do we do now?"

"Are you still open to forming an Alliance of sorts? Let's show them that we can work together. That's what these people need." Both Imogen and Luke smiled at him. "What?" he asked.

"It's just, that's leadership right there. I know I don't just speak for myself when I say that I truly, honestly, feel like I could follow you. And I'm a magic user!" she finished.

"I don't always feel like a good leader. I've done things I'm not that proud of," he replied solemnly.

"To keep you and Kayla alive, for the right reasons – correct? I've already pledged my loyalty to you, Blake, and Imogen? She's good people," Luke added. Imogen smiled at him.

"Thanks Luke. I wondered if you still thought well of me."

"Always have. It's your father I don't like."

"Why stay then? Sorry, that's personal."

"For you and Wyatt, and the fact that I do want our races to work in harmony, in peace."

"You stayed for us?"

"You were just kids, and he was starting to push you in directions that I wasn't altogether happy with."

Silence filled the car.

Blake spoke up first. "So we're just going to prove that I exist today then, yeah? When we get back, I'd like to bring Kayla in on our discussions about how we can promote an alliance between our sides."

"And Wyatt," Imogen tagged on, looking shocked at herself for suggesting it.

"Yeah, him too."

"My dad won't be happy. We should do this without him, at least until we come up with a concrete plan he can't dismiss."

"Is she safe there with him?" Blake asked, and he knew Imogen understood his meaning.

"Wyatt annoys me to death, but he has her back."

THE TRIO WALKED INTO a library that had been closed to the public. Bookshelves lined three of the four walls and tables he assumed were normally placed in the middle of the room were pushed to one side to make space for about eighty people. Some talked in groups, and some threw antagonising looks at others. There were a few mixed-race groups trying to talk to each other, engaging in tension-filled conversation. He couldn't imagine news of yesterday's attack had done much to unify them.

An older woman spotted Blake and moved towards him, offering her hand. Her long salt-and-pepper hair was tied back in a low, sleek ponytail that matched her tailored outfit: grey trousers and a pale green buttoned up jacket.

"Hi, I'm Chrissy. I manage the library here. How are you feeling?" she asked in a gentle voice, and he thought she might be another shifter. He didn't find it as easy identifying female shifters. Apart from a couple he'd seen around the hotel, most shifters he'd met were male – he didn't have much to go on.

"I'm better now, thank you," he replied.

"Good, good. Do you mind if I introduce you now?"

He threw a quick glance at Imogen, who smiled in support. "Sure, go ahead."

"Hello everyone!" she raised her voice and the noise quickly died down, all faces turning their way. Imogen stood to the left of him, but Luke stood way off to the side, scanning the area for threats. "The shifter Prince has arrived, and I'd like to welcome him and thank him for taking the time to come to us today," she finished, beckoning him closer. He stepped forward with Imogen beside him and cleared his throat. If he was to become the shifter Prince everyone thought he was, he'd have to get used to speaking. His mind quickly flashed to Kayla. He wished she was there with him; she'd know what to say, both to him and the crowd.

"Hi, I'm Blake, or at least I was brought up with that as my name. I know a lot of you remember the Prince being called Killian." He paused, and a few people nodded their heads as he spoke. "I know I was meant to be here yesterday, and we do apologise for that – I'm sure you know that we were attacked."

He looked to Imogen who nodded at him, encouraging him to go on.

Someone from the audience asked, "What happened? If you don't mind me asking?"

"Magic users attacked us, and I'm not putting any blame on them here, just stating fact. I've been hunted by my own kind since I found out who I was, but magic users poisoned me with silver." After he finished, there was an influx of questions.

"How did you escape?"

"How are you so well?"

"Why weren't you brought up knowing who you were?"

Blake held up his hands. "Look, I'll explain everything I know. I don't want to lie to you or withhold anything." He spoke the truth then, as he knew secrecy had been far too prevalent. Trust had to start somewhere.

He told them he was brought up human and had only recently shifted for the first time, how he was hunted by shifters, had his family kidnapped by them, and then met Marcus and his daughter. He finally finished by explaining it was Kayla who had saved him. He didn't divulge her secret about the magic strains – he wanted to be truthful, but he had to protect her.

When someone whistled, saying that she must be a powerful elemental, a surge of pride swelled in his chest. Yes. She was magnificent, and not just because of what she could do, but because of who she was.

"Where is she? The one who saved you?" someone else asked, and something made him bristle at the tone.

"She is . . . resting. Imogen came with me instead."

"And what of the Alliance? How will the Alliance work now that you're here?" the same voice asked.

"Like this: communication, openness, a willingness to fight back against those who wish to silence and segregate us."

"How do we know you are who you say you are?"

Blake turned around, pulling his t-shirt over his head to reveal his shoulder blade. There was a collective gasp followed by murmurs. Even Imogen snuck a glance at the Alastair royalty mark.

"Nice," she murmured. Blake re-dressed and faced the crowd again.

The woman who asked him to prove who he was stared at him, uncomfortably so, and then her lips were moving – except he couldn't hear any words. Imogen sucked in a sharp breath and rushed forward, putting a hand on his shoulder just as a shimmering golden arrow aimed straight for his chest. The arrow wasn't real, vibrating with magical energy, but he was sure if it hit him, its tip would strike true. It smashed into Imogen's shield and dissipated.

A roar shook the room as a couple of shifters growled at magic users, many of whom stood with their hands raised in surrender, but some held magical energy at their fingertips, ready to fire if needed.

"Stop!" Blake commanded, and most of the shouting ceased. "Enough, stand down!" He didn't know what possessed him to take over like that, but something rushed through his blood and both the shifters and the magic users turned around. The woman who'd attacked him was held by a shifter who pushed her towards Blake.

"What should we do with her?" the shifter asked.

"What normally happens in these situations?"

"Kill her."

"No, that won't happen. We have to stop killing each other. Luke?" Luke came over, and Blake whispered in his ear. Luke nodded and moved away, pulling his phone out. "Why did you attack me?" he asked the woman. She scoffed at him.

"Because we don't need shifter royalty. We don't need another Alastair banding all the wolves together. You'll just get them all on your side and then wipe us out!"

"How have I given that impression?"

"It's just what you are. Shifters think they're better than every other race."

"No, my closest . . . person . . . is a magic user. I've made friends who are magic users," he said, looking at Imogen. He prayed Kayla was still his person.

"Then they need ending, too!"

He growled instinctively at the threat against Kayla. The witch may not have known who Kayla was, but the warning was there. He swallowed his aggression and took a moment to compose himself.

"I want us to work together. I want to protect us all. You won't be able to stay here. Some of these people don't look happy with you, but I don't want you harmed. It will take time to prove myself, but I hope I do. I want to unite the shifters and make peace with the magic users. I've asked Luke to arrange transport to take you to where you live. I'd pack a bag and then leave. Perhaps later, you might see that we want the same thing."

"Oh yeah? And what's that?"

"A world without fear," he finished, and she looked taken aback.

Luke came inside and said Mal would be there in thirty minutes.

Questions rose up again, all at once.

"I'm happy to answer what I can," he said, and the long half hour commenced.

CHAPTER TWENTY-TWO

BLAKE

BLAKE, IMOGEN, AND LUKE arrived back at the hotel late in the afternoon. The questions had been relentless at the library, but Blake hoped he'd done a good job of answering what he could. They were surprised he was raised as a human, but some saw it as a good thing. Mal arrived, true to his word, about thirty minutes after he'd been called and took the witch back to gather her things.

Before Blake left, he'd asked the people there to respect his decision to leave the witch alone, and he hoped, for the sake of any sort of a truce, that they did. One thing was clear to him: The fighting had to stop.

The three of them had missed lunch, so they made their way to the dining room and into the kitchen. The chefs were in the midst of preparing dinner, but they shoved a whole load of leftovers from lunch at them. They carried what they could back to a table and dug into sandwiches, meats, and salads.

Talk was easy and varied as they chatted. Nothing about the Alliance was mentioned. Instead, they discussed everyday things and got to know one another. He liked Imogen and hoped they could even become friends. Her life hadn't been easy, and he admired her strength of character – now that she was beginning to show it. Luke was great, too, and one of the only shifters he actually knew and trusted – one who hadn't tried to kill him, that is. He didn't know what it was, exactly, that told him Luke would be loyal to him, but he decided to trust his instincts as Kayla often told him to do.

"You guys aren't going to manage any dinner," Imogen declared, watching the boys plough through leftovers.

"Oh we will!" Luke grinned, and Blake wondered if it was the first time Luke had looked so relaxed. Imogen playfully rolled her eyes but stopped, glancing at something behind them.

Blake turned his head. Wyatt stood awkwardly in the dining room doorway. When Wyatt saw him looking, he walked over. He held a piece of paper, passing it from one hand to the other.

"What's with you?" Imogen asked, dropping some of her playfulness. Her tone seemed to jumpstart Wyatt again, and he scowled.

"Well, hello to you too, Immy," he sneered. She tsked at him.

"Where's Kayla?" Blake asked, checking behind Wyatt to see the doorway empty. Blake's unease grew. He couldn't feel her presence.

"Ummm . . ." Wyatt trailed off. Blake growled.

"Wyatt!" he snapped.

"What's this?" Imogen bit out angrily, snatching the paper from Wyatt's restless hands. She opened it and began to read.

"You better start talking, Wyatt!" Blake demanded. He turned to Imogen when she let out a groan. Her eyes shot up to Wyatt's, something indiscernible passing between them. "What?" Blake shouted, his fear and anger entwining.

"Blake, she . . . she's gone," Imogen said softly, holding out the note.

Blake,

I'm sorry to do this, but I must leave. The Alliance between you and Imogen is incredibly important, and I want to do my duty, too. I think you and Imogen will make a great team to unite both our races in these dark times.

There are no hard feelings.

All the best,

Kayla.

Blake dropped the typed note, and Luke leaned over to read it.

"I'm so sorry," Wyatt whispered. Blake pushed to his feet and grabbed Wyatt by his shirt, bringing him closer to his face. Pure anger fuelled his actions.

"What were you doing? We trusted you to stay here and watch her!"

"She wanted space, man. I was just giving her space! When I went to check on her, she was gone, and all that was left was this note. I looked everywhere, asked everyone, but she'd disappeared. I'm sorry. I'm so sorry."

"Blake," Luke said, placing a hand on his shoulder. After a hard shake, Blake let go of Wyatt.

"She wouldn't have left. She wouldn't have left me," Blake said quietly to himself, but the others heard.

"Blake, I . . . I would have left, too, if I was in her shoes," Imogen said. Blake snapped his head around to face her. "It's just, we all know how much you meant to her and how much she wanted an Alliance to work. If I thought I could potentially be standing in the way of that? Or if I had to watch someone I cared about move on with someone else? I would leave. I'm sorry. I'm sorry it came to this. I can ask our tech guys to try and track her down . . ." she finished weakly.

"Maybe she'll contact us in a few days after she's had some time and space?" Wyatt offered, but Blake whirled on him.

"Don't you ever dare speak to me again! You were supposed to stay with her! You could have talked her out of it!"

"Blake!" Luke barked, but he kept his distance. Blake was grateful, because he wasn't sure what he would have done otherwise. His wolf was dangerously close to the surface.

Blake growled, and he knew his eyes were golden when both Imogen and Wyatt took a step back. He grabbed the note off the table.

"I'll be in my room," he ground out, stomping off to the lift.

When he pushed through the door to his room, he slammed it shut and punched the wall next to him, letting out an angry roar. Pain flared in his fist, but it was nothing compared to the tightness he felt in his heart. He'd finally had the courage to tell her – show her – how he felt, and she'd still left him.

Bits of plaster rained down to the floor from the hole he'd put in the wall; he even heard tiles fall from the other side in the bathroom. With another growl, he stalked over to the bed and flopped down, crushing the note in his fist.

Her scent rose up around him and the memory of their last moment together surfaced. She'd wanted him. He could sense it, taste it. Why had she left?

He closed down his thoughts, staring vacantly at the ceiling.

HE WASN'T AWARE OF the exact time, but he knew it had been a few hours when he heard Imogen and Wyatt outside his door. The pair clearly forgot he had shifter hearing.

Wyatt whispered, and not very quietly, "No, you knock and talk. He doesn't want to hear from me."

"God, you are *such* a baby," Imogen replied, but there was a sharp knock at the door. Blake chose not to reply. "Blake? I thought you'd like to get some dinner, maybe?"

Imogen tried to get him to engage with her, but he ignored her efforts. Kayla's note was still crumpled in his fist. He unclenched and smoothed it out, holding the paper in front of him.

She'd typed a note.

After all this time, she didn't even leave a handwritten note. Typing one up was clinical, emotionless, and he still couldn't believe she'd be that way after the moment they'd had.

His wolf whined. Kayla. Pack. Kayla. Ours.

And then it clicked. She *wouldn't* be that cold. To others maybe, but not to him.

He jumped up and yanked open the door, sending Wyatt and Imogen scrambling backwards.

"Blake, I thought you weren't going to–" Imogen started.

"How did she type a note?" Blake asked quickly, and they both frowned at him. "Where would she have been able to type and print a letter?" he clarified when neither spoke.

"Um, we have a computer room that we can use for sending messages, playing games and stuff. It's not guarded or anything. She could have easily gone there," Wyatt offered, but Blake pushed past them and hurried towards the room Kayla had slept in alone.

"No, she wouldn't do that. She was too . . . emotionally charged. She wouldn't have gone to find a computer room that I didn't know about either and type and print a note. She'd just write one and leave.

Something isn't right." He didn't wait to hear what the other two would say in response as he opened the door and walked into the room. "Where was the note?"

Wyatt answered from behind him, "On the bed."

Blake tore off the duvet and pillows. Nothing. He opened the wardrobe to find nothing but hangers.

"What are you doing?" Imogen asked.

"Looking."

"For what?"

"I don't know. Anything. She wouldn't leave me. She wouldn't." He turned back, muttering it over and over, almost pleading with them to believe him. Wyatt nodded.

"Okay, what can we do?"

"Search for anything off, anything that isn't quite right," he said, turning back to move the mattress. Imogen went into the bathroom and opened the cupboards.

Blake knelt by the nightstand and rifled through the drawers, then he bent to look under the bed. He stilled. He reached out and grabbed Kayla's spell book, the one that had belonged to her mother.

"Blake?" Wyatt questioned, concern bleeding into his tone as he came to stand near him. Imogen emerged from the bathroom. "What's that?"

"Her mother's spell book; she wouldn't have left this here. It means too much to her."

"Did it fall out by accident? She was probably in a rush to avoid . . ." Wyatt went quiet, and Blake growled.

"In a rush to get by you? Then why spend time finding the room to type up and print a note? She would have double, triple, even quadruple checked for this."

"What are you trying to say?" Imogen asked.

"That she was taken," he ground out, gripping the spell book.

"But by who?"

"Marcus."

Imogen gasped, "No, he wouldn't! He couldn't!"

"He saw her as a threat, and he wasn't the most welcoming or accepting of her. He did something. I know it."

"Wyatt? He couldn't, could he?" Wyatt looked down at her for a long few seconds.

"I think he could. I'm sorry, Immy." He went to touch her arm, but she pulled out of his reach.

"I'm going to speak to him. He shouldn't be a suspect until we have actual proof – evidence."

She stomped to the lift. Blake and Wyatt followed, their faces lined with dark expressions. As the lift carried them to the lobby, Blake struggled to keep his wolf at bay, and it wasn't until the doors pinged open that he realised he still held Kayla's spell book. He vowed to keep it safe for her. He vowed to find her.

Imogen surged down the hallway and knocked on Marcus's door before walking straight inside.

"Dad," she announced loudly. Marcus looked up from his desk. The man frowned and had the decency to look a little concerned. Blake stepped forward.

"Where is she?" he growled. Marcus blinked, putting his pen down with deliberate care and then leaned back in his chair.

"I don't know what you mean."

"Yes, you do. Don't play coy with me!" Blake used his shifter hearing, and Marcus's heartbeat was hammering away faster than it should have been for someone who claimed not to know anything.

"I'm not playing at anything, and I don't like your tone."

"My tone? You did something to her! Where is she?" Blake shouted again, stalking over to the desk. The door opened behind them, and they all turned as Luke entered the room.

"Sir, we have a breach on the wider perimeter."

"Observe first, and if needed, send out a group," Marcus said dismissively. Luke looked confused for a moment but then elaborated.

"Sir, I must not have made myself clear. We have a breach, a large breach, and we are about to be surrounded by hostiles."

That got Marcus's attention, and he marched around to where Luke stood.

"You three are to stay here until I am back, is that understood?" Marcus yelled at them.

"What? No, if there's an attack, I can help!" Wyatt argued but Marcus whirled on him.

"If you are on *his* side then no, you cannot help. You will stay here where I know you'll not be making any trouble." Marcus walked out and locked the door behind him.

"Great," Imogen said, throwing her hands up in the air. "He has a magical lock on the study. We can't get out."

Blake moved over to Marcus's desk and sat down.

"What are you doing?" Wyatt asked.

"Looking for Imogen's evidence," he said as he rifled through a drawer and opened the next one, the computer sprang to life and asked for a password. "What's his password?" he snapped.

"Um, I don't know, try my name?" Imogen said.

Blake typed it in but was refused entry. "Something else."

"Try my birthday," she suggested, rattling off the date. Again, it flashed: 'access denied.' "Okay, try the date of the original alliance."

Blake typed it in and gained access to the desktop. He brought up the task manager and selected the last thing Marcus had been on, some form of private messenger that allowed anonymous messages.

He growled, struggling to keep his wolf beneath the surface.

>Get rid of her.

>Done. Those wolves you sent my way are vile creatures.

>But they'll get rid of her for us. She shouldn't possess the power she does. It isn't natural. I want confirmation when she's dead.

The messages between Marcus and the unknown sender circled around his head. Get rid of her. Vile creatures. Isn't natural.

Dead.

Marcus was setting Kayla up, and he hadn't been there to protect her; his wolf paced inside his mind, agitated, guilty, murderous.

"Here is your proof," he spat, and they both stared at the screen. Imogen sucked in a sharp breath.

"No! Oh my God," she sobbed, spinning away from the desk. Wyatt stood directly behind her, and she covered her face with her hands as she cried. Wyatt placed an arm around her as he, too, stared at the screen, his face ashen.

"We need to find her," Wyatt breathed.

"I'm making a leap here that it has something to do with the breach. Marcus didn't seem concerned until Luke indicated it was on a large scale – what if he was expecting shifters on the outskirts of the property? What if they're the 'vile creatures' that were sent for her?"

"You think she's out there?"

"I think Marcus would get himself as far away from suspicion as possible and dump her for the shifters to catch. If Luke's team has only just noticed the breach, then they might still be out there. I have to get to her before they . . ."

"I'm so sorry, Blake. I'm so sorry," Imogen mumbled from behind her hands.

Blake closed his eyes and took a deep breath; his voice still sounded rough, but his words were kinder.

"It's not you, it's Marcus. We need to get out." Blake stood, putting Kayla's spell book in his back pocket as Imogen moved away from Wyatt, wiping her eyes.

"We can't get out," she hiccupped.

Blake replied from the window as he shoved it open. "Yes, we can."

"Blake, that's a three-storey drop! Maybe you could stick the landing as a shifter, but we couldn't," Imogen cried, and Wyatt's face lit up.

"We could, Immy, if we jumped together and you shielded us!"

"I'm not sure I could do that, and what if I lost contact with you during the fall?"

"That won't happen. Shall we?" He headed towards Blake as he looked out the window.

"This is mental, guys. We can't jump from a three-storey window!" Imogen shrieked a little too loudly.

"Hey," Wyatt said softly, grabbing her hand, "you got this, Immy. You won't let me go."

"How do you know that?"

"Because who else would you be able to annoy all the time. You *need* me," he said exaggeratedly, and she rolled her eyes. "That's more like it," he said, smiling.

"Are we ready?" Blake interrupted, climbing onto the ledge. He didn't quite wait for a response before dropping to the ground. He was glad he didn't take too long to think about the move, because if he had, he probably would have stumbled. A quick, sharp jolt whipped up his legs, but after testing his weight, he knew he was okay.

He looked up. Imogen sat on the ledge, scooting over as Wyatt climbed out. Wyatt held up his hand, and Imogen took it in hers. Blake hoped Wyatt was right when he said Imogen could shield them, and he held his breath when they made the leap. They landed with a thud, Wyatt splayed on top of Imogen, but still holding hands.

"Ew, get off me!" Imogen shrieked, and Wyatt sprung up, straightening his clothes.

"God, don't you love it when I'm right and people sing your praises?" he said to no one in particular.

"Loser," Imogen muttered, and Blake saw the answering smile on Wyatt's face.

"Where to, shifter?" Wyatt asked him, and Blake looked around the area. "Use your senses, man. You got this."

"When did you become so encouraging to everyone?" Imogen muttered.

"I've always been a delight, didn't you know?" he retorted, but Blake tuned them out and closed his eyes, taking a deep breath.

Kayla. He had to find Kayla. His wolf perked up and whined, wanting to see her. He knew how the wolf felt. He was empty and lost without her.

As he remembered their kiss, the hairs on the back of his neck stood up. He sensed her. It wasn't so much that he could hear or smell her, just that his entire being was homing in on her. He tried to gauge if she was hurt, but he couldn't sense anything – numbness overtook him like ice.

He opened his eyes and stepped up to the bickering pair, holding out Kayla's spell book.

"Imogen, look after this in case I need to shift. I don't want to risk it."

Imogen ceased her quarrelling with Wyatt and tucked the book in the waistband of her jeans. "Did you sense her?"

"Sort of. This way," he said, leading them in the right direction.

The three of them silently entered the woods behind the hotel as the sun sank in the sky.

CHAPTER TWENTY-THREE

KAYLA

KAYLA WOKE WITH A START and instantly scanned her foreign surroundings. The darkening sky made it harder to see, but there was enough moonlight to paint a bleak picture. Trees surrounded her, their bare branches like skeletal arms reaching for something unknown. A rope was knotted around her middle, securing her to one of the tree trunks. Alarm set in as she remembered her last conscious moments.

Marcus had drugged her. He'd caught her by surprise, but instead of helping her join the task force like he'd said, he told her he was going to get rid of her, and then she felt a sharp sting in her upper arm. The bastard! He'd knocked her out, and she must have been unconscious for most of the day, as it had been morning when Marcus betrayed her. Not that she was surprised by his actions.

She held in a scream of frustration and tried to connect with her magic; maybe she could use her new telekinetic power to loosen the bindings. She frowned. Her magic seemed . . . dull. She couldn't call it to the surface. The hum was gone. Its vibrancy? Gone. She started to panic. Her magic had been blocked again, just like the last time she was kidnapped.

For a split second, she thought about screaming for help, but not only would it get her a sore throat – and she had to admit, if Marcus had spent all that effort drugging her and dragging her out there, she wouldn't be heard – she feared what else might appear. A hazy memory of Marcus saying something would come for her surfaced, that he would make it seem like she had gone outside to bravely defend the compound. But from what? Would Blake believe that?

Throwing her head against the wood in exasperation, she let out a small growl, and the action reminded her of Blake. He was probably back from the meeting and panicking because she was absent. Crap! She hadn't agreed to stay. He probably *would* believe she'd leave after what she'd said earlier, because she didn't want to see him and Imogen together. Great. The one person who always came for her probably thought she'd abandoned him, and he wouldn't go looking for her. Marcus had picked his time too God damn well. Coincidence? She thought not.

Her head jerked up when she heard a sharp snap to her right. Something told her that whatever was close wasn't friendly, and she didn't even have her hands to fight, let alone her magic.

Male sniggering drifted through the woods and she caught sight of three shifters, all as big and ugly as the last. The first one reminded her of one of the shifters who'd kidnapped her six months ago and brought her to where Blake's adoptive parents were being kept – his familiar leery grin told her she was right. His black hair was gelled back, making him look like some fifties gangster. He probably thought he looked good.

"Ahh, we meet again," he sang, and his voice made her skin crawl.

"What do you want?" she asked as bravely as she could manage.

"We've been informed that you're not wanted, and we've been contracted to dispose of you."

She refused to answer him in any way, continuing to glare at him.

"But we could make a bargain?" he suggested with a laugh.

"No thanks."

"Oh, but you haven't even heard what I've gotta say." He squatted down beside her, brushing some of her hair away from her face, stroking her cheek at the same time. She flinched away from the contact, and he inhaled with closed eyes. "Such a mix. You're so exotic."

"She certainly smells it," one of the other two, the one with part of his ear missing, said breathlessly, a glazed look in his dark eyes.

"Kayla, is it? I hope you don't mind me calling you sweetheart instead?" The man knelt in front of her and smirked. She tried not to spit in his face. "Now, we love to catch a magic user, but we don't always get to play. Have to be quick so they don't use magic on us but that's been taken care of this time, so we're looking forward to going slow. You're going to know exactly how much we despise your disgusting race," he finished, caressing her neck with his stubby fingers, and dread sent her stomach roiling. She wanted to hurl, but she kept her mouth closed.

"Shall I untie her?" the third shifter asked excitedly. Gelled Hair nodded as he kept his eyes glued to hers.

"You can't use your magic and you can't take on three shifters, but I can see in your eyes that you're a fighter, and I'll be honest. That's getting me excited. Go on, I dare you. Fight me," he whispered in her ear. Her arms and body sagged forward with the release of the ropes.

Her mind whirled through her options: fight and risk more pain before death? Go limp and pray for either a quick death or a chance to get away?

Blake's face filled her mind, and she closed her eyes to bring his image closer. She thought back to their kiss – God, that kiss – and tried to hold on to the happy memory. The shifter pushed her back until she was lying in the cold dirt, he leaned down on top of her, sniffing her neck like a dog.

She whimpered and struggled to hold onto her memory, her image of Blake. The guy raised his fist and she squirmed against him, feeling nauseous, trying to push her body away from his, but one of the others held her arms down so she was defenceless.

"GET YOUR HANDS OFF HER!" a voice roared nearby. Her heart kicked in her chest at the sound of his voice and she twisted, looking for him. The man above her growled dangerously and sat back on his haunches. With his weight gone, she was able to turn her head, and breath escaped her.

Blake stood a few metres away, tall and furious, his shirt stretching taut over his muscles as he bunched his fists at his sides. His glorious mouth stretched into the angriest sneer she'd ever seen, and as he trembled, his rage poured off him in tangible waves.

His molten eyes glowed so vividly she wondered how he was keeping his human form.

"Blake," she whispered in awe, but her voice trembled.

His eyes locked with hers and his need to protect ran unchecked, the rage directed at the shifters who planned to do awful things to her. He shifted gracefully and she looked on in panic as the muscular white wolf raced towards the three brutish killers. They rushed to change forms, and she caught one last glimpse of his golden eyes.

That wasn't Blake, an awkward seventeen-year-old boy struggling to come to terms with his newfound abilities and responsibilities. He knew exactly who he was, and in that moment, he was very, very dangerous. He was heir to the shifters. Powerful. Protective. That wasn't Blake Collins. No. That was Killian Alastair.

Chapter Twenty-Four

Blake

BLAKE DARTED CLOSER TO where he sensed Kayla, tuning out Wyatt and Imogen as they shot insults at one another.

He took another deep breath, and then he felt her: her worry, her anxiety, her fear. He marched faster, despite Imogen's complaints that she was struggling to keep up. He couldn't slow down, not yet.

As he got closer, he finally heard her heartbeat, and words pierced his mind that made his blood run cold. His wolf was dangerously close to the surface. He took off at a run, ignoring Imogen's pleas to wait for them. Running in his human form, he reached a small incline and knew she was on the other side. Three long strides brought him to the crest, and he saw red.

Kayla was beneath a man. A man who threatened to hurt her. Her whimper almost made him lose his head. He fought for control.

"GET YOUR HANDS OFF HER!" he roared. He wasn't sure where the power came from, but he sensed it flowing through him.

She whispered his name, and in that moment, he wanted to gather her up, hold her close, and never let go. His wolf was begging to be released – to show the men what they deserved and prove that Kayla belonged to him.

He met her terrified eyes, unable to deny his true nature any longer. He let the wolf take over.

And then he was charging in his wolf form, intent on killing.

The three men quickly shed their human forms and ran to meet him, and he let out a sigh of relief. If they were all charging at him, Kayla was safe. The smallest one got to him first, as he was quick and agile, but Blake used his bulk to send him flying. He didn't even turn around to see how he landed as the other two stopped just short of him.

All three wolves growled at each other, lips curling viciously before one of them leaped at him, landing on his back. He couldn't get a grip on the other wolf even as he thrashed from side to side. The last wolf used the opportunity to attack from the front and Blake ducked, narrowly avoiding the jaws intended for his throat.

CHAPTER TWENTY-FIVE

KAYLA

KAYLA WATCHED THE DEADLY dance of wolves in fear. Jaws snapped and claws swiped. More than once, Blake flinched and yelped, blood splattering the ground. The wolves moved so rapidly, but Blake's white fur was fast becoming washed with red.

"Kayla!" someone wheezed beside her. She twisted her head as Imogen and Wyatt approached, darting past the wolves.

The two of them crouched low in front of her, concern on their faces.

"What happened? Are you okay?" Imogen asked, grabbing onto Kayla's shoulders. Kayla had only ever cried in front of Blake, but she was spent, and tears fell from her eyes. Imogen pulled her in for a hug and stroked her back. "Shh, it's okay. It's okay, Blake's got this, and we'll get you out of here."

"No! No! We need to help him!" Kayla said urgently. One of the wolves seemed to be down permanently, and Blake was being circled by the other two. Their sides puffed heavily as snarls filled the air, and then they were clashing against each other, but something went wrong. Blake fell, and one of the wolves landed on top of him.

Blake's wolf cried out, and her heart stopped. She reached out and clutched Wyatt's arm.

"I've been drugged. I can't do magic, but you can! Help him!" she panicked. They moved in to attack Blake again as he tried to rise.

Wyatt's hand shot out and focused on something Kayla couldn't see. Blood slid unnaturally over the ground to one of the wolves' legs, wrapping around a paw. A bloody hand took shape on the wolf's foot and Wyatt pulled his arm, yanking the wolf backwards. Wyatt surged forward, landing on the wolf while it struggled in the sticky pool of blood.

Wyatt was able to get his arms around the wolf's neck and the two were locked in a battle of their own. Kayla spun her attention back to where Blake was struggling with the last wolf.

As Blake went crashing to the ground again, he looked up and met Kayla's panicked eyes. New determination set in and he pushed up, swinging around and locking his jaws on the wolf's jugular. A sickening snap echoed through the clearing, and the wolf's body returned to its human state.

Wyatt dropped his opponent, who had also shifted back, and braced his hands on his knees, panting heavily.

"Blake?" Kayla breathed, wanting him to come to her, wanting to see if he was okay, but he stayed locked in his wolf form. He stood over the black-haired shifter who threatened her.

Kayla frowned, wondering what Blake was doing, but then he shifted into his human form and straddled the man, pummelling his fists into the guy's skull. Wyatt ran over to stop Blake, but Kayla sensed his rage, and as he reared back to punch, Wyatt was sent flying.

"Help me up," she said to Imogen who pulled her to her feet. She was unsteady, so Imogen placed an arm around her waist. When they reached Blake, Kayla dropped to her knees in front of him, trying to ignore the pulped flesh. "Blake," she said softly, calmly, trying to get his attention.

Blake breathed harshly, spittle flying out of his mouth as his face contorted with fury. She scanned his ripped shirt, the cuts and scratches trying to heal.

"Blake, please, you're scaring me," she whispered, and Blake's fist froze mid-air. He slowly lowered it and looked up at her, his face an open mask of pain, but it wasn't physical pain. "It's okay, I'm okay," she said, trying to get him to see that she was, mostly, unharmed – she knew he needed to hear it, see it.

Blake blinked quickly and then moved so fast she barely saw it. He knelt in front of her, taking her face in between his bloody hands. He half grunted; half growled. His wolf was near the surface again. The agony in his eyes nearly broke her. She placed her hands over his where they rested on her face.

"It's okay, I'm okay," she repeated. She was trying to soothe him but having him that close caused her voice to wobble, and before she knew it, he pulled her into his lap, his arms going tight around her. Twining her arms around his neck, she ran one hand through his hair, crushing him against her. Blake mirrored her actions, wrapping his hand in her hair to hold her even closer. He buried his head in the crook of her neck, his other arm banding around her waist. "I'm sorry. I'm sorry for what I said."

She breathed unsteadily, losing her battle to keep the tears at bay. She wanted to be strong for Blake, but in his arms, she knew she could come apart and he'd hold her together. She knew he felt the same, his ragged breathing exposing his emotions.

"No. I'm sorry," he mumbled, his voice mostly back to normal.

"Don't you dare. Don't you dare. This isn't your fault."

"I let them . . . you nearly . . . God, Kayla . . ." he moaned, his tremble running through her body.

"I'm right here. I'm right in your arms. Don't . . . don't let me go just yet," she finished, not ashamed of how she sounded. They both needed it. His arms tightened their hold in response.

"I've never been so scared. Never. You're mine to protect, and I failed you."

"You couldn't."

"Kayla . . ." he moaned once more, and then his lips were on her neck, placing a tender kiss there.

He leaned back a fraction to take her face in his hands again, brushing her hair out of her eyes.

"Are you really okay?"

Feeling like they were the only two people in the world, she trailed one hand across his cheek, his chin.

"I will be," she said breathlessly.

"Guys? Are you all right?" Imogen asked. Wyatt and Imogen stood to the side, the bodies of the three shifters between them. Kayla shuddered, and Blake hugged her again.

"Sorry," she mumbled towards them, not releasing her hold on Blake, and he didn't release his on her. "Thank you, Wyatt," she said, remembering what he had done to help.

"Anytime," he replied with a shrug, but she knew the bravado was a front when his usual carefree tone was absent.

"Kayla, I'm so, so sorry my father did this to you. I know he was worried, but I didn't think he'd do . . . this." Imogen gestured to the bodies.

"What did he think he was trying to achieve here? That we'd think you just left, as he conveniently got rid of you?" Wyatt asked absentmindedly. Kayla shrugged.

"He said he was going to make people think I had come out here to protect us but was killed in the process. He lied about offering me a position in the taskforce – I was going to take it," she replied, closing her eyes and resting her head against Blake's as she faced Wyatt and Imogen.

"You were still too much of a risk to his plan. Your power, your bond with Blake. I'm so stupid! I should have done more. I knew he could see your connection," Wyatt chastised himself.

"He can't get away with this. He can't," Imogen announced.

"We'll go back, call a meeting with Luke, and see where we go from there. We can't just accuse Marcus and kick him out. He practically runs this place," Wyatt said, but Imogen's eyes went wide.

"The breach! If this was the breach Luke mentioned, then they'd be here by now, and didn't he say that it looked like quite a few hostiles were closing in?"

"We need to get back. If something's wrong, we need to know," Wyatt said, just as a faint alarm sounded in the distance.

Blake and Kayla frowned.

"What's that?" Blake asked.

"A warning," Imogen answered. They took off. Blake stood with Kayla, but when she wobbled, he scooped her up in his arms and marched on. Kayla wrapped her arms around his neck.

"What are you doing?" she asked, smiling.

"You were unsteady on your feet. Besides, I'll be faster carrying you than I will be waiting for you to walk."

"I can . . . manage." She said it, but she didn't believe it. Apart from the drugs in her system she was mostly okay, but her legs were still shaky, and she wasn't exactly hating being in Blake's arms. God that made her sound pathetic.

"Don't reason it away, Kayla. I can see those cogs turning. Just let me help you. My wolf needs it."

"Okay," she said quietly, resting her head against his shoulder.

It wasn't long before the smell of smoke wafted through the trees.

"Is that smoke?" Wyatt asked, and Blake sniffed the air.

"There's a fire somewhere," Blake answered. Imogen gasped.

"The alarm. It's not a warning . . ." And then she ran. Wyatt shouted after her and followed with a torrent of curses.

Blake frowned.

"The hotel's on fire?" Kayla asked.

"It could be. Should we be going towards it? I'm struggling with the idea of heading toward potential danger with you," he admitted, shifting her slightly. His arms tightened around her.

"We should follow them. We should help if we can, there are a lot of innocent people in the hotel, Blake. Good people."

"What if we see Marcus?"

She was quiet for only a moment. "I won't stop you."

With that, Blake sped on to catch up with Imogen and Wyatt.

As they got closer, they found the hotel covered in flames that stretched and danced against the night sky. Screams and shouts rang through the darkness as the fire rose higher, and the group gaped at the blazing building. They stepped through the last of the trees at the back of the hotel, flinching away from the heat.

Imogen gasped. "My dad! Wyatt?"

Wyatt raised his hands towards the blaze. "I can't control all of this. If Kayla's magic was working, too, maybe, but . . ."

It didn't stop him from trying, and soon some of the flames nearby started to die down. Kayla motioned for Blake to put her on her feet; she felt stronger, but she was glad he kept his arm around her waist.

"Perhaps I can still transfer some of my magic? Or connect like we did before?" Kayla shouted over the roaring flames.

"No!" Blake yelled. "You're too weak, and your magic is blocked. You could hurt yourself, drain yourself like you did before!"

"I have to try!" she replied, but before they could argue, a small path carved towards one of the doors. Wyatt concentrated, his face covered in a fine sheen of sweat.

Imogen sprinted forward, and they all shouted after her.

"Immy, no! I don't have a handle on this!" Wyatt cried. She turned around just before she reached the door.

"I trust you," she said, darting inside.

"Fuck!" he yelled, his hands trembling. "Kayla, I'm struggling. Fire isn't my speciality – I need to hold this door clear for her!"

Kayla reached for Wyatt, desperate to help however she could, but a loud boom sounded within the building. The far side of the structure caved in, shaking the foundations. Blake removed his arm from around her and started towards the door.

"Blake? What?"

"I can find her, just keep a path open!" he shouted over his shoulder as he ran into the inferno.

Wyatt and Kayla stared on in shock as another blast rocked the hotel, and Kayla's heart constricted painfully. The last image she had of Blake was his broad back disappearing into flames.

END OF BOOK 2

RHIAN EDWARDS

SOUL BOUND SERIES

ALLIANCE OF ENEMIES

3

ALLIANCE OF ENEMIES

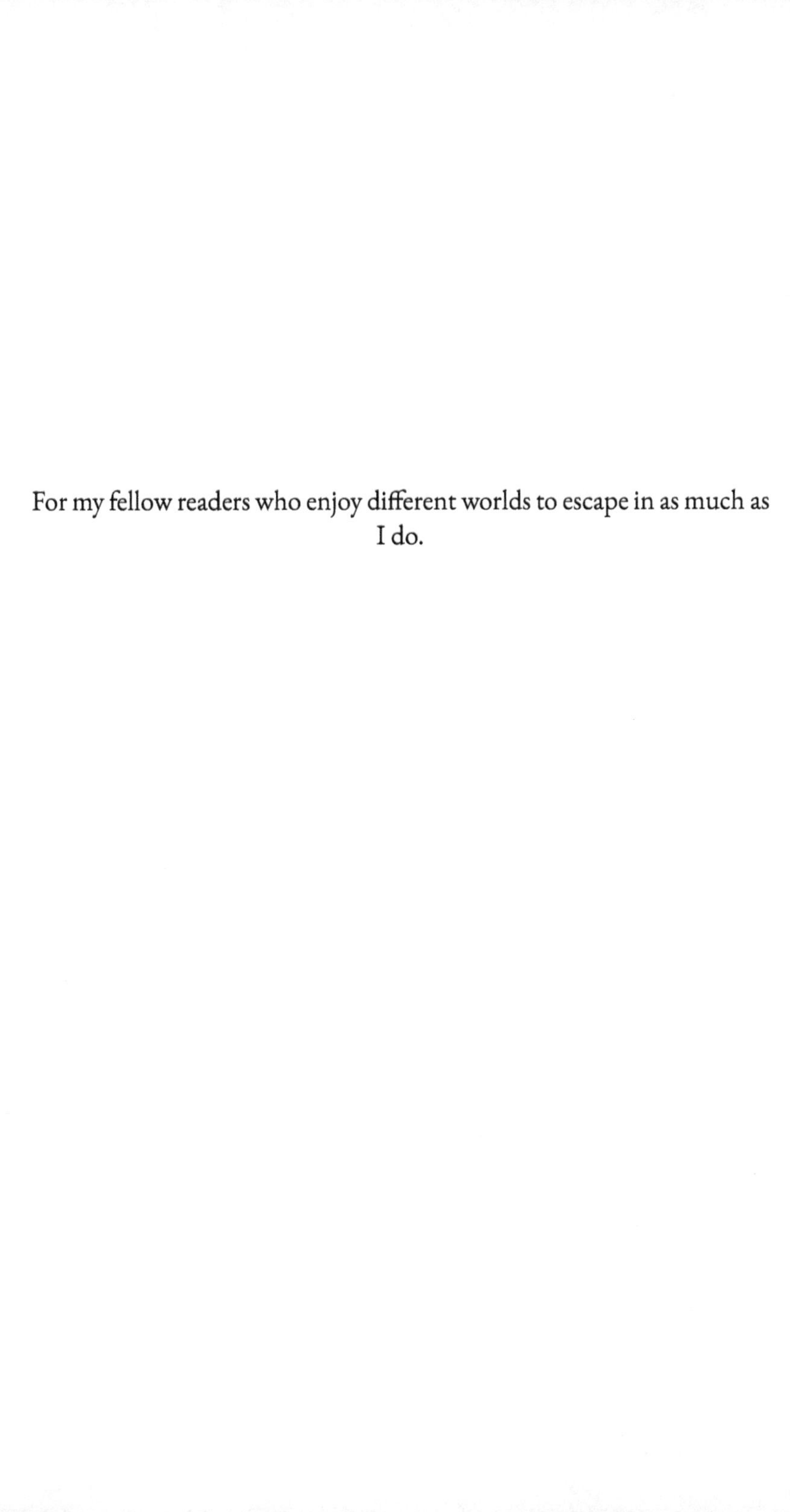

For my fellow readers who enjoy different worlds to escape in as much as I do.

CHAPTER ONE

IMOGEN

HER HOME, THE PLACE in which she had grown up, was unrecognisable. The fire savaged everything in its path. Nothing was spared. Not the sofas in the lounge area where she'd spent many a night with some of the other young magic users. Not the dining room where one of her father's shifter aids, Mal, would always sneak her an extra cupcake. Not the reading room where she went to relax and escape. And not her father's office where she came to a stop, barely able to make out the familiar surroundings through the amber haze.

"Dad!" she screamed into the fire, smoke racing into her lungs.

She stumbled into the corner of the desk, snatching her hand away from the scorched wood.

"Dad!" Her voice strained, the word scratching at her throat.

Her dad wasn't there. She lurched away from the heat, coughing as she fell out of the office and into the hallway inferno. Imogen crawled forward, unable to stand with the smoke drowning her lungs and the fire licking at her body.

Wyatt's stricken face as she ran into the hotel filled her mind. But she had no choice. Her dad was there – she was sure of it. There was no doubt he'd come to find her, thinking she was where he'd left her when he went to investigate the perimeter breach. Except she hadn't been in the building at all. She'd gone with Wyatt and Blake to rescue Kayla from the shifters her father had hired to kill her in the woods behind the hotel.

Her leggings caught on something, and pain flared through her thigh. She touched the area, her hand coming away slick. Tears gathered in her eyes. She wasn't trained. She wasn't strong. She wasn't powerful. She injured herself at the first sign of danger, crawling in the depths of a flaming building with no way out. Oh, the things Wyatt would say if he could see her now.

Wyatt.

She gulped, a fresh wave of tears spilling down her cheeks. She'd left him to control the fire, and it dawned on her just how perilous the situation was.

A groan ahead of her grabbed her attention. She crawled faster, ignoring the heat, and saw a body collapsed in a heap on the floor. It was a man. Her dad.

"Dad!" she cried, heart pounding.

She pushed him onto his back, shaking his shoulders, fear gripping her throat in a tight knot.

"Dad," she whispered, hiccupping.

He remained motionless. Defeated, alone, she laid her head on his chest, clutching his jacket in her hands.

CHAPTER TWO

BLAKE

HEAT. UNBEARABLE HEAT, BORE down on his skin. Thick black smoke curled around his body. His throat ached – begged – for air, but there was none to be had. He crouched low, coughing and rapidly blinking cloudy tears out of his eyes – not that his vision improved. His shifter abilities were working overtime to give him some aspect of visual superiority, but the fire raged feverishly through the repurposed hotel and the fumes boiled viciously above him. He raised an arm to his brow, swiping sweat-drenched hair from his forehead, panting between lung-rattling coughs. Squinting, he swore he saw a human-shaped shadow moving erratically through the murky darkness. Imogen? Calling out wasn't an option as the smoke would drown him. He rushed forward with the heat of the flames teasing his skin.

He cursed Imogen, questioning his own sanity after he'd pursued her into the fiery blaze. She'd sprinted inside to rescue her father, and even though Blake had no love for the man after what he'd nearly done to Kayla, he couldn't let Imogen die, too.

Just thinking of Kayla tied up in the woods, waiting to be tortured and killed by shifters, made his blood boil.

Yeah, he couldn't care less what happened to Marcus.

His head jerked around at the sound of wood splintering. Behind him, a large wooden beam crashed to the floor, and a wave of heat and sparks peppered his clothing. He slapped at them and scrambled away, crawling as fast as his oxygen deprived muscles could manage. If he was struggling with the abilities his shifter nature gave him, how was Imogen? He pushed the thought away when a low cry reached his ears. Shutting his eyes, he listened closely. Not only did he have no clue where he actually was in the building, he couldn't see a blasted thing – at least not anything useful. If he never saw a flame again, it would still be too soon.

He heard the sound once more and he followed its direction, scooting past fiery tendrils that reached out to grab him.

Imogen! He paused when he saw her kneeling next to a body. While he didn't want to see Imogen hurting, he prayed the body was that of Marcus's. He hurried his pace, coming to a stop next to her. She held her father's hand in one of her own, tenderly stroking his cheek.

"Dad? Daddy?" she croaked, coughing the words out.

Blake laid his hand on her shoulder and met her wide eyes. Fear – not for herself, but for her father – shone in their depths. Tears tracked down her dark skin, making paths through the thick layers of muck and ash.

Marcus spluttered, his head thrashing from side to side with a painful wheeze.

"Imogen?" he murmured, his voice strangely small in the roaring crackle of the blaze.

Sweat dripped into Blake's eyes. Down the hall, a plume of sparks shot into the darkness, indicating that something else had collapsed. He didn't have much hope for the ceiling above them, and he tipped his head back to see rolling clouds of ink-coloured smoke. He tugged on Imogen's arm.

"We have to go," he rasped.

"I'm sorry . . . I just wanted . . . the best for . . . you." Marcus mumbled incoherently. He was more injured than Blake had first thought. That suited him. Even if Blake wanted to, he wasn't sure he could get them both out of the hotel.

"Imogen! No time." Blake pulled at her arm, rubbing his wrist across his eyes to wipe them free of smoke. Marcus noticed him, and they locked eyes. It could have been the smoke or the waves of heat, but Blake thought regret flashed on the dying man's face just before his eyelids fluttered shut.

"Dad!" Imogen screamed, shaking his shoulders. Over the noise of the blaze, Blake heard him moan, but he knew Imogen hadn't. How could he explain to her that her dad was close to death and they would be, too, if they didn't get out?

"Imogen, please," Blake begged. He wasn't beyond throwing her over his shoulder and running out.

Imogen flung herself at Blake with wild eyes, clutching his arms. "Help him, Blake!"

Time was of the essence, but it was still her father. Shit.

"He's too far gone," he began carefully, pulling her closer to the ground where the smoke wasn't quite as thick; he needed to get the words out without the incessant coughing. "I can't get us all out. I can't."

Understanding filled Imogen's gaze. She glanced at her dad's still body, his relaxed face, his shut eyes. She bowed her head and wrapped her arms around Blake's neck, sobbing against his chest. Her laboured breathing worried him as she turned towards her dad, placing a kiss on his forehead.

Blake grabbed her hand and shuffled forward, her body stuck to his like glue; if they got separated again, he didn't fancy his chances of finding her a second time. The fire spat at them as they attempted to navigate the searing inferno, red-orange flames reaching out to catch them in a deadly embrace. Imogen dragged behind him more and more, her movements sluggish, her breaths coming in shallow wheezes. He needed her to concentrate on her shield, but grief overtook her abilities.

Blake tucked her into his side, one arm wrapping around her middle so he could shoulder her weight. The building shook around them as more of the walls came down, ravaged by fire. As soon as they turned down one path, it was covered with parts of the rapidly collapsing building.

Another path cleared ahead of him, and he sensed magic was at play. He got to his feet, knowing he needed to move fast, even though the air was thick with smoke when he did so. Imogen leaned against him heavily, barely moving her own feet. Blake dragged her beside him and her head rolled forward as he stumbled under her weight.

C'mon, he said to himself. He had to get out. Kayla was waiting for him. At the thought of Kayla, the path widened for them, and a faint trace of lavender pierced through the overwhelming stench of acrid smoke. He took a small, gruelling step forward, blinking sweat out of his eyes, shaking with concentration and effort.

"You have this, Blake. Your abilities – your strength, your speed, your senses – increase every day." He recalled Kayla's words when she was trying to encourage him to use his shifter advantages, back when it was just the two of them.

"When you're around I'm better. Perhaps I'm feeding off your magic? I can't seem to get the hang of this on my own," he'd replied.

Kayla had put her hands on her hips and looked at him pointedly, raising one of her brows. *"You're never alone, Blake. You've got Alastair blood. I've seen you in action, and you're way stronger than other shifters because you have determination, purpose, and this quality about you. It's like you have this strong sense of self."*

"Sense of self? I highly doubt it. My life has done a complete 180. I have no idea who I am and what I'm supposed to do." He was drowning. He was lost.

Kayla had stepped forward into his space, her eyes expressing some truth he hadn't seen at the time. She raised her palm and placed it gently over his heart.

"Here. This is you. And remember, you're never alone . . ."

The sensation of her hand lingered. He tightened his grip on Imogen. They had to get out.

Another beam came loose and crashed into them from behind. Blake took the brunt of the force as they were knocked to the ground. Their path closed up ahead, but he rushed to push the blazing beam off them. His back screamed as he rose up on his forearms. The flame-riddled wood rolled and trapped his legs. Imogen lay still, face down on the floor as Blake shoved the beam away, releasing an agonised roar as he did. Panting, he turned Imogen over and frowned at her fluttering eyelids. His blistered hands trembled, but he ignored the pain and wrapped her arm over the back of his shoulders to hoist her up.

Blake took a step forward, trusting that Wyatt and Kayla would be able to sense where they were. It wasn't much, but a small halo around his foot pushed back the flames pecking at his skin like greedy vultures. Another step. Another halo. His clothes caught on stray flames more than once, but every time he took a step, the flame was extinguished. Kayla.

Blake stumbled to his knees, nearly losing his grip on Imogen as his charred hands quivered. He knew the tears that tracked down his face weren't from the smoke.

A glimmer of hope surfaced when a small, thin path opened up to a door. An exit. Blake's sudden relief was quashed when flaming debris rained down from above, blocking their only way out. He turned, and the path he'd followed was swallowed whole by flames as they slid closer, eager to engulf them.

I'm so sorry, Kayla. He closed his eyes, bracing for the moment the fire claimed him.

CHAPTER THREE

KAYLA

FLAMES DANCED AGAINST THE night sky, casting eerie shadows. She stood motionless. Blake ran into the burning building like he'd forgotten something, not like he was risking his life. She was so mad at him. Mad that he could tell her to be careful but didn't give his own safety a second thought as he ran towards danger to save their friend. Even though it made him who he was, it didn't diminish her frustration.

"I can't hold it!" Wyatt grunted, dropping his hands and bending over at the waist to rest his palms on his knees. "Shit!" he growled, anger spewing into his words. Standing up straight, he brushed his uncharacteristically messy blonde hair back and shook his hands out. "You got this, dude. You got this," he murmured to himself.

"Wyatt! Kayla!" Luke shouted as he and Mal rounded the corner.

"What are you doing? You need to get out of here!" Mal ordered, but Luke frowned.

"Where's Imogen, Blake?"

Wyatt pointed to the building, panting. "In there. I'm not powerful enough to counter whatever magic is fuelling the flames, and Kayla's been drugged. Her magic isn't working."

"What?" Mal spluttered. His confusion was reflected on Luke's face.

"Marcus knocked me out and took me into the woods where he'd arranged for shifters to kill me. These guys found me in time, but we came back and . . ." Kayla trailed off.

Luke ran a hand through his short hair, the first physical sign of frustration she'd ever seen him display. "That makes sense. He'd been acting off, and that perimeter breach didn't add up. When we got word of the attack on the hotel, we came rushing back. I lost Marcus in the building trying to evacuate everyone. Mal and I guessed you guys had escaped before the fire as the office was empty, but Marcus wouldn't leave without looking for Imogen first."

"Is everyone else safe?"

"Yes. We followed procedures, and the rest of the taskforce are leading them to our safe compounds. Marcus though . . ."

"That's why she ran in," Kayla finished.

"It doesn't matter about any of that if we can't get them out!" Wyatt snapped.

Kayla shuffled forward, still weak from the drug Marcus had given her to hinder her magic. She placed a hand on his shoulder. "Let me help."

Wyatt faced her, chewing the inside of his cheek. His eyes held a world of worry.

"But –"

"But nothing. It's worth a try. If we can clear a path for them . . ."

Wyatt nodded and grabbed her hand. "Try and channel to me. I know the drug is preventing *you* from using your magic, but I remember what your magic felt like during training. It's strong. Maybe you can funnel a bit to me so *I* can use it."

"Anything."

Wyatt turned his hands towards the building, closing his eyes. He breathed deeply. Despite her aches, Kayla did the same, keeping her hand in his. She was lucky the shifters who had come to kill her hadn't been able to do much before Blake arrived. She'd been tied up for hours and it was causing most of her pain. She hated feeling weak and useless.

She had no idea if she was transferring magic to Wyatt or if he was taking it from her, but he was controlling a section of fire, moving it away from the door to leave it clear for Blake and Imogen. Fire wasn't his strongest element, but Wyatt was still a powerful magic user – probably one of the strongest she'd seen.

Fire was supposedly her strength, but the drug had rendered her incapable of magic, so all she could do was watch. Her heart galloped in her chest.

A crash from within sent a spark of fear coursing through her veins. Was Blake okay? She felt the heat of the blaze from where she stood. She locked her knees to keep her trembling legs upright.

"That's as far as I can extend the magic," Wyatt said dejectedly, his voice heavy with pain.

Kayla frowned. "Are you giving up?"

"Kayla . . ." he said, tears welling.

"No, Wyatt. You don't give up! You don't get to give up! Blake's in there! Imogen!" she shouted. What would she do without his help? If Blake were here, she'd kick his ass for being so reckless.

"I can just about keep the doorway open, but what about inside? Look at the building, Kayla. Does it look like anyone is coming out of that?" He stormed a few paces away and ran agitated hands through his hair. "She was wrong. She shouldn't have trusted me!" With a scream of frustration, Wyatt crouched and his back shook. His strangled sobs echoed her own turbulent feelings.

"It's not your fault, mate," Mal said.

Luke watched her closely. "Kayla? What would Blake do or say in this situation? About your magic?"

She paused. "That he trusted me."

"Well, I trust you. We all do."

"Why?"

"Because Blake does. And Wyatt's strong, too. You can do this. Both of you."

Kayla swayed, her focus on the flames. "We're doing it all wrong," she murmured, an idea beginning to form.

Wyatt looked up at her from where he'd buried his head in his hands. She sat cross-legged opposite him.

"What?" he replied, sinking to the ground to mirror her. His bloodshot eyes studied her gravely, as if he didn't know what else to do. Kayla grabbed his hands.

"Magic is about intent. Purity," she explained, recalling her mother's advice years ago. "We need to go to them. We're connected in so many ways. We need to use those connections to sense where they are and carve a path to us. We need to trust what we can't see."

Wyatt's eyes brightened. "Let's do it."

He closed his eyes and focused, and Kayla followed suit. She stretched out her senses – not unlike Blake with his shifter abilities – while pushing what she could of her magical essence towards Wyatt.

It wasn't long before she felt Blake's mind, filled with turmoil, distress, and worry.

"Keep doing what you're doing, Kayla. I have a picture in my mind. I can send my magic there."

She nodded, which was pointless given how he also had his eyes shut.

"I can't do much, so just keep focused on Blake. I'm trying." His voice was strained. She had no clue if Imogen was with Blake, and she guessed Wyatt didn't know either. They both just had to hope he'd found her.

Their heavy breaths merged with the hissing of the fire as she focused on Blake, but Wyatt's sudden sharp inhale and a loud explosive boom from within the building had her nearly jumping out of her skin. Her eyes snapped open. The right corner of the hotel completely crumbled. Tears sprung as a sharp pang of pain shot through her heart.

"Kayla!" Wyatt snapped, grabbing her face between his hands. A feverish, mad look entered his wide eyes. "Give me everything you've got!" he commanded. The deep, controlling tone shocked her into obedience. She kept her eyes connected with his, and their magic merged and mingled. She knew her magic was straining to get out, to be released. She knew it wanted Blake.

Wind brushed her cheek and magic teased her skin, the hairs on her arms rising in anticipation. Her magic wasn't free yet, but it was there, just under the surface.

Wyatt's eyes grew brighter as she felt weaker.

He was pulling the magic to him, and she was letting him have it.

Yes. Take it. Help Blake.

Wood, brick, and plaster erupted from the building, throwing them both to the ground and severing their connection. Her head thrummed.

Kayla pushed up on her arms as Wyatt stirred. Luke and Mal were by their sides in an instant, but they paused as two people stumbled away from the building and staggered towards them. The male figure dragged a slighter, female body, and Kayla's heart lurched into her throat.

"Wyatt!" she breathed, not sure her voice was stable enough to share what she was seeing. Wyatt mumbled something as he sat up, bumping her shoulder as he did. His face was the palest she'd ever seen, but his dim eyes shone when he saw the figures. She smiled. She knew she wasn't hallucinating.

Wyatt helped Kayla stand as the shifters ran ahead. She would have joined them, and she suspected Wyatt would have, too, if they had been able. Blake's features became visible as the smoke began to clear. He was covered in layers of ash, dirt, and smoke, and his clothes were tattered. Imogen was limply slung against him, and while Blake should have had the strength to easily carry her, she sensed the level of concentration and effort he was expending to keep them both upright was taking its toll.

"Blake!" she cried out, her throat constricting painfully. His head tipped up but he stumbled, falling to the ground with Imogen. Neither moved. She gripped Wyatt's hand hard and they moved their drained bodies quicker than they should have been able to.

Wyatt dropped down beside Imogen, gathering her up in his arms. Mal checked her pulse, his face relaxing after a few seconds.

"Wyatt?" Imogen mumbled, her eyes blinking rapidly.

"Shh, you're okay," he whispered to her, gently brushing back her hair. Imogen curled into him and wept. At the exit, there were no other signs of life. Marcus hadn't made it.

Blake groaned. "Kayla?" he mumbled. She placed her hand on his shoulder, encouraging him to turn over. She would have rushed to roll him over herself to get a look at his face, but she could barely stop her arm from shaking. Exhaustion and cold seeped into her muscles.

"Blake?"

With a pained grunt, Luke turned Blake to his side. Bloodshot eyes stood out from his face, patches of smoke and ash painting his features. She reached for his hand but froze when she saw his blistered palm.

"They'll heal," Blake said.

She nodded, swallowing tears. She knew he didn't need them. "Can you sit?"

"With help."

"Always," she replied, trying to sound normal. Except nothing was normal.

"What happened?" Luke asked, glancing at Imogen as he lowered his voice.

Blake briefly looked over to where Imogen was huddled against Wyatt. "We found Marcus."

"Was he . . .?"

"Nearly. I couldn't have gotten them both out even if . . ."

"It's all right," Kayla responded, squeezing his shoulder. Blake leaned forward and rested his head against her arm, closing his eyes. He exhaled a shaky breath, but it sounded clearer by the minute. She said a silent prayer of thanks for his shifter abilities.

"Imogen? Are you . . .?" Kayla slowly trailed off. She was about to ask if Imogen was okay, but after watching her own parents perish, she knew exactly how Imogen was feeling. And it was not 'okay.'

Imogen sat up and twisted her body away from Wyatt's, wiping her eyes with her charred clothing.

Wyatt rubbed her back, but Imogen wrenched away from his touch. His face fell, but he didn't try again.

"Am I what? Okay? Screw you!" Imogen spat. Kayla recoiled, not expecting the venom in her voice.

"I'm–"

Wyatt quickly jumped in. "I think we ought to find a car and get out of here before whoever did this finds us."

"It wasn't – it wasn't an accident?" Imogen asked, the hostility draining from her voice.

"No," Luke answered. "Mia rang us to say they were being attacked by a group of elemental magic users who were setting the hotel on fire. She started evacuation procedures and ordered the remaining task force to stop the magic users." Kayla was relieved to hear that Mia, Wyatt's magic user friend who'd helped her and Blake the week before, was the one evacuating the others. She was a trustworthy ally.

"Did they catch them?" Wyatt asked.

"They'd run off by the time we arrived, and we had to get everyone out and safe first."

"Any idea who it was? Did Mia recognise any of them?"

Luke shook his head. "She didn't see faces, but they must have been part of the magic group who are constantly trying to stop us. They're always sabotaging our missions. They didn't like what we did here. The taskforce has been working tirelessly to find them."

"The timing of it . . . could it be linked with what Marcus tried to do to me?" Kayla added.

Imogen sucked in a deep breath. "Oh, so this is his fault, too? Why don't we just blame him for everything else while we're at it!" Imogen stood up and paced away a few steps, keeping her back to the others.

"About that car, Wyatt, great idea. I don't think we should stay here," Blake said, trying to diffuse the tension.

"What should we do?" Mal asked. He looked at Blake who promptly frowned.

"Why are you looking at me?"

"Because you're the shifter prince."

"Okay, well, um . . ." he glanced at Kayla, and she rolled her eyes.

"We need to find out who did this and stop them – especially if they are against an alliance. We can't have a group of magic users going to these lengths against other magic users and shifters."

"We also need to head to London," Wyatt added.

"Huh?"

"There's a peace meeting; Marcus was in communication with other pro-alliance groups. I don't have any intel on it, though, as he kept everything secret."

"How do we find out about this meeting?" Blake asked.

"Ben," Kayla answered. "Ben is the person my parents entrusted to continue their work. Blake and I were going to meet with him after we'd rescued his family from some shifter hunters, but Ben was compromised because of us. We severed all ties to protect the work he did."

"What about now? Isn't it still dangerous?" Mal said.

"Yes, but securing an alliance is the most important thing right now, and your resources are burning to the ground as we speak. It's a risk we have to take."

"Will this Ben be able to help you?" Luke asked.

Kayla nodded. "He has the information we need."

"But what about everyone who lived at the hotel? Are they safe?" Wyatt questioned. Luke and Mal shared a look.

"We were doing a last sweep around the building to see if Marcus had come out, and then we were supposed to be catching up with everyone. We've had to split up into groups – the taskforce are leading smaller groups to safe accommodations," Mal said.

"Then you need to meet up with them and ensure everyone made it to safety," Blake instructed.

"But we need to make sure you are safe, too!" Luke argued.

"The people who support us are important. Without them, our work doesn't matter. It's risky going to Ben, but we have no choice. Once you've made sure the people here are safe, we will meet up, and hopefully we'll have the information we need. We have to be at the meeting before the hunters and those against an alliance can stop us."

"It just doesn't sit right, leaving you on your own."

"I have a powerful elemental and a Kayla." Blake grinned. "Luke? The people here will be looking to you for leadership. Go and settle them, make them feel safe, and then we'll finish this."

"He's right, Luke. When we leave them, we'll put the taskforce in charge. Mia can oversee it – it's what you've been training her for," Mal agreed.

Luke nodded, rubbing at the stubble on his chin. "Okay. I don't like it, but okay. Wyatt, when you're settled with Ben, email me – I'll have a mobile by then. If you get one, too, we can communicate via phone, which'll be much easier."

"No problem. Is there a car we can take?"

"Yes, round the front."

Kayla glanced at Imogen who still had her back to them, arms wrapped around her middle.

"You go and get a car. I'm going to . . ." Kayla jerked her head in Imogen's direction, hoping the boys understood.

Wyatt frowned but nodded.

"Look after our prince." Mal smiled and hugged her.

"And yourself," Luke added as he, too, grabbed her for a quick hug. She nodded.

Luke gave Imogen one last look, but she never turned around. His eyes clouded, but he didn't approach her.

The guys walked around the smouldering remains of the hotel, and she was thankful Blake was moving with more grace than when he had come out of the building.

"That was uncalled for," Imogen whispered when they were alone. Imogen sat down and pulled her legs up to her chest, wrapping her arms around them. "I was . . . it . . ." She swallowed and closed her eyes.

"You'll see him in your head every time you close your eyes, but it'll get easier. You'll stop picturing what you just saw and you'll remember him in a better light. The better times. Promise."

"I forgot you lost your parents."

Kayla gave a small smile. "Don't be afraid to talk. To me, to Wyatt, it doesn't matter, but don't bottle it all up."

"Not Wyatt," Imogen said. "I mean, not him. I'd rather talk to you. Oh god, that's if you want me to. I know – he – I . . ."

"Still your father, no matter what he did," Kayla reassured her. Sure, the guy had tried to kill her, but he paid the ultimate price and left his daughter grieving in the process.

An engine rumbled in the distance. Her head jerked up to see Wyatt and Blake driving a small car towards where they sat on the grass. She supposed tire marks were inconsequential now that there were bits and pieces of the building decorating the once-immaculate lawn. Kayla helped Imogen up and they joined the boys in the vehicle.

THEY'D ONLY BEEN DRIVING an hour or so, but the tension was palpable. Imogen sat in the front passenger seat so Blake and Kayla could sit together in the back. No one spoke.

They were heading towards Oxford where Kayla knew Ben was staying. She prayed their presence didn't put Ben and his work at risk again, but it was a gamble they had to take.

"When will Kayla get her magic back?" Imogen asked out of nowhere, startling them from their individual thoughts.

Wyatt frowned in the rear-view mirror just before he spoke. "Um, maybe a day or two." His hands tightened on the steering wheel, and Kayla knew he was frustrated that Imogen was distancing herself from him. He may not have been blood, but the two had been brought up together.

"That's good," Blake said.

"I know that you might not think it but my dad, he . . . he wasn't a bad person." Imogen's voice wavered before she cleared it with a cough. "I don't want what happened to be the legacy he leaves behind."

Blake's hand curled into a fist. Kayla brushed her fingers over it, shaking her head to prevent whatever he was about to say. Yes, he had a right to be mad. She, herself, had more reason than anyone to hate Marcus. But the man responsible was dead. She knew what losing a parent felt like, and if their support allowed Imogen to process her grief, then so be it.

"It won't be, Imogen. We'll focus on what he stood for before." She didn't need to say anything else. They all knew 'before' meant 'before he went crazy and tried to have Kayla killed.'

Blake laced his fingers through hers, and the slow, circular motion of his thumb on her skin lulled her to sleep.

CHAPTER FOUR

Blake

It was late, and Wyatt was getting tired. Blake suggested stopping for the night to rest – they were all beyond exhausted – and unsurprisingly, the others agreed.

Wyatt and Kayla went inside to book a family room for the night at a cheap, roadside hotel. People wouldn't really pay them much attention, but as Blake and Imogen were still covered in smoke, ash, and sweat, they decided it would be best to send the cleaner ones to the front desk.

Imogen and Blake sat in silence as they waited. Blake wanted to talk to Imogen, he really did, but he got the feeling anything he said wouldn't really help. Thankfully, it didn't take long for Kayla to make her way back out to them.

"Wyatt's gone to check the room out. I've come to get you guys," she said. She'd slept for the last forty minutes of the journey, and it seemed to have done her a world of good. Her cheeks were rosy, her eyes were bright, and she was certainly more relaxed.

Blake stretched his stiff muscles as he got out of the car. The smoke inhalation was making his body sluggish, but some food, a long sleep, and perhaps a run would help. Kayla led the way inside, and Imogen and Blake were careful to keep their faces turned down when they passed other guests. It was late at night, but there were still some people about.

Their room was on the third floor and they took the lift, none of them having the energy to bother with stairs.

Their room had two double beds, a small desk with a TV, and basic kitchen supplies. The tiny kettle would probably only fill one of the miniscule cups the hotel provided. The biscuits were a good shout, though. Blake opened a packet of chocolate chip cookies and devoured both within seconds. When he turned to face the others, they were all staring at him.

"What?" he asked, swallowing the last few crumbs. "I've expended a lot of energy. I need food."

"I think we all do," Wyatt replied.

"Pizza?" Kayla asked, holding up a leaflet that had been left on the desk. The pizza place delivered to the hotel, so Kayla placed an order for four large ones – Blake assuring them he could polish off anything left uneaten – and then he took a shower while they waited.

When he was done, he tied a towel around his waist and left the bathroom so Imogen could shower. The door shut behind him, and the water started up again. Kayla was looking in every direction but his, and Wyatt cleared his throat.

"Perhaps I'll go in search of some clothes – or a washing machine? Something at least," Wyatt suggested. The blonde elemental magic user scooped up a pile of clothing and hastily left the cramped room.

Blake smiled and moved closer. She crossed her arms over her chest but met his gaze at last. "You all right?" he whispered, gently tucking some hair behind her ear. Her eyes drifted shut for a moment.

"I will be. I'm glad you're okay, but . . ."

"But what?" he frowned.

"I'm still mad at you for rushing into that fire."

Blake blinked. He hadn't been expecting that response. "I had to. Imogen had gone in and–"

"I know, I know," Kayla sighed, covering her face with her hands as her body sagged. Blake stepped forward and wrapped his arms around her waist. He needed her touch, and he couldn't help himself. His wolf wanted the contact.

He placed his chin on top of her head. "You're right. I'm sorry. It was reckless, and I acted without thinking."

"It's just who you are. You're ruled by your emotions. It's not necessarily a bad thing, as I think that's what will make you a good King Alpha. Just . . . for me, I wish you weren't like that."

He placed his fingers under her chin and lifted her head. Words escaped him. He knew she was right; he couldn't promise that he wouldn't run off to save someone without thinking about it first. His birth father had said something similar to his uncle, but the memory was quickly chased away when he looked into her deep brown eyes.

They were beautiful.

He lowered his head before he even realised his intention, any insecurity washing away when his lips met hers. Their first kiss was fuelled by anger and fear. Their second kiss was fuelled by relief. But now? Now he was kissing her because he wanted to. Her hands uncurled and spread over his lower stomach; she dragged her fingers across his abdomen, pulling a satisfied growl from his throat. Her answering smile against his lips did nothing to hold back the needy wolf inside him as he clutched her to his chest.

In the distance he heard a startled yelp and then a pointed cough, but it wasn't until Kayla gasped and leaned back that he twigged Wyatt had stepped back into the room.

Wyatt froze, staring at them both with wide eyes. Blake didn't let go of Kayla's hips even as she pulled away from him. He was too busy controlling the possessive wolf that was itching to bite off Wyatt's head.

"All right, wolfy. Stand down, boy. I'm not the one making out with a girl in the middle of a shared room," Wyatt said, more like his usual self. He shut the door and dumped the contents of a shopping bag on one of the beds.

Imogen walked out of the bathroom, hands fluttering at the towel she secured around herself as she surveyed the scene in front of her. Her brows furrowed, but she relaxed when she noticed the clothes on the bed. Wyatt roughly gestured to the fabric.

"I found a shop two minutes down the road. Got us all some pjs – there wasn't much choice, but I've shoved all of Imogen's and Blake's clothes in the washer. There's a washing room near the lobby. They should be done in about an hour."

Imogen carefully made her way to the bed and plucked out a pair of red flannel pjs. She retreated into the bathroom to change without saying another word. Blake grabbed a pair of dark blue bottoms and a grey t-shirt that stretched tight across his torso. As he finished putting on the shirt, Kayla glanced away, her cheeks stained pink.

Kayla quickly took the black strappy top and the thin teal-green bottoms, leaving Wyatt with the same blue joggers Blake had on and a white tank.

When Imogen exited the bathroom, Kayla nipped in to change, but Wyatt had no such problems stripping to his boxers to get into the clean nightwear.

"Wyatt!" Imogen chastised, spinning away from his nearly naked form.

Wyatt grinned at her back. "Making you uncomfortable, Immy?"

Imogen rolled her eyes and sat cross-legged on one of the beds when Wyatt was clothed again.

Kayla walked back into the room, rolling the top of her bottoms so they came up to her hips rather than half-way up her torso.

The shrill tone of the hotel phone plunged the room into silence.

Fear tightened each of their faces as Blake approached the phone. He picked up the receiver, jaw tense.

"Hello?"

"Hi, your pizza is at the reception," a cheery female voice sang down the line. His shoulders sagged, and he watched as one by one the others relaxed, too.

"Thank you." He hung up and turned to the room. "Pizza's downstairs," he declared.

Kayla snapped her eyes towards where Imogen sat on the bed, picking at a spot on the bed covers, and then to Wyatt who sat in the desk chair, studying the hotel information.

"I'll help," she said, slipping her shoes on. He didn't need any help carrying boxes, but there was no way he'd want to be alone with Imogen and Wyatt either. The air practically sizzled between them – it was making his wolf agitated.

BLAKE GROANED AROUND A warm mouthful of bread, tomato

sauce, and cheese. He knew the others were just as pleased with the meal judging by the looks of ecstasy plastered on their faces. He and Kayla sat cross-legged on the bed, knees touching. They were on Kayla's pizza box as he'd already finished his. Wyatt lounged in a chair near the desk, and Imogen was laid across the other bed.

"Is everyone okay if we discuss what we're gonna do when we get to Kayla's friend?" Wyatt asked, swallowing a bite of pizza.

Imogen perked up but Kayla tensed beside Blake. He squeezed her knee, hoping to comfort her.

"Yes, I think that's wise," Kayla answered, sounding more confident than Blake knew she felt. Was that how she always was when she made the plans? How had he never noticed? A swell of pride rose in his chest and he found himself grinning at her. "What?" she asked, smiling at him.

He shook his head. "Nothing. Go on, Wyatt."

"When we get to what's his face–"

"Ben."

"Yes, Ben's. I think we need to look at how we get Blake's Alpha status. It would help us at the Alliance meeting."

Three sets of eyes stared at Wyatt.

"How will that do anything if people clearly don't want to work together?" Imogen snapped.

"Well, that's why we should do it. Show people that we have a King Alpha again. He can use his status to get the shifters to commit to a peace treaty of sorts."

Imogen huffed and shoved a slice of pizza into her mouth.

"So, how is this peace summit actually meant to work, Wyatt?" Kayla asked. Blake could almost see her brain working, planning something.

"A group of shifters and magic-users across the country have been in talks to get together and solidify connections. More of us than you'd think want peace. We've been building relationships with these . . . umm, I want to say leaders, but I think you know what I mean. They're 'in charge' of groups of people, like Marcus with us, and we decided we should meet and form our own alliance of sorts. Marcus wanted to use the meet to show off Blake and Imogen, probably gain some sort of status from it, which is entirely *not* the point."

"We should go and explain who Blake is. Seeing him as King Alpha might just be the edge we need to forge an alliance," Kayla announced.

"Where is it? When?"

"In a month. London."

"London . . .?"

"That would be why we need Ben. While I knew about the meet, I was never given any details. I'm hoping he can tell us more. All the chats were done on secure sites – I have no idea who these people are. Marcus hoped the month would be enough time to solidify his plans with Blake and Imogen."

Blake blinked at Wyatt in disbelief. "He expected me to just get over Kayla's so-called disappearance within a month?"

"Can we not?" Imogen said, sitting up on the bed. "He made a mistake, okay?"

"I'm sorry you're hurting. I am. But I'm not sorry that he's dead. He was planning to kill Kayla, and he would have succeeded if I hadn't gotten to her in time!" Blake's wolf was close to the surface and Kayla placed her hand on his back. He resisted the shift, using her comfort to support him.

Imogen crossed her arms over her chest. She fought to keep her tears at bay.

Blake broke the tense silence, asking, "Shall we get some sleep? It's late."

"We'll get to Ben's tomorrow and we'll fill him in so he can help us find the peace summit," Wyatt suggested, collecting the now empty boxes of pizza. "Where's everyone sleeping?"

Blake was about to speak up when Imogen jumped in. "I'm not sleeping in the same bed as Wyatt. Girls' bed and boys' bed."

"Okay, yeah," Kayla agreed, giving him a small smile and shrugging apologetically.

Oh, what a fun night it was going to be.

CHAPTER FIVE

IMOGEN

IT WAS DARK, BUT the lights on the phone and TV cast enough of a glow for her eyes to adjust. She'd been awake for hours, lying in the bed and hoping sleep would come. But it evaded her. Every time she shut her eyes, she saw her dad in the fire and the fear came back. The grief was constant, but it was mired with resentment and frustration. She was so angry at her dad for what he tried to do to Kayla. At first, she didn't believe what Blake had been insinuating; the messages they'd found on his computer – coupled with her dad's confession that he was sorry – confirmed what her gut instinct was trying to tell her.

How could she be grieving and relieved at the same time? He hadn't been the best father, not for a long time. He'd used Wyatt for his magic and had no qualms about manipulating her to get the shifter/magic user hybrid babies he so desperately wanted, plus the Alastair fortune. She wasn't sure Blake knew that he had money. She doubted he even knew where it was. She didn't either, but according to her dad, it would have been hers one day.

She'd never wished for power or money – she just wanted a father.

She sighed and turned over to find Kayla's sleeping form beside her. In the other bed, she knew Wyatt and Blake were both asleep. The sounds of soft, rhythmic breathing greeted her ears, and she closed her eyes to try and do the same.

Her eyes snapped open. It was no use. Her brain wouldn't shut off. Her dad. The fire. Kayla. Ben. Who was this Ben? Did she trust him? She'd been so used to following her dad's commands that it was alien to be the one deciding what she should do next. Did she want to be a part of what the others were going to do? She wasn't sure.

A memory from when she was twelve resurfaced. Her dad made her memorise a phone number and drilled into her that she should contact that number if anything happened to him. It had been buried in the depths of her mind but was now clear as day. He'd been so secretive; no-one was to know. Not even Wyatt. At the time it had upset her, but when Wyatt came back from his training, they rarely spoke – unless it was to argue. They were good at that.

Her mind went back and forth on whether she should ring the number. Wyatt would want to be consulted, but she didn't think it was a good idea to involve him. Her dad had been quite specific. The others wouldn't understand anyway, ringing a number her dad had left her. They would probably think it was bad, but her dad wasn't evil. He got carried away, yes, but he wanted peace between the supernatural races. The person on the other end of the phone had to be an ally, someone he trusted to help her.

Decision made, she slipped out of bed and grabbed a key card from the desk. She knew she'd have to be quiet to not wake the shifter, even though she imagined he would be in a deeper sleep so his body could repair the damage done from the fire. She'd been able to use her magic to shield some of the effects on herself, but he'd taken the brunt of the weight that had collapsed on them. If it wasn't for Blake, she'd have been crushed by the beam and the fire would have eaten her alive.

She swallowed a lump in her throat. They needed help. Who were they kidding? They were just a bunch of lost kids, and they had no clue who this 'Ben' really was. They were trusting Kayla's word that he was a good guy. Imogen knew she was doing the right thing.

Taking one last look at the boys' bed, Blake with his arm slung over his face and Wyatt on his front, hand dangling over the edge, she slipped out of the room and made her way downstairs.

In the lobby, she approached a bored-looking night clerk at the front desk. He sat lower than the high countertop and made no effort to stand and greet her.

"Hi," Imogen said, and he looked up at her with barely any interest.

"How may I help you?" he drawled, lazily blinking at her as he waited for her to reply.

"I was wondering if I could use the phone? My . . ."

"Sure," the guy said and stood up, moving the phone from the lower shelf to the top of the counter. Imogen smiled warily. She'd been expecting to beg. "I'm going to take a leak anyway." The guy sauntered off, leaving her alone. Okay then.

She picked up the headset and recalled the number, punching in the numbers carefully. She blew out a nervous breath as it rang. Looking at the clock, she wondered if she should have waited. It was eleven forty, far too late at night to be waking someone. But as the ringing continued, she knew that if she waited, it would be too late. The others had spoken about leaving at first light to drive the rest of the way to Oxford.

"Hello?" a deep, older male voice answered, sounding mildly annoyed. At least he didn't sound like she'd woken him. She tapped the counter while she built up the courage to speak. *You got this, Imogen.*

"My name is Imogen, and my dad, Marcus, told me to ring this number should anything happen to him." She enunciated the names carefully, giving the man behind the voice time to digest the information. God, she hoped it wasn't a wrong number.

"You don't say."

Imogen blinked back a hint of worry at his unsurprised tone. "Pardon, sir?"

"Dear old Marcus's daughter, ey? What happened to him?"

"Um, we were attacked by shifters, and there was a fire," she supplied, not sure how much she should tell him and not wanting to go into much detail regardless. "Forgive me, but I don't know who you are?" she asked, posing it as a question in the hopes that she didn't sound rude.

"I'm an old friend. Where are you now, then? Who's with you? That ward of his made it out alive?" he asked. She was suddenly wary when he referenced Wyatt. The man's tone certainly didn't suggest any positive feelings towards him. But she couldn't lie. She needed help, and it was the last thing she could do that went with her father's wishes.

She exhaled and told him the truth. "Wyatt's with me. Also Blake.

He's a shifter. And then Kayla, another magic user." When she finished, it occurred to her that she didn't know if her father's contact was a shifter or a magic user. She didn't even know what his name was. "What's your name? Please?"

"That's quite the . . . quite the selection of company," he spat, ignoring her question. She detected a hint of . . . annoyance? Anger? "Where are you now? I'll send someone to pick you up, bring you to safety. We magic users have to stick together, don't we?" Well, that answered what he was. She didn't respond straight away, warring with some internal voice that sounded remarkably like Wyatt's. *Don't do it, Immy,* it warned. "Imogen! Where are you?" the man barked and she jumped.

"Blake is a good shifter. He's on our side. My dad thought he could help with an alliance."

"Oh, don't you worry about that. We'll make sure your dad's murder is avenged."

"What? I-I didn't say that."

"No, but you can't let the shifters that did this get away, can you? Now, tell me where you are, and I'll bring you somewhere safe where we can talk and discuss how to stop those that did this to you."

It was around then that she'd usually go to Wyatt or her father for advice on what to do next – she'd never made an executive decision before. The closest she'd come was when she told Blake that she'd support however he wanted to proceed with an alliance. She closed her eyes and counted to five. She could do it. She could make a decision to help her and her friends.

She told him – a complete stranger – the hotel they were staying in and the room number. Then she went back to the room and climbed silently into bed, praying that the man her dad had told her to contact was trustworthy.

Dad, you better not be letting me down again.

CHAPTER SIX

BLAKE

HIS EYES OPENED WIDE, taking in the near pitch-black room. Kayla slept next to Imogen in the other bed. Wyatt was at his back but as far away from him as possible, hanging off the other side. He wasn't especially pleased that he was sharing a bed with the guy. He would have much preferred Kayla, but Imogen hadn't wanted to share with Wyatt. He could sort of understand – those two got along as well as a cat and a mouse.

He frowned into the darkness, swearing something had pulled him from sleep, but what? Tuning into Kayla's heartbeat – something he did automatically throughout the day – he realised she was waking up.

"Blake?" she whispered into the darkness. He knew she was healing, and hopefully the drug she'd been injected with was working its way out of her system. In fact, he thought he detected a faint trace of lavender, a scent he was beginning to associate with her magic. Maybe the drug was wearing off?

"Yeah, I just woke up," he whispered back, trying not to wake the others.

"Me too. Everything okay?"

"Not sure. I feel like something woke me."

"Trouble?"

"I don't know. Knowing us, probably."

Kayla sighed. "That's true."

"How are you doing?"

She only paused for a couple of seconds before answering. "I'm actually feeling pretty good, all things considered. I thought I was gonna feel pretty terrible for a bit longer, but I'm not as achy and I think some of my cuts and bruises have healed. Feels like some of your shifter abilities have rubbed off on me!" she joked, careful to keep her voice down.

Blake chuckled softly. He wondered about the drugs she'd been injected with and if there would be any lasting effects. "Your magic?" he queried.

Again, she was silent for a few seconds while she figured out a response. "I can feel it inside me, buzzing to get out. I just can't call on it yet. That's good progress, I suppose."

"I'm relieved," he admitted.

"Relieved? Were you worried?" She shifted in bed, most likely to face him. He turned on his side, too. He was glad that his body had been healing while he slept – his extra abilities helped him to see her a bit. Her features weren't clear to him in the dark, but he knew she was smiling at him. He could sense it.

"Of course."

"Says the guy who ran into a burning building."

"Why, were you worried?" he teased.

"Terrified."

Her reply was so instant, so serious that his smile fell.

"Kayla, I–" He stopped. Something caught his attention from outside the room. A noise that felt like it was trying not to be a noise. Like someone was desperate to be quiet.

"Blake? Everything all–"

"Shh," he snapped. He didn't want to sound harsh, but he needed to concentrate. She stopped talking, trusting him completely.

There was commotion in the hallway, but it was the early hours of the morning – it should have been quiet. Sitting up in bed, he strained to hear more. He could only make out muffled voices, his ears struggling to pick up the words.

A gun clicked. He sprang towards Kayla, grabbing her hand to pull her from the bed, and thrust her behind him just as the door opened and the lights switched on. Five bodies piled into the room.

"What the hell?" Wyatt yelled, throwing the bed covers off. Imogen rubbed her eyes and gasped, pulling the duvet up to her chin, her eyes wide with fear. Blake would have done something, anything, but a gun was trained on his head. "Who the bloody hell are you?" Wyatt shouted at the intruders. Two men stood close to Wyatt and Imogen, and two women chanted by the door.

"Done, sir," one of the women announced.

Wyatt slowly got out of bed. "Was that a bubble spell? To stop others from hearing anything inside this room?" he asked harshly. The woman side-eyed him carefully.

Two men slowly edged around the sides of the room, getting closer to Wyatt and Imogen. Blake couldn't do anything; he'd be leaving Kayla alone if he did. Besides, he couldn't split himself into three anyway. There was no way he'd leave Kayla's side, so he had to hope Wyatt and Imogen could look after themselves. He prayed Imogen had recovered enough to use her shielding magic.

He growled in frustration, and the guy holding a gun to his head raised one brow. The man was older – perhaps in his forties – with light brown, cropped hair and dark, calculating eyes. He was clearly the one in charge, and Blake's gut told him they were all magic users.

As if she could hear him, Kayla confirmed his suspicions. "Magic users."

"Got the cuffs ready?" The guy with the gun spoke over his shoulder to one of the women who'd performed the so-called 'bubble' spell. She moved to his side.

She wordlessly handed him a pair of silver handcuffs. They weren't like the normal police ones he'd seen before; the bands were thick and dark. The word 'shackles' sprung to mind.

"I'm going to put these on. Don't give me a reason to be violent," the man ordered, passing his gun to the woman, neither of them taking their eyes off Blake. Kayla's hand tightened around his. She hadn't let go since he'd grabbed her.

As the guy took a step forward, Blake took one back. He was more in line with where Kayla stood. He couldn't move any further or he'd be behind her.

Blake growled as the guy drew closer. "What makes you think I'll just let you put those on me?" he asked through gritted teeth.

"Who are you?" Kayla demanded from beside him.

"We're here to collect you, bring you to safety. But the shifter needs to be leashed."

"Hey!" Blake snapped. Imogen sucked in a sharp breath and Kayla's frowned at her.

"You're not going to cuff him, mate," Wyatt said, sounding like his ever-cocky self.

A smile ghosted the man's lips. "Says who? You're just a bunch of kids. Now, let's get you leashed up," the guy repeated. It didn't escape Blake that two of the magic users had been edging closer to Wyatt and Imogen during the exchange.

The leader lurched forward to put the cuff on Blake's wrist, but Blake snatched it away and swung at the guy. It was with his left hand, as his right was holding onto Kayla, so when the guy easily dodged and countered, Blake was left with no other option. He dropped her hand to block the incoming fist.

It was like a silent signal had been given. The two inching closer to Wyatt and Imogen went to grab them. The woman holding the gun moved towards Kayla but surprised him by lowering the weapon to reach out and seize Kayla's upper arm, pulling her away from the fist fight. It didn't make sense to Blake, but the distraction cost him as the leader landed a punch on his jaw. His head snapped to the right and his wolf rose up, pushing against his skin. If Kayla wasn't so close, he might have let it free.

Kayla yelped and pried the hand off her arm, eliciting a scream from the woman holding her. Both Blake and the leader turned towards them, noticing a red handprint on the woman's forearm. Kayla's hand was glowing. Had she been able to bring her magic forth? Was the drug wearing off? Blake frowned at her. She gaped at her hand and then slowly raised her eyes to look at him.

"Watch out!" she yelled. The leader came at him again. He'd been so preoccupied with Kayla's distress that he ended up constantly on the defence. The leader was keeping up with him, and while Blake knew he was mostly healed from the injuries sustained by the fire, he didn't realise just how sluggish he'd become.

He shook his head as fog filled it.

"Stop! Stop!" Imogen screamed from somewhere to his right. "He said no one would be hurt!"

Blake frowned. What did she mean? Did she know who these people were? He didn't have much time to process what was happening. Punches rained down on his face and a foot landed in his ribs, sending him down to his knees.

"Leave him alone!" Kayla ordered. A scream cleared the fog from his mind. He looked up to see the woman who had spelled the room swatting at her flaming jacket.

Kayla's body sagged. She wiped sweat from her brow. Wait. Had that woman been using magic on him?

Confusion spread just like the fog had. In his distraction, the leader stepped forward and snapped the first cuff on his wrist. He let the wolf into his eyes, but his attention was diverted.

"Stop or she gets a bullet," the woman Kayla had burned snapped. He flashed his focus to Kayla, who was standing with her hands raised in surrender. The gun was trained on her. Blake froze, growling when the leader came forward to put the second cuff on his wrist and bind his hands together.

A shiver ran down his spine. His eyes returned to normal. The wolf whined and protested within him but he was just out of reach.

"You've locked my wolf away!" he shouted at them. A weird mix of feelings washed over him. He'd had this done to him before when his adoptive parents had utilised a mage to push back and hide his natural change. He didn't want to be smothered again; he'd only just learned about his wolf and didn't want to be separated.

His emotions were mirrored in Kayla's eyes. She knew exactly how he was feeling.

"What do you mean they've locked your wolf away?" Imogen repeated, her face going pale.

Wyatt looked from the cuffs to the leader before he addressed him. "You didn't . . . those cuffs are meant to be really, really rare."

"Shut up!" the leader barked. "We're going downstairs to the vans. You'll come with us, and for your safety," he said, motioning to everyone but Blake, "the shifter will stay cuffed until we reach our destination."

"And where is our destination?" Kayla asked confidently and her eyes flashed to the gun before looking back at the leader.

"Ask her. She called us," he smirked, nodding his head in Imogen's direction.

Kayla's mouth went slack and Wyatt smacked his forehead with his palm. At least Imogen had the sense to stare at the floor and look guilty.

"Immy, you're an absolute idiot."

CHAPTER SEVEN

KAYLA

"I REPEAT: IMMY, YOU'RE an idiot." Wyatt tutted, blowing out a breath and rolling his eyes.

They were bundled in the back of a van. Another van. Kayla wondered if she'd been cursed in some previous life to be kidnapped over and over again. At least there were seats this time. The three of them sat in a row, Wyatt between the two girls. It was a good thing he separated her and Imogen, really. Blake had been taken to a different car and her stomach flip-flopped at the thought of what they could be doing to him.

Wyatt drummed his fingers on his thighs as the van sped down the road. Kayla had no idea where they were going; she'd seen signs for London at one point, but she eventually gave up. Many places had signs for London – it was the capital. Her thoughts kept circling back to Blake, distracting her from their journey. Once or twice, she'd looked behind them to see if the car he'd been put in was following them, but she couldn't really see. Maybe his van was a few vehicles away.

Both of the women she'd burned sat in the front seat. To be fair, she'd only intended to scald the one performing a spell on Blake. The woman she'd injured first had been a complete shock in terms of the specific elemental magic involved. She was surprised that her magic had come through at all. She could feel the drug wearing off and flexed her fingers, trying to draw on some of the restless magic at her core.

Wyatt covered her hand with his. He whispered to her over the music their captors had put on. "I heard them spell the vehicle when we got in. If you use magic, it'll misdirect and hit us."

She sagged in defeat. "Who are these people?" she asked.

"Would you care to elaborate, Immy?"

Kayla was surprised at his tone. She was expecting him to sound as frustrated and as angry as she was. Instead, his voice was only mildly annoyed.

"It wasn't meant to be this way."

"What wasn't meant to be this way?" Kayla snapped back. "Please, do tell."

Imogen flinched. "They said no one would be hurt. I promise, they did. I never would have agreed to anything if I thought they'd hurt him."

"And how did that work out for you?" Kayla hissed.

Wyatt gave her hand another comforting squeeze. "Imogen, we really need an explanation of what's going on and what sort of danger Blake is in. Do they . . . know?"

There was a whole row of seats between them and their captors, but Kayla was glad Wyatt lowered his voice and didn't explicitly refer to Blake as being the Alastair heir. Did they know?

Imogen shook her head. "I didn't say that."

"That's something at least. Who are they?"

"I – I'm not sure. My father made me memorise a phone number when I was twelve and I promised to ring it should anything happen to him."

"Why wasn't I told about this number?" A thread of hurt laced his tone.

"I don't know. He made it very clear I wasn't to share it with you."

"Charming. He was never a father figure to me, was he?"

Imogen shrugged but didn't speak.

"So, you rang this number and spoke to who?" Kayla interrupted when Wyatt became too lost in his own thoughts.

"He never actually said a name," she responded, frowning, "but he said he was going to pick us up and bring us to safety."

"Well, they obviously didn't include Blake in that, did they?"

"Look, I am really, really sorry. I thought I was making the right decision!"

Wyatt turned to face Imogen. "And what decision was that? To go behind our backs? Decide something without us? I thought we were a team?"

A moment of silence stretched between them as Imogen and Wyatt stared each other down.

"What about the fact that you guys were making all these decisions to go to Oxford, go to the peace summit? Did I get a say in that?"

"Immy! You were there for all those conversations! You should have said if you didn't want to do that!"

"Would it have made a difference, Wyatt? Would you have chosen me over your new friends?"

"What is this about? I thought we wanted to work with Blake and Kayla? Unify the sides without you having to go through what your dad wanted?"

Imogen went quiet, fighting some internal war. In one respect, Kayla wanted to offer Imogen words of comfort, but at the same time, she couldn't ignore the fact that Imogen had put them all in danger.

"Imogen, I'm sorry you felt that way. I'm sorry about you losing your dad. But you have to realise that this was a mistake, and we have to free Blake. Will you help us do that when we get to whoever you spoke to?" Kayla asked. Her tone was still icy, but she did her best to soften the words.

"Yes, I will. I'm sorry. I'm so, so sorry." Tears ran down her cheeks.

"Thank you."

Imogen turned to look out the window, and Kayla heard the sobs she tried to keep quiet. Wyatt reached for Imogen's hand, interlocking their fingers. Neither spoke. Neither acknowledged they were touching. They didn't even face each other. Kayla didn't know the nature of their relationship – fraught and full of insults from what she'd seen – but it was the first time she sensed a deep connection between them. Maybe there was a chance they could all escape as a unit.

The team that Wyatt spoke of.

THE CAR CAME TO A stop, and they were ushered out of the vehicle onto a white gravel driveway. A circular flower bed provided some sort of directional flow, leading to the single-track entrance and exit they'd come down only moments ago.

Kayla looked up at the house in front of her. Mansion was the only word she could think of that adequately described the size and impression of the mid-eighteen hundreds estate. Brickwork curved into turrets at each corner of the building, and large windows were spread along the ground floor on either side of a massive wooden door. Even from where she stood, she could tell the imposing door was intricately designed. It would take a great deal of energy to break it down, and that was assuming it wasn't magically shielded. She wouldn't put it past them to have such a precaution in place.

They were secluded, and their kidnappers clearly had money and resources to keep them prisoners if they wanted to. Ben wouldn't even know they were missing; she hadn't told him they were coming.

A silver car pulled up behind them. One of the men yanked Blake out, his hands still bound in front of him. The harshness of the movement and blatant lack of care caused Blake to stumble to his knees, landing with a heavy thud. The leader of the group came around the other side and hauled Blake up to his feet. Dried blood stained Blake's top lip and chin.

"Blake!" She rushed over, but the man who'd yanked Blake from the car put his arm out to stop her. She crashed into it.

"No one goes near the shifter," the leader sneered.

"You clearly couldn't keep your hands off him!" The corner of Blake's lips twitched at her quick retort. "You okay?" she addressed Blake. He nodded at her, his eyes hooded with concern. She sensed his worry was over her welfare and not his own. She needed him to be thinking more about himself to get out of his situation.

"Are you?" he asked in return.

"They've not harmed us."

The two women herded Wyatt and Imogen closer to Kayla. Imogen made to move towards Blake, an apology written on her face, but Wyatt gripped her shoulder. She seemed to understand and stood quietly, studying the ground.

"Ah, hello Imogen," a voice boomed. A man made his way across the gravel. He was older, around the same age Marcus was, and he walked confidently with his head held high. His shoulder-length grey hair was neatly styled in a low bun, and a well-groomed silver beard covered the lower half of his face. A long black coat flowed behind him, opening at the front to show a black suit and an ice blue shirt. As he drew closer, he turned his brown eyes to Kayla, and a shiver danced down her spine.

They were cold, calculating.

Kayla did not trust him one bit.

Wyatt's grip on Imogen's shoulder tightened, and his jaw stiffened. "Are you the person Imogen spoke to? The number Marcus made her memorise?" Wyatt asked, his voice hard and devoid of emotion. The man turned those piercing eyes on Wyatt.

"Wyatt, I presume?"

"You presume correctly," Wyatt replied in the same tone.

"Hmmm." The unknown man pursed his lips in thought. His eyes darted to Wyatt's hand on Imogen's shoulder, but he returned his focus to Blake. Kayla wasn't sure if anyone else had seen the lightning quick study of his.

"Why did you have Blake handcuffed?" Imogen blurted, her voice trembling.

The man turned to her and smiled. Kayla saw right through the forced display of emotion. "Because he's a shifter, and we can't risk the danger he poses to us."

"But he's not a danger," Kayla interrupted, earning a shrewd look from the man. "It was Marcus who handed me over to shifters. He hired them to get rid of me. It wasn't Blake. And it wasn't Blake who caused Marcus's death!"

"That may be so in this specific instance, but do not underestimate shifters. They are a risk to us all," he concluded, a layer of ice coating his voice.

Wyatt jumped in. "What do you plan on doing with us?"

"I'm hoping you'll all come to see my point of view and join me." He sighed.

"Including Blake?"

The man was silent for a moment. "That remains to be seen."

Kayla locked eyes with Blake. That didn't sound promising.

"Let's go inside and discuss this some more, shall we?" he asked, sweeping his arm in the direction of the mansion. A large, fake smile was plastered on his face.

Wyatt frowned at the man. "I know you – don't I?"

The man's grin grew wider. "I wondered when you'd recognise me."

"Elijah."

CHAPTER EIGHT

WYATT

"IF EVERYONE WOULD FOLLOW me," Elijah confidently announced. He had the same air of arrogance he'd possessed when Wyatt knew him over twelve years ago as an advisor to Marcus on the magic user council.

Imogen's mouth had gaped open when he said Elijah's name. Immy was only six years old when Elijah left, but the name would have been familiar. He couldn't believe she didn't know who she'd been speaking to – his voice had aged, but that tone? It was the same self-imposed superiority as always.

Guilt swept through his body when he thought of Imogen ringing that number in secret. He blamed himself for their predicament. Could he have spotted her worry before she made the decision to go behind their backs? Could he have been more supportive about losing Marcus? There was certainly no love lost between him and Marcus, and he wasn't grieving his death. He knew Immy didn't like what her father had been forcing her to do, but she still loved him. Love had a way of digging its heels in, even when it was in someone's best interest to move on.

She turned to him, a lost, spiralling emotion tumbling through her deep brown eyes and straight into him. Shit. The brat was looking to him for help – stability – and he'd give it to her in a bloody heartbeat. Damn responsibilities. He rolled his eyes, just to let her know he was feeling somewhat annoyed.

Elijah moved towards the open front doors, which would've looked more at home on a castle. Wyatt reluctantly followed but stopped when Blake was hauled in a different direction.

"Where are you taking him?" Kayla demanded of Elijah's goons.

Elijah stopped and called over his shoulder, "Shifters aren't welcome here. They don't get the same . . . privileges." He didn't elaborate as he nodded at Blake's abductors, some unspoken command passing between them, and Blake was dragged away. The shifter struggled in their tight grasp.

"Stick with Wyatt!" Blake shouted back to Kayla.

Cheers, man! Appreciate the pressure of looking after your girl! Great. The responsibilities were just piling up.

"C'mon Kayla. Let's go see what Captain Douchebag wants."

"You know this guy?" Kayla asked under her breath, catching up to Wyatt as they followed Elijah into the building. That was just like Elijah. So confident and cocky, assuming they would follow. It didn't matter that they were indeed following him. It was just the implied expectation that Wyatt didn't like. They didn't really have a choice.

Jerk.

Imogen stayed close to his other side, quiet and pensive. He glanced down, worried about where her troubled thoughts were taking her. He needed her to hang on a bit, just while he figured out how to get them all out of this mess. God, he seriously hoped Kayla was forming some grand plan in her head.

"Unfortunately," he answered. "He was Marcus's subordinate when the Alliance was being finalised with the Alastairs. Marcus was the mage councillor, and Elijah was his second and advisor."

"What happened? What do we need to know?"

"From what I remember, there was some sort of incident with Elijah and the King Alpha. He was banished by the King Alpha and Marcus severed all ties . . . supposedly."

Imogen grabbed onto his arm as they walked, her voice urgent. "I didn't know it was him. I didn't."

He didn't know why, but his stomach tightened at her desperate expression. She needed him to know, but fear was painted across her features. She never needed to worry – he always believed that face. He'd been able to read that face for years.

"I know."

Kayla snorted but kept her mouth shut as they stepped over the threshold and into a large foyer with marble flooring, a glass chandelier, and a sweeping oak staircase. It would have been beautiful, something to marvel at, if Elijah hadn't been waiting for them, hands clasped behind his back and a huge grin on his face. Wyatt yawned, feigning boredom. He knew it was getting to Elijah when a muscle ticked in the older man's jaw.

"We'll be heading straight to the meeting," Elijah announced, continuing down a long and impressive hallway.

"What meeting?" Kayla asked, moving to Elijah's side. Wyatt would have pulled her back, but he didn't want Elijah to notice. Thankfully, Imogen stayed next to him.

"You'll see soon enough."

Elijah stopped and pulled open a heavy door to his right, holding it for them to walk through. The room was wide and long with an extensive table situated in the middle. Four magic users sat on one side – at least, Wyatt assumed they were given Elijah's hatred of shifters. A stern, well-dressed woman stood behind the seat at the very end of the room. She held an iPad and placed a glass of water at the head of the table. Elijah sauntered into the room and sat at the place of honour, sipping the water.

"Thank you, Margaret," he said to the woman. She smiled appreciatively. "Please, take a seat," he said to them, and gestured to the empty side of the table. The chairs faced the line of magic users, each with a stony, unwelcoming expression on their face.

Wyatt sat between the two girls, impatient to find out what was going on. A horrible sense of foreboding clenched his gut and he bounced his knee up and down in an attempt to calm himself. Imogen looked down, noticing his nervous tic, but didn't say anything.

No one spoke. Kayla looked like she was about to say something when a door opened, and Blake was dragged in to stand at the opposite end from Elijah. Blake wasn't offered a seat, his hands were still shackled, and two magic users held him in rough grasps. Kayla's hands gripped the table in front of her.

"Let the trial begin, shall we?" Elijah smirked.

"What?" Kayla shrieked. Blake's head snapped up to focus on Elijah while Wyatt struggled to comprehend what they'd walked into. A trial.

"A trial for what?" Wyatt asked warily.

Elijah didn't disguise his grin when he answered. "We will be reviewing what kind of threat the shifter poses to our society. Proceed," he said to the panel sitting opposite them.

A tall slender man stood up, rearranging his glasses. He held a clipboard in front of him.

"Nature: shifter. Violence: high. Attacked the retrieval group–"

Kayla interrupted, "You guys forced yourselves into our room! What were we to think?"

"Possessive tendencies towards others, verbally abusive during transportation, unknown history of potential violence."

"You can't summarise somebody like that. Elijah, please?" Imogen pleaded, finally finding her voice.

"These are just observations we've made within the past few hours. It doesn't look good, you have to admit," Elijah responded.

"But Kayla hurt some of your 'retrieval' team, and you're not putting her on trial!"

"Imogen!" Wyatt barked. Did the girl have a death wish for them?

"Yes," Elijah mused. "I can only assume that the shifter manipulated her emotions to make her fight for him."

"He did no such thing!" Kayla argued and Blake growled, his eyes flashing yellow. Wyatt sensed that if the spelled cuffs weren't on him, Blake would have shifted and ripped out Elijah's throat – oh, how he'd love to see that.

"He is an animal – he follows instincts rather than thought. Can't you see that?" Elijah directed his last question at Imogen.

Imogen spluttered. "Instincts are important, Elijah. Why are you doing this? I thought you wanted peace?"

"I do, but most shifters are barbaric, more animal than human. We can't have them risking everything we've worked so hard for in this world."

Wyatt cringed. He'd never liked Elijah, always thought he was way too crazy to be an advisor, but he sounded as mad as Marcus wanting to use

Imogen to breed hybrid babies.

"What are you saying?" Wyatt asked slowly.

"Victoria? Summary?" He addressed one of the panel members and a slender woman in her forties stood, smoothing down her pencil skirt.

"We have concluded that even if we did further research into his origins, this shifter poses a significant threat to the magical community and to humans. We believe that his base instincts will one day overpower what little sense of control he possesses right now. Furthermore, his ability to manipulate others to his cause is a danger to our mental wellbeing. We recommend putting the shifter down."

"Down? Down where?" Kayla asked, but Wyatt's stomach twisted. The woman sat, and Elijah took a sip of his water while Wyatt's heart thumped in his chest.

"Thank you. Based upon your recommendations and my own thoughts, I hereby sentence the shifter to death."

"Wait," Kayla breathed, her hand clutching at her chest.

"You will be taken to a private cell and held there, cuffed for our protection until the execution date–"

"What's going on?" Kayla interrupted, but Elijah ignored her.

"–in three weeks. That should provide sufficient enough time to ensure procedures are followed and affairs are in place."

"This can't be happening . . ." Kayla whispered, turning to look at Blake, who had a similar look of utter disbelief on his face.

"Margaret? Can you please contact the relevant bodies to start planning the event?" Elijah said. Wyatt's fury rose at Elijah's blasé attitude. He'd just sentenced somebody to death, for Christ's sake.

"Elijah!" Wyatt snapped, standing up, his chair scraping behind him. "You cannot do this. Blake is nothing but a supporter of peace between our communities. He saved Imogen even though it was Marcus who tried to set up Kayla's death. You cannot be serious!"

"Oh, but I am, boy. And you'd do well to remember who's in charge here. I would hate to have a magic user stand trial," Elijah said, looking pointedly at each of them, "but I will for the safety of this community and for the security of our future."

Kayla stood abruptly, her chair grinding against the hard stone flooring like Wyatt's had. "No!" She moved towards Blake but was stopped by another magic user who had been standing guard at the door. As soon as Kayla's arm was in the man's grip, Blake thrashed against his captors, but the handcuffs' power blocked his strength and abilities.

Blake roared in anger, and the two holding him began to lose their grip as they dragged him back to the other exit. Wyatt pulled Imogen up with him to move towards Kayla.

"Blake!" Kayla screamed, and the papers on the table burst into flames. She gasped and realised at the same time as Wyatt that the drug must have worn off. Kayla narrowed her eyes at the two still dragging Blake backwards.

"How interesting. Now, enough of that!" Elijah shouted and raised his arm, aiming at Kayla. Elijah snapped his fingers, and as he did, Kayla's eyes rolled back. She slumped to the floor.

Blake roared, his body vibrating with fear when he realised he didn't have the strength to escape. Blake's eyes darted around the room, coming to rest on Wyatt.

"Look after her!" he shouted as the doors slammed shut behind him.

CHAPTER NINE

KAYLA

KAYLA WOKE UP WITH a headache the size of Africa. She rubbed her temples with her fingertips until she realised she wasn't waking up in the hotel they'd driven to last night – she was in a small blue room. A short desk, a chest of drawers, and the single bed she was lying on were the only pieces of furniture decorating the space. She got out of bed fully clothed and made her way to the door.

Locked.

She thumped her fist on the door and shouted, "Hey! Let me out!" There was no reply, and if she was being honest, she wasn't expecting one. Elijah had locked her away so she wouldn't be able to free Blake.

Tears sprung to her eyes, Elijah's words haunting her: *"I hereby sentence the shifter to death . . ."*

How had everything gone so wrong so quickly? How long had she been out? Elijah had used some seriously strong mojo on her; she remembered the click of his fingers and the strangest desire – an urge she couldn't fight – to fall asleep. She even worried about Wyatt and Imogen. Okay, she wasn't Imogen's biggest fan at the moment, but she was still concerned. If they were somehow together, then they were probably okay. Unlike herself.

After trying and failing to escape, she sat on the bed and rubbed her hands over her face. Was her magic back yet? She'd managed to set some papers on fire, and she'd tapped into it at the hotel – maybe the drugs were finally out of her system?

She held her hands out in front of her and willed her magic to come forth. She visualised drawing on her magic, utilising both her mage and elemental powers. She squeezed her eyes shut and focused on her breathing. Blake was clear in her mind, but thinking of him made her heart hammer, so she pushed thoughts of him to one side and concentrated on the magical hum that was gaining momentum.

Just as the tingle reached her fingertips, a key scratched in the lock on the other side of the door. Kayla stood, prepared to fight whoever came in. She raised her hands and prayed she could keep her magic close to the surface for long enough.

To her surprise, Imogen and Wyatt hurried into the room, quickly shutting the door behind them. Kayla frowned, wary of what might have happened since Elijah had knocked her out.

Wyatt looked relieved to see Kayla, his body sagging when he saw her awake.

"Thank God you're okay – I was worried about what kind of magic the bastard used on you," Wyatt said, coming over to hug her.

"I'm okay – I think. How long was I out for?"

His eyes apologised first. "A day."

"A day? Jeez." She ran a hand through her hair, but it reminded her of Blake, so she settled for tucking some of it behind her ears. "Blake?" She folded her arms, looking at Imogen.

"Fine for now. And don't worry, she's on our side," Wyatt replied, answering Kayla's unspoken question.

"How do you know?" she asked him, and Imogen looked embarrassed as she hid behind Wyatt.

"I just do. She knows she made a mistake. Besides, we need to work together to free Blake. Imogen has a plan."

"Really?" Kayla responded disbelievingly.

Imogen stepped forward, hands clenched together in a prayer position. "I'm truly, truly sorry, Kayla. I honestly didn't mean for any of this to happen."

Kayla pursed her lips. "What's your grand plan then?"

Imogen pulled a pouch out from her back pocket and unzipped it. Inside was a syringe and a small vial full of light blue liquid.

"What the heck is that?" Kayla accused, stepping back.

Imogen's eyes flashed with pain. "Elijah wants me to drug you with this."

"To block my magic?"

"No, it'll make you more . . . amenable, and he can then bend you to his will."

"You bitch!" Kayla spat. She rushed forward, grabbing Imogen around the neck and pushing her up against the door. Imogen dropped the pouch and slapped at Kayla's arm as she struggled to breathe. Smoke started curling its way up from where Kayla's hand came into contact with Imogen's skin.

"That's enough, Kayla!" Wyatt ordered. He marched over and yanked Kayla's arm away. Imogen immediately covered her red-tinged skin with both hands and coughed; Wyatt rubbed her shoulder, asking if she was all right. She nodded.

"You expect me to react how? She just said she was going to drug me and she admitted she was working with Elijah! Why else would he get her to do it?"

"Because she's trying to stay on his good side and get us intel, Kayla!" Wyatt shouted back, quickly lowering his voice and looking to the door.

Kayla sighed. She knew she was reacting poorly and without thought, but the fear of what Blake was going through was eating her alive. She rubbed her middle, easing the knots in her stomach.

"I'm sorry. I'm just . . . worried."

"We all are, but we gotta keep our heads. We're in the middle of a viper's nest right now."

"Imogen, I apologise," Kayla said, trying to sound sincere.

Imogen nodded. "Maybe we're even?" she asked, her voice timid. Her lips lifted in a tiny hopeful smile.

Kayla sighed and held her hand out. Imogen took it. "Even," Kayla agreed. Wyatt put his arms around their shoulders and pulled them in close.

"My two girls, friends again!"

"All right, you big sap. What's the plan then, Imogen? I sure as hell ain't being drugged again."

"I was thinking I could say that I'd done it, but we would dispose of the contents, and then you would pretend to be acquiescent and . . . submissive," she started with an apologetic smile.

Kayla snorted, but when Wyatt gave her a pointed look, she apologised. "Go on."

"If Elijah thinks you're working for him, you'll gain access to more information about where Blake is being held."

Wyatt held his hand up. "But Kayla, you need to be really, really careful. He saw you create fire, so he knows you're a powerful elemental. I think he wants power, craves it, so you would be valuable to him."

"Noted. What about this . . . execution date?" Kayla said, stumbling over the words. "Why wait three weeks if Blake is such a big risk?"

"I have . . . theories, but I don't think they'd help us at this point," Wyatt answered.

"Right. You guys need to contact Michael and Ben."

"Who's Michael?" Imogen asked.

Kayla looked at Wyatt, placing a hand on her hip as he squirmed.

"Err, a friend, another magic user . . ."

"Is he some big secret?"

"No just . . . ugh, all right! I liked having something you didn't know anything about, okay? Marcus would send me to him for intel and we just got on – I liked having a friend outside of the hotel."

"I hate to interrupt, but both Michael and Ben will be able to contact others to come and help us. We need to find out where and how Blake is being held, and then all the weak points in their security. If we need brute force, then we get the guys to find it for us. We cannot let Elijah know who Blake is."

"Agreed," Wyatt concurred.

"It'll be best if Wyatt shows some signs of unease with both of us," Imogen suggested.

"That won't be a problem. Seeing you suck up to Elijah and Kayla become his pet? Yeah, it won't be hard to act disgusted."

"Yes, Wyatt, but you need to tread a fine line there. You need to slowly 'come around' to his way of thinking. Do it too fast and he'll suspect something. Do it too slow and he'll probably find a way to 'conveniently get rid of you.'"

Wyatt rolled his eyes.

"How are we doing the drug thing?" Kayla asked.

"I'll flush the liquid down the toilet, but I'll need to – you know – the needle?"

Understanding dawned. "Oh crap. Stick me with it?"

Wyatt sniggered. "That's what she said." Both girls elbowed him. "Couldn't be helped!"

Imogen looked at Kayla apologetically. "Yes, sorry."

Imogen got to work making an obvious needle mark on Kayla's arm while Wyatt got rid of the contents of the vile.

"You think you'll be okay, Kayla?" Wyatt asked as he returned to the room.

"Yeah. Just wait here until I'm summoned, right?"

"Sarcasm. Yup. You're all right!"

"Will you . . . will you try and find out how he's doing? If you can?"

Imogen and Wyatt briefly looked at each other before agreeing.

"We should probably go before Elijah realises we're both missing," Imogen said, zipping up the pouch.

Before they made it to the door, Kayla rushed over, hugging them tightly. "Stay safe," she whispered.

They smiled and slipped out of the room, leaving her alone again.

CHAPTER TEN

BLAKE

HE'D BEEN STUCK INSIDE the cell for three, maybe four days with only a bread roll and a bottle of water each afternoon. The 'cell' was his nickname for the God-awful accommodation. It wasn't quite a prison, but it might as well have been. Grey walls, bars over the one small window, a thin mattress – no frame – and a toilet. All in one room. The toilet wasn't even in a separate little cubicle or something. It was pretty much a jail cell, but instead of bars for a door, well, there was an actual door. Silver linings and all.

The first few hours he'd been in there, he'd scraped the skin off his fists trying to get out, but they simply replaced the door he'd managed to put a hole through. It had taken a lot out of him to even get that far, as his shifter strength was held back by the stupid manacles. He was grateful for the training he'd always done with his dad, but the door was hard as a rock. His stinging hands cruelly reminded him of that fact. They'd not given him anything for his wounds, so he'd used some of the water to rinse off the blood and pick out shards of wood.

During his first full day he searched for a way out, but the bars were fixed in place with cement and there was nothing in the room he could use – not even a pin. He'd woken up that morning with the intention to just lie there all day. What else was he to do but wait for his execution? He wasn't weak, but by God did he struggle to hold back tears. How was he expected to react?

He wondered how Kayla was. She was never far from his thoughts. A few times he swore he felt her, sensed her emotions, but those moments were fleeting. He wondered if he needed his wolf to have that connection with her – maybe that was all she was attracted to. His wolf. No. He pushed the negative thoughts out of his head. Kayla wouldn't let him die, not after everything they'd been through. He just had to have faith.

Knowing he'd need his strength if he were to escape, he started on a light workout: a few press-ups, crunches, squats, that sort of thing. His muscles had to be ready, but he didn't have the energy to do cardio, too. If he was only going to get a bread roll a day, he had to be wise about how much he put his body through.

He'd only done a few minutes of exercise, but he was covered in a fine mist of perspiration. Taking a few sips of water, he sat down on the mattress to rest.

When he heard a key turn in the lock, he sat up straight, wondering if it was his daily allowance of bread. Instead, Kayla walked in, holding a tray. He shot to his feet. Two guards stood outside the open door, watching closely.

"Kayla! You're okay!" He smiled at her as she placed the tray on the floor by the mattress. He briefly glanced at the meal, finding a bread roll, a small bunch of grapes, and another bottle of water. "How are you?" He rushed through the words, wondering how much time they had. In fact, he wondered how she'd even managed to get there in the first place.

A wide smile stretched across her face. "I'm well, thank you. How are you?" Blake frowned.

"Kayla? What's going on?"

"Everything is good, thanks." She smiled again, but it didn't quite reach her eyes. "Please, do eat up."

"Why are they even bothering to feed me if they just want me dead?" Something close to anger flashed through her eyes, and then she tilted her head to one side, listening.

There was a blinding flash in the hallway, and an explosion rumbled somewhere in the building. Shouts of surprise and alarm filled the air, and the two guards looked at Kayla.

"Stay here," they commanded. They shut the door and Kayla bowed her head. Blake heard soft, hurried whispers, and as she lifted her face to his, her eyes flashed with magic. She leaped at him, wrapping her arms around his neck. He barely kept them both upright.

"Oh, Blake! I'm sorry I had to pretend." She spoke quickly, pulling back to take his face in her hands. "Are you okay? Have they hurt you?"

"Not since I was put in here. What's going on? Have they done anything to you?" He studied her eyes, drinking them in.

"Long story short, Imogen is pretending to drug me so I'll do what Elijah wants without question. He probably thought sending me in here like that would get to you. Wyatt is causing a distraction somewhere, but he helped me learn a bubble spell to hide our voices from anything that might be recording. We only have a few minutes."

Blake's head spun. "Okay, I think I'm just about following."

"We're working on getting you out. Imogen is contacting Michael and Ben, who can assemble an army if we need it. You won't die here," she finished, her voice thick with emotion.

He tried to smile reassuringly at her. "I know you wouldn't allow that." He raised his wrist, the short chain between the shackles meaning he had to use both hands to brush some of her hair back. It was becoming a habit, and the soft, silky strands made him want to pull her close again. He knew they didn't have long, so he ducked down for a kiss. Her lips were warm and inviting, even as they grew urgent.

When the initial hunger was sated, she pulled back, resting her forehead against his.

"You need to eat what they give you. One of us will sneak in more when we can, but you need to keep your strength up. And be ready – I don't know when it will happen, but just be ready!" Voices approached the cell and she sprung away from him, plastering that fake smile back on her face. The doors opened and an irate Elijah barged in. Blake curled his lip at him.

"Hi Elijah!" Kayla chirped. Elijah studied her carefully.

"Have you given the prisoner his food?"

"Sure have!" she replied with forced cheeriness.

Elijah looked back and forth between them and gestured for Kayla to join him. She moved forward with only the slightest of hesitations. It was only because Blake knew Kayla that he noticed her falter, but she recovered quickly and leaned into Elijah's side.

Blake growled, unable to hide his reaction despite knowing Kayla was only pretending. "What do you want, Elijah? Sending her in here like this? What's the point? I'll be dead in a few weeks anyway. And why even bother with the pathetic food?"

Elijah's answering smile was poison.

CHAPTER ELEVEN

Imogen

"IMOGEN!" ELIJAH'S VOICE RANG through the kitchen, making her jump. She picked up the tray of food she was meant to be delivering to Blake with nervous hands, but she made sure to hide the chocolate protein bar in her waistband. She deliberately held her face in a neutral expression as she turned around.

"Elijah, everything okay?"

"Of course, dear. Maggie here will take the food to our guest." An unremarkable middle-aged woman stepped forward and took the tray from Imogen. She tried not to huff that she wouldn't be able to give Blake the bar, and instead turned to Elijah with a smile. He was watching her carefully.

"Is there a problem?"

"No, no. I just wanted to discuss Wyatt with you."

"Wyatt?" Imogen squawked. "What about him?"

Elijah motioned for Imogen to follow him. He walked lazily out of the kitchen, heading towards his office.

"Wyatt seems to have . . . settled. Better than I thought."

Imogen waited for him to continue, but the pregnant pause grew uncomfortable. "I'm not sure what that has to do with me."

"Hm, perhaps nothing. I expected more of him, I suppose. Do you know how he is? He seemed awfully worried about the shifter."

Imogen stared at her feet, gulping down the lump in her throat.

"Yes, I think he thought the shifter was on our side, but ever since . . ."

"Oh, my dear. Yes, the fire. The fire that claimed your father's life. If it wasn't for shifters taking over the hotel, perhaps it would still be standing. Maybe your father would still be here."

She controlled her breathing. Swallowed her tears. Buried her grief.

"You're absolutely right." *Asshole*, she added in her head.

Elijah's personal assistant appeared down the hallway, her sharp heels clicking on the hardwood floor. While her face was impassive, the woman's eyes sent a message of sorts to Elijah. Distractedly, he waved Imogen away.

"I'll see you later. Keep an eye on dear Wyatt, would you? Make sure he is . . . adjusting as he should." Elijah met the woman halfway, and they scurried into his office.

Imogen spun on her heel, but she bumped into someone standing directly behind her. She sucked in a breath, raising her hands with her shield already in place when she looked up into Wyatt's scornful face.

"Jesus, Wyatt. Are you trying to give me a heart attack? Where did you come from anyway?" She placed a hand over her racing heart as Wyatt frowned, his gaze fixed on Elijah's office door.

"What did he want?" he asked gruffly, lowering his voice.

"I don't know. That secretary of his just appeared, and they looked serious about something."

"No. About you. What did he want with you?"

"Huh? Were you watching us or something?"

Wyatt's piercing green eyes finally landed on her face.

"Yes."

"Why were you were spying on me?"

"Spying? Immy, he's a dangerous man. Did you think I wouldn't be keeping an eye out for you?"

Imogen was taken aback. She honestly hadn't been expecting that reaction – a reaction that suggested he was shocked she'd doubted him in the first place.

"Um, yeah, I suppose that makes sense."

"Well? What did he want?"

Imogen blinked. "Oh, to ask about you. I don't think he believes you've fully converted. Maybe you need to be a bit more like your usual self to throw him off?" Wyatt sneered. "Yes, like that."

"I'll ease up on the act, but I've got a thin line to walk. Was that all? He thinks you're on his side, right?"

"Yeah, he mentioned my dad again."

"Hey," Wyatt murmured. "Look at me, Immy," he commanded. "I know you're going through a really hard time right now, but you're a strong person. You can do this."

Imogen squared her shoulders. "Did you get the address from Kayla?"

He continued to stare at her, boring a hole in the top of head as she avoided his eyes.

Wyatt sighed. "Yeah. You think you'll be able to get the message out tonight?"

"He doesn't suspect anything, but even so. Perhaps you should cause some kind of distraction so he doesn't catch me?"

"I can do that."

"Did you discuss with Kayla what I need to say in the message?"

"Yes. She believes it'll be best if we wait until Blake's execution date."

Imogen winced. "But that's nearly three weeks away!"

"Yes, but Elijah is planning a public execution right outside. If we do it then, there are fewer barriers to overcome to get to Blake, and that means we can sneak our allies onto the grounds under the pretence of them watching the execution."

"So, two and a half weeks from now?"

"Yes."

"I'll send it tonight – the sooner everyone knows the plan, the better."

Imogen shuffled past Wyatt but he grabbed her hand, paper rustling between skin.

"You still need to be careful, Immy. Keep your shield ready."

Imogen nodded and moved away, praying she could sneak onto Elijah's computer later that night.

THE MANSION WAS ASLEEP, but by God did every step she took

echoed like a homing beacon determined to reveal her position. The old floorboards creaked, threatening to expose her plan to sneak into Elijah's office.

She pulled a set of keys she'd temporarily borrowed from Elijah's assistant out of her pocket and unlocked the door, flipping the lock shut behind her when she made it inside. Faint moonlight poured through the large bay window, and she quickly rounded the desk and moved the mouse, bringing the computer screen to life.

The password screen opened and she entered what she was nearly certain he'd typed in earlier that day. She held her breath.

The home page popped up.

It didn't take her long to open her email account and write out the key details – along with Kayla's codes for Ben and Michael to know that it was legit.

She was about to wipe the internet memory like Wyatt had instructed when footsteps stopped outside the door. A key scratched in the lock.

Imogen's hand flew to her open mouth. Crap!

"Elijah!" Wyatt's voice was rushed, his quick steps coming to a stop in the hall.

"Wyatt?" Elijah's gruff voice snapped dubiously.

"I just wanted a word."

Imogen used the precious time to hastily wipe her digital footprint from the computer and log out. She stood, flapping her hands in panic when she realised her exit was blocked. She turned to the window. The office was only on the second story. She could do that.

Climbing out took a bit of manoeuvring, especially shutting the window behind her while balanced on a very small ledge. Thank God the wall was covered in ivy.

She'd never been one to excel at rock climbing, but she knew the basics from hanging out with Mia. Surely climbing down ivy worked the same?

Her view of the room vanished just as the office door opened. The voices stopped abruptly, and she froze.

"Goodnight, Wyatt," Elijah snapped.

She didn't hear Wyatt's reply, but she moved as quietly as she could down the ivy, knowing that if Elijah glanced outside, she'd be in full view. The ivy itself wasn't difficult, but the tangled vines beneath the leaves proved difficult. Her foot stretched down, searching for another foothold, but it slipped and her breath came in short bursts. She was about to scream when two strong hands grabbed her hips.

"Let go, I've got you!" Wyatt whispered from behind her.

"Oh, thank God," she murmured, letting her weight fall into Wyatt's hands. He pulled her off the ivy and pushed her against the greenery, his body following suit. "What the–?"

Wyatt's hand covered her mouth, and he tipped his head back. She listened, and sure enough, Elijah opened the window above them, peering out into the still night.

In reality, it was only seconds, but it felt like she spent hours praying he wouldn't notice them.

When he shut the window, Wyatt lowered his hand.

"You don't think he saw us, do you? Why did he open the window?" she asked.

"He's not daft. He probably sensed something. Did you send the messages?"

"'*Are you okay, Imogen?*' Oh, I'm absolutely fine, thank you," Imogen mocked and then sighed. "Yes, yes. But I don't want to do that again. My heart is about to burst out of my chest."

"I overheard someone saying he was going away for a couple days, so we'll check for a reply while he's gone and make sure Ben and Michael can set things in motion for us."

Imogen rolled her eyes. "Fine. But maybe this time you'll go inside, and I'll keep watch."

"Yes, because catching me inside won't arouse suspicion."

"It's hardly innocent finding me in a locked room on his computer, is it? You'd just prefer if I was caught and not you," Imogen huffed and crossed her arms over her chest.

"You're right. I don't want to be caught. I'd rather be on watch. I trust myself to protect you if needed."

"But I can't be trusted to watch out for you?"

"That's not what I . . . you know what? Fine. Yeah. That's exactly what I meant."

"Screw you, Wyatt."

"Whatever you say."

She growled as he flashed his signature cocky grin.

"I'm going to my room." Imogen turned and stomped as loudly as she dared towards the estate, trying very hard to ignore the tall blonde trailing behind her. She clenched her fists and refused to turn around – even his silence was infuriating! It was one more thing he could do better than her, and she knew with one hundred percent certainty that if she did turn around, his grin would confirm that he knew it, too.

CHAPTER TWELVE

BLAKE

Three weeks later

BLAKE WALKED DOWN A long, barren corridor with two guards on either side of him holding onto his arms. He contemplated how messed up his life had become. They didn't have to hold him. Being shackled, weakened, and anxious made him quite agreeable.

True to their word, Kayla, Imogen, and Wyatt had slipped extra bread, cheese, and veggies to him when they could, but it was barely enough to sustain a child, let alone a seventeen-year-old shifter. His wolf whimpered deep within his mind, and he hated that it was tied down – again. The restraints on his wrists itched and rubbed at his skin, exposing raw flesh beneath them.

The door ahead led outside, and then beyond that? His execution was to take place. His execution. His death. He trusted the others, but what if they hadn't managed to find a way out for him? They were cutting it pretty close.

In his last few hours, he'd tried to think of positive things: Kayla, his parents, his brother Charlie, and all the other people he'd met who'd given their loyalty to him without question. He didn't deserve it. The shifters deserved more than a dumb kid on his last leg.

He stumbled. He was about to be killed. Would it hurt? Would they make Kayla watch? The guards gripped his arms tighter and pushed him forward.

"Stop making this difficult!" one of them snapped. Difficult? *He* was making it difficult by walking to his death? If he'd had the strength, he would have thrown the guard into the wall and punched the other one in the face for eating his meagre supply of food in front of him the other day. The guard had spat at him, so maybe Blake would do the same.

They opened the doors, and his vision of victory disappeared. The light was blinding. Blake blinked, allowing his eyes to adjust. A crowd of people stood in the courtyard, chatting amongst themselves and drinking glasses of bubbly as if it was a celebration. He hated them. He hated them all.

The guards took a sharp turn to the left, marching Blake to the place where they intended to murder him. They'd erected some sort of platform, and two large poles with iron hoops drilled into the sides stood front and centre. Blake imagined the shackles would be attached to those hoops and he'd be forced to stand with his arms outstretched.

He gulped as they made their way towards the podium. Elijah stood with two magic users Blake recognised from his so-called trial. Blake would have loved to wipe the arrogant smirk off Elijah's face; the way he held himself and spoke to the other two made his blood boil. The man looked calm – serene, almost – like he wasn't about to kill someone.

Blake was yanked up the stairs, and his footsteps vibrated along the wooden planks. Elijah turned to face him.

"Ahh, there you are," Elijah announced. "Get him secured!" he ordered. The two guards disconnected the chain between Blake's wrists and yanked his arms back, dragging him towards the two poles. He swallowed a hiss of pain as he was positioned like something Leonardo Da drew.

He fought, trying to yank his arms away, but the iron bandings would not budge.

"Do you seriously think you're going to get away with this?"

"I think I already have," Elijah said, motioning for the guards to step back. He leaned into Blake's personal space, asking, "Isn't that right? Killian?"

Blake's eyes went wide. Elijah knew who he was.

"How?" he breathed.

"I've been collecting data on you for some time, wondering if we might find each other. Honestly? It was a stroke of luck getting you here. It wasn't quite how I intended to do things, but I could see as soon as I met you that you would never agree to my plans. Shame really."

"What plans?"

"You're about to be executed. Are you sure that's what you want to ask me?" he mocked.

"What. Plans?" Blake repeated, growling.

Elijah rolled his eyes, but Blake suspected he relished the chance to gloat.

"I get your shifter powers for starters. That's why I had to wait until now. The spell takes time to prepare."

"Spell? You're a mage."

"I thought I could use you to get the shifters to work for me, but you're useless, as your loyalties are so heavily tied to that girl. Now she *is* powerful." A faraway look entered Elijah's eyes. Blake growled again. "You see? That is precisely the reason I can't use you alive."

"What about her?" Blake snarled through clenched teeth.

Elijah gazed into the distance, but it was just for effect.

"Eventually, she should come around to my ways. I'd like to see how her magic develops – it's definitely intriguing."

"She'll never come around to your ways, Elijah."

"Oh, but she will. I have the means, and if she doesn't . . . I'm not opposed to killing other magic users who stand in my way."

Blake lunged at Elijah, but the man casually stepped back and laughed. Blake was furious. He needed to tell Kayla that she had to get out of there and not worry about him anymore. Get Imogen and Wyatt to go with her if she could. He scanned the crowds, looking for her; he didn't know how well his senses were working, but something told him she was nearby. He could smell her floral scent, and his gut twisted with an intense need to see her.

There were at least eighty people in the crowd, chatting amongst themselves. It was a sunny day, so many were wearing hats or caps, making it hard to spot anyone. Wyatt offered drinks to people, smiling at them. Blake gulped and hoped it was all part of the pretence. Imogen was nowhere to be seen.

Elijah stepped to the edge of the podium and opened his arms.

"Welcome, everyone. I am honoured that you could all make it," he began, addressing the crowd. The murmurs died down as people listened to Elijah. "It is unfortunate that this shifter could not be rehabilitated and instead fell back on his animalistic and violent nature. It was a difficult decision, but one I made for the safety of our people." Elijah even had the nerve to look emotional. "It is with a heavy heart that I must condemn this shifter to death. In doing this, we take one step closer to ensuring the safety and survival of our tremendous race. We won't be destroyed, we shall prosper! This is the time of magic users, my friends!"

A huge cheer rose up from the mesmerised crowd. Blake couldn't believe how much bullshit they were eagerly lapping up from Elijah. The man was delusional at best. There had been no 'rehabilitation' – not that Blake needed any.

Elijah continued when the cheer died down. "To ensure this creature's violent nature is purged from the Earth, I will have a cleansing spell performed at the same time as the execution." Elijah turned his back on the crowd and smirked at Blake.

Blake leaned around Elijah to shout to the crowd. "He's lying! He wants my–"

"Silence." Magic disturbed the air, and Blake found himself unable to speak. He tried, but nothing came out. It wasn't hard to convey his anger through his eyes, and Elijah smirked at him before he turned his face to the sky. The woman who stood behind him at the trial stepped forward and chanted in a language he didn't recognise. Latin maybe?

Blake searched the crowd again, desperate to see Kayla, but at the same time, he hoped she wasn't here. Just as he was about to give up, he spotted her standing amongst the crowd. She was still, calm even. He frowned. She caught his eye and a slow smile crept over her face, making him all the more confused. Kayla swore she was pretending to be drugged. Had Elijah found out somehow? Was she being drugged for real?

She slowly raised her hand to tuck hair behind her ear, never taking her eyes off his, then she moved a closed fist to the opposite shoulder. That was the sign Luke and Mal had used to pledge their loyalty to him. Was she trying to tell him something?

Someone else discreetly placed a fist over their chest. Then another. About twenty people spread throughout the crowd copied the movement, each of them wearing caps and oversized coats.

In his peripheral vision, Elijah stretched a hand towards Blake, hovering his palm over Blake's heart. He knew his death was imminent. He jerked his head, urging Kayla to turn away, to run. But she didn't.

Elijah's hand made contact with his chest. Searing, white-hot pain pierced his upper body, and a garbled cry was pulled from his throat. His knees buckled, and if he wasn't being held up by chains, he would have collapsed to the ground. The pain began its tortuously slow attack, creeping into his arms, his legs, and his head. His blood boiled, mirroring the fiery bursts of pain electrocuting his defenceless body.

Nothing compared to the agony – not the burning of his flesh when he was trapped in the hotel, and not even the snapping of his bones when his shift was magically hindered. He prayed for the end. He craved death.

In some distant, cognizant part of his brain, Blake registered that Elijah had begun chanting. The spell coated his skin and poisoned his ears; it was a miracle he could even make out Kayla's words.

"NOW!" Her loud, confident voice broke through the dark pain wracking his body. Shouts of surprise echoed around him. Were people fighting? His trapped wolf strained against the chains that bound him as snarls and howls emerged from the crowd.

A commotion broke out on the podium. The wooden panels shuddered beneath his feet, and he caught himself against the chains. Blake fought the magic and lifted his head, blinking past his blurry vision. The crowd exchanged blows as wolves tore through the chaos. On the platform, several guards grappled with an onslaught of attackers, but Blake was too weak to figure out who was who.

His breathing slowed, and while the pain still raged through his veins, it wasn't as intense. Sleep tugged at his mind.

No. That couldn't be right.

He had to be strong.

Fight. Don't accept it.

Blake shook his head and growled in frustration. He looked up at Elijah and glared into his pure black eyes.

Kayla rushed up to them, panting.

"Elijah, if you could keep your hands to yourself, that would be great!" she quipped, livelier than he expected. Her voice was music to his ears, but he admitted to himself that even if she'd been crying, it still would have been the most melodic sound he'd ever heard.

Kayla moved to swat Elijah's hand and thus disturb whatever dark magic he was channelling into Blake, but Elijah snapped his head in Kayla's direction. Elijah's hand dropped to his side, and the blistering pain dwindled to a blissful simmer.

"You'll regret this," Elijah hissed.

Kayla put her hands on her hips. "No, I won't. You think I've been taking that drug? You think I've been a good little girl these past few weeks, doing whatever you wanted?" she teased.

Elijah tilted his head to one side and chuckled. "I know why you're so desperate to save him, and I know he's the Alastair heir. But once he's gone, there will be nothing in my way."

"Except me."

Elijah's face twisted with a horrible smile. "I doubt it." Elijah aimed his hand at Kayla and clenched his fist. Her eyes went wide as her hands scratched at her throat. "I doubt that very much."

CHAPTER THIRTEEN

KAYLA

ELIJAH'S MAGIC CUT OFF her access to oxygen, his tight fist mimicking what was happening to her throat.

Blake moaned, sagging in his chains. She lifted her arms into the position she'd seen Wyatt use to call on his air magic, and then slammed her palms towards Elijah. His magic wavered, freeing her. She sucked in a breath and allowed her anger to fuel her as she swung her leg right into his manhood. He covered his groin with his hands, face turning a puce colour. Channelling some of Blake's fighting style, she drew her fist back and let it fly at his face. She remembered to untuck her thumb at the last moment and smiled as Elijah fell off the podium and was swallowed up by the chaos.

She hoped someone would finish him off before he was able to recover and use his magic. She turned her attention to Blake who hung limply from the chains.

"Blake!"

He opened his eyes and focused on her, a smile tugging on one side of his mouth.

"Hey angel," he drawled.

Kayla rolled her eyes. "He really did a number on you, didn't he?"

Wyatt had taught her a spell that would override the cuffs, and she poured her magic into the iron bands around his wrists. Her magic hummed from within, happy to be near Blake again. She tried not to dwell on how . . . satisfied her magic source seemed to be whenever she was close to him – that was for another time.

A sharp electric current zapped the iron bands and they popped open, clanging against the wooden pole. Blake started to fall, but she hooked her arms under his, manoeuvring him to the edge of the podium.

The uproar continued behind her, and she prayed she had enough allies within the crowd. She hoped no one was hurt because she'd asked them to come. Well, she hadn't directly asked; Imogen was the one who'd managed to get a message to Ben and Michael, and they in turn had contacted shifters and magic users to aid them. It didn't take much persuasion when they realised the shifter heir was in danger.

They were nearly to the steps, Blake's weight slowing her down, when one of the guards appeared in front of her. He snarled, crouching down to touch the wooden platform. The panels rippled, sending both her and Blake tumbling. Blake rolled off the back of the podium, but she couldn't see if he was hurt because the guard was on top of her in a flash. She used her fist again, infusing the hit with some concentrated air magic, and it connected with his nose. He yelped, covering his face, and Kayla climbed to her knees. The guard regained control and lashed out with his elbow, catching her cheek. Blood rushed into her mouth and a dull ache throbbed along her jaw. The guard came at her again, but she blocked his attack and snaked one hand around his bicep. She called her fire forward and the man flailed and screamed as she fell back.

Something inside her said she should be mortified, but she was beyond caring. They would have happily killed Blake. They deserved more. The man crumpled and Kayla kicked out with her foot. His head snapped backwards, and he fell to the floor, unconscious. She crawled to the edge of the podium and dropped down beside Blake, who knelt on all fours.

"What's wrong?" she asked, placing a hand on his shoulder.

"Disorientated. Can't focus."

"You're free of the chains now, Blake. Use your shifter abilities to heal – and quickly." While they took shelter behind the podium, the fight raged on, and she knew they were nowhere near safe yet. She hoped Wyatt and Imogen were okay; she hadn't seen Imogen before the ceremony had started, and she was getting increasingly worried about her.

Blake sat back on his heels and nodded. "I'm not strong enough to move yet."

"Don't worry. I got you." She placed her palms on either side of his head, infusing him with some of her magic. She had no idea what she imparted to him, only that her essence felt the need to share it. His colour came back immediately, and his eyes were already brighter. A smile spread over his face as he studied her, and she leaned in, placing a chaste kiss on his lips.

"What was that for?" he asked, amusement in his tone.

She shrugged. "I was in the moment. You good now?"

"As good as I can be."

Kayla stood and held out a hand for Blake, but he managed without a problem. They both crept to the edge of the podium and looked around. She had no idea who was winning, but the fighting hadn't stopped. Magic exploded through the air, mangling the courtyard in the process, and wolves snarled and snapped their teeth in return. She didn't want a massacre, but they'd had no choice.

"You guys all right?" a voice whispered. Blake and Kayla both jumped even though she knew who it was. Luke crouched down behind them. "Good to see you free of those chains." He spat the last word.

"Thanks for being here," Blake responded.

"Mal and I made sure everyone from the hotel got somewhere safe. I can't tell you how relieved I was when Michael contacted me – well, until he told me you were set to be executed."

"I'm glad you're okay and I'm glad you're here, but how are we getting out of this? What's the plan?" Luke leaned around him and looked at Kayla. Blake smiled, shaking his head. "Should have known. What's the plan, Kayla?"

She rolled her eyes. "Distract and rescue. Fight, then escape. I can't say it's the most elegant of plans, but it's been difficult to form them through multiple different people."

"It's fine. You've done amazing," Blake told her.

"Ready to . . .?" Kayla bared her teeth and curled her fingers into faux claws.

"We're not cats, Kayla," Luke deadpanned, and Blake held in a chuckle.

"I know that! I meant are you ready to shift if you need to? I'm more concerned about you, Blake, after being in the chains for so long."

"I'd hold off the shift until your adrenaline peaks and you can feel your wolf more keenly. Let the natural state of things work in your favour. If the wolf has been held back for three weeks, a forced shift may take too long," Luke suggested.

Blake nodded. "Got it. Natural instinct."

Kayla unfolded from her crouched position just as a guard landed next to them. A brown wolf followed, snarling at the whimpering guard beneath its paws.

"No! Please!" he begged, but the wolf paid no attention and swiftly bit into the man's neck. The wolf turned its yellow eyes on the three of them and lowered the front half of his torso to the ground in an elegant bow.

"Is it . . .?" Blake asked.

"Acknowledging you," Luke answered.

Kayla grabbed Blake's hand and crept around the body.

"Thanks," she mumbled to the wolf, and the furry beast loped away to join the fight.

Luke shifted and placed himself in front of Kayla and Blake – not that it helped. Bodies swarmed them from all sides. Kayla recognised some of the guards from around the mansion as they tried to grab her. She centred herself, drawing on the limited combat training her father had given her, and called upon her magic.

Her fists collided with jaws, her elbows with ribs, and every time she got a punch in, she infused her limbs with magic. The air element pushed her foes further away. Her fire scolded them. Her mage magic tore at their minds. She wasn't even sure what else her power was doing, but she knew they were getting closer to the gates.

She found herself separated from Blake, but she was distracted as three enemies appeared in front of her. She twisted her hand and thrust it towards them. A tornado of wind hit one of the men and his head flew backwards, blood spurting from his mouth. The second guy didn't wait, rushing in before she had time to recover. She just about managed to duck under his swinging arm, but he grabbed hold of her jacket by the hood and yanked her back to his front. His thick arms banded around her middle and upper chest, barricading her against him. He leaned back and lifted her off the floor until she couldn't force her way out, and her legs kicked uselessly. The third man approached with a knowing smile. He thought they had her. It was too close to use her magic – if the guy holding her was burned, who knew what would happen to her.

The third guy thrust his fist into her stomach and she gasped, drawing a painful breath. He bracketed her head between his hands as his partner squeezed her body tight against his own. Through the haze of fear and pain, she rifled through her mind for a spell she could cast. She hadn't memorised her mother's spell book yet, and most spells were defensive. Witch magic was often used to nurture, not fight.

She braced herself, and just as the first tendrils of pain licked at her consciousness, a slender rust-coloured wolf dove at her attacker, aiming for his jugular. His garbled screams soon died down. The one holding her sensed he was outnumbered, and he began dragging her away. She dug her heels in, hoping the wolf would finish what it was doing and help her out. The wolf lifted its head, ears twitching, and made eye contact with her. Bright eyes flashed as it bound towards her. The wolf picked up pace and caught the man's leg in its powerful jaws. Kayla fell to the ground with her attacker as he tripped, and the rust-coloured wolf growled. The man scrambled away, and the wolf watched him run before shifting to his human form.

A young lad – around the age of fourteen or fifteen if Kayla had to guess – replaced the wolf. A familiar smile spread over his face, and his dark skin was much clearer than the last time she'd seen him as an eleven-year-old boy.

"Oliver?"

His grin widened. "The one and only!"

The fighting around them had slowed down as Elijah's men began to run off, and Kayla rushed to hug the boy. She hadn't seen him since her dad relocated him and his father after the murder of his mother.

"Jeez, you've gotten big!"

"I know. I shifted!"

"Why are you here?" she asked leaning back to look at him.

"Ben. He contacted the person I was staying with to see if he knew anyone who would help. I overheard and decided to join the fight – I heard your name and couldn't just sit back. You were right before, Kayla. We should fight for what we believe in. Screw the consequences!"

"Woah there, calm down. None of that, please. Let's stay safe and get out of here, yeah?"

Oliver nodded with a grin, shifting back into the rust-coloured wolf. He stayed by her side, dispatching a couple of guys trying to join the main foray. She had to admit they made a great team.

Kayla faltered on her next attack and Oliver jumped in to protect her, but her eyes were drawn elsewhere.

Blake was surrounded by at least eight magic users. He'd already shifted, but even his large wolf would struggle against the eight attackers circling him. One of them spoke too low for her to hear, but whatever they said, the spell was powerful. Blake's body jerked and he let out a high-pitched yelp. One of the others moved forward, arm outstretched.

At first, Kayla couldn't compute what was going on. Not as the guy wrapped a hand around Blake's neck. Not as the glint of pointed silver flashed in her direction.

And then it made sense.

"NO!" she screamed.

CHAPTER FOURTEEN

BLAKE

A SCREAM PIERCED THE air, startling the man poised to plunge the dagger into his throat. Blake still couldn't properly move his limbs, his legs jerking underneath him with whatever magic had been cast.

While the guy was distracted, Imogen moved towards them, aiming her hand at Blake as she made direct eye contact. Before Blake even knew what Imogen was doing, the man plunged the knife down, but something repelled him away from Blake. Another magic user ran forward, but nothing could harm Blake.

He looked up at Imogen again and it hit him. She was using her shield magic on him from afar. Her arm shook; he knew the magic was taking its toll. Had she even been able to project her shield before?

A woman snuck behind Imogen quick as a flash. He tried to warn her, but she was too fixated on her task. He attempted to shift back, but his body refused to obey.

The woman lifted an arm, shouting words at Imogen. Imogen's eyes rolled back in her head as she melted to the ground, immobile.

"IMOGEN!" Wyatt yelled, rushing to her side and rolling her over. Blake's shaky legs carried him only a few steps before Kayla's shout stopped him.

He spun, heart racing. She was under attack but she was distracted, her eyes darting everywhere, missing their advances. Why was she not focusing? Was she looking for him?

Blake shook off the last of his tremors and rammed into one of her aggressors; he went down, and Blake stomped on his head, knocking him unconscious. Kayla pushed the other guy into Blake's path with her magic. He quickly got rid of him, but when he looked to see where Kayla was, she'd disappeared.

He found her frantically weaving in and out of the thinning crowd. Luke was working with another shifter and a magic user to push back the remaining members of Elijah's guard.

Wyatt called for Blake, struggling to fend off another magic user. Instinct kicked in. Blake jumped into the foray and dragged the attacker by his arm, yanking hard. The guy screamed, but Blake shut him up when he swiped a claw across his neck.

As the guy sank to the ground, Blake bounded over to Wyatt who knelt over Imogen.

"She's been knocked out by a spell of some kind, but she hit her head when she fell; there's blood. We need to get her out of here," Wyatt said, looking around. His eyes landed on a clear path to the gates. "I think it's time we make our exit."

He scooped Imogen into his arms, but Blake whined. He couldn't leave without Kayla.

"Go. Find her. I can get us out of here and meet you," Wyatt ordered. Blake awkwardly nodded his canine head in agreement.

Luke appeared behind him in wolf form, and Blake threw his head in Wyatt's direction, telling Luke and the shifters with him to follow. Luke held back when Blake didn't join them, but Blake nudged him with his snout, encouraging him to leave.

Kayla popped into view, her body tense as she continued her frantic search.

"OLIVER!" she shouted, examining the area. She moved bodies, looking into faces and throwing them aside as she went. Blake trotted closer, weaving in and out of corpses and avoiding the few people who remained standing. Luckily for him, the majority of those left on Elijah's side were walking around inanimately thanks to some mage magic.

He didn't think his footsteps were quiet, but she jumped when he appeared, throwing her arms around his neck as she realised who it was.

"You're okay!" He nudged her arm and looked to the bodies, hoping she understood. "I can't find Oliver. He's young. He shouldn't have been here!"

He couldn't offer her words in his wolf form, so he nuzzled into her side and she buried her hands in his fur. A quick yip caught his attention, and as he lifted his head, a dark brown wolf barrelled into them both. All three crashed to the ground. A large plank of wood flew over them, exploding into a million splinters when it collided with the stones they'd been standing in front of.

Kayla's eyes widened, looking at the wolf who saved them. Blake tensed, ready to attack should he need to, but something glinted in the other wolf's eyes: recognition.

The wolf dipped his head before running off to fight the magic user who had sent the wood hurtling towards them. Kayla used the distraction to continue her search, scrambling a few paces away. Blake was torn between helping the wolf or helping Kayla.

Kayla's sudden, keening cry made the decision for him. He sprinted towards her. He made it to her side as she fell to her knees, frantically brushing away debris. The body of a boy lay in the rubble, his face blank and eyes shut. Kayla pulled him to her chest.

"I'm so sorry," she cried, tears running down her cheeks.

Blake shifted back to his human form and pressed two fingers against the boy's neck. "His pulse is weak; I don't know if he'll make it." He gently laid his hand on her shoulder. "We should leave, Kayla, I'm sorry." She snatched her shoulder away, cradling the boy tighter.

"No! Not without Oliver. He didn't deserve this. He didn't. I won't leave him alone here."

"Okay, okay, I'll take him with us." He gently pried the boy away from Kayla, lifting him into his own arms. Kayla froze on the ground. "Kayla, come on. I need you to get up," he pleaded.

"Here, let me," a familiar voice offered. Blake started as Josh appeared next to him, covered in dirt and a few cuts, but otherwise okay. The last time he'd seen Josh was when he'd first learned Josh was a shifter – at the time, he hadn't even known he was one himself. Blake knew Josh had escaped from the shifter hunters who'd been after them, but he'd heard nothing since. He couldn't believe his best friend was there. He wanted to punch Josh for never telling him about the world of shifters then grab him in a tight hug. But that would have to wait.

Josh nodded at Blake, but his eyes reflected the same emotions. Josh lifted Kayla to her feet. He moved her arm around his shoulders so he could support her as they walked. Speechless and confused, Blake joined them, carrying Oliver out of the main gates.

CHAPTER FIFTEEN

KAYLA

SOMEWHERE INSIDE, KAYLA REGISTERED that Josh was helping her. She wasn't all that surprised. She'd known he'd contacted Imogen when the plea had gone out through Ben, but she still wasn't quite sure how he had access to those channels. Either way she was grateful. Blake could do with a friend.

Friend.

Oliver. Oh, God. It was her fault, wasn't it? She helped get Oliver to safety years ago, and now he was gravely injured. Because of her.

She was vaguely aware of their journey out the gates, and she watched as Wyatt helped Blake with Oliver. Wyatt led them to the rendezvous point deep within the woods surrounding Elijah's mansion.

He had made sure to organise enough vehicles to get them all out of there once they were back together. Luke helped, too, calling in some of his older contacts.

Kayla looked around at the sea of faces, noting that some were missing.

"How many?" she asked nobody in particular.

Wyatt answered, "They all knew what they were signing up for. Every one of them would be relieved to know we'd gotten Blake out–"

"How many?"

Wyatt sighed. "Six."

Josh settled Kayla on a fallen log while Blake laid Oliver on the cold, hard ground. Mia ran forward with a middle-aged woman Kayla thought she recognised, and they both knelt beside the boy. The woman waved her hands over him, closing her eyes. Was she the healer from Marcus's hotel?

Blake, Josh, and Wyatt discussed something in the distance, but her focus was on Oliver.

Fingers clicked in her face. Scowling, Kayla forced her eyes to meet Mia's. Why was Wyatt's friend there? How did she get there?

"Heidi needs to know what happened! Did you see anything?" Sweat dripped down Mia's tense face. Kayla frowned. The nearly eighteen-year-old's frustration seemed out of place as she shook Kayla by the shoulders. "Kayla! Heidi is trying to save your friend. Did you see what happened?"

"N-n-no," she whispered.

Her father would be disappointed. Oliver, too. She'd let them both down.

"Kayla?"

She refocused on Blake who crouched in front of her, his eyes soft and reassuring. He gently ran his hand up and down her thigh, resting it there when he knew he had her attention.

"Mmm?"

"Oliver isn't gone. He's fighting. Watch."

Kayla looked at Oliver – truly looked at him. Sounds and sights she hadn't noticed before came crashing into her senses. Mia was busy tending a wound to Oliver's stomach. Heidi chanted above him. Heidi. Heidi was a healer.

"What . . . what do I do?" she whispered.

"You've done amazingly, Kayla. Think you can hang in for a bit longer?" Kayla nodded. "I'm going to speak to Luke and find out what's happening, okay?"

"Yes. Yes."

"Will you be okay here with Wyatt?"

Kayla nodded, and Josh and Blake moved to stand by Luke. She ignored them when they turned their heads in her direction.

She jumped as a nearby engine rumbled. "We're near the road, but far enough back that no one can see us," Wyatt said.

About fifteen. There were about fifteen people there.

Two men appeared by Oliver, but as they made to pick him up, Kayla flew to her feet.

"What are you doing?" she cried.

"We've got another vehicle that we're using to transfer our injured. It's taking time because we need to do it slowly and not draw attention to ourselves. It's okay, Kayla. They're taking Oliver to a better facility close by, one that agreed to help us." Wyatt spoke slowly, quietly, resting his hand on her shoulder. Heidi and Mia stayed with Oliver, climbing into the car after him.

Wyatt sank to the ground, resting his back against a fallen log.

"Sit down, Kayla. You need to rest." She did as she was told but frowned. She hadn't seen Imogen.

"Where's Imogen?"

"Getting her head checked out."

"What? What happened!"

She guessed Wyatt heard the growing panic in her voice when he quickly soothed her and said Imogen would be all right. "She hit her head. Mal took her down the road to get some medical attention. She needs a few stitches, so he's paying a doctor to help them out. A mage went with them to help change their appearances and provide a cover story. Don't worry. Our serious injuries are being sent to allies; minor ones are being treated here." Wyatt flashed his signature smile when he finished.

"Don't worry? I can't do that. Look what happened," she replied, clenching her hands together. Wyatt pried them apart so she wouldn't hurt herself. "Everything is my fault."

"How is everything your fault?" he snapped. "Blake was in danger. We all knew the risks."

"Because I asked. . ."

Wyatt huffed. "Hate to break it to you, but this rescue had nothing to do with you and everything to do with Blake. No one wanted to lose the heir to the Alastair throne. I get it was more than that for you, but that's why these people risked their lives – that's why some lost their lives. Not because of you."

Wyatt's words wormed their way into her head and spun around in circles. She was numb. She didn't say anything else as they waited.

Imogen soon returned with Mal, looking pale but alive. Wyatt jumped up as she approached, embracing her before she could protest; Imogen's eyes widened, but she relaxed into the hug.

"I'm okay. Tender, but okay," she said softly, stepping away from Wyatt.

Blake and Josh wandered over and Blake caught her eye. She fell into the depth of emotion swirling within his gaze. He didn't know the people who had come to save him, but their deaths were taking a toll. She was only adding to the burden.

"Are you okay?" he asked. She tried to nod her head, but she didn't think her efforts worked. His frown deepened.

"Blake?" a blonde girl in her twenties with a pink streak in her hair shouted. She'd been standing next to Luke, who now frowned at her.

"Amy?" Blake blurted. Amy was the woman who'd helped him and Kayla when they first went on the run. A smile blossomed on his face. Amy jogged over, looking Blake up and down to check that he wasn't injured. Luke accompanied her, coming to a stop next to Amy.

"Blake! I'm so glad to see you're okay! And you, Kayla! I'm so happy you're both all right!" Amy pulled Kayla into a hug.

Luke smiled tightly at them both.

Luckily, she didn't have long to think about what she should be saying, because Mal announced that the last cars had arrived.

"What's the plan now?" Blake asked.

"We're going to Oxford as planned. We can't let this change what we set out to do. We're running out of time," Wyatt answered.

Blake glanced at Imogen who shifted uncomfortably.

"I'll go with Amy and the others," Luke announced. "Make sure everyone is safe and then I'll meet you guys later, just like we planned before. We can't let Elijah get away with what he's done."

"Agreed," Wyatt said, nodding at Luke.

Blake held his hand out, and Luke shook it. "Thank you, man. For all you did to help me."

"Wasn't a problem at all." Luke led Amy and the others to the cars, and they all pulled away until there was only one vehicle left. Many people offered Blake the sign of their loyalty as they drove off.

Wyatt headed over to the last car and turned back to the others. "We going then?"

CHAPTER SIXTEEN

BLAKE

HE COULDN'T BELIEVE HE was back with his best friend; it took everything in him not to bombard Josh with questions. Besides, he had to stay focused on Kayla. She was unusually quiet, but she had valid reasons. His wolf recognised that she took those losses personally, but that knowledge didn't help quiet the restless creature.

She sat on his right, his best friend to his left, and Imogen and Wyatt sat up front, whispering to each other. A part of him was surprised to not hear their usual bickering. He didn't listen to their conversation, though. Instead, he chose to tune in to Kayla. He held her hand in his, gently rubbing his thumb in small circles on her skin. Eventually, with the contact and the movement of the car, she fell asleep, her breathing soft and rhythmic. For the first time in a while, he felt content: Her heart beat at a steady pace.

"She asleep?" Josh leaned around him to peer at her, his eyes dipping to their hands. Kayla snuggled into Blake's shoulder. "Think you've got a lot to tell me, mate."

Josh sat back in his seat, a confident smirk on his face.

"What's that look for?" Blake replied, smiling. God it felt good to see him again.

"You want me to say it out loud?" Josh flicked his eyes towards the front, keeping his voice low.

"Wyatt and Imogen already know."

"Know what?" he asked coyly.

Blake frowned. "Well actually, we've not really spoken about it."

Josh snorted. "Never thought I'd see the day when you, of all people, were stuck on a girl." He shook his head and grinned.

"Whatever." Blake shifted uncomfortably.

"Wait. You're more than stuck on her, aren't you?" He leaned closer, his eyes widening a fraction. "You're bonded with her! A wolf bonded with a magic user. Oh man!"

Blake frowned. "Why do people always sense that about us? What does it mean?"

"Jeez, I forget you weren't brought up as one of us. Has no one explained it to you?"

"To be honest, I just thought it meant we had a connection – which we do. My wolf . . ."

"Go on," Josh encouraged when Blake stopped.

"My wolf always wants to be near her, and I can sense her, like always. Even when she's far away."

"That sounds like a bond, dude. Bonded wolves aren't rare or anything like that, but they aren't too common either. Bonded wolves tend to stay together for life, and I was always told they're more in sync with each other than anyone else. Just like you said you are with her."

"Is there anything wrong – negative – with being a bonded wolf?"

"Just unusual possessiveness." Blake snorted. "Take that as a yes then."

"It's not my fault. It's the wolf."

"About that. You do know that this is the first example – at least the first I've heard – of a wolf bonding with a magic user?"

Blake leaned against the headrest and let out a sigh.

Wyatt chimed in, saying, "We're stopping for fuel, guys."

"I'm busting!" Imogen squeaked from the front, bouncing in her seat.

Blake leaned over Kayla, squeezing her hand. "Hey, wake up. We're taking a break."

She moaned softly and stretched, looking out the window. "Oh," she murmured.

"Kayla, come with me to the ladies? I'm about to pee my pants!" Imogen squealed as they all got out the car. Kayla didn't have much time to answer before Imogen twined their arms together and marched off.

"Am I to assume those two are okay again?" Blake asked Wyatt as they walked into the building, aiming for the coffee shop.

"They made up when they worked together to get you free. Imogen is sorry. For what it's worth."

Blake nodded, knowing that he should forgive her, especially after what she'd done to help him escape. His wolf was still a little miffed, however.

The guys grabbed takeaway hot drinks, sitting at a table in the middle of the services while they waited for the girls.

"So, you must be Blake's best friend, huh?" Wyatt asked Josh.

"The one and only."

"And you're a wolf, too?"

"Yep."

Blake jumped in. "But he didn't tell me he was a wolf."

"You still bitter about that?" Josh asked him with a smile.

"Only a little. You could have told me – I had no clue I was a shifter. Knowing you were one could have given me a heads up."

Wyatt laughed. "You didn't know Josh was a shifter? And Josh didn't know you were one either? That is so messed up!" Both Josh and Blake stared at Wyatt until Wyatt put his hands up in surrender. "Okay, easy there, boys."

"I want to know more about you and Kayla," Josh said, winking at Blake.

"What more can I tell you?"

"Um, well, for starters, how this all happened?"

Wyatt held his hand up. "Oh, same! Same! I'm intrigued about your bond. Never before has a wolf bonded with a magic user."

"Good one. I'm interested in that part, too."

Josh and Wyatt looked at Blake expectantly and his hands started to sweat.

"I have no idea. I have no idea if Kayla even knows, so please don't say anything to freak her out – she's in a delicate place right now."

"Oh, I think she knows something is up with you two already," Wyatt said.

"Yes, but a bond? What does that even mean for her as a magic user? She may not have the same sort of . . . attachment to me as I do to her. What if she doesn't want it? What if she's forced into this bond?" Blake rambled.

"I don't think that's an issue." Josh said confidently. Blake frowned but couldn't ask him to clarify as the girls returned to the table with sandwiches and snacks.

Imogen sighed. "It was the best we could find."

Josh rifled through the selection, grabbing a sandwich and crisps. Blake did the same, opting for a panini. He watched as Kayla nibbled at her sandwich, her eyes focused on the packaging. It wasn't normal. Normal Kayla would've been searching the room for exits, going over the plan. Discussing what they might need.

He didn't know what he was doing until it was done, but he relaxed his leg against hers under the table. A current of electric heat ran through him, waking up his wolf. Kayla sat up straighter, glowing softly, and her cheeks took on more colour than they'd had for hours.

He smiled to himself when Kayla joined in Wyatt's conversation with Josh about fuel. Would it be too much to hope that she wouldn't reject their so-called bond?

NIGHT HAD FALLEN BY the time they pulled up to the end of a long driveway. The house was set away from the road; large hedges and trees offered protection, and it was incredibly well hidden. They decided to drive closer but stopped when a cottage with a thatched roof came into view. The walls were made of crumbling stone and the small green garden was bordered by a white picket fence. All the lights were off, and the place was quiet.

Nobody said anything as they studied the building. Blake wondered if it would look slightly less imposing during the day when the bright colours of the garden would stand out more.

"He's expecting us, right?" Blake whispered.

"He should be, but we didn't tell him we'd been successful at the rescue. Didn't have a chance," Wyatt replied.

"Sense anything?" Kayla asked Blake.

Blake nodded. "Only one person as far as I can tell."

"I concur," Josh added.

"Anyone else slightly freaked out?" Imogen asked.

"For once, Immy, I think I agree with you," Wyatt answered, shivering.

Kayla leaned forward so she was closer to the front. "I think we should split up to go inside. It could be a trap."

"I agree," Wyatt replied, turning round with a big grin.

"I'll go round the back. I can shift if I need to," Josh offered.

"I'll go with you. Blake and Kayla go in the front," Wyatt said. Imogen opened her mouth to argue. "I'm getting to you. Patience."

Imogen huffed and folded her arms. "Assuming I'm staying with you, aren't I?" she asked sourly.

"Actually, I was thinking with Blake and Kayla."

Imogen raised her brows at him. "Sure," she replied in a sceptical voice.

"You don't sound so sure?" Josh asked Imogen with a laugh.

Wyatt interrupted, "I normally make her stay with me, to keep her out of trouble and all that, but she seems to find that quite well herself these days. Regardless, she has her shielding powers. She's better off with those two."

"Cool." Josh nodded at Imogen. Blake wasn't certain, since it was dark after all, but he was pretty sure Imogen blushed.

"Okay, out now," Wyatt snapped.

They piled out of the car into the darkness. Only the faint light of the moon and stars lit the path to the front door of the cottage.

Josh held his fist out to Blake. He bumped it automatically, and then Josh took off on a slow jog around the property with Wyatt close behind. A smile spread across Blake's face at the familiarity of their ritual pre-game move.

Imogen whispered through the darkness as she slid closer to him. "What's the plan?"

Kayla stifled a laugh.

"Um, I was thinking of just, you know, walking through the front door," he answered.

"Really?"

"C'mon, I'll go first," Kayla stated.

Blake grabbed her as she moved past him. "Hey, is that wise?"

"Well, yeah. I'm more expendable than you."

His growl was low and instinctual. Imogen took a step back, but Kayla leaned closer.

"Not. To. Me," he growled.

His eyes were glowing, reflecting off her own. She brought her hand up to his cheek.

"Imogen? Why don't you go between us? Then you can shield us both if necessary. I can use my magic, and Blake's strong enough to defend against a surprise attack from behind."

"Sounds good to me," Imogen said, scuffing her foot against the ground.

"How does that sound to you?" Kayla asked Blake softly. His wolf receded, and he nodded. Reluctantly, he let go of her arm. Imogen followed Kayla and he took the rear.

A soft whine echoed through the seemingly vacant property when Kayla pushed open the gate, and the three of them entered the garden. Even with his shifter hearing and senses, he only detected one body within the cottage. Josh and Wyatt were probably still making their way inside.

Kayla laid her palm on the white wooden door, using her other hand to try the metal handle. Locked. Kayla closed her eyes and whispered some words – he didn't know what they were, but he recognised the scent of her magic as it ignited. The door clicked open. She quickly glanced back at Imogen and Blake before slipping inside. Imogen followed, and Blake went in last. He turned around to push the door shut, but his senses flared.

He heard a grunt and Imogen flailed past him, dizzily sliding to the floor. Kayla yelled out in surprise before her voice was cut off; Blake surged forward. A man in his thirties held Kayla pinned against the wall, one arm across her sternum and the other holding a dagger above her face.

Blake growled, eyes glowing gold. His fists curled as he fought for control over the wolf who desperately sought to attack the man. It was too close. Kayla might get hurt.

The man spared him a cursory glance but remained focused on Kayla as Wyatt and Josh burst through the back door. Josh's eyes glowed in response to Blake's, but Wyatt clasped a hand on his shoulder. The man looked to Blake again, his brows tightly drawn together.

"I can sense intent: Yours doesn't match the others. Who are you?" he snapped.

"B-b-en . . . it's us!" Kayla managed to rasp out.

The man's eyes darted to Josh and Wyatt, then to Blake, looking him up and down. He finally studied Kayla again.

"Don't tell me you're Kayla?" he asked in an accent Blake couldn't quite place. Kayla's feet found purchase, and she breathed in deeply. The man lowered the weapon, loosening his grip on Kayla, but not letting go entirely.

Blake growled, his body rigid.

"Uh, Kayla?" Josh mumbled, pointing at Blake. The man frowned as Blake's growl continued in a low, dangerous rumble.

"Let go, Ben. Step back. Don't run," Kayla instructed, her voice calm.

Ben obeyed, but his eyes never left Blake's.

"Dude, quit staring a shifter down when he's agitated! Do you have a death wish?" Josh added.

Blake moved in front of Kayla when Ben retreated, his muscles still tightly coiled for action. His wolf was beyond agitated. Kayla stepped around him and placed a hand on his upper arm. A short burst of electricity ran through him and immediately calmed his roaring beast. Blake took a deep breath.

"How'd you get such a possessive shifter?" Ben asked.

CHAPTER SEVENTEEN

KAYLA

KAYLA ENCOURAGED BLAKE TO take a walk around the property with Josh to cool down – assuring him they were fine inside and the incident was just an automatic response to people trying to get onto Ben's property. It seemed to work, and Josh placated the wolf side of things.

Ben continued to apologise profusely to Imogen who sat in an armchair in the cosy living room, an ice pack to the back of her head. Kayla remained quiet, studying the cottage while Ben and Wyatt spoke. The room contained worn-down furniture, a new flat screen TV, and surprisingly smooth interior walls. She'd expected more exposed brickwork. Ben clearly spent a lot of time there and put effort into the upkeep of the building.

When Josh and Blake returned, Blake immediately moved to sit beside her on the sofa. Josh took Blake's other side. Blake leaned forward with his arms resting on his legs, hands clasped together. He studied Ben intently.

"Again, I am sorry for the misunderstanding," Ben said for the hundredth time. Blake nodded, and Kayla sent a silent thanks to Josh.

"We should have found a way to let you know we were coming – things happened so fast," Kayla said.

"Don't apologise. I was on high alert – it's just habit to assume anyone on the property is coming after me. I'm sorry. I'm glad you're okay though, and you got Blake out." Kayla lowered her head, trying not to dwell on the people they lost in the process.

Wyatt cleared his throat. "Not everyone made it, but thank you."

"I'm sorry to hear that."

"Thanks," Kayla whispered, refusing to meet anyone's eyes.

"What's the next course of action? Has Elijah been neutralised?"

Blake scoffed and Wyatt jumped in to answer. "Unfortunately not. I do have an idea about what we should do next. I broached it with Blake, Kayla, and Imogen before . . . well, before Blake was captured, and I still think we should do it."

"Go on, I'm listening." Josh perked up, too. He'd never heard the details before.

"Marcus was planning to attend some sort of peace meeting between the races in London. He didn't tell many people about it because he didn't want to spook Blake – he knew he had to get Blake and Imogen on board before attending. I honestly think the meeting was a great idea, but it's in two days. Have you heard of it?" he asked Ben.

"I heard rumblings about a peace conference of sorts. I haven't been able to focus on it though with my normal work and helping to coordinate Blake's escape from Elijah. I'm sorry." A shadow of guilt flashed across Ben's face. He tried to smile at them, but it came across as more of a grimace. Kayla studied the dark circles beneath his bloodshot eyes. She didn't know him before he took over her parent's work, but she couldn't help but wonder if it was the additional responsibility that made him look so tired. Her parents often took turns pulling all nighters; their jobs were not ones that could be 'switched off.' Did Ben ever sleep?

"That's okay. I know what city it's happening in but not where specifically. Marcus had control over all the communications. If everyone agrees, I think we should locate the place, join the peace meeting, and offer our help. Blake will be with us; he'll help lead the shifters." Wyatt stopped and looked to Blake, who nodded in response.

Josh put his hand up to speak. "What makes this meeting special? How are we so sure the meeting's purpose is to develop a treaty or some form of alliance?"

"The meeting has been arranged by leaders – for want of a better word – of pockets of those who believe in equality. They've been fighting back and trying to support both races. I'm praying none will be like Marcus – sorry Immy," Wyatt said, tagging an apology on at the end.

"You're okay. My dad did some horrible stuff, and it was following his orders that nearly led to Blake's death." Imogen looked anywhere but at Blake and Kayla.

"So this could be our best shot at finding others who want an alliance?" Josh asked.

"I think so. What about you, Ben?" Wyatt directed at the quiet magic user.

"I think if enough numbers come, it could work. All we need to do is persuade people that an alliance will work. More people want to band together than not – fear just gets in the way."

"That's what I said," Kayla mentioned as she gave Ben a small smile. It felt weird after all that time to be talking with him in person.

"We can arrange details tomorrow, and it gives me a chance to reach out to contacts and track down the meeting place. I have a couple spare rooms you are all welcome to stay in."

Imogen leaned forward. "Kayla! I'll share with Kayla!"

Kayla ignored the sad eyes she knew Blake was giving her and agreed to Imogen's request.

"Oh, lovely. I get to share a room with two shifters," Wyatt deadpanned.

Josh flashed a wide grin, making sure to show his teeth. "We won't bite."

"HEY, KAYLA?" IMOGEN ASKED softly when they were changing into some spare clothes of Ben's to sleep in.

The room they were sharing was a basic spare room: a double bed, a chest of drawers, and a wardrobe. The wardrobe housed spare linens, and Kayla grabbed a towel so she could freshen up in the bathroom.

"Yeah?" she replied to Imogen as the girl flopped on the white bedspread.

"I am truly sorry, you know? I didn't mean for any of . . . any of what happened to happen." Imogen hung her head, fiddling with the loose blanket.

Kayla sighed. She couldn't hold a grudge forever; she'd agreed to move past it when she worked with Imogen to free Blake. She'd always known that they would need help from others, she just wished it hadn't been Oliver who suffered the consequences.

"I can't say I'm over it all. What happened to Oliver . . . that wasn't fair. But I agreed to forgive you. Imogen, things happen. You did something you shouldn't have, but you did it because you thought we needed help. I can't be mad at that forever. You want peace between the races as much as I do. I can't say when, but I can promise that I will be able to put it all behind me." Kayla's voice was soft, sensing the need for compassion.

Imogen nodded her head, sniffling a little. She reached up to take her ponytail out, her long black hair falling haphazardly around her shoulders.

"Change of subject?" Kayla asked, trying to lighten the mood. Imogen giggled.

"Gladly!"

"Your hair's a mess." Kayla smiled.

"I know!" Imogen replied, laughing harder. "What have we come to?"

Kayla put the towel down on the bed and sat beside her, shrugging. "Who knows. Want help?" She pointed at Imogen's mass of hair.

"Please!"

Kayla plaited Imogen's hair as Imogen babbled on about never having had a sister, a mum, or even a childhood friend to do her hair with.

"It's like a rite of passage though, playing with hair, isn't it?" she asked.

Kayla snorted. "It's not a big deal. Mum used to do my hair all the time. Plaited it to keep it 'practical.'"

"But isn't that bonding time? I never got that with my mum."

They were moving into dangerous territory, discussing parents. "What about Wyatt? You saying he never plaited your hair and painted your nails before?"

Imogen cackled so hard Kayla nearly lost her place in the plait.

"HA! Oh please, he would have run away screaming had I asked. We were never close."

"You've said that before, but I always see Wyatt wanting to help you."

"Really?"

"Yeah, don't you see it?"

"No, I never really thought about it like that before. I always figured I was a thorn in his side – a burden he felt obliged to be around."

"Why would you think that?"

"Because my dad took him in. I think Wyatt feels like he had to help me because of what my dad did for him."

"No offense, but your dad didn't do too much for him, did he?"

"I suppose not," she mumbled, fiddling with the blanket again. "You really think he genuinely looks out for me?"

"You two are weird," Kayla responded, shaking her head as she started on the second plait.

"Hey! You're the one going around pretending you don't have a connection – a bond – with a wolf. Now *that's* weird."

"The connection, or the fact that he's a wolf?"

Imogen let out an exasperated huff. "Both, to be honest."

Kayla finished the second plait, and Imogen turned to face her.

"I don't get what we have. We haven't exactly had many opportunities to discuss it."

"Maybe you should. Did he ever tell you what we spoke about on the way to the meeting my dad had set up, when you were taken?"

Kayla shook her head. "No. I'm not even sure what we should be doing with the original alliance."

"The alliance as it was . . . is gone. That was between mine and Blake's parents, and neither of us want that. Who would want two people forced together to lead them into peace? What does that actually say?" Kayla shrugged. "Blake and I wanted to form a different kind of alliance – a consensual alliance. Luke and I knew you two had a bond, and that doesn't happen as often as it once did within the shifter world. What if that's the alliance we need?" Imogen reached out to cover Kayla's hand. "What if this bond is nature's way of saying shifters and magic users should work together? Like you and Blake."

"But I'm a magic user. We're not meant to be bonded. We don't have that in our world. I don't like the thought of a bond, something supposedly out of my control, forcing my decision in things."

Imogen raised her eyebrows at Kayla. "So you're saying you don't like Blake." Kayla squirmed where she sat.

"No, not that exactly."

"Maybe you should ask about shifter bonds before you make a judgement about them."

"What if Blake doesn't want to be with me? What if it's just his wolf because his wolf thinks we're bonded?"

Imogen rolled her eyes and huffed. "Then speak to him, let him have a say. Jeez girl, you're worse than me!"

SHE REALLY WASN'T LOOKING where she was walking when she slammed into a solid wall of muscle that was exiting the bathroom.

"Gah!" she cried as strong hands steadied her. She looked up at blue eyes with a ring of gold around them. She should have just known it would be Blake she'd bump into. She was pretty sure her cheeks were on fire; Imogen's words had wormed their way into her mind, and she was now thinking about Blake in so many inappropriate ways. Get a grip.

"Hey, you okay?" he asked, brows drawing together.

"Mmmhmm."

"You wanting the bathroom?" She nodded. "Are you sure you're okay? You're acting a little . . . off?"

"Oh, what? Me? No, I'm fine, honestly. Just been a long day, hasn't it?" Kayla said, clutching the towel closer to her body, hoping it would offer some barrier between herself and the heat coming off Blake. The urge to lean in and hug him was far too great.

"You could say that again," he replied, running a hand through his damp hair.

"It must be nice to have Josh around." Blake's eyes pinched slightly, and Kayla winced. "I meant, for you. Not for me. Not that I don't like the guy, I do. He's a great friend. To you. I barely know him. I'm just happy for you . . ." she trailed off, studying the floor intently. How stupid could she be? Josh had crushed on her when she'd first turned up at their sixth form academy. Blake wasn't happy about it and constantly brought it up in the beginning. Why on Earth would she bring it up now? A shadow fell over her feet, and she inwardly groaned. Josh stopped beside her.

"Hey, bathroom free?" he asked.

Blake folded his arms across his chest, standing tall. "Not the time, man. Kayla was about to use it." Blake's jaw was stiff and she knew it didn't escape Josh's attention.

"You all right, mate?"

"Ahh, probably best if you came back later, Josh," Kayla added as Blake glanced away from them both. Josh looked between Kayla and Blake, his eyes widening slightly.

"Umm, is something going on between you two?" Josh asked.

"What? No. Why do you ask?" Kayla said quickly, and Blake turned back to face her, his eyes holding a tinge of hurt.

"Actually," Blake began, "we were just discussing you."

"What? No. We weren't!" she replied a little too loudly. Josh smirked.

"Oh yeah? What were you talking about?"

Oh, this could not get any worse. Blake growled deep in his throat. Okay. It could definitely get worse.

"Nothing! Why do you always have to make things worse?" she cried and then realised what she'd said. "I'm so sorry. That was uncalled for. I didn't mean that. You came all this way to help Blake, and I'll forever be grateful for that." She smacked one hand over her face.

"I can see I'm in the middle of something, sooooo I'll just come back later." Josh backed away and retreated into the room the boys were staying in.

She peeked at Blake and was surprised to find him already watching her. The golden ring around his blue eyes pulsed.

"Are you okay with Josh? With me?" she asked timidly.

"Why wouldn't I be?" He tilted his head to one side.

"Well, your wolf seems to be close to the surface."

"My wolf is just agitated when Josh is around you. I can't always control him."

Kayla nodded her head, tucking some hair behind her ear. He'd said his wolf was agitated. Not him. It wasn't because he was worried about Josh being around her. It was his wolf being possessive. Not Blake. She sighed. Imogen was wrong.

"I better get in the bathroom before Wyatt comes and steals it," she tried to joke but neither moved. Blake stood firmly in the bathroom doorway, staring her down.

Footsteps bound up the stairs, and then Ben appeared.

"Oh, Blake, I was looking for you. Mind if we have a word?"

"Sure," Blake replied, still not taking his eyes off her. Kayla looked anywhere but Blake's face, just wanting to get into the bathroom and shut the door on the awkward embarrassment. Eventually, Blake huffed and moved aside, following Ben downstairs.

Kayla hurried inside, locking the door and leaning against it. She slowly slid to the floor, letting out the breath she had been holding. The towel slipped from her arms in a heap, and she held her head between her hands.

What on Earth had that been about?

CHAPTER EIGHTEEN

BLAKE

BEN WAS AT THE bottom of the stairs when Blake jogged down to meet him, throwing on a t-shirt as he went.

"Thanks for this. Was going to go into my office if that's all right with you?"

"Sure."

Blake followed him through a steel door, which was odd for a cottage, but he stopped short when he entered the room. It was not just an office. An office didn't have a bank of cameras and monitors like a guardroom. Ben shut the door behind Blake as he stared, mouth hanging open.

The office similarities ended with a desk and a computer. Ben sat on the edge of his desk, gesturing for Blake to take the worn armchair. A small table sat beside the chair with a lamp and a tattered book. Behind the desk, a row of filing cabinets filled the short wall.

Dark paint and no natural light should have made the space feel small, but instead it felt cosy with warm lighting, a snug armchair, and hardwood flooring.

Blake studied the monitors and recognised the driveway, the rooms downstairs, and the landing. He was pleased there weren't cameras in the bedrooms. Or so he hoped.

"I don't have cameras in the bedrooms," Ben began, reading Blake's mind. "That would be an invasion of privacy. I do, however, keep an eye on downstairs and the landing just in case."

Blake blew out a breath and leaned back. "I gotta say, I wasn't expecting this."

Ben smiled.

"I'd make a joke, but I don't think it would be appropriate. This room is custom built so I can keep track of the house and surrounding areas, but also . . ." Ben got up to stand in front of a control panel. He pressed a few buttons, typed in a code, and then a map appeared on one of the screens with a blinking red dot hovering over one point. "I can keep track of my clients here, too. Any news I hear about disturbances, I plot them on the map and use it to re-locate people."

"That is kinda cool. You *have* been busy."

"I wanted to progress the amazing work Kayla's parents started, bring it into the twenty-first century." Ben sat back down in his chair, facing Blake. "The room is also lined with silver."

"What?" Blake started.

Ben held his hands up. "It's enough to stop shifters from listening in, not enough to weaken you or anything like that. Promise. Speak to your wolf. He's fine, isn't he?"

Blake tuned in to the wolf inside, noting it was content enough to feel somewhat safe. He settled into the chair and nodded.

"What did you want to speak about?" he asked.

Ben was quiet for a few moments, studying Blake as he began to fidget.

"Kayla," Ben said eventually. Blake's heartbeat sped up, and his wolf's ears pricked.

"What about her?" he asked in a guarded manner.

"I think you two have a bond."

"So everyone keeps telling me."

Ben gave him a tight smile. "I think you guys have a very strong, very deep bond. I've not seen one like it before."

"And what do you know of shifter bonds? No offence."

"None taken," Ben said smiling. "Part of my gift as a mage is reading emotions and the energy you give out."

"Like auras?"

"Not quite, but if it helps you to understand."

"So why was it so important to tell me this now?"

"Because I'm worried it's going to make you a target."

"Aren't we already targets?"

"You don't mean to, but you're giving off energy, both of you, and it's indicating this huge bond between you. I don't know what this will mean for Kayla and her magic, bonding to a wolf. I have no idea if cementing that bond will make that signal, that energy, even brighter."

"Is this going to be a problem for us?"

"Yes. It'll draw those who don't want an alliance to you both like a moth to a flame. I sense that even though you've not been together for a very long time, the death of one of you would be catastrophic to the other."

Ben reeled back, and Blake guessed his eyes must have flashed.

"Sorry," Blake muttered.

"Don't be. If you and Kayla are who I think you are, I'd expect nothing less."

Blake frowned. "Who you think we are?"

"Has anyone explained the shifter bond legacy to you?" Ben asked and shifted uncomfortably.

"Not really, no."

"Well, shifter bonds are relatively rare. They've been on the decline for years."

Blake nodded. "Yeah, I got that bit, I think."

"Being soul entwined is something else altogether and is considered a myth amongst most."

"I'm sorry? Soul entwined?"

"Shifters once that said bonds could be traced back to soul entwined pairs. Very powerful and connected beings. Bonded pairings can be broken, given enough time and space. If one dies, it can affect the other if they have been together for many years, as time only deepens the bond. But being soul entwined means your souls come from the same place."

"Like being split in two? Those stories?"

"Sort of. Being soul entwined is a much deeper connection. You connect on every level. You are attuned to their needs, their wants, their desires. But you can also be clouded by them. Jealousy is a common trait amongst shifters. Your protectiveness will be instinctual. Your wolf's sole purpose is to protect that other being."

Blake understood. He felt connected to Kayla in ways he never could articulate. His wolf was also stupidly attached.

"That makes sense," Blake said quietly, almost to himself.

"You feel it then?" Blake nodded. "Blake, I'm saying this because no matter how much time has passed, the death of one could kill the other or send them into madness. Your souls – your very essence as Kayla would see it – are connected to each other. Never has a shifter bonded with a magic user, and now a shifter has become soul entwined with a magic user. That's some powerful magic."

Blake rubbed his hands over his face. "I'm not sure I'm following why you're telling me all this."

"Because I believe you need to take the royal oath."

"The royal what now?"

"The royal oath would give you access to your family's power. It would strengthen your abilities and your standing. Bonded royal wolves are incredibly powerful. The bond heightens an Alpha's abilities. I can only imagine what it would be like to take the oath as a soul entwined shifter. While it's true that this is unchartered territory, I have reason to believe it would equip Kayla with more power, too, and stabilise her own magic."

"So I should take the royal oath and officially become King Alpha to protect Kayla." Ben nodded. "Do you realise how much this is to take in? I'm not even sure I want to take this oath. I'm not sure I can handle that sort of responsibility! I've never said that to anyone before, not even Kayla. She'd be so disappointed in me."

"It is a lot of responsibility, and I am sorry it's fallen on your shoulders. But our Creator has a way of helping us. If you are soul entwined with Kayla, you should trust her to take some of this burden with you. After all, this affects her, too."

Blake groaned. He leaned over in the chair. "Oh God. How is this fair to her? Being dragged into this like she is? Does she even want a bond, let alone a soul-deep one? Doesn't her magic want to find another magic user? Surely her 'essence' wouldn't be happy with my wolf? What if she feels forced into this because of a stupid bond, soul thingy?"

"That's a lot of questions, and some I think you should share with Kayla. I told you because I truly think taking the oath is your best chance at strengthening yours and Kayla's capabilities."

"When? How?"

"As early as tomorrow if this peace meeting is to take place. I've already been looking into it. I can have it all arranged."

"Can it be done quietly?"

"I would recommend that it *is* done quietly. We don't want to alert anyone who may oppose this. Once you've taken the oath, it cannot be undone."

Blake said he was thankful for the information, but his mind whirled. He asked to sleep on it, let it sink in – not to mention he needed to know what he should and shouldn't tell Kayla. It was all too much, spinning around his head until he was dizzy. As he lay in bed, he tuned in to Kayla's heartbeat down the hall and let it lull him to sleep.

CHAPTER NINETEEN

KAYLA

BLAKE WAS DOWNSTAIRS WITH Ben, and Imogen was arguing with Wyatt in the boys' room over something she'd rather not get involved with, so she went back to her room and dug out her mother's spell book. It was quite frankly a miracle it had survived all they'd been through. Imogen still had it tucked into her jeans when she escaped the hotel fire, and between them they'd been able to keep it hidden from Elijah.

The familiar, worn cover may have been a little dirtier than it once was, but when she opened the book, her mother's perfume greeted her. Her lips tipped into a smile as memories – good memories – of her parents came to mind.

She turned to a spell she wanted to work on. The door lock spell was firmly wedged in her head, but if she wanted to make use of the spells, she either had to have the book in hand or recite them from memory. It wasn't practical to always have the book with her, so she knew she'd have to start memorising the ones that could come in handy. She stopped on a spell that removed light from a room which, under certain circumstances, could be helpful. The spell wasn't long but learning it by heart was difficult. The downside of witch magic, she supposed.

A knock at the door interrupted her.

"Can I seek refuge?" Josh asked, peeking around the door. She could hear the argument in the next room.

"Are they still going at it?"

"Oh yes."

"What on earth do they still have to argue about?"

"Something about who would be the best bait."

"Bait?"

Josh shrugged. "I know. None of us have discussed a situation where we would even need to use bait . . . can I?" he asked, gesturing next to where she sat on the bed.

"Oh, yeah. Sure."

Josh walked into the room and sat beside her, leaning over her to look at the spell book.

"Whatcha doing?"

"Trying to memorise a spell."

"About that. Is it true you can do all three magics? Blake told me, and don't worry, he said if I told anyone he'd personally kill me. I believe he was being quite serious."

Kayla squashed the smile that threatened to escape.

"That's Blake for you, and yes, I can."

"That is awesome! Want any help?"

Kayla accepted and showed him the light snuffing spell. When she finally recited it accurately – and plunged them into temporary darkness – Josh asked about her mage magic.

"Err, I don't know."

"You don't know what your mage magic can do?" Kayla shrugged. "Have you used it before?"

"Only with Blake; I got into his mind and spoke to his wolf."

Josh's jaw dropped. "Can you speak to mine?"

"I – I'd rather not," Kayla mumbled, fiddling with the frayed edge of the spell book.

"Why? It's bloody cool!"

"How is controlling someone cool?" Kayla's voice rose.

Josh frowned. "Controlling someone?"

"My dad, he adjusted and wiped memories, altered perceptions; he affected people's free will. I don't want to be like him."

"But how will you know what you can do if you don't try? So far, it seems like your magic only helps people! Try on me."

"What?"

"Try on me. I'm happy to be a willing participant. Best to find out what you can do in case you can use it in defence."

Kayla thought for a moment, and she couldn't deny the small part of her that wanted to see if she could talk to another shifter's wolf.

She nodded.

"What do you need to do?"

"I think I need to touch you." She laughed when Josh raised an eyebrow. "Steady on there!"

"I should be saying the same to you! All right, go for it."

She reached out, placing her palm against the side of his face and closed her eyes. As soon as she concentrated, the pull of the wolf inside Josh appeared, calling to her.

"Woah," Josh murmured.

And then she was in.

Much like inside Blake's mind, she stood in a dark, open space with monitors to her left, each screen displaying a different memory. She smiled at one with a younger Blake, but before she could take a step closer and watch it, she heard a heavy pant nearby.

"Josh?" she called out quietly.

A sleek, chestnut-brown wolf sauntered forward, emerging from the darkness. It stopped a few paces away, wary eyes studying her, and then its tongue lolled out of its mouth.

"You had me worried there for a moment!" She moved towards him and tentatively held her hand out to stroke – instinct she supposed – but froze just before she made contact. "Is this okay?" she asked, looking into Josh's yellow wolf eyes.

He dipped his head, which she took as a yes. After a quick stroke, Josh watched her intently and nudged her hand.

"Yes, yes I know I should practise something, but I don't want to." She listened, looking at Josh intently, and seemed to understand what he was asking. Kayla huffed. "Fine." She stood up and closed her eyes. "Shift."

When she opened her eyes, she was back in the bedroom at Ben's, and something soft brushed her hand. She stood up as Josh shifted into his wolf form.

Josh's wolf leapt off the bed and spun quickly, wagging his tail. Kayla giggled and the wolf headbutted her thigh twice.

"Okay, okay! Jeez! Um . . . sit?" Josh's wolf tipped his head to one side, but he stayed firmly on all four paws. Kayla coughed. "Sit," she commanded more firmly, ensuring eye contact.

Josh slowly lowered himself until he sat on the floor. His eyes widened.

"Holy Moses . . . I did it! Oh, um, you can shift back."

Josh's fur receded until his human form took over. He stood up and whooped.

"That was so cool! When you focused, I had no choice but to sit!"

"I don't think that's cool – you had no choice. Do you realise what that means?"

Josh frowned. "It means we have another weapon to use. Surely that's what we want?"

"To control people? No. That's not what I want. I'm not using my mage magic. Ever."

"You might have to, Kayla. We know you'd never do something to deliberately harm someone, but sometimes it's necessary."

"Where does it stop though, Josh? My dad thought it was necessary to push back Blake's wolf, erase his and my memories – completely alter them. He thought he was doing something to shield us, but all it did was leave us unprotected. If I hadn't been able to help Blake, who knows what would have happened. The shift was tearing him apart!"

"I get that, but your mage magic helped him."

"Only because I was able to command his wolf and override what my dad did. This sort of magic, this sort of control, shouldn't be used. Now that I know I'm taking away someone's free will? I can't do that."

Josh scratched at his chin. "I understand, but please don't dismiss it. You're powerful, Kayla. Don't be afraid to be who you are because of it – I know you'll use your powers for good."

Kayla said goodnight and got into bed, Josh's words churning in her head. She was finally certain that her mage power was connected to shifters – she could control them if she so wished. It was dangerous and scary. Would she become like her dad, thinking she was doing the right thing?

CHAPTER TWENTY

KAYLA

OPENING HER EYES MADE no difference to what she could see – which was nothing.

"Hello?" she asked cautiously. She knew she was standing upright, and when she'd called out, the sound echoed around her. She was definitely not in the room she'd gone to sleep in.

"I better be dreaming," she mumbled.

"Open your mind, sweetheart."

Kayla spun at the sound of the familiar melodic voice. "Whoa. Who said that?"

"Open your mind."

"My eyes are open," she responded sourly. What sort of bossy dream state was she in?

"But not your mind."

"I just want to wake up in the same place I fell asleep."

"Okay then. The hard way it is." The voice sounded disappointed.

"Wait. What?"

Kayla's view dizzily came into focus as her eyes and mind struggled to process what she was seeing. A huge clearing dominated the middle of a thicket of trees, protecting the area around a hand-built house with a thatched roof.

It was the sorcerer's house. Again?

"Why am I here?" she asked the faceless voice.

There was no answer inside her head, but giggles echoed through the clearing. Three children around the age of eight spilled out of the cottage door. Kayla frowned. Were these the sorcerer's children?

The first girl darted past, dark blonde hair trailing behind her as she ran ahead of her siblings. Her dark green eyes were squinted in concentration as she pumped her legs and disappeared into the forest.

"No fair!" the boy called as he, too, started running. His long, tied back hair was nearly the same colour as Kayla's. The boy didn't see Kayla as he jogged past, but he frowned and slowed down, his blue eyes darting around the area where she stood. She didn't move, and the boy continued his chase.

A loud, irritated sigh to her right had her looking down at the third child, a girl with long chestnut hair. She tutted, shaking her head, and then looked right at Kayla.

Kayla sucked in a sharp breath, taking a step back.

"Siblings," the young girl murmured. She studied Kayla intently with eyes that weren't just similar, but almost exactly the same as her own. The same shade of brown, the same calculating gaze – even the eyebrows drawing together in the middle. Kayla knew her own face. The young girl was deep in thought, but she was trying not to show it.

"You can see me?" she asked and the girl nodded. "How? I'm not really here." The young girl raised an eyebrow. "I mean, this is a dream?"

"I'm real!" the girl claimed, crossing her arms over her chest in what Kayla knew was a defensive move. It was her own.

"Okay then, but *how* can you see me?"

The girl shrugged her shoulders. "How would I know? I'm a child." The girl had a good point. "Anyway, I'm going now, as my brother and sister will be waiting and probably trying to kill each other without me there." She rolled her eyes.

"Well, it was nice meeting you," Kayla responded when the girl made no move to leave.

Nodding, the girl stepped forward. Her foot caught on a tree root and she tipped forward, arms windmilling. It was instinct, but Kayla reached out to grab the girl.

The vision filled her mind instantly.

Incoherent images flashed by too quickly to make sense of. A wolf? Bursts of colour? A castle? Was that a dagger? A current of fire raging red, amber, yellow with streaks of blue, gold, and green swamped her vision. The vortex of flame expanded and consumed familiar faces: Imogen, Wyatt, Oliver, Michael, Amy, Mia, Luke, Mal, Blake.

She wiped her cheeks, fingers coming away wet, but instead of tears, blood stained her hands. Unable to scream, unable to think logically, Kayla spun, moving through the fire to find her friends.

Three figures stood before her in a circle, their silhouettes dancing within the roaring, magical flames. Kayla tried shouting, but nothing came out.

The figures held hands, and dark, black shapes circled them. Kayla shuddered. The malevolent evil of the darkness reached out to her as the shadows slammed into the trio one by one.

Screams reached her ears. The three convulsed, their heads thrown back, bodies tense. Their faces were hidden but they stayed connected.

The black spirits, or whatever they were, disappeared within the circle, and then a blinding explosion erupted from the trio.

Kayla was thrown back and consumed by immense power. Two other bodies also flew away from the trio, pushed back by the powerful blast. Her last thoughts were ones of shock, horror, and recognition. They were older, but two of the siblings from the clearing were the last faces she saw before pain shattered her fragile, human body.

KAYLA OPENED HER EYES and drew in a shuddering breath as Imogen's soft snores vibrated through the room. She unclenched her tense hands and found them wet. Sitting up, she inspected her palms. It was dark but the curtains were thin, and the bright night sky provided enough light to see that her hands were just sweaty. Her breath of relief was instant.

Knowing her heart was beating a hundred miles a second, she climbed out of bed and tiptoed down the hallway, pausing outside the boys' room.

"Blake," she barely whispered, but the door opened immediately.

Blake's pinched blue eyes searched her face, and despite the worry coming off him in waves, his presence instantly calmed her.

He reached out, cupping her elbow in his large hand as he turned to shut the door behind him.

"What's up?" he asked, assessing her for injuries. He only had one hand on her, but his heat and energy flowed through her and brought down her thundering heartbeat. She nodded to herself.

"Bad dream."

His face softened. He moved his head in the direction of the stairs; Kayla followed behind him as they made their way into the kitchen.

Blake put water in the kettle and switched it on, leaning back against the worktop and crossing his arms over his chest. She tried to ignore the way his muscles bunched. She didn't need her heart racing again.

"Want to talk about it?" he asked softly.

She shrugged. "Not sure. It was . . . different."

Blake busied himself making hot chocolates for them.

"It was a dream, a nightmare. They're not real."

His advice was practical, smart, logical, but she couldn't shake the feeling that she'd witnessed something from the future. Goosebumps ran down her bare arms when Blake handed her the steaming cup of chocolate.

She smiled instead of answering, unsure of what she could say. The more she tried to remember the dream, the shakier the details became. Maybe he was right. Maybe it was nothing.

"Thank you," she told him over the rim of her mug, taking a sip.

"Shall we sit for a bit?"

"Please," she responded, hesitant to go back to sleep just yet.

They moved into the living room, taking the same sofa. Kayla pulled her legs up beneath her, and Blake's thigh rested against her side. Neither flinched or pulled away from the contact. Was it becoming their norm?

"What?" She giggled when Blake smiled into his mug.

"Just thinking about the old days, before we met Wyatt and Imogen and all that."

"What about 'all that'?" she narrowed her eyes at him.

His smirk grew. "Nothing."

"Blake," she warned, fighting a smile.

"It's just nice to have this again, with you. Plus, you don't seem to sleep well without me." He flashed his award-winning smile at her over the top of his mug, and her mouth dropped open.

"I was just about to say I missed those times, but now . . ."

"I'm joking!"

"And I can manage perfectly well on my own, thank you! I only came to you because I knew you'd sense my heartbeat, and I didn't want you barging in and disrupting Imogen."

"If you say so." He smiled again.

"I do!"

They drank their hot chocolates in companionable silence.

"How is Imogen?" Blake asked, looking into his empty mug.

"I think she's doing okay, all things considered."

"I should be nicer to her; it's you who has more reason to be upset with her, and you're being so friendly."

"We both have a reason to be angry with Marcus, not Imogen – as easy as it would be to share that blame now that he's gone. I lost my parents too – in a similar manner, no less. That clings to you. I also know what it feels like to learn things about your parents after they die and feel torn between grief and anger. I mean, my parents lied to me and hid your wolf, but they didn't try to kill anybody so I can't imagine that part."

"You're a better person than me. Wish I could just get over it." He closed his eyes and rested his head against the sofa. "Or rather, my wolf needs to get over it."

She frowned, deep in thought, glad he couldn't see her face. There went that distinction between him and the wolf. If she had to, she'd guess it was the wolf that was angry at Imogen for her connection to Marcus, the man who'd tried to kill her.

She steeled herself and asked the question on her mind. "Why do you always talk about your wolf separately? Don't you think the same?"

He turned his piercing eyes on her. "Sort of. I'm better at managing my emotions. He clings to instinct and feelings, so we butt heads. I'm still not happy with Imogen, but human me can forgive her and understand what happened. Wolf me wants to destroy any connection to that man as soon as possible."

"Oh," she replied quietly. "Are you okay with Josh now?" she asked, trying to fill the quiet void but regretting it when Blake's jaw tensed.

"Another subject the wolf and I can't process the same way," he mumbled, eyebrows drawing together.

"Why?"

"It doesn't matter."

"Yes, it does." Her voice came out in a whisper.

"You," he eventually answered, and her stomach clenched. Was he wondering how to let her down? Had he realised it was the wolf influencing his actions and feelings before?

"Oh."

Blake's leg bounced up and down against her folded one. "Screw it," he announced and leaned over, one arm reaching out to cup the side of her face, drawing her closer.

Their lips crashed in a hot, desperate attempt to convey something neither could articulate. He breathed her in, his warm hand curving around the side of her throat, resting at the nape of her neck. His thumb stroked her cheek and she leaned into his palm. Blake's earthy scent wrapped her in a cocoon of warmth and longing, so much so that when he pulled back, resting his forehead against hers, she couldn't stifle a small whine.

Their breath mingled. He ran his fingers over the back of her neck, sending pulses of energy dancing down her spine.

"I just need time with my wolf to work through some things. Can you give me that? Please?"

She didn't know what he was begging for, but even through her worries, her insecurities, her doubts, she knew she'd give him that. She'd give him anything, and it scared her.

She nodded, and a tension she hadn't known he'd held vanished.

He placed a soft kiss on her forehead, pulling her close to cuddle.

They both struggled with words, but there had to be something there. His energy was reaching out to her. She could feel it, and her magic hummed peacefully. Maybe she should take it as it was.

Warm and content in Blake's embrace, her eyes fluttered shut, and she felt their connection click and solidify, waiting to be activated. She wasn't sure how she knew. Maybe it was her unique magic. Whatever it was, her magic buzzed excitedly, and for once she was confident in her control over it.

CHAPTER TWENTY-ONE

BLAKE

"I'VE FOUND SOMEONE WHO can perform the oath ritual for you, and he can do it today." Ben lowered his voice as he spoke.

Ben had found Blake and taken him to one side while the others were busy making noise in the kitchen during breakfast. Blake leaned back against the hallway wall, blowing out a long breath.

"That was quick."

Ben's eyes softened. "We need to tell the others. I know you wanted to wait, but this is important."

Blake nodded and followed Ben into the kitchen where scents of French toast and cinnamon greeted him. Kayla looked up from sprinkling sugar over hers, a genuine gleeful smile reaching her eyes. He walked over and pressed close to her side. He couldn't deny it wasn't a deliberate action – his tense muscles relaxed when her unique scent mingled with his. He picked up two plates and brought them to the table, tucking in as he waited for the others to sit down, too.

Josh and Imogen were chatting animatedly by the fridge, and while she rummaged through it, Ben grabbed a coffee from the side.

"That's the last of the syrup!" Imogen whined from the fridge door, holding the apple juice and watching Wyatt drain the syrup bottle over his toast.

"So?" he said. Blake bet Wyatt knew it was the last of the syrup and exchanged a sideways glance with Kayla.

"So? Did you not think to see if anyone else wanted any?"

"Well, perhaps if you weren't so busy talking, you might actually have gotten some," Wyatt snapped. Blake frowned.

"You mean while I was being friendly, which is what you asked me to be in the first place?" she spat back, and even Ben looked awkward at the exchange.

Wyatt laughed. "You don't think it's strange that I have to remind you to be nice to people?"

"Well, look at you telling me to be nice when you've just finished the last of the syrup! You're so selfish!"

Josh stepped closer towards the pair. "Woah there, guys. Is there something more going on here than syrup? Is everything okay?"

Both Imogen and Wyatt turned to face Josh.

"Shut up!" they shouted in unison. As they continued yelling at each other, Josh brought a plate to the table and began eating.

Pointing a fork at the pair, he mumbled around a mouthful of food, "They have issues." No one disagreed.

"You always need someone to come to your rescue, don't you? If it's not me, then someone else your father has instructed to do so."

Imogen sucked in a harsh breath. "Don't bring him into this!"

"Too late, *Princess*," Wyatt teased, and Imogen's eyes narrowed.

"You promised to stop calling me that years ago!"

"Ahh yes, but I only did so because your dear old Dad paid me to stop after it upset his precious little girl."

Beside Blake, Kayla winced.

"Dad paid you? You accepted money from him?" Imogen asked in a small voice.

"Yeah, why not? He didn't exactly give me much else, did he? Why not take his money? Getting extra cash to stop calling you certain names, or so I would take you places, or help you with your work, earned me a nice bit of pocket money."

"He gave you a home. He gave you a family."

"Ha, what family?"

Imogen nodded her head and took her plate to the table. Wyatt followed and sat as far away as possible, a stormy expression etched deep on his face.

"Blake, shall we share what we discussed?" Ben asked, trying to turn the focus away from Imogen and Wyatt.

"Umm, yeah," Blake replied. He should have said something to Kayla last night, but he couldn't bring himself to do it. They'd barely admitted their feelings for one another. Moving from that to declaring they were soul entwined and needed to take an oath that would bind them forever was kind of a stretch.

"I spoke to Blake last night," Ben addressed the table, "about taking the royal shifter oath."

"Now that's what I'm talking about!" Josh whooped, clapping a hand on Blake's back. Kayla was quiet.

"But we'd need a priest, one versed in the shifter ways and one who wouldn't be afraid to do it. Not to mention only a handful have the ability and the power to perform the oath," Wyatt said.

"I have someone who can do it. He actually performed Alpha Kieran's oath – Blake's father."

"Really?" Blake asked.

Wyatt's eyebrows rose. "Wow."

"Kayla? What are you thinking?" Josh asked, and Blake flexed his hand, calming his wolf. Josh was just being friendly.

"I think getting Blake to take on Alpha status was what we wanted all along."

Ben nodded. "More than that, we discussed how taking the oath would give you guys the extra boost, extra credibility when going to the peace meeting. It would be foolish to think a meeting of this magnitude wouldn't come up against opposition." Ben slid a file to Wyatt, who opened it as he listened. "This is what I could find about the peace meeting. There is a lot to indicate an attack by both shifters and magic users opposing an alliance.

"That's ironic," Wyatt mumbled, his eyes scanning the information.

"Quite."

"So, take the oath, get access to his Alpha heritage, win over everyone?" Josh asked hopefully.

"More like take the oath, gain the Alpha abilities, hope it's enough to go against the idiots planning on stopping an alliance. Are we getting out of this without a fight?" Wyatt asked Ben, and he grimaced.

"I don't think so, no."

Ben looked to Blake, but he shook his head, praying the guy wouldn't bring up the connection with Kayla and how taking the oath could strengthen them both. She freaked out about her own abilities; taking strength from him might be too much for her to handle, even though he knew she was more than capable of wielding such power.

He sagged against the back of his chair. Was he ready for the power? The responsibility? Could he really take on Alpha status and lead the wolves to peace?

Kayla rested her hand on his arm and gave him an encouraging smile.

"You can do this," she whispered as the boys continued to discuss tactics. "Are we doing this today, then?" she asked the group aloud.

"I think it's best," Ben answered her.

"Right then, what do we need to do?"

CHAPTER TWENTY-TWO

KAYLA

KAYLA FOLLOWED THE OTHERS into the old, abandoned church. The priest they met didn't look like any she knew, but not many people could perform an oath of that magnitude. She was surprised he was still alive, given how the magic users would have done their best to destroy anyone who could potentially call an Alpha forward.

The priest led the way down the aisle, his white hair bobbing as he ducked into a back room. They all piled in after him and he clasped his hands together in front of his body as she turned and shut the door behind them. His smile didn't quite reach his eyes when he thanked her.

"Thank you, Axel, for doing this so quickly," Ben said, shaking the older man's hand.

"I was surprised when you contacted me, but nevertheless, I'm more than willing to help in any way I can."

"We appreciate the risk you're taking."

"I've managed to live a long life – goodness knows how – but helping out young Blake here is something worthwhile. I'd rather go out with a bang." He smiled sadly at them all, and Kayla was touched at his use of Blake's chosen name.

"You performed the oath with my birth father?" Blake asked.

The man's eyes danced momentarily with a memory none of them could see.

"Yes. A great man, and a great woman your mother was, too."

"Thanks. I don't remember them so it's nice to hear," Blake replied shyly.

"The oath is a simple ritual, but it evokes a lot of power. Your mark will change as you accept the power bestowed to you by a higher being through me. I will be speaking a very ancient language, one you won't recognise, but as you accept the oath and all that comes with it, you will understand and be able to complete the oath in the language. It's important you use the language as the knowledge comes to you."

Blake nodded. "Does it involve . . . blood?"

The man barked out a laugh. "No, my friend, it does not."

Axel looked to Kayla and she saw a knowing glint in his eye. Did he know she'd used Blake's blood before in spells?

"Do we need to do anything?" Josh asked.

"Just give us some room. The power of the oath is strong, and it will be testing Blake's mind, heart, and body for acceptance as well as his capability to house such responsibility."

"What happens if the power denies him? Can that happen?" Kayla asked, tucking hair behind her ears and dancing from foot to foot.

"It can. But I know Blake is strong enough, not to mention he has Alastair blood." Axel turned back to Blake. "Show me your mark, Prince."

Blake pulled his shirt over his head. It wasn't until she spotted Imogen's smirk that Kayla realised her cheeks were hot. Imogen caught her eye and raised a brow, but Kayla studiously ignored her.

"Blake, I'll have to use your birth name throughout the ritual, if that's okay?"

"Yeah." Blake nodded tensely, glancing at Kayla who stood the closest of everyone. She gave him what she hoped was a reassuring smile.

"Do you understand what the oath is? The responsibility it brings to your door for you to bear, and the connections it will establish and strengthen?"

Blake nodded.

Axel raised his arms up and spread them wide, but before he started his chant, something crashed from within the main part of the church.

Pews scraped across the floor, and shouts rang out.

Ben turned away from Blake. "Josh, Wyatt, Imogen, I need you to go and see what that is. If we've been found, can you hold them back?"

Josh rolled up his sleeves while Imogen nodded, her face paling.

"How did they find us?" she whispered.

"Why don't we go ask them?" Wyatt replied snarkily.

"Let's go," Josh growled as he shifted and ran through the door Wyatt opened. Imogen moved to follow but Wyatt pulled her back, storming through first.

"We should probably do this quickly," Kayla suggested.

"My dear, I was just thinking the same myself," Axel replied.

Magic reached out to her. Wyatt was engaging his powers. They were under attack. She should be helping, but as she looked at Ben, he shook his head and nodded in Blake's direction. He was right. She needed to focus on him. If others came through that door, she and Ben would be needed to protect the ritual.

She hadn't realised Axel had been chanting until Blake grunted and dropped to his knees. Black lines from the mark on his shoulder started growing, adding more detail across his shoulder blades, but then they quickly retreated. He panted, the muscles bunching beneath his skin, reminding her of when his body had first tried to shift but couldn't.

"Something's wrong," she whispered, instinct guiding her assumption. Blake cried out as the mark once again tried to change but snapped back; he fell forward, resting on his hands. She knelt beside him, placing a hand on his back. "Something's wrong!" she snapped louder at Axel. Axel's eyes dimmed; she hadn't even realised they'd grown brighter.

"He's not in sync. His body, heart, and mind are pulling in different directions, and he's putting up a barrier."

Blake grunted. "Not deliberately."

Kayla moved her hand to his forehead when he sat back on his knees, hoping she could infuse him with some of her magic – it seemed to work last time.

Axel gasped. "Ben, you were right!"

Kayla flicked her eyes between them both. "Right about what?" Something clenched deep within her stomach.

Ben stepped forward, apprehension written all over his face. "I suspected something when Blake and I spoke about you."

"Me?" she squeaked.

"You are soul entwined. That means both your hearts, minds, and bodies need to be in sync with each other before he can take the oath. I thought you had a strong bond and told him that the oath would enhance both of your abilities, but being soul entwined is something else entirely."

Kayla's mind reeled with information. Something her dad said long ago came back to her.

"But isn't being soul entwined made up by the shifters?"

"No." Axel stepped in. "But it hasn't been seen in centuries, so many believe that lie."

"What happens now?" she whispered. Blake shuddered beside her. "He can't stay like this forever."

"He can't take the oath without you."

"I'm not a shifter! I can't take the oath!"

The door rattled, but Wyatt shouted through it. "Got it!"

Ben paced. "Axel, what can you do?"

"It's not something I've personally come across before, but I can do it. Kayla needs to accept the role of shifter Queen and all the responsibility that comes with it. Only then will the oath accept Blake as Alpha."

"Again, I'm not a shifter!"

"That doesn't matter. You are his soul entwined. The oath will rip him apart if he tries to accept without his soul entwined. Without you."

Kayla stood, hands in her hair. "This is a lot. This is too much. I'm nobody's Queen! No shifter would accept me!"

Blake moaned where he knelt, hands on either side of his head.

"What's happening to him?" she asked, sinking next to him again.

"His head is struggling, too, Kayla. Your distress is his. The oath is continuing to test him, but he cannot pass it without you."

Kayla fought frustrated tears as she watched Blake's face scrunch and tighten with each passing moment. She wished he was lucid enough to discuss this with him. Was this what he wanted? To be bound to her forever?

The door shuddered again.

"We need to hurry," Axel whispered.

Kayla nodded her head. Mind made up.

CHAPTER TWENTY-THREE

WYATT

WYATT LANDED ON HIS butt after the witch uttered a spell that threw him backwards, sending him into a row of pews. He tumbled over the hardwood benches and groaned. His magic surged forward. Calling on air, he pushed at the witch coming for him.

In his peripheral, Josh fought two more magic users: a mage and a witch by the looks of it. The wolf was managing to hold his own against the magic, but Wyatt couldn't work out how the witch's spell on Josh failed. It had been a stun spell, yet Josh was unharmed, and he clamped his jaws around the witch's arm.

Then it dawned on him.

Swivelling his head, he watched as Imogen fell to her knees, her arm crashing down beside her. She had been focusing her shield on Josh. She'd done that before for Blake, but where had the new ability come from?

His eyes widened when a magic user came up behind her. "Immy! Watch out!" he shouted. She looked at him briefly, but it was too late. The female magic user grabbed Imogen by the head, muttering in her ear. Imogen flailed but stayed glued to the floor.

Wyatt jumped up, his hand pointing at the bank of lit candles beside him. Marching forward, he drew the small flames together, pulling the energy into a ball, and thrust his arm at the witch behind Imogen. The fire ball flew into her, disrupting the witch's spell. Imogen surged forward, breaking her fall with her arms just before her face slammed into the stone floor, but she didn't waste any time. She kicked out behind her, sending the witch crashing to the floor. A loud crack jolted through the air, and the woman went still.

Wyatt used his air magic to force the woman out of the building, and then used what connection he could with the broken wooden furniture to block the main doors.

He scanned the room for anyone else, grabbing Imogen's arm to pull her up beside him. Surprisingly, she let him. He looked down at her ashen face.

"You okay?"

She nodded, rubbing her temple. "Yes. Go help Josh."

He did as she asked, hand lingering as long as he could before he added his power and fighting ability into Josh's brawl. It wasn't long before they subdued the other two magic users.

Wyatt panted, catching his breath, and Josh shifted back.

"You good, man?" Josh asked.

"Yeah. You?"

"I am thanks to Imogen. Thanks for the save, by the way." He spoke over Wyatt's shoulder when Imogen approached the pair.

"You're welcome." Her voice sounded stronger than it was a moment ago, which helped relieve the last dregs of tension in Wyatt.

Wyatt was about to say something when an invisible blast from the back room hit them. Wyatt knocked into Imogen, her yelp mixing with his grunt. He tried to regain his balance, but it was futile as the energy pressed down on him.

Falling back as one, Imogen's hand gripped his shoulder. Just before they slammed into the floor, Imogen's protective shield curved around him.

CHAPTER TWENTY-FOUR

KAYLA

COOL TILED FLOOR SOOTHED her flaming cheek. A stabbing sensation throbbed at her shoulder and down her side, even as it dulled from the peak of its agony.

She'd accepted the oath with Blake, and the full force of the power had slammed into her and forced its way into every ounce of her essence, merging with her magic. Every atom in her body felt raw, like it had been torn open to join with the Alpha oath. Her mind had exploded and then been stitched back together, but a static energy hummed in the background. When she probed at it, she felt Blake's wolf, as exhausted and spent as she was.

Even though her body had taken a beating accepting the oath, she knew it was Blake who still bore the brunt of the pain as its intended host. She also knew he would have drawn as much of it from her as possible. She flexed her fingers and opened her eyes. Blake lay on his front beside her, unconscious. His hand was wrapped around hers. Not wanting to move much more than her eyes, she cast a glance down the length of his body, relieved when his back rose up and down.

Black streaks of soot stretched out from where they were joined. Without a doubt, he had taken what pain he could from her.

And she still felt like she'd been torn apart.

"Blake?" she whispered hoarsely, tears forging a lump of unspoken emotion in her throat.

She braced her upper body on shaking arms and slowly pulled her legs under her so she could kneel. Reaching over, she brushed some of his long, shaggy hair away from his face and ran her hand over the markings on his back. His ink tattoo spread and curled around his upper arm now and down his side in intricate patterns.

"Kayla!" Ben exclaimed.

Her exploration of the mark halted. Ben held Axel up as the old man wheezed and shook.

"Is he okay?" she asked, nodding towards Axel.

"I think so; there was some serious power going on in the room. He had to channel it."

Kayla gulped, wondering how the old man was still alive given how she felt, but Axel had said the Oath power would assess the intended host. And if that wasn't Axel, maybe he was strong enough to be the conduit.

"What about Blake?" Ben asked, lowering Axel to a sitting position on the floor.

"Um, I think he's okay."

"And how do you feel?"

"Like I've been hit by a high-speed train. I'm okay, but my shoulder and side hurt. I'm guessing I've been marked like Blake?"

Ben frowned in thought. "It's possible."

Scratching pattered above her, a soft tip-tapping clatter growing louder with each passing moment. She looked at the skylight above them, daylight streaming through the glass.

"What's that?" she whispered just before the face of a snarling tan wolf came into view. "Shifters!" Two more wolves appeared in the skylight and they began scratching and jumping on the glass, spittle flying everywhere as their lips curled up.

Ben and a dazed Axel looked up. "They don't like what we've done," Ben muttered, his body frozen to the spot.

"No one ever does," Kayla uttered back, anger simmering low in her belly instead of the fear she'd expected.

"I'm guessing they don't like the fact that shifters and magic users worked together – or the fact that a new Alpha has been initiated who is working with us."

"How are they even finding us?"

"Your power, together. The oath became a beacon. I was afraid of this happening."

The glass cracked into a wide spider web. "We need to get out of here," she ordered, even though she worried about the state of the main church and the others.

She pushed at Blake, hoping he would wake up, but the glass shattered, raining sharp edged weapons over them. The wolves fell in; their furious snarls filling the space. Ben immediately planted himself in front of a defenceless Axel as one wolf turned to him and two started towards her and Blake.

She contemplated moving away from Blake to draw the wolves' attention away from his unconscious body, but the darker of the two wolves narrowed its gaze on Blake's back where his mark had settled. The wolf's lips curled up even tighter, a rumble in its throat growing louder still.

She couldn't abandon Blake's side and leave him exposed.

The darkest wolf bunched his muscles and sprang towards Blake. Instinct had her stretching her hand out, reaching for her magic, and a bolt of lightning shot from her palm. The wolf let out a yelp of pain as she drew her hand back, staring at it.

"It's the oath; your powers are heightened now because your souls are entwined – you are connected and can draw energy from each other." Axel shouted the information to her. She shook her head. She had no time to dwell on her enhanced powers.

She drew on her magic again, feeling the soft caress as it slipped up from her core and slid over her arms to her palms. Vibrations raced along her skin when she asked the magic to bring forth her fire. It was the most confident she'd ever felt with her magic.

Flames leapt from her palms but didn't burn her skin. She flexed her fingers, wiggling them, and the flames followed her patterns. Clenching a hand, the flames merged into a ball of fire, and she released it at the second shifter.

It screeched and scrambled back, flames coating its body in a red and orange blaze.

Ben's yell of surprise caught her off guard as more wolves tumbled in through the opening above them, descending on Ben and Axel. The old man fell beneath the furry bodies and disappeared from view.

"Axel!"

Kayla drew up her magic again to attack but didn't leave Blake's side. She paused. What if she hurt Ben or Axel instead? Did she have enough control?

The door behind her to the main church burst open. Her head whipped around lightning fast. A large brown wolf barrelled through the room and leapt into the mass of coiling bodies, snarling and ripping at anything non-human.

"Holy smokes!" someone exclaimed from the doorway. Wyatt stumbled in after Josh's wolf and began waving his hands. His eyes jerked to where Kayla knelt, fire caressing her palms. Imogen's brown eyes widened at the scene before her as she appeared behind Wyatt.

"Blake!" Imogen exhaled on a sharp squawk when she noticed his unconscious body.

"He's just out. Imogen, come shield him so I can help Ben and Axel!"

Imogen rushed over, wasting no time, and Kayla and Wyatt approached the vicious shifters. She spotted Josh ploughing through wolves, but as soon as he cleared them from where Axel lay, they reappeared again.

There were now at least ten by Kayla's estimation. She no longer hesitated and let the magic fly, surprised at its golden hue. Fire and electricity tore from her palms to get rid of the wolves on the edge of the assault.

A cream-coloured wolf leapt at her from the tangle of furious wolves on top of Josh. She fell to the ground, and the wolf snapped its jaws inches from her face. Her arms trembled with exertion as she held back the creature. How was she keeping it away from her?

The wolf snapped and snarled, dripping thick ropes of saliva onto her face. She sent a bolt of magic into the wolf and the stench of burning fur assaulted her senses. Grey smoke rose from where her hands connected with the creature.

Its yellow eyes went wide. It yelped and collapsed on top of her, its full weight bearing down on her slight frame. Despite having had the strength to hold back the razor sharp teeth when the shifter had been alive, she failed to move the body as it transformed into a human. Tears sprung in her eyes. The man's vacant expression stared her in the face, but the pressure on her lungs fell away as Imogen grabbed at her arm, pulling her up.

"Quick Kayla!" she screeched.

Kayla frowned, but it dawned on her what Imogen was doing. "Blake!" she yelled at her.

"Got it covered, but not for long. Help Axel!" Imogen scooted back to Blake's body, standing loosely as she prepared to fight whoever came close.

A cry behind Kayla had her spinning in Josh's direction just as he disappeared beneath a hulking grey wolf. Kayla rushed forward, fists raining down on the wolf, causing it to falter and shake its head. It turned towards Kayla, and in an instant, fire coated her hands.

She couldn't believe the power rush she felt. The adrenaline. Her lips curved as she took aim. Magic and beast collided. The wolf was strong, grazing her shoulder with dagger-like canines. She let out a short cry of surprise as a quick blast of pain shot through her, but she moved it aside, boxed it up, and drove her flaming fist into the wolf's jaw. His whimpering whine pierced the air when he fell, landing with a thud. He didn't change back to his human state, but he stayed motionless. That would have to do.

Josh's whine caught her attention and penetrated her bubble of adrenaline-filled victory. She looked around to find Wyatt finishing the last of the wolves off. A couple scampered out the broken door, unable to go back through the roof they'd dropped down from. Some lay in their human forms, dead. Others, like the grey wolf at her feet, lay motionless, but they wouldn't be out for long.

Wyatt's chest heaved. Imogen nodded at her. Relieved Blake was okay, Kayla turned her attention back to Josh who stood on shaking legs.

"Josh?" she asked. Josh shed his fur and knelt with his head hung low. He reached a hand to the back of his neck and rubbed it, but it came away red. "Oh god!" She rushed forward to inspect the nasty wound at the base of his skull.

"I'll be fine. Just a few more moments for the concussion to die down, and by tomorrow the wound should be fully healed."

Her eyes clouded with worry. Wyatt came over and gently touched her shoulder.

"What about you?" Wyatt asked.

"Just a graze. I'm fine."

"Guys." Ben's low, dark tone interrupted the injury assessment. It didn't take a genius to figure out something was wrong.

Wyatt helped her to her feet, and the three of them made their way over to where Ben sat, holding Axel's head gently in his lap.

"Is he . . .?" Wyatt whispered.

Ben looked up and nodded. Kayla took a step back when Josh's hand came up to support her. She pulled away, moving further from Axel. Axel who had given her and Blake the oath. Her thoughts were selfish ones and guilt flooded her. Who would be able to tell her about the oath and what it would mean for her now?

She closed her eyes, but they flashed open when Blake moaned. She rushed to him.

"Blake?" she asked gently as she knelt beside him. He pushed up on a shaky arm, and with her help, managed to get into a sitting position. He looked around the chaos of the room.

"What did I miss?"

"We got attacked."

"What's going on?" he asked, his voice hardening when he focused on Axel's body.

Wyatt came over and explained, and Blake's eyes went dark as he finished. Kayla placed her hand on top of his, knowing he needed the comfort as much as she did.

"We need to get going before others arrive," Wyatt said quietly.

Ben finished wrapping Axel's body in a cloth he found inside a cupboard with Imogen's help. An apology was written all over his face.

"Kayla, I . . . I'm sorry to ask this, but we need to destroy the evidence of this room. We can't have the human world knowing about this."

Kayla's brows drew together. "You want me to set fire to this building, don't you?"

Ben nodded his head, unable to verbalise the words himself. Her mouth opened to protest, but she couldn't say anything.

"This is the sort of thing Mia and the taskforce would be called in to help with. They'd actually have the time and manpower to do this properly, respectfully," Wyatt muttered, almost to himself, before sighing. "Want me to help?" he said to her, and she nodded. She didn't think she could do it on her own. Physically, sure, and with her heightened power, even more so. But emotionally? She was grateful for Wyatt.

Josh and Ben helped move Blake away from the room; they took him outside so he was away from the mess. Imogen didn't know who to stay with, but with her shielding powers she was better off with Blake, and so she left with them.

Wyatt gently took Kayla's hand in his and she started the fire, growing it until flames were touching the ceiling. Once the flames were established, he helped guide the blaze around the room, making sure to cover the bodies. They did the same in the main church.

As she left, she couldn't help but feel something had begun there, despite it being the final end for Axel. She tripped, and if it wasn't for Wyatt holding her up, she would have fallen.

"We had to, Kayla," was all Wyatt said when they met the others and watched as the hungry red beast devoured the building. Imogen turned away when the spire collapsed. They left the area deep in thought. Quiet. Pensive. And for Kayla: riddled with guilt as her new powers coursed through her body.

CHAPTER TWENTY-FIVE

BLAKE

BLAKE BRACED BOTH HANDS on the side of the sink in the bathroom back at Ben's. He'd just finished cleaning and freshening up after . . . well, after the oath, the attack, the fire. He clenched the porcelain tighter until a sharp crack pierced the air.

He'd been unconscious when everyone around him risked their lives to protect him, and he hated it. He ran agitated hands through his long, wet hair and grabbed another towel off the radiator to dry it.

Axel had died. Josh and Kayla were injured, and who knew what else could have happened while he was asleep?

Kayla remained quiet the whole journey back and pushed for everyone to get cleaned up ahead of her. She wouldn't look him in the eye, much less speak to him, and he and his wolf weren't okay with that.

He felt their bond now more than ever; it was like a physical tug constantly pulling him closer to her. It was the only reason he let the distance she was putting between them exist. He knew she needed space. He may not have known how deep their connection was before, but now that he understood, he was trying to respect it.

Even if that meant leaving her alone. But eventually, he would speak to her. They needed to discuss their bond. It wasn't just some small thing she'd accepted for him – she'd accepted a role as the shifter queen.

He hadn't been in much of a place to deliberate it earlier, but he'd listened to what Axel had been saying, knew the confusion and turmoil she was going through. He needed to tell her that it was what he wanted, regardless of the alliance between the shifters and the magic users. All he wanted was to accept her. Why was it so difficult to voice that?

The oath had been clawing at him, taking him completely by surprise. He wasn't expecting it to be so . . . raw.

It continued to test him even when he understood he couldn't take the oath without Kayla by his side, and he was terrified of it attacking her essence the way it had his. At first, his wolf had been resistant, anxious, but then he grew angry that the oath was attacking Kayla in the same way. Blake grabbed onto her hand, not knowing what he was doing, and drew what he could away from her. The oath – he suspected it knew Blake was the main host – happily ran through him even as it continued to test Kayla.

At one point, he was sure the oath wasn't just a 'power,' but a living organism with thought and purposeful actions. He sensed the curiosity towards Kayla when she brought up her magic as a defence – or was she showing the oath her magic, getting them to accept each other? He didn't know, but her screams as the mark burned and branded them both were clear as day.

The last thing he remembered before waking up was falling to the cool floor. Kayla collapsed beside him with her face pinched tight and eyes shut. He remembered trying to reach for her, but he could no longer fight off the darkness as it spread to his human form. Grabbing her hand had been his final act of connection before unconsciousness claimed him.

He finished dressing before moving downstairs where the others milled about the kitchen. Soft words filled the space while they got drinks and snacks. Even Wyatt was quiet as he hopped onto the kitchen island with a bottle of water in hand. In the corner, Ben and Kayla were deep in conversation, and it took a considerable amount of restraint to not listen in. Instead, he moved to where Josh had his head in the fridge.

"You all right, man?" he asked his friend. Josh leaned back, a half-eaten carrot sticking out of his mouth. He held a block of cheese in the crook of his arm, and some sandwich meats and butter in his hand. "Hungry?"

Blake asked, the corner of his mouth tipping up.

"Always. Want something?"

"Nah," he replied, his eyes darting to Kayla. Her concentration was centred on Ben, and his wolf whined. Josh tracked Blake's gaze as he moved to the counter next to Imogen to make a sandwich.

"Hungry for something else?" He winked while buttering bread.

Blake hit him lightly on the arm. "Watch it." He smiled at his best friend.

Imogen turned around abruptly from the coffee she'd been making and almost spilled the contents down Josh's front. Josh reached out an arm to steady her as she spluttered and shook her hand.

"Oh my gosh!" she cried.

"You burned?"

"No, no . . . just a bit red. I'm sorry!" Imogen's eyes were wide. She checked Josh over to make sure nothing had spilled on him.

Josh's chuckle was deep and low; Blake wasn't even sure if Imogen had heard it.

"I'm okay, if that's what you're wondering. It would take more than a few drops of hot coffee to take me down."

Blake rolled his eyes behind Josh's back, but Imogen's tense body relaxed, and she smiled to herself.

"Is everybody here?" Ben's voice filled the room. Imogen jumped once more but kept control of her drink.

"Yeah, why?" Josh answered, biting into his sandwich.

"We're going out for the rest of the evening. Blake and Kayla are staying here." He looked pointedly at Kayla, but she glanced at the floor, folding her arms across her chest and nursing a small scowl.

Josh turned to Blake and smirked. "No problem," he said as he clapped a hand on his shoulder.

"But I've just made coffee! Why do we have to leave these two here?" Imogen whined.

Wyatt rolled his eyes as he leapt off the counter. "Clearly missing the subtle vibes, Immy. Let's go."

"But–"

"I'll buy you a damn coffee," Wyatt huffed. He waited in the kitchen doorway for her to move. She looked into her drink and then back up to him.

"A proper nice one," she instructed, dumping the drink in the sink. "With cream and sprinkles if you so desire . . . as long as you move your ass quicker than a snail's pace."

"I don't move that slow!"

Blake was surprised to find their bickering a familiar comfort. Kayla had still yet to look up from her study of the floor.

"Talk. Both of you," Ben instructed. He left, shutting the front door behind him and plunging the pair into silence.

Blake coughed. "So, um . . ." Again, he found it absolutely ridiculous that he was struggling to talk to her. They'd found such synchronicity when living together, but this new part of whatever their connection entailed made him nervous.

"I need to clean up," she said and made to move past him. Instinctively, he reached out to take her arm in his hand, lightly tugging her to face him.

"We should talk, Kayla. What happened . . ."

"I'm well aware, thank you," she snapped, finally turning her large eyes to look at him. "But I need a breather." She yanked her arm away with unnecessary vigour, considering he wasn't holding on tightly. "We chose the alliance; we didn't choose for our souls to be bound together," she finished, her eyes glaring at him as her mouth flattened into a thin line.

He stepped forward, but she retreated; both he and his wolf froze.

"Kayla, I–"

"I'm going to clean up. Don't follow me," she instructed, flying up the stairs.

HE LEFT HER TO IT, much to his wolf's disappointment, but the longer she took, the more agitated his wolf became. Blake paced the living room as he fought the need to tune in to her. It would be an invasion of her privacy. He couldn't do it when she'd specifically asked for space.

Her sob echoed in his mind, and his wolf strained to get to her. Had he just listened in without meaning to? As he thought about her, the crying became louder.

He was going up, her wish be damned. Taking the stairs two at a time, he was outside the bathroom door in seconds. Running water cascaded from within. He gripped the door handle and took a deep breath.

Pain. Sorrow. Panic.

Her emotions leaped out to him.

"Kayla, I'm coming in," he warned and pushed open the door.

She sat against the side of the bath in the clothes she'd borrowed from Ben yesterday, knees pressed against her chest. Wet hair curled in thick strands, tumbling haphazardly over her shoulders and face. A towel was scrunched up under her chin. Blake walked in without saying anything and leaned over her to shut the shower off before sliding down to match her position. Where their knees and arms touched, a warm tingle spread from the contact, instantly calming the pacing wolf inside his mind.

Blake didn't speak while she cried, her breath hitching on tired hiccups. Each new sob pierced his gut and tore at his heart. She was crying because of him.

Not knowing what to do but needing to be close, he stayed where he was. Eventually, slowly, her body pressed against his until her head rested against his shoulder. From there, he could no longer stand to be idle and wrapped his arm around her back, pulling her into him. As she moved her head to his chest, she gripped onto his shirt, and he pulled her legs over his so she was in his lap. He cradled her for a few moments before standing with her in his arms.

He took her across the hall into the girls' room to gently lay her in the bed. They'd still not spoken, but he knew she didn't need words right then. He'd show her what she meant to him with actions. She laid her head on the pillow, her gorgeous eyes no longer leaking tears. He pulled the duvet up around her.

He reached out and stroked her hair, tucking it behind her ear. She closed her eyes at the contact and something tight constricted in his stomach – a feeling of utter protectiveness over her. He sensed how spent she was and turned to leave, but her hand shot out, grabbing his.

"Don't go," she whispered, her voice raw.

Like he'd done a hundred times before, he turned back and slipped into the bed, turning on his side to face her. She took his hand where it rested between them.

"I'm sorry," she whispered.

"Why on earth are you apologising?" he murmured.

"I just – I was selfish. I failed to think about you over my own emotions. I know I hurt you."

He couldn't deny she hadn't. She was likely feeling the hurt coming off him, just like he could feel hers.

"I'm hurt because you are hurting, I couldn't do anything about it, and I feel responsible. Don't worry about me," he said, stroking some of her hair over her shoulder.

"But that's the thing, Blake. I worry about you all the time. I can't stop worrying about you, and now . . ."

"The whole soul entwined thing?"

She nodded. "It's not like I can hear your thoughts or anything – I just *know*. Before, I did feel connected to you, I can't lie about that, but this is just intense. I'm not sure what my own thoughts and feelings are anymore. I'm so confused."

"Want me to tell you mine?" She nodded and focused on his eyes. "I sense an unwillingness in you to accept that I could ever like you the way you like me. I know there's a block within you that isn't allowing you to fully feel. Kayla, I'm pretty sure my wolf wanted you from when we first met, sensing our connection."

"But that's your wolf. I would have always supported you in the oath, always. It's not that I had to take the oath with you. It's the fact that you're forced to be connected to me because of this soul entwined bond. I don't want you driven into something you didn't want because of your wolf. I don't want to be the one to take away your free will."

"Since when have me and the wolf ever disagreed that much? Sure, I wasn't happy with how 'okay' he was when we killed, but I didn't disagree with it. Every life I've taken has been for a purpose. My wolf is happy with that, and I know it was for a reason – I'm not as happy with it as he is, but I agree that they should have died. My wolf *is* me. I talk about him as a separate being, and he is to a degree. But we are one and the same."

Her eyes looked up at him, less clouded than before. "So, what do you feel – about me?"

The corners of his mouth quirked up. "That I've wanted you from the beginning. I don't feel trapped in this oath and this bond with you, Kayla. I feel liberated. Free."

She mirrored his smile. "You do?" She rolled onto her back and covered her face with her hands.

"Yes!" he answered and pulled her into him. She rolled over with a yelp and rested her hands on his arm as he caged her in close. "Don't ever doubt you and me. Don't ever doubt my feelings. Don't ever doubt the things I'd do for you. Just . . . don't ever doubt us."

"Us? There's officially an 'us?'"

Blake rolled his eyes. "Enough talk now."

He bent down and placed his lips on hers, moving his hand to cradle the side of her head, thumb stroking over her cheek. She nestled in closer until his other arm snaked under her waist. He used the position to draw her body flush against his. Her hand stroked down his side and around his back, grabbing the shirt he wore in her fist.

"I want to see," she murmured against his lips.

He reluctantly pulled away, just enough to tug the shirt over his head and dump it on the floor. She pushed him until he lay face down on the bed, but he turned his head to watch her while she studied his back.

Her delicate fingers traced the mark, starting where his first mark originated and then following the patterns down his arm. Her touch was light, but it sent tremors straight to his middle. His eyes closed when she followed the markings down his side and back again, but he hadn't realised he'd grunted until her hand stilled.

"Does it hurt?" she gasped, pulling away.

"No."

"Does it feel . . . different?"

"Yes." He was going to have to use more than one syllable words soon.

She chewed on her bottom lip. "Will you show me?"

Nodding, he reached up and pulled her lip from her teeth with his thumb before she pulled her top over her head, keeping the fabric close to her naked chest. He snaked an arm around her and pulled her to his side as they settled together on the bed again, and then with his free arm he began an exploration of her marks – very similar to his own. As he traced them, her mouth opened on a gasp and her eyes closed.

"Oh," she whispered.

He smiled. "Oh, indeed."

When she opened her eyes again, they burned with hunger. She kissed him fervently, cupping his strong jaw in her hand. He danced his hand over her marks, swallowing her moans as he did.

"Hey," he whispered, leaning back just enough to tell her the words he so desperately wanted to say. “I love you.”

Her smile was instant and spread across her entire face. “I love you, too.”

Their soft touches became passionate embraces, and both of them began a different kind of exploration.

CHAPTER TWENTY-SIX

IMOGEN

IMOGEN HELD HER COFFEE between her hands while Wyatt, Ben, and Josh discussed something about the peace meeting over breakfast. She didn't feel like she could contribute given the circumstances, and guilt weighed down on her heavily. Wyatt had put a stunning amount of emotional distance between them. Sure, they'd always argued, but she thought he was part of her family. She was under the impression that he would stick with her in the tough times. But apparently not. Learning he'd taken money from her dad to stop calling her names had been the proverbial nail in the coffin.

As she sighed and took a sip, Blake and Kayla walked into the room hand in hand. Kayla's cheeks were tinged pink, but her smile couldn't have been any wider.

After leaving Blake and Kayla alone for a few hours last night, Imogen was forced to share a room with Wyatt and Josh when they'd arrived back at the cottage the night before. The bedroom she'd stayed in with Kayla was a 'no-go zone.' Imogen wasn't stupid – Kayla had been getting busy with the shifter.

Relief and happiness for them both calmed her nerves and quieted the guilt for just a moment. It was obvious the two were meant for each other, and now that they'd taken the oath, Imogen was further away from her dad's contract than ever. Plus, not so surprisingly, she liked Kayla.

Josh leaned back in the kitchen chair and stretched, winking at Blake. Wyatt whistled.

"Well hello, love birds," Wyatt sang. Kayla rolled her eyes as she left Blake's side to pop bread in the toaster.

Josh held out his fist to Blake, who turned to check that Kayla's back was to him before bumping Josh's with his own. They shared a goofy smile, but they toned down their grins when Kayla returned with glasses of orange juice. She paused, looking between the two friends, then settled her eyes on Imogen.

"Good night?" Imogen asked, a grin on her face.

Kayla shrugged. "So-so." She plastered her lips together after she answered.

Wyatt burst out laughing.

"Right, should we get on?" the ever-practical Ben suggested.

Now it was Imogen's turn to roll her eyes, and Kayla stifled a giggle by shoving some toast in her mouth.

"What do we need to do?" Blake asked, his tone dipping into the serious voice he often used.

"The meeting is tonight. I know where it is and when – that's great – but we need to get outfits and figure out security."

"What do you mean security?" Blake questioned.

"We need to know what security they have, given there's a strong chance they'll be attacked."

"Why can't we warn them?" Kayla interrupted.

"I suggested that," Wyatt answered, "but then they may cancel the whole thing, and we need an agreement in place. It took months to get enough groups to agree to come together to work out a peace deal. Many are worried that they'll be stopped and killed, so if we say that they'll be attacked, it will confirm their fears. God knows how long it will take to get enough people to agree to a meeting again."

"Good point, but what about Elijah? We don't know where he is. He could be planning to go to the meeting himself, and who knows what he'll do? Turn them against us? Kill everyone?"

"Oh, I agree. Ben found something, didn't you?"

"Yes, Elijah will undoubtedly be there. I heard back last night from an old friend who has connections. We'll have to work the event quietly, avoid Elijah if at all possible, and get the others to see how dangerous he is."

Blake snorted. "So, the impossible?"

"Exactly right, my friend." Josh clapped a hand on Blake's shoulder and grinned.

"Why do you look so happy?"

"I'm up for a fight." He winked.

"I've already tried having a word with the 'oh-so-crazy-one,'" Wyatt apologised, shaking his head in mock distaste. Imogen recognised the smirk on Wyatt's face.

Ben coughed. "Anyway. The boys and I will go and grab suits; girls, I can give you some money to pick up dresses. It's a black-tie event, so think fancy."

Imogen placed her mug down and squealed. "Yes! A thousand times yes!"

"Oh, dear lord, you've set her off," Wyatt mumbled in a condescending tone. Imogen chose to ignore him.

"Are you . . . one of those girls?" Kayla asked, leaning back in her chair.

"You're going to have so much fun, trust me!"

"Not too much fun. The old guy is giving us an hour in the centre after Blake and Josh have done a sweep," Wyatt happily supplied.

Kayla turned to Blake. "Is that wise?"

"I've taken the oath, so I'm much stronger now. We'll be good," he replied, taking her hand in his.

Ben stood up. "Right, let's go. We don't have loads of time here."

They quickly piled into two cars and met at a shopping centre not too far away. While Josh and Blake left the parking structure to do a quick sweep of the building, Imogen meticulously ignored Wyatt. The pair stood on either side of Kayla and Ben, who were busy discussing the oath.

Imogen shivered when the wind whistled through the concrete parking tower, making her wish she had her thick fluffy coat from home. The thought soured when she remembered what state her coat would currently be in.

It only took a few minutes before Josh and Blake returned.

"Think we're as clear as we can be," Josh explained.

Once inside the shopping centre, Ben gave the girls a credit card and allowed them to go off by themselves. The boys sauntered off the other way, but Blake turned back to wave at Kayla. She smiled and giggled like a schoolgirl.

Kayla turned to Imogen. "What?" she asked playfully.

"You are so giddy in love right now. Acting like a kid with her first crush."

Kayla sighed. "I feel like it. Anyway, let's get this over with."

Imogen dragged her to a few stores on the ground floor before they made their way into an evening dress shop on the next level.

"Oh, this is much better," Imogen exclaimed, eyes lighting up at the displays of long elegant dresses and sequined masterpieces hanging on the walls.

She towed Kayla over to a pastel-coloured rack of gowns and rifled through it.

"Honestly, Imogen, it doesn't matter what the dress looks like."

Imogen snorted. "Yes, it does! You're now the shifter Queen – you have to make an impression." Kayla's face paled. "Oh, I didn't mean anything by that! You'll be great no matter what you wear. It doesn't matter!" She spoke too quickly, words tumbling out of her big mouth.

"No, no. You're right. First impressions matter. I can't let Blake down, can I?"

"I somehow doubt you could ever let him down."

Kayla cleared her throat and nudged Imogen towards the rack. "Find me a pretty dress, please."

"Coming right up!"

They entered the changing rooms with a dozen dresses between them, but Kayla eventually settled for a blush pink chiffon gown. It hugged her chest and curved down her waist, flowing out from the hips to allow for movement – the girl had been very specific about her need to run and fight if necessary.

Imogen had opted for something a bit glitzier. She chose a deep red number that hugged her curves. A small slit at the bottom of the dress would have been okay under any other circumstance, but she would cut it up to her thigh to allow for movement should she need. And, if she was being honest with herself, the slit would show off her legs. Wyatt would so not approve. Ha! Take that, Wyatt.

"You okay?" Kayla quizzed as they left the store with bags in hand.

"Yeah, I suppose," Imogen sighed.

"You can like, talk, if you want, to me," Kayla mumbled, stumbling through her words.

"Thanks, I'm fine." Imogen frowned.

Wyatt once told her that she needed help with everything – including being nice to others. Maybe she should open up to Kayla, as she was the only one around who ever backed her up. "Just had a lot going through my head: my dad, the meeting, the alliance, Wyatt," she tacked on at the end.

"Wyatt? Because of what he said?" Imogen shrugged. "You do know he does it to wind you up . . . have you ever thought about how he might be feeling right now?" Imogen opened her mouth to argue but stopped herself.

"No, I haven't. Am I a bad person?"

"Gosh, no! Sheltered . . . kinda, but not a bad person."

"Well, maybe Wyatt shouldn't have contributed to that sheltering and taken payment from my father!" Imogen huffed.

"Hmm. I'm just playing devil's advocate here, but maybe Wyatt did that to maintain some form of communication with Marcus. The man didn't treat Wyatt like a son, even though he raised him. I get the impression that Wyatt actually wanted his approval, and you'll hate me for this, but I think Wyatt is trying to help you grow and find your own two feet. He wants you to be independent."

"Well, he has a funny way of showing it."

"He's just lost a father figure, too. Sure, he was treated horribly and shunned by the man, but he was still in his life and now he's gone. You are all he has left. Maybe he's trying to protect himself from you."

Imogen stopped walking and pulled a face at Kayla. "Protect himself from me? I'm useless. I can't hurt anyone!"

"No, but what if you leave him or treat him like Marcus did? Wyatt could be distancing himself so that when you do leave him, he knows what to expect."

"He thinks I'll leave him?"

"Have you guys actually discussed what you want to happen after this? Like, what do you each want out of life?"

"I – I don't know. My life and actions have always been decided by someone else. Whatever Wyatt wants though, I'll be a hindrance. I should leave and let him be the person he wants to be. I'm not blind to how my dad treated him. He'd be better off without having some weird responsibility for me."

"I don't think he feels responsible. I think he feels connected to the last person he knows."

Imogen stayed quiet, unsure of how to respond. It made her think too much about Wyatt, and she wanted it to be clean. Simple. It definitely sparked the idea that after the alliance was sorted, she would go off on her own and find her true calling, leaving Wyatt to find his without her as a distraction. She would be no one's responsibility but her own.

"C'MON ON, GIRLS!" WYATT yelled from the bottom of the stairs just as Imogen finished fixing Kayla's hair. They were both dressed and made up for the evening. Apparently, everyone wanted to make it a night worth remembering. She rolled her eyes. She just wanted everyone to agree to a decent peace alliance with Blake and Kayla as the shifter leaders – nothing to do with her.

"We're coming! Jeez," she shouted, and Kayla smirked at her.

"Let's go before the guys get worked up. They probably want to get this over with."

"Same here! I've lived with this hanging over me all my life. I can't wait to be free of it. Sorry," she added when she realised Kayla was the one stuck with the burden for the rest of her life.

"It'll be worth it for peace and . . ."

"Blake?" Imogen asked. Kayla beamed.

The girls descended the stairs side by side. They were greeted by Josh in a well-fitted black suit, dark hair swept to one side.

"You look smart!" Kayla gushed, and Josh winked.

"I wouldn't let Blake hear you compliment me."

"Too late," Blake announced, coming out from the kitchen in a form-fitting grey three-piece suit. His voice was deep and serious, but the smile on his face was evident as his eyes flashed at Kayla. He held out a hand for her and she took it, allowing him to draw her into his chest.

He gave her a quick kiss on her cheek, murmuring something in her ear. With Josh's smirk and Kayla's blushing cheeks, Imogen didn't want to guess what he'd whispered.

"You look lovely, my dear," Josh said, distracting her from her thoughts.

"Not so bad yourself," Imogen threw back easily.

She giggled with Josh as Wyatt and Ben stepped out of Ben's study.

Her eyes travelled down Wyatt's navy suit, white shirt, and matching blue tie. Wyatt usually dressed well, but she'd never seen him in a tailored suit before. When she glanced at his face, his eyes were busy roaming her body. He looked up, saw her watching, and shot her a curt smile before turning away to the front door.

"We ready?" Ben asked, and they made their way to the cars.

Imogen sucked in a deep breath, anticipating what the night would hold. She prayed Elijah wouldn't turn up, that everyone would come to an agreement to stand up against the elitists – the hunters. If enough of them joined together with Blake and Kayla leading the wolves, would that be enough?

CHAPTER TWENTY-SEVEN

BLAKE

BLAKE HELD OUT HIS arm for Kayla to take as they approached the high-end hotel. Her face lit up with a smile, but he wasn't sure if it was nerves or desire that caused her heart to race.

"You'll do great," she whispered.

"With you by my side," he answered, letting her know with his eyes how much he meant it. Kayla was his rock. Her steps faltered and her smile fell, but before he could ask if she was all right, Ben stopped them.

"Now, as we enter, I think it's important that we try to stay together as much as possible, or at least move in pairs. Most people here truly want an alliance, but if Elijah is inside and he has his own people working to stop the new alliance, then we could be in trouble. We have to prevent a fight from breaking out, as we cannot afford for these group leaders to go back underground again."

"Bunch of cowards," Wyatt muttered.

"I don't see you doing anything different," Imogen retorted. Wyatt huffed, but not before he shared a look with Kayla. Did Imogen truly not know that Wyatt had been working with Mia and the others in pursuit of a better alliance?

"Let's go!" Ben ordered and took the lead at the front of the group. They entered the revolving doors of the grand hotel.

Small talk and laughter from a room to their left greeted them. A doorman stepped forward. His black trousers, white shirt, and red and gold waistcoat stood out. He dipped his head ever so slightly.

"May I see your reservations, please?"

Ben produced documentation that he'd been emailed to prove he had contacts within the meeting; the doorman smiled and swept his arm to the side.

"This way," he said and led them to a pair of large double doors. When they opened, Blake glanced around, identifying extra exits and any suspicious behaviour. In his peripheral vision, Kayla did the same.

Imogen's mouth hung open. "This is gorgeous!"

"Beats our hotel!" Wyatt responded, and for the first time, neither bit the other's head off.

Imogen was right – the room was exquisite, and Blake could see why it had been chosen. It was a large ballroom with hardwood floors and sizable windows looking out onto the quiet street. Long, velour curtains were artfully draped on either side of the windows, held back with golden rope tied into expert bows. A live instrumental band played soft background music on the small stage opposite the double doors where they stood.

The room was full of people in suits and dresses. Some had genuine smiles on their faces, while others wore pinched expressions, eyes darting around the room erratically.

"I'm going to find my contact and learn when the main meeting is taking place; I think many of the leaders and their aides will meet in a separate room to hash out details for a plan moving forward." Ben made to leave and Josh moved beside him.

"Remember, stay in pairs." He repeated Ben's earlier words back to him with a grin. Ben nodded at Josh, and they both disappeared into the sea of people.

"So . . ." Blake began.

"Let's mingle!" Wyatt sang. "What? We should speak to as many people as possible, show our faces, let them know you're King Alpha now."

"How will they know?"

Wyatt rolled his eyes. "Shifter senses, dude."

"Oh. What should I say?"

"Just be yourself. Show them you're not a tyrant. Show them you want peace. It shouldn't be hard given it's the truth."

Blake rolled his shoulders back. "Be myself. Got it."

The four of them moved into the crowd and smiled at the first people they encountered. It was mostly shifters by the looks of it. They introduced themselves to a couple, and the pair froze.

"You're . . ." the blonde woman murmured and the man beside her beamed, holding out his hand for Blake to shake.

"I'd heard the shifter prince was alive! I can't believe you're here and you took the oath! We have a chance now of this properly working!"

The woman's eyebrows drew together as she studied Kayla. "Wait!" she gasped. "Are you two . . .? I thought it was a myth, but then how could you take the oath with him?" The woman gushed like an excited child.

"Um . . ." Kayla stumbled, which wasn't her usual style. "We have a connection, yes."

"And she took the oath with me," Blake finished.

The woman and the man placed their fists over their chests.

"King Alpha, Queen Alpha," they uttered breathlessly. Kayla stilled beside him, less used to the term than he was.

"Thank you." Blake tilted his head in what he hoped was respect.

"We shall let you move on and speak to others; thank you for coming over to us," the man said, retreating with his excited wife.

"If everyone loves you like that, we'll be fine," Wyatt said.

"More than. They loved you too, Kayla," Imogen added.

Blake looked at Kayla as she gave a tense smile to Wyatt and Imogen. He squeezed her hand, reassuring her.

"Blake!" a deep voice rose from nearby. He turned his head just as Luke appeared. The tall shifter barely fit in his tight suit. He tugged a blonde woman behind him who looked amused at his rushed pace. Blake recognised Amy's eye roll when she stumbled to a stop beside Luke. She straightened her tight black dress, taking a sip from her glass when she finished.

"You made it," Wyatt said.

"Thanks to you. I got your message with the details just in time."

"No problem."

"I'm so glad you're all here, though. It's getting tense. There are a lot of shifters and magic users here who have never worked with each other and given the high rate of murder between the two groups, many are wary. Understandably."

"Oh my god," Amy whispered, placing a hand on Luke's arm.

"What?" he asked, concerned.

"These two! We were right about them being soul entwined!"

"Soul entwined . . ." Luke breathed, and his eyebrows rose to meet his hairline. "The oath!"

He smiled at them both, clapping Blake on the shoulder and embracing Kayla.

"Is that okay? Are you all right with that?" Blake asked, his heart beating faster.

Luke's eyes nearly bugged out of his head. "More than all right! I'm so honoured to know you – to know you both. I can't quite believe we have a magical Queen Alpha!"

Kayla's head dipped as she pulled her hand out of Blake's. "Excuse me. I just need to go to the bathroom," she mumbled, making a hasty exit.

Imogen turned from her conversation with Amy and frowned, watching Kayla leave. "Wait!" she called. She stepped forward to follow, but Wyatt grabbed her elbow.

"You've lost sight of her now."

"Then we should find her together."

"I'll go with you," Amy started to say, but Blake stopped her.

"Wyatt, you go with Imogen so I can fill in Luke and Amy," Blake suggested, trusting that Kayla would be okay. She just needed a few moments to compose herself. Wyatt nodded and left with Imogen.

"What's going on?" Amy asked.

"We think Elijah is going to be here with others who believe in his stance. We're worried he'll stage an attack of some kind, but we have no proof or evidence – just the knowledge that he isn't who he says he is. We couldn't afford to freak out all those who came here for an alliance. Will you be able to keep an eye out and help us intercept any problems?"

"Sure thing," Amy confirmed.

Luke grimaced. "Elijah won't accept an alliance. Judging by what he attempted with you, I'd say he definitely has a plan in place. Does he know about the oath? That strengthens your position."

"We're not sure. We were attacked by wolves and magic users, but they weren't working together. Some of them got away."

"Let's assume he knows and is hoping to stop you tonight. If the wolves heard that not only was the shifter prince alive and had taken the oath, but a magic user killed him, that would put an end to any alliance discussions."

Amy grimaced. "Did you have to say the word 'killed?' Don't worry, Blake, we won't let anything happen to you or Kayla," she added after she'd scolded Luke.

Thinking of Kayla made his stomach tighten, and his wolf pricked his ears. Where was she?

"Hello, Blake," a deep, arrogant voice announced. It took all he had not to shift and leap at the man.

He turned slowly.

"Elijah," Blake ground out between clenched teeth, barely holding in a snarl.

The man had a smug smile on his face.

"Having a good time?"

"What do you want?" Blake asked, glancing around the room. Only Luke and Amy were as tense as he was. Nobody else understood the danger. "You don't want an alliance."

"Maybe I've changed?" Elijah answered with a shrug, flashing a smile at Amy and Luke. Amy clamped a hand on Luke's forearm when he growled..

"You haven't changed. You hate the shifters just as much as you did before. What are you planning?"

"I'm not sure you should be accusing me in that tone considering the circumstances." Elijah sighed, rubbing the back of his knuckles on his dinner jacket and inspecting his nails.

"What circumstances?" Blake managed to tone down the volume, but his hands curled into fists. He couldn't lose it – Elijah would love it if he did, and it would only further Elijah's argument that shifters were dangerous. "You won't win. These people want to work together, and we'll stop those who think they are superior to everyone else."

"We'll see about that. It won't be long before you show your true nature, and most of these magic users will beg to be led by me – someone who is strong enough to make the hard decisions. Could you? Could you put the shifters before yourself? Before the one you are bound to?" Elijah asked, a triumphant smirk permanently plastered on his face. Kayla. His wolf whined, wanting to leave Elijah and look for her. Something wasn't right.

But Blake stood his ground, rooting his feet in place.

Elijah walked away. Even his confident gait implied he was better than everyone else. Blake would have followed, but a breathless Wyatt and Imogen rushed over.

"Was that . . .?" Wyatt asked, his eyes narrowing on Elijah's back.

"Yes."

"He's got something up his sleeve for sure," Amy added.

Imogen waved her hands frantically in front of her. "Never mind that. We can't find Kayla!"

Blake whirled on her, his eyes flashing golden. "Elijah."

"Elijah was just with us?" Amy muttered, her brows drawing together.

"But he wasn't when Kayla first left," Luke said, thinking out loud.

Blake growled, but only his group could pick up the sound over the noise in the room. "He had something to do with it. I can sense that something isn't right."

"Maybe she's okay? Maybe she just moved past us when we were looking for her?" Imogen offered, but the three shifters shook their heads. "What?"

"He's soul entwined to her, Immy. That means he has a sixth sense about her well-being."

"I always have. It's just stronger now." Blake looked around the room, hoping to see her walking towards them, but his growing sense of dread told him otherwise.

"Imogen and Luke, come with me to look for her. We might need Imogen's shield magic. Wyatt and Amy, you two stay together. I think it's wise to pair a shifter and a magic user together for strength. It'll also solidify the idea that we can work with each other. Everyone okay?" Blake instructed.

Luke and Amy nodded, and Wyatt grinned. "Knew you were leadership material!"

Amy rolled her eyes and looped her arm through Wyatt's. "Come on, Mr Magical. Let's keep our eyes out for trouble."

"His name is Elijah," Wyatt retorted as the two moved into the crowd.

"Let's go," Blake ordered.

CHAPTER TWENTY-EIGHT

KAYLA

KAYLA'S HEAD THROBBED. SHE gingerly touched her temple, and her brain tried to pound its way out of her skull. She pulled her arms in close when a shiver ran through her body. Scraping her hands over the cold, hard floor, her eyes sprung open and quickly adjusted to the dimly lit room.

She was lying on a slab of concrete, facing a wall of shelving units that held what looked like cleaning supplies: bleach, sprays, cloths, that sort of thing. Above her, a single bulb cast dim light into the room. No windows. One door above a short flight of wooden stairs.

Kayla sat up and waited for the room to stop spinning. She felt around the floor for her bag but came up empty, scanning the area by the stairs in case she'd dropped it. Had she fallen down by accident? What had she been doing just before she blacked out?

The door creaked open, allowing bright light and noise from the party into the basement. When the door shut, surprisingly little sound made it beyond the walls. A man's heavy footsteps pounded down the stairs.

Kayla looked up, her eyes going wide when he stood before her.

"Elijah!"

He grinned. "You didn't hit your head too hard when you fell down the stairs, then," he joked, putting his hands in his pockets. "Perhaps I shouldn't have knocked you out when you were standing at the top."

"Why is it only me you keep forcing unconscious?" she grumbled, shaking her head to get rid of the lingering fogginess.

Elijah shrugged. "Only works on highly vulnerable states of mind. Yours seems to always be ripe for the picking."

"That's what happens when you sentence people I care about to death . . . what am I doing here, Elijah?"

"You're here because I brought you here."

Kayla raised a hand, about to summon her magic when a new, dull pain throbbed in her temples. As she drew closer to her magic's essence, the throbbing became more intense. She gripped the side of her head, wincing.

"What have you done?" She looked down and found a black circular pattern etched on the back of her hand, sharp thorn-like shapes jutting out from around the circle.

Elijah let out a quick laugh. "A spell I performed to stop your magic; it stays inside you and can't get out."

"But . . ." she muttered, a frown tugging at her lips.

"But I'm a mage? Well done. Ten points to you!"

"I'd forgotten you were chanting over Blake when you meant to kill him. How do you have the ability to recite a spell? That's witch magic – how did I forget that?"

Elijah rolled his eyes.

"Another spell to stop you from remembering. That way, if you saw me performing witch magic, your memory would simply let it go."

"How? How are you doing both mage and witch magic?" she asked. She knew that engaging him was dangerous but it gave her more opportunity to work out an escape. It didn't help, however, that she wanted to know what he had to say. Was he like her? Could he wield multiple strains of magic?

"I stole it. Didn't you realise there are some dark magics out there? How great is that?"

"Are you going to steal mine?"

"Is the Pope Catholic?" he snapped back. "Of course I am." He moved to the wall of units and nudged a duffel bag from the corner with his foot.

"What will happen to me?"

Elijah shrugged. "You'll become a shell. That's not my problem, though."

"You can't just take my magic!" she argued, fear clawing at her insides.

"Oh, but I can. Would have taken Blake's alpha abilities, too, but waiting seems to have helped me out," he explained, squatting by the open bag. "He's more powerful now. Both of you are actually. Waiting till now worked out for the best. Plus, taking your magic first will weaken him and cause him pain – now that *is* something I look forward to. Filthy creature." He grimaced on the last word as he unveiled a container of blood red sand.

Elijah was talking about the oath, about being soul entwined. If something happened to her, Blake would feel it. Could he feel her now? She couldn't sense him. She looked down at the black brand on her skin. Was it blocking their link?

"You just want to be powerful?" she asked. She couldn't quite believe it was all because one man wanted more power. "Why?"

"Because it's destined," he answered simply, standing up. "Lie back," he commanded.

Her eyes narrowed. "No."

"Lie. Down," he repeated, his arrogant sneer contorting into a thin line.

"I said no."

Elijah was quick, flicking his fingers at her. A force hit her body, sending her flat to the ground. She moaned when her head hit the concrete, and a ringing echoed inside her ears. Elijah chuckled, which gave her enough strength to open her eyes and glare at him. Despite not being able to get back into a sitting position, she still had control over her limbs. For the moment, at least.

"Better," he sighed. He poured red sand around her in a circular shape.

"Why is this so important to you?" she asked, her voice holding steady despite the fear she felt. If she was going to lose her magic, she had to know what for. There had to be a reason.

"No one is winning. Not the shifters or the magic users. Once the filthy mutts are gone, I will be able to rule the magic users as they should be. Shifters should never have been allowed to exist. They muddy the waters. I'm tired of hiding in the shadows of monsters and humans," he scoffed, grabbing wide candles and placing them in a ring around her.

"Humans? We protect our supernatural world from them; we all know what would happen if they found out about us!"

"Well, no more. Once the shifters are gone, magic users will be free to rise up with my command, break the chains our ancestors forced upon us to hide us like cowards. We aren't cowards! Humans should be the ones cowering beneath *us*!" Elijah's eyes lit up manically. He lit the candles one by one. "Your magic will help me gain the power I need to prove myself to the other magic users. Blake's power will ensure I can destroy the wolves. At one point, I'd thought maybe he and I could work together – obviously he wouldn't know the ultimate goal. Luckily for me, I found a spell that would allow me to harness his shifter abilities."

"The first time you met us, you sentenced Blake to death!" she yelled as he placed shells and artifacts around the ring.

"I've had my hand in your journey for a while now. Who do you think ordered Blake's capture?" Kayla thought back to when his family had been taken. The shifters who took them never knew who Blake was and had been instructed to keep him alive. Elijah was responsible for that?

"You hired Oz?"

"Yes," Elijah answered, pulling a face.

"You worked with shifters?"

"A necessary arrangement. I much preferred working with Marcus despite his shortcomings and annoying, needy attitude. He actually thought I wanted Blake and his daughter to fulfil the original alliance contract." Elijah shivered dramatically as he rifled through a thick textbook, its yellowed pages curling up at the sides.

"You . . . and Marcus . . ." Kayla said, connecting the dots in a slow, painful realisation. "You were the one working with Marcus? You were the one who wanted to kill me?"

"No. Through Marcus, I learned of your gifts. While he thought you were an atrocity, I saw your value. It wasn't hard to trick the old fool into thinking we were working together to get rid of you. Those shifters were meant to bring you to me so I could take your power, and that would caused enough of a distraction for my magic users to get in and destroy the hotel. I couldn't have those people trying to find you, could I? Of course, the stupid mutts decided to get themselves killed. This is why you should never work with shifters. But when you both ended up on my doorstep, ha! You'd put yourselves in my hands so that I could take both of your powers."

"You wanted to kill him!"

"Side effect of the spell to extract his power as the Alpha heir. I thought that was my destiny until you both escaped, and then I realised I had been given another gift: your soul entwined bond!" Elijah's eyes danced with excitement.

"What? Your destiny?"

"I was granted a premonition, one that must have come from the Creator. The premonition was about a soul entwined shifter being the key to unlocking the most powerful being on earth."

"And you think that's me?"

"NO!" Elijah screamed. "It's me! Why else would I be given this premonition if it wasn't to show me what I was capable of? Being soul entwined bolsters your power, and you are already incredibly powerful, Kayla. The premonition showed me that I've been asked to be a vessel for this power. Chosen by the Creator."

"You're wrong."

"It's a shame you can't see the truth, my dear, but I will be taking your power and I will be taking Blake's, and I will achieve my destiny."

A tear slid down Kayla's cheek as she fought to control her breathing. She knew Elijah was bad, but his plan was utter madness. All of the turmoil and pain they'd endured was because Elijah wanted to kill the shifters and control the humans. How could he think that was his destiny? The Creator was about protecting the world, not destroying it.

The woman with silver eyes materialized in her mind, reminding her what she had said when Kayla was struggling to control her magic. Kayla had a purpose. Had a reason for being. But she refused to believe it was all so Elijah could take it away from her. She'd had her abilities given to her by the Creator. She hadn't stolen them like Elijah.

Elijah chanted from the book, and she could already sense the growing seeds of darkness spreading in the room.

She pulled on the strongest thread of her magical essence, knowing it was connected to Blake. The thread vibrated and pulsed faster, and she drew what she could through the connection. Her muscles trembled with energy, her lungs filled with oxygen, and when she opened her eyes, her vision had sharpened. She strained against her invisible bonds and rolled onto her side with considerable effort. As she panted, the first hands of dark energy touched her skin, crawling over her body and sinking beneath the surface.

She fell back, screaming as it tore through her. The connection went dull, darkness wrapping around the thread and thrusting her into a world of pain and silence.

CHAPTER TWENTY-NINE

BLAKE

IMOGEN RUSHED OUT FROM inside the girls' toilets and held up a small white bag splattered with a handful of red dots. His wolf howled, but Blake fought to keep calm.

"It's not much blood," Imogen offered helplessly.

"It's still hers."

Josh rounded the corner, frowning at the three of them.

"What are you doing?" Josh and Blake asked at the same time.

"Ben's discussing you with some of the leaders. He wanted me to come and get you. Is that Kayla's?"

Blake tightened his hands into fists as he nodded.

"She's been taken," Luke explained. As he told Josh what was happening, something tugged at Blake's core. Small, weak, but most definitely there.

He took a step back and turned to move down the long, empty hallway.

"Blake?" Josh called out. They all trailed after him.

"I can feel her," he replied breathlessly, turning down a corridor used by the hotel staff. "I know . . ." He stopped abruptly. The connection tugging him went cloudy. He could sense it, but he couldn't use it.

"Damn!"

"Was she close?" Luke asked.

"Yes. Try the doors."

They opened doors in the corridor and were met with staff rooms, offices, and toilets until Imogen yelped. Blake rushed over as she cradled her hand delicately.

"The door is spelled. I wasn't prepared," she explained.

"Can you open it?"

"I can now," she replied, closing her eyes briefly before putting her hand around the chrome handle. She smiled to herself and yanked the door open. The three shifters barrelled through.

Someone chanted from within the darkness: Elijah.

It took only seconds for the shifters' sight to adjust to the dim lighting, and as Blake's did, his wolf rushed forth. Four white paws hit the wooden stairs, leaping to land outside of the ring in which Kayla was lying. He bared his teeth at Elijah, whose eyes widened in rage. The man barely flinched when Josh and Luke landed beside him, Luke still in his human skin.

"Get her," Luke ordered and rammed into Elijah. The book flew from the mage's hands.

Blake bound towards the circle but flew back, repelled by an invisible force. A low growl scratched at his throat. He lowered his head and rammed the wall again.

Luke's cry cut through the air, and his body skidded next to Blake. He came to a stop, twitching.

Elijah stepped through the barrier preventing Blake from getting to Kayla and hauled her to her feet. She was barely able to hold her own weight as she swayed dangerously, eyes still closed. A soft moan came from her lips.

Elijah smirked and chanted a quick spell.

"Wait!" Imogen screeched, but Elijah disappeared into thin air – taking Kayla with him.

"What the –?" Luke asked as he stood.

Imogen's body sagged. "I recognised the spell, a vanishing one. It took me a second because I didn't know he could even do witch magic!"

"It's not your fault," Luke reassured her.

Josh and Blake shifted back.

"Where is she?" Blake asked.

"I don't know."

"You must have some idea!" Blake snapped.

"I'm sorry, I don't. Wyatt might know . . ." She trailed off, unsure.

Luke picked up the book Elijah had been reading from and flicked through the pages. "This is some dark magic," Luke muttered to himself.

"We have to find her. We don't know what Elijah is planning on doing with her," Blake said, stomping up the stairs.

"No arguments there," Josh huffed.

The door opened and Wyatt halted abruptly before he fell into the basement.

"What the–?" he began but then shook his head. "Never mind. Someone just told me Elijah has a freaking helicopter on the roof!"

"That's where he's taking her!" Imogen deduced.

"Taking who?" Wyatt asked as Blake and Josh brushed past him. They skidded into the lift across the hall.

"Get in!" Josh yelled, holding the doors open.

Soft elevator music filled the crowded space. The shifters twitched, eager to let their wolves free. Wyatt bounced on his toes, uttering curses at the 'slow moving piece of junk.'

When the doors finally pinged open, the group raced out into the night. Wind whipped at them as the helicopter's blades rotated, humming to life as two figures darted towards it.

"ELIJAH!" Blake roared. The man froze and slowly turned to face them with Kayla's arm tight in his grasp. More alert, she tried to go to Blake, but Elijah yanked her back to his side.

Elijah raised his right fist, and four magic users jumped out of the helicopter. He smirked at Blake and flashed his hands at the group. Electric power flung from his fingertips. Imogen took the brunt of the power, absorbing it into her shield and falling back into Wyatt who held her up.

"You're too late," Elijah shouted over the roar of the helicopter. "She can't use her magic, and soon it'll be mine to control!"

"Go!" Imogen told them. Wyatt turned to her.

"If she can't use magic, she can't protect herself. Get to her and use your shield to protect you both." He rushed through his words. Imogen nodded. Wyatt didn't linger and raced off behind the others.

One of Elijah's men whirled his hands – a move Blake recognised. He was calling on the elements. Blake shouted an order to Wyatt, who raced to release his magic first. The man flew back, skidding painfully across the tarmac.

Wyatt whooped. "Yeah! Plenty of elements up here for me!"

Josh shifted and darted back and forth between two of the magic users near him and Wyatt, working in sync with the elemental.

Blake went for Elijah and Kayla. Elijah started chanting but Kayla shoved at him, hooking her foot around the man's ankle, tripping him. He caught himself before he fell, lashing out at Kayla and swiping his hand across her face. Her gasp shot through Blake.

"Stop!" she yelled across at him. "Help Luke! Elijah spelled him!"

He skidded to a halt, panting, and looked over to find Luke with one of Elijah's magic users. Luke fell to the ground, gripping his head as Elijah's muscle man stood over him. Blake shifted as he ran, his paws thundering over the roof.

He used the power in his back legs to fly through the air, aiming for the magic user. The pair fell to the ground in a heap, but before he could check that his opponent was fully out, Luke leapt forward. Onto him.

Blake shifted back, unsure and shocked, blocking an attempt to punch him. He pulled both his legs in and put force behind the kick to push Luke away.

"Luke! What the hell, man?"

Out of the corner of his eye, Wyatt slammed a flurry of violent air into Elijah. As he stumbled away, Imogen ran to Kayla and threw up her shield, holding onto Kayla's hand. Blake's shoulders relaxed momentarily, but he tensed when Luke groaned. His friend stood back up, his muscles taut and bulging under his skin.

"He's. Using. Me," he ground out between clenched teeth. Blake frowned but realisation dawned. "Forcing. Change. Can't. Stop."

"Luke, back down!" Blake commanded, not ashamed that he put some power behind the words. Luke shivered, but it didn't stop his advance. "Luke, stop!" He tried again.

"Not enough," Luke breathed, launching himself at Blake.

His friend was trying to kill him. Luke shot around Blake at an alarming rate, showcasing just how proficient he was at combat. Blake barely blocked jabs as they came at him and narrowly missed being caught in a headlock. It wasn't just that Blake didn't want to hurt Luke – the guy was a fighting machine, and he was hard to defend against.

Luke tripped Blake and hauled him back by the scruff of his neck. His face contorted with rage, fighting against the magic Elijah had used on him.

"Kill me before I kill you!" he spat, releasing Blake. Luke grunted, his arm shaking at the physical exertion of the action.

Blake sucked in deep breaths and tried to think of a way out. His Alpha powers weren't working on Luke. They weren't overriding the magic. Magic. Kayla. He needed Kayla.

"Kayla!" he shouted and turned sharply towards her. "Bond. Oath. Need you!" he managed to communicate, racing to stay ahead of Luke who was dangerously close on his heels. Kayla and Imogen ran together, staying connected as they raced towards him.

Blake collided with Kayla, taking hold of her free hand and spinning around to face Luke. He felt his eyes glow and power surged through his body as he took a deep breath. Luke growled.

"Stand! Down!" Blake commanded, his voice deeper than he'd ever heard it before. Power rocketed towards Luke. He stumbled, falling to his knees. A gold mist cascaded from his body and dispersed into the air. Blake squeezed Kayla's hand, bracing himself for Luke to attack again when the man sucked in a sharp sob.

"Thank you," he cried, and Blake's body sagged in relief.

"You good?" Blake panted. Luke nodded and apologised, jumping up to embrace Blake.

"Elijah's getting away!" Kayla cried out.

CHAPTER THIRTY

KAYLA

SHE POINTED BEHIND THEM, still trying to catch her breath. Not being able to use her magic clawed at her insides, despite being able to draw on some of Blake's strength. Wyatt's shouts and creative curses filled the air as he tried to get to Elijah.

"On it," Luke growled, racing to join Wyatt and Josh.

Blake leaned into her, cupping her cheek with his free hand. He searched her face, looking for injury or distress, and she couldn't deny the sense of relief at having him near again.

"Are you okay?"

"Yes, but Elijah tagged me. I can't use my magic – I can still connect to you, though. I've been pulling on your strength." She quickly rushed through her words, holding up her hand to show him the additional mark.

"Really?"

She rolled her eyes, needing him to sense the urgency. "Yes! We need to stop him!"

"How?" Imogen asked.

"Force," Blake ground out, dropping Kayla's hand. "You be careful and stick near Imogen!" He ran ahead of the girls.

"Let's go," Kayla said to Imogen.

Josh and Luke ran as wolves, snapping at the two remaining magic users. Elijah growled in frustration as his two cronies' attention was directed elsewhere. He waved his hands just as Wyatt did the same, releasing energy. Air collided with mage magic and exploded outwards, knocking Wyatt and Blake off their feet.

Kayla tried to use the distraction, but her power couldn't escape.

"I'm useless! I can't fight!" she spat. The girls stopped when Elijah got to his feet and laughed.

"Do you really think you can beat me?" he asked, wiping dirt from his jacket and cracking his neck. He muttered foreign words under his breath.

Imogen sucked in a sharp gasp. "No!" she screamed, holding both her hands out towards Wyatt as Elijah released a spell. The spell hit her shield and sent sparks into the air. Wyatt held his arms up instinctively, but when he remained unharmed, he looked over at Kayla and Imogen, his eyes wide with shock.

Blake crept behind Elijah and grabbed him, one arm banding around his neck.

Kayla frowned. If Blake had hold of Elijah, why was he struggling? Elijah didn't have shifter strength.

Smoke rose from Blake's skin where it touched Elijah.

"Imogen! Can you shield Blake?" she shouted, pointing at the pair. Imogen lowered her arms and panted.

She shook her head. "I can't. Not if they're already touching. I'd just be protecting them both from further magic attacks."

Josh's wolf yelped and fell to the ground. Wyatt pushed the approaching magic user back with his elemental magic and helped the massive wolf up.

Kayla stared down at her hand. "We're connected," she whispered to herself. She closed her eyes and found the thread she knew linked her to Blake – the one she'd been able to use despite the mark on her hand. She pulled and found Blake's eyes on her, glowing golden. He grunted with pain but managed to nod at her. He could feel what she was doing, and it gave her strength.

She pulled her elbows into her sides and pointed her palms up to the sky, feeling for the natural draw of energy. She directed her magic through the connection with Blake, and it flooded the line, pulling parts of her essence with it. It wasn't painful – at least she thought it wasn't until she heard Blake's cry.

Her eyes flew open and Blake's flashed an icy silver. It reminded her of the woman from her dreams: The Creator.

Blake stumbled, holding his middle as energy expanded from him like when she'd struggled to control her magic. It pulsed outward, knocking Elijah and the two magic users to their knees.

"It targeted the enemy," she whispered. Then she yelled over to Blake. "Send it back!"

"What are you doing?" Imogen asked breathlessly, wincing when Wyatt and Josh took down one of the magic users. She quickly looked away when one of them slammed a fist into Josh's jaw.

"I can use the connection with Blake to override Elijah's mark . . . I hope."

Blake closed his eyes and took deep breaths; she felt a swell of pride at his ability to put all his trust in her, no questions asked.

Power trickled back through the connection, slowly at first, then faster as her mind encouraged it. Mage magic slid over her body, swirling around the mark. A sharp, stabbing pain seared her skin, but it faded as she turned her hand to see the mark had shattered. She smiled.

"Oh my god! Your eyes, Kayla. They're golden!"

Kayla stood tall, calling on her elemental magic. She waved her hands the way Wyatt had taught her, pushing back the magic user near Luke. Luke looked over his shoulder at her, his eyes wide.

"Wyatt!" Kayla shouted, hoping he'd follow her lead. She called on her fire element and whipped it around Elijah in a vortex of flaming fury. Elijah fought back, pushing at the flames.

The pressure eased as Wyatt took control of the fire. She called on her mage magic and her witch powers together; they effortlessly joined within her core as memories surfaced.

Not her memories.

The original sorcerer's.

Words of a spell echoed in her mind. She repeated them over and over, forcing them towards Elijah even as he fought against the field of flames around him, screaming in anger. Rage swelled within him, which only fuelled her power.

Imogen gasped and ran to Blake and Luke, who attacked the last of Elijah's magic users, but Kayla couldn't focus on Blake. She had to trust in his abilities without her.

Her arms shook. She forced more power at Elijah even as he fought back. Wyatt shouted, dropping to his knees as he, too, struggled to keep control of her fire.

Something wet trickled from her nose, dripping into her mouth. She ignored the blood spilling down her face and sucked in a deep breath.

She let it out. She let everything out. Her scream ripped through the night.

Her power merged with her flames and exploded, illuminating the star-filled sky. Shouts of surprise rang out as the force flung her to the ground like a broken ragdoll.

CHAPTER THIRTY-ONE

BLAKE

"IMMY!" WYATT SHOUTED THROUGH the black smoke.

Blake's eyes quickly adjusted as Imogen got to her hands and knees, coughing beside him.

"I'm good!" she hacked back.

Blake scooped Imogen up and planted her by his side. Through the thinning black smoke, he could see Wyatt leaning over his knees, coughing. Luke slowly climbed to his feet a few metres away. He couldn't locate Josh, but across the roof, a female form lay still on the ground.

"Kayla!" He rushed to her side, his heart in his throat. As he dropped to his knees, she sucked in a large breath, coughing as she came to.

"Blake?" she mumbled, opening her eyes. She surveyed the scene and looked back at him. "We did it?"

"Let's go see. Can you move?"

She nodded but he helped her anyway, wrapping his arm around her waist. Wyatt had joined Imogen and Luke, and they limped over to the group.

"Where's Josh?" Wyatt asked.

"I've not seen him," Blake said, scanning the roof. Luke did the same.

The smoke was dissipating, but not quickly enough.

"Let me help," Wyatt said, waving his hands. The smoke parted, spilling over the sides of the building. Elijah was nowhere to be seen, but Josh's wolf lay in a heap on the other side of the roof.

"Josh!" Blake shouted. Kayla nudged him and he ran over with Luke, assessing Josh for injuries. The others followed.

"I can't see anything obvious," Luke said, running his hands through Josh's fur, feeling for broken bones.

"Why is he still in wolf form? Is that a good thing?" Imogen asked.

Kayla knelt beside Blake. "Want me to see if I can get inside his head?"

He searched her face for signs of worry after the magic she'd just done, but her eyes held his with confidence. He nodded and she placed her fingers on Josh's canine head, closing her eyes to concentrate.

Imogen bit her nails while Wyatt folded and unfolded his arms. Kayla opened her eyes and slid her hands through Josh's fur.

"He's okay. Concussed, I think. His head was a bit jumbled. Why don't you see if you can rouse him?" she suggested to Blake. He didn't know if he could command a wolf to wake, but then again, he hadn't known he could take Kayla's power and send it back to her – yet he'd somehow done it.

He took a deep breath and searched for the Alpha power deep inside of him.

"Wake up, Josh," he said, his eyes glowing. The power of the Alpha stirred. "Wake up!" he commanded again, using the extra strength the oath had given him.

Josh stirred with a low whine.

Everyone let out a collective exhale. Kayla leaned into Blake, stroking his back. Josh shifted into his human skin.

"You all right?" Wyatt asked when Josh rolled onto his back, frowning at the group around him.

"What happened?"

"Kayla says concussion, mate. Personally, I think that was always there," Blake joked, and Josh laughed.

"Elijah?"

Wyatt looked at a large black shadow smeared across the roof.

"Well, this is where he was standing when . . ." he frowned, then shrugged, ". . . whatever magic we had exploded."

"You don't think he's alive, do you?" Imogen asked in a quiet voice. Wyatt shot her a look and rolled his eyes.

"I'd say no, given there's nothing left but ashes. People don't survive that kind of explosion, and they certainly don't survive becoming ash." He kicked at the ground, and a cloud of dust rose into the air.

"So, we did it?" Josh asked, sitting up.

"I . . . I think we did," Kayla responded, a smile blossoming on her face.

"Um, what's going on up here?" Ben called from behind them. He stood in the doorway to the stairwell, holding up a finger as he leaned over his knees. Amy appeared behind him without having broken a sweat.

"Everyone okay? We sensed something wasn't quite right, and the magic users knew some pretty powerful magic was being cast. I managed to track you guys to the elevator, but it wouldn't work," she explained.

"We had to stop Elijah," Kayla replied, and Ben's head snapped up, eyes darting around the roof.

"Where?"

"There." Wyatt smiled, pointing to the spot of ash.

Ben's face paled. "I can't believe you stopped him."

"Hey!"

"No, I mean. It's done – we can make the peace treaty without the threat of him hanging over us!"

Ben flashed a smile at the group and Kayla returned it. Blake guessed they were both thinking of the work her parents used to do – work that Ben had taken over.

"Let's go, then. They won't wait forever downstairs!" Amy clapped her hands and herded Wyatt, Imogen, and Luke towards the stairs. Blake helped Josh up and followed Kayla inside.

"Wait guys! The lift works. I just pulled the emergency stop button so no one else could come up," Luke said.

"Oh, thank God," Wyatt and Ben said in unison.

Once downstairs, they were ushered into a large meeting room. Several men and women sat around a long table in the otherwise sterile room. Luke and Amy stood behind Blake and Kayla at the head of the table, and Josh stood behind Wyatt and Imogen as they took seats. Ben grabbed another chair from the back of the room.

Expectant faces turned to look at Blake, and it was hard to forget the last time he'd been in a roomful of people around a table. He gulped, but the shifters in the room identified themselves by placing their arms across their bodies, fists resting at their collarbones. They were allies.

A man in his fifties lowered his arm and smiled warmly.

"Blake, it's an honour. Ben told us about what you've been through, what you've sacrificed to be here. We want to work with you to see how we can move forward as one supernatural entity rather than a fragmented society."

"That's all we want, too," Blake replied, looking at Kayla.

"I still can't believe a magic user was chosen to take the oath alongside you – or that we have a soul entwined mixed race pairing," a woman with short blonde hair exclaimed. When Blake glanced at her, she shook her head. "Sorry, where are my manners? I'm Lina, a mage. If you don't mind, we were just discussing the idea of setting up a mixed council so we're all held accountable?" She phrased it like a question – like they needed his permission.

"Look, I may be King Alpha, but I'm still just a teenager. All I want is for us to work together and stop people from hunting us."

The man who'd spoken before chuckled softly. "I think we can all agree you're a good guy," he started, gesturing around the table at the nodding heads, "but you're someone we – especially the shifters – look up to for advice. Your opinion here matters. We will follow your lead."

Blake stared at his hands under the table. He'd known there was a possibility he'd be asked to lead, he just didn't think he was up to it.

"Look," a woman with greying hair and kind eyes said. "We now have a King Alpha and a Queen Alpha. A perfect mix of shifter and magic user. I believe you were meant to lead us out of this."

Kayla sat up at the mention of her title. "Forgive me, but will the shifters not want to reject me as their Queen?"

Several of the shifters in the room shook their heads. A young female shifter spoke up. "On the contrary, I think it's the best thing to ever happen. Soul entwined pairings are a gift from the Creator. We should respect that, and I for one am excited!"

"So, what happens next?" Kayla asked.

Ben cleared his throat. "I've told them about your magic, Kayla."

"What?" Kayla breathed, her eyes widening. Blake placed a hand over hers.

"This is a good thing. I wanted them to see you as a worthy match." She looked at the friendly faces around the room, some smiling, some nodding. None afraid. "And we've had some ideas. With you and Blake heading the council, we could form a united front to lead the supernatural community into a new era. One that focuses on growth and advancement."

"Protecting the world as the Creator originally designed," she whispered, thinking back to when she'd met the silver-eyed woman.

"Exactly."

"And how would this council be decided? No offense, but we got into this mess because people wanted power and control," Wyatt added, leaning on the table.

The first shifter who'd spoken cleared his throat. "For now, we'd decide how many would be on the council and pick amongst ourselves, as we have ties to lots of large groups of people who all share a common goal. It would help connect us. When things settle down, I think we're all in agreement that council positions are voted on by the supernatural community. Or at least, some form of choice is given. It shouldn't be a birth right to be on the council – except for Blake and Kayla."

"Why us?" Blake asked.

"Because the King Alpha powers along with the oath are passed through blood."

"I like the sound of a council, but we cannot have the corrupt individuals we had before. Look at Marcus and Elijah."

"That's why we want this to be a joint effort – a joint council between shifters and magic users, along with the King and Queen Alpha. No one should have the kind of power we let people have before. Even you," the man said to Blake.

"Totally agree. Kayla and I need to be held accountable just as much as everyone else."

"There's going to be backlash, a resistance to change. What are we going to do about it?" Wyatt asked.

Shrugs filled the room along with discussions about how to police the chaos. Wyatt was right. If they didn't have a plan for how they would fairly establish some form of law and order, no one would follow them.

"Um," Kayla began. Blake smiled at her, encouraging her to speak up.

"The taskforce," she said more clearly, and noise died down.

"What's that, Queen Alpha?" a male magic user asked.

"One good thing Marcus did was set up a mixed taskforce. Wyatt, you know more." She turned to him.

"Yes, Marcus had a taskforce I worked closely with. They monitored and gathered intel, acting quickly when possible to rescue those targeted for assassination. They provide support and relocation to many. The taskforce are extremely talented shifters and magic users."

"Ahhh yes, I'd heard about this," the older shifter said. "Perhaps this is something we could set up? Our own supernatural police force almost. They could help on the ground by ensuring the rules that protect our community are followed, protect the weak and vulnerable from attack, and monitor those who are flagged as potential threats. Thoughts?"

Some people smiled. Some nodded in agreement. Someone turned to Blake and asked for his thoughts on the matter.

"I agree. I think we need a unified body of people, like this taskforce, to act within the wishes of the council. We can't have shifters and magic users running around, declaring who's right and who's wrong, conducting their own trials for their own benefits." Kayla clutched his hand tighter. "The taskforce should be independent and bring those who need trial to the council. They should be the ones to gather all manner of evidence, which we'll deliberate on. We should also have a jury made up of randomly selected individuals – like the humans do – to help us in our decision process so that nothing is down to us alone. It should be a joint effort. How we punish those threatening our society is another matter, and not one I think we can decide on now."

"I like it," Wyatt agreed, as did the others. "Who's going to run it? I can speak to Mia and get the existing taskforce details over to you. They should be the first people chosen, as they've done the job already, and they can train more from there." Wyatt looked around the room until Blake spoke up.

"What about you?"

"Me?" he squawked.

"I'm happy with that," someone at the table announced, and they all verbally agreed that Wyatt should lead the taskforce. Wyatt ran a hand through his hair as he blew out a long breath.

"Really?" he implored, looking straight at Blake.

"You'd be great."

"Perfect for the job," Kayla added.

"Okay then, I guess."

"So, we just need to decide on a council and how it'll work moving forward," Blake addressed the group.

The blonde-haired mage, Lina, put her hand up. "I personally think the previous magic council had it right, in that each magic strain should be represented. Plus, we now have Kayla with all three strains. Maybe three shifters, too?"

Murmurs of agreement and the low timbre of voices rumbled through the room. All those present discussed pros and cons, decided on a course of action, and the start of a fairer ruling system. The council would be about justice, equality, and ensuring every voice was heard, governing jointly to ensure the survival of both races within the supernatural community and the human world.

IT WAS EXTREMELY LATE when they got back to Ben's cottage, but Blake buzzed with excitement for what was to come. He was nervous about the amount of responsibility bestowed upon him, but with Kayla and the support of a council to hold him accountable, he felt better.

Imogen teased Wyatt while Josh made coffee, and Ben retreated to his office to start the process of sharing the information of the newly formed council.

They had their work cut out for them, but with Luke and Amy working with those at the meeting to organise events across the country, he was starting to feel optimistic about positive change.

"Hey, want to take a walk?" he whispered to Kayla as Wyatt and Imogen escalated from teasing to bickering. Kayla raised her brows at the pair and nodded at Blake enthusiastically. Josh finished making coffee and watched Wyatt and Imogen, eyes bouncing back and forth like he was following a tennis match, quietly chuckling to himself when insults were hurled around.

"Gladly!" she replied.

CHAPTER THIRTY-TWO

KAYLA

BLAKE LACED THEIR FINGERS together, and they started their stroll around the cottage. The full moon cast a glow over the yard, highlighting the different plants and herbs growing along the side of the building. She enjoyed just being with Blake, and her breath was taken away when they moved into the gardens. She'd not had a chance to explore yet.

She had no idea the cottage backed up to a field with a large expanse of grass, lined with beautifully aged trees. There was even a small pond; the soft trickle of running water was music to her ears. She closed her eyes, breathing in the fresh air.

"Ben did well to find this place, didn't he?" Blake asked.

"Very."

"What a night."

"You can certainly say that again." She giggled.

Blake sighed. "I'm sorry. I'm sorry Elijah took you, and I'm sorry for what he did to you. I should have been able to stop it."

Kayla turned to face him. "Blake, I don't want you dwelling on that. What happened, happened. It was mostly my fault for going off on my own. Plus, I do have a habit of being snatched – you'd think I'd have learned enough by now to, you know, stop that." She tried joking, but her tone was more serious than she intended.

Blake tugged on her hand, curling her body into his. She relaxed into the embrace, resting her head on his chest and listening to the solid beat of his heart.

"I want to talk about our future," she whispered to him, worrying when his body tensed. She pushed back slowly. "What's wrong?"

"I need to know that you're okay with this. That you want this. I was always . . . I don't know, destined to be King Alpha and have that responsibility. But you weren't. I don't want to take those choices away from you. We're in for a bumpy ride with the new council and everything else. I would understand if you decided that wasn't your path. Nothing means more to me than your happiness. If taking up this position with me doesn't bring you that, then you deserve to go and find what makes you happy. I don't want to be the reason you're not." His voice cracked. He brought a hand up and brushed his knuckles across her jaw, flattening his hand against her check. His thumb gently stroked across her tingling skin.

"But what do you want?" she asked in a small voice, barely above a whisper.

"I . . . I want you. I want you to realise just how special you are. I would choose you over and over again. I want you to stay with me, but not because of the Creator, not because we are soul entwined, and not because we took the oath together. I want to be with you because you are my Queen, my world, my life. All of those other things? They're just bonuses, and all they do is confirm what I've known the whole time."

He swiped at a tear running down her face. She searched his emotion-filled eyes. Everything he said and felt poured through their bond.

"Funny thing about being soul entwined is that we were made for each other, and I can't think of a better person to share this journey with. Yes, the Creator gave me this power so I could stand with you. I'm soul entwined and bound to you with the oath. While I need you because of those things, my heart wants you and will always choose you no matter what." She ran her hands up his chest and wrapped them around his neck, standing on her toes. "Blake Collins, I choose you and whatever this life brings us."

His smile was instant, and she grinned back at him. He answered her silent prayers, lowering his mouth to hers sealing their fate with a kiss.

END OF BLAKE & KAYLA'S STORY

Click or scan the QR code and join the newsletter for bonuses (includes the prequel short story to the Soul Bound series!) https://rhianedwardsauthor.com/newsletter/

NOTE FROM THE AUTHOR

Thank you so much for reading the Soul Bound series! I hope you loved diving into Kayla and Blake's world as much as I enjoyed writing it. This was the series I started just after having my son and it means the world to me that it's now complete and out there.

If you enjoyed this book, I would truly appreciate if you'd consider leaving a review on Amazon or Goodreads. I can't express how important reviews are to authors, and we love hearing what you all thought.

And, if you're as nosey as me and want to be in the know about all new book releases, bonus extras, freebies and all other sorts of fun bookish stuff, come join my newsletter: rhianedwardsauthor.com

I'm also on Instagram, TikTok and Facebook so come and say hi, I'd love to keep in touch!

YOUR NEXT READ

A NEW NA FANTASY ROMANCE!

She is born to rule a kingdom. He is competing to be in her elite royal guard.
Together, their love becomes treason.

Nineteen-year-old Rayleigh Kalastone may be heir to the Balmore throne, but her controlling and secretive mother has done nothing except treat Rayleigh with icy disdain. So, when the guard trials start to find Rayleigh four lifelong protectors, she sneaks out of the palace to spy on the contestants. She never expected to meet Wren Netero, a talented warrior entering the trials. He's lethal, sinfully gorgeous, and forbidden.

But as the trials progress, dark druids continue their relentless assault on the kingdom's borders before launching a vicious and bloody attack on the palace. One thing is certain: they didn't get in without help.

Drawn into a world of deceit, questioning loyalties, and an enemy growing in power, Rayleigh must learn who to trust, who to love, and who to destroy before Balmore falls to ruination.

The Guard trials are only the beginning.

Find Reign of Blood and Shadows at: https://books2read.com/u/mB8nKv

Acknowledgments

This series, or at least Kayla and Blake's story is now complete and I couldn't end it without saying a great big thank you to some people. It's amazing how many people help to finish a book when you start to actually think about it. I wouldn't have had this opportunity without my husband and children. They motivate me and give me the space to work on my stories so I am forever thankful. My parents were some of the first people to ever believe in me and so I owe them for protecting my spark when it first ignited.

I have some pretty awesome friends who had the unfortunate task of reading very early drafts (sorry!) but without their honest feedback, these characters wouldn't be where they are today.

Being in the writing community has gifted me with knowing some of the best people. I don't think I've ever felt as loved and supported and valued as I do now. I couldn't possibly list you all and all you've done because we'd be here forever but whether we met on courses, or social media, know that you are cherished! From those who beta read to those who listen to my plot rambles – thank you!

A final thank you to you, my fellow readers. Thank you for taking a chance to read Kayla and Blake's story and I hope you fell in love with them as much as I did.

ABOUT AUTHOR

RHIAN is a YA/NA fantasy romance author so you can expect romance, a dash of humour, and a lot of supernatural twists.

Stories were Rhian's lifeline growing up, and not much has changed now she's in her thirties. She has always enjoyed supernatural elements, anything romance, and of course, a happy ending. She believes there is nothing that calms her more than having her head in other worlds.

When Rhian isn't writing, she is busy being a mum to two gorgeous toddlers and chasing around an energetic golden retriever.

CONTACT WITH RHIAN EDWARDS:
Website: https://rhianedwardsauthor.com
Instagram: @rhian.edwards.author
YouTube: www.youtube.com/c/RhianEdwardsAuthor
TikTok: @rhianedwardsauthor

www.ingramcontent.com/pod-product-compliance
Lightning Source LLC
Chambersburg PA
CBHW020344310726
48979CB00015B/2493/J
* 9 7 8 1 9 1 5 7 1 9 0 8 9 *